A Long Ways from Home

by Mike Martin

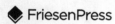 FriesenPress

Suite 300 - 990 Fort St
Victoria, BC, V8V 3K2
Canada

www.friesenpress.com

Copyright © 2016 by Mike Martin
First Edition — 2016

Also by Mike Martin
The Walker on the Cape
The Body on the T
Beneath the Surface
A Twist of Fortune

Cover Photo Credit: Anne Riggs

ISBN
978-1-4602-9199-3 (Hardcover)
978-1-4602-9200-6 (Paperback)
978-1-4602-9201-3 (eBook)

1. FICTION, MYSTERY & DETECTIVE

Distributed to the trade by The Ingram Book Company

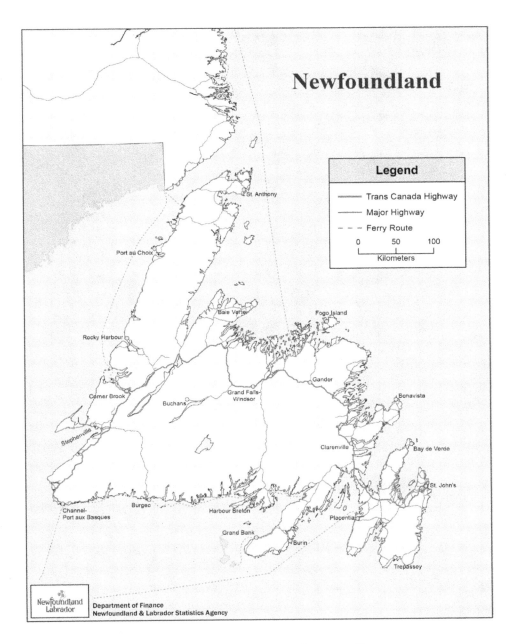

Newfoundland

Legend

— Trans Canada Highway
— Major Highway
- - - Ferry Route

0   50   100
Kilometers

St. Anthony

Port au Choix

Baie Verte

Fogo Island

Rocky Harbour

Gander

Corner Brook

Grand Falls-Windsor

Buchans

Bonavista

Stephenville

Clarenville

Bay de Verde

Burgeo

Harbour Breton

St. John's

Channel-Port aux Basques

Placentia

Grand Bank

Burin

Trepassey

Newfoundland & Labrador Statistics Agency, Department of Finance,

Government of Newfoundland and Labrador, 2016.

Dedication

To Joan, as always.
Without you there would be no Sgt. Windflower.

Acknowledgements

I am forever grateful to have people to help me on this writing journey. They include fabulous beta readers Mike MacDonald, Andy Redmond, Robert Way, Lynne Tyler, Denise Zendel, Karen Nortman, Evan Cathcart and Lise Winer. And Elliott Youden for his helpful advice and editing at the end.

Chapter One

A low, heavy rumble punctured the idyllic quiet of the lonely highway outside of Deer Lake, Newfoundland. There was little other traffic, maybe because it was the middle of the day, or maybe because people knew better than to interfere with the procession of motorcycles that RCMP Sergeant Winston Windflower could see coming over the hills.

He was impressed, despite himself. Nearly two hundred shiny and beefy Harley Davidson motorcycles ridden by equally beefy but much dirtier men, with a handful of women hanging on the back for dear life. Impressive wasn't really the word. Formidable was more like it, thought Windflower, as he and his fellow police officers snapped photos and fell in behind the zigzagging parade in their cruisers and SUVs.

He had dealt with biker gangs when he was stationed at the Halifax Airport. Different gangs but the same modus operandi. These guys, the Bacchus Motorcycle Club, were the cut from the same cloth. That's what he'd been told in the morning briefing. They were professional criminals who liked to be called businessmen, except their business was prostitution, illegal drugs, extortion and severe brutality.

The Bacchus crew had been in Newfoundland for their yearly 'run'. This was as close to a family holiday as it gets for the outlaw bikers. They had been travelling around this part of the province in a pack for the long weekend, causing as much havoc and chaos as they could. That meant taking over a few parks and camping areas and terrorizing the adjacent town or village while drinking as much liquor as possible. Of course, they chased the local women, toyed with the ones who wanted to be caught, and gladly fought any of the local men who saw fit to object.

The Royal Canadian Mounted Police were concerned about these behaviours and tried to check them at every step along the way. This included meeting them when they arrived off the ferry in Port-aux-Basques, and handing out as many tickets as possible for even the most minor violations of the law. The bikers called this harassment but the Mounties saw it as a deterrent; not a very good one, but all they had. They wanted to send a message to Bacchus that they were not welcome in this province.

The weekend visit by the bikers was an irritant, but what happened all of the other days of the year was what the police officers were most worried about. These yearly 'runs' served another purpose for Bacchus. They were a way to check-up or inventory their criminal empire. It was a time to weed out any weak links and to reward the most loyal people who worked for them. This year part of the Bacchus getaway involved a 'patching over' ceremony. This was when the big gang allowed some of its affiliates to graduate into full membership in the club.

There was an elaborate and semi-secret initiation rite, which most often involved lots of drinking and one disgusting or degrading act after another. At the end, the initiates had to pledge eternal loyalty to the club, above friends and family. Above everything. Because after this point they would only be responsible to their new family in the Bacchus Motorcycle Club, for the rest of their lives. There was only one way out of this club. That ceremony had taken place yesterday at a park in Bishops Falls. Now the bikers were heading home, and the rest of their allies and associates were giving them an escort. So, too, were the RCMP officers.

This was the last stop for Sergeant Windflower and his crew, who had been brought in from all over the province to assist the police in central and western Newfoundland. Another team of officers would take over from here and ensure that all of the outlaw bikers from out of the province actually left for the trip back to the mainland. As Windflower watched the motorcade he felt a sigh of relief and mentally started drifting back towards his home and his life in Grand Bank. He shook hands with his fellow officers and said his goodbyes.

They were all feeling pretty pleased about their efforts to minimize the damage the roving bikers could have caused in the journey around their part of their world. Windflower shared their relief. It could have been a lot worse, he thought. Little did he or the other police officers realize what had happened while they were watching the main show. Two days later, long after the Bacchus crew had left the province, they would find the bodies. A man and a woman, both bound head to foot and shot dead in the woods near the same campground where the motorcycle gang had recently been partying.

Chapter Two

Windflower didn't know about this yet, as he travelled along the Trans Canada Highway eastward towards his turnoff near Goobies. He was more focused on getting back home and back into his old routine in the sleepy town of Grand Bank. He had been on this posting for six years already and had cajoled his boss and friend, Acting Inspector Ron Quigley, to let him extend his stay for two more years. That would allow him to figure out his next move, which certainly included getting married to his sweetheart Sheila Hillier. Mayor Sheila Hillier, he thought.

Sheila's foray into municipal politics came about when the former mayor died in office from a heart attack. Sheila was elected in a run-off to finish his term and was now getting ready to run again for the full-time position in elections this fall. The transition to political life had been relatively easy for both of them. Sheila was a hard worker and a natural with people, and Windflower had learned to keep his mouth closed when political discussions arose at the dinner table.

That allowed them to keep a polite separation of work and family life. And since the Town of Grand Bank was technically his employer, that not only kept the peace, but his job intact as well.

The wedding was planned for the fall after the election and Sheila had already done most of the preparatory work. The church and reception were booked, and the invitations were in the mail. His Auntie Marie and Uncle Frank had already confirmed their attendance. In fact, Frank was coming a bit early. He claimed it was to help out, but Windflower figured it was to get a start on the festivities before his aunt arrived. A few old friends from his earlier RCMP days were also expected. He hoped Guy Simard from Halifax would be able to come. They were friends from many years ago and Windflower had learned much of how to be a policeman from his friend when they worked together at the Halifax Airport.

One person who might not be at the wedding was Windflower's long-time sidekick, Corporal Eddie Tizzard. Tizzard had been lucky to get a perk assignment in Grand Bank for the last six years, but now it was time for him to move on. He didn't know where he would be posted yet, but the rumour mill had him slated to go to RCMP Headquarters in Ottawa. That was because Tizzard could speak fluent French, Spanish, and a little Italian. Those skills were always in demand at HQ. Windflower was not looking forward to losing Tizzard. Eddie had become his right-hand man and things wouldn't be the same in Grand Bank without his friend.

Windflower's cell phone buzzed and he glanced to see who was calling him. He didn't pick it up, wary of the distraction while driving, but noticed the call display said Sheila. He would call her from the service station at Goobies, just before the turn-off for the road to the South Coast. He would gas up there, grab a coffee and then be home in about two hours. He passed quickly along the highway through Gander and then Terra Nova National Park. Too bad he didn't have Lady, his dog, along with him. That collie loved to splash in the water at their favourite picnic spot near the visitors' centre.

Instead, he drove through the park and before too long was

pulling up at the gas pumps at Goobies. As usual there was a line-up of cars, trucks and even a few motorcycles. One solitary biker stood out in particular. She was tall with long blond hair wound up in a braided ponytail. She was sunburnt, probably wind burnt would be more like it. Windflower thought she nodded at him as she deftly maneuvered her big bike, with a small trailer behind it, across the parking lot and back onto the highway. Windflower followed her with his eyes as she turned left and then another quick left to the same highway he was about to take home.

He filled his mug with 100% Colombian, rocket fuel, the locals called it, and bought an apple flip from the pastry tray. He took a large bite from his snack and called Sheila to check in.

"Hi Winston. Are you on your way home?" Hearing that cheery voice never failed to raise Windflower's spirits or to remind him what was important in life.

"I'm at Goobies, on my way. It will be good to get home. I missed you."

"I missed you too," said Sheila. "I've got a small roast in the oven and the smell of it reminds me of you."

"So you associate me with the smell of burnt meat," Windflower said.

"Not just the aroma, the whole thing," she said. "Pick up a loaf of molasses raisin bread if they have any in the store, will you?"

"I didn't see any, but I'll check in the back before I head home."

"That's great, Winston. I'll see you in a couple of hours."

"Bye, Sheila, see you soon."

Windflower went into the convenience store and walked to the back. As he rounded the corner a woman baker was wheeling out a rack of freshly made bread. Windflower grabbed a loaf as she went by. It was so fresh it was still warm to the touch and steam was condensing on the plastic wrap. He almost opened the package to taste test it, but satisfied himself instead with the last bite of apple flip, paid for his bread, and headed back onto the highway.

The road to the Southeast coast of Newfoundland was stark and incredibly scenic at the same time. There was very little traffic, and with the exception of the small community of Swift Current, there was nobody living on the vast tracts of open land. That often lulled Windflower into a kind of a driving trance, especially when the fog rolled in at parts of the highway that were open to the bays of the nearby Atlantic Ocean. It was a great place to think, especially for Windflower. Right now he was grateful for the opportunity to do just that.

At the same time, he also knew he had to stay alert for the ever-present highway danger of moose, the eternal scourge of Newfoundland drivers. During the daytime it was fairly easy to spot the large creatures that were really just another form of cattle grazing by the side of the road. As evening grew closer to dusk they tended to blend into the scenery.

People described the moose as jumping up out of a ditch or appearing out of the fog to meet them in their path. Windflower had seen plenty of them and he had also seen the damage these massive animals could do to a car travelling at high speeds along the highway. In many of these collisions, the moose walked away but the occupants of the vehicle did not.

Luckily for him, the day was bright and clear almost all of the way, and traffic in both automobiles and moose was light. He travelled through the beautiful curves in the road near Swift Current and down towards Marystown in no time. Traffic in Marystown was slow and busy, especially near the Tim Hortons coffee shop and drive-through. It was the only real traffic tie-up in the town that served as home to a shipyard and the centre for regional government services. It was still small by any measure, about 5,000 people, but big enough for a Walmart and the always popular coffee outlet.

Windflower thought about one more coffee for the last leg of his journey but didn't want to fight the line-up to get one. Twenty minutes later he could see Grand Bank on his horizon. Home, he thought, that is my home.

Chapter Three

As he neared the Grand Beach turnoff he was surprised to see a motorcycle with an attached trailer parked by the side of the road. Maybe that was the same one he had seen up near Goobies, but he couldn't be sure. It wasn't strange to see cars parked along here because he had heard it was a great spot for picking berries. So maybe the motorcycle owner was picking a few berries, thought Windflower. This time of year, in late summer, the yields might be small, maybe a few wild raspberries or a local delicacy called bakeapples.

Bakeapples looked something like large yellowish or orange raspberries growing on ankle-deep plants. When they were fully ripe they turned a soft golden orange. Windflower had tried to describe it once as having a kind of honey, apricot flavour, but the truth was nobody could really capture exactly what they tasted like - they were unique. All the locals agreed, however, that bake-apples when made into a jam were 'sum good b'y'. An expression that in the Newfoundland dialect meant pretty darned delicious. Windflower agreed with that assessment. He joined in that activity whenever he could by spreading bakeapple jam over thick slices of homemade bread.

There was even a local festival named after this humble berry in the nearby community of Garnish. Windflower loved the Bakeapple Festival which featured a number of community events, including what they called 'Breakfast on the Wharf'. It was no longer held on the side of the wharf because it had rained on the celebrations far too often. Moving it to the community centre hadn't dampened Windflower's appetite for fried eggs and baloney along with some of the famous jam to spread on his toast.

The aroma of the freshly baked bread in the backseat of his car and the memories and hopes of another breakfast on the wharf in Garnish only whetted his appetite. He had one more task to complete before he could get what he felt he so richly deserved. That was to see his other female companion. Lady, his four-year-old collie, rushed to greet him when he opened the door to his house in Grand Bank.

"Hello, girl," said Windflower as Lady ran a few victory laps around him to celebrate his homecoming. "Did Tizzard look after you well while I was gone?" Lady's response was to run into her bed and come back with a leash between her jaws.

"Okay, Lady. We'll do a short walk now and a full one later on. Come on." As soon as Windflower opened the door she was out like a shot. The pair did an abbreviated walk around the block and although Lady was not completely satisfied, two Milk Bone biscuits diverted her attention, and Windflower was able to sneak out while she munched happily on her treats.

He drove the short distance to Sheila's, and by the time he pulled up at her house he was certifiably starving. When he opened the door and smelled the roast beef he felt his knees go weak.

"Hi, Sheila," he called out as he took off his hat and coat and hung them on a hook in the hallway. "That smells fabulous."

Sheila came out of the kitchen with her apron on and went to Windflower to meet his embrace. "I'm glad you're home." She hugged him closely.

"Me too. Dinner smells delicious."

"I could probably have come out here naked and you would have still talked about dinner," said Sheila with a laugh.

"No, I might have asked for my dessert first though," Windflower said

"Go get cleaned up. Dinner is almost ready."

Windflower gave her another squeeze and went to the small bathroom in the hall to wash up for dinner. By the time he got back, Sheila had placed two bowls of vegetables on the table along with a small, perfectly-browned roast. She handed him the carving knife and fork and went back to the stove to pour the gravy into a serving dish.

The sharp knife slid smoothly through the peppered crust of the meat revealing a ring of growing pink towards the middle. Windflower tried to keep from drooling as the room filled with the aroma of the meat and the newly released juices. He placed a large slice on each of their plates, which Sheila had already prepared with scoops of mashed potatoes and steaming vegetables. She poured a ladle full of gravy over the meat and smiled at Windflower.

But he was long gone to meat heaven and for a few minutes all Sheila got in return was the murmured sighs of her hungry man. Finally, the muted Windflower awoke and raised his plate to Sheila for another slice of meat. "This is so good, Sheila," he said as she handed him back his refilled plate. "What did you use for spices?"

"Nothing special. Some black and white pepper, salt, thyme, garlic powder and onion powder. Plus, my secret ingredient."

"Secret ingredient?" mumbled Windflower with a mouth full of beef.

"If I told you, I'd have to kill you," said Sheila. But by now Windflower had drifted back into his food, and she knew all conversation with Windflower would be one-sided and futile until he was done.

Once Windflower's appetite had been satiated he gave Sheila his undivided attention. She gave him an update on the latest plans for the wedding, including who had confirmed they would attend and those sending their regrets. One of the positive replies was from Guy Simard, who sent along a little note saying he and the missus would happily be attending the festivities.

"And by the way my cousin, Carol, is coming to visit," Sheila said. "She's a bit of an outlaw in the family. Rides a big motorcycle. Has never been married. She lives up north in Ontario now but every couple of years takes a big trip on her Harley. This year she is heading down our way. I was expecting to see her show up by now."

"What does she look like?" asked Windflower.

"She's tall, pretty. The last time I saw her she had long blond hair. Liked to wear it up in a ponytail."

"That's interesting. I might have seen her at Goobies. Or someone fitting that description anyway. But I didn't see her on the way down. Maybe she stopped off in Marystown along the way."

"Maybe," said Sheila.

Then Windflower remembered the motorcycle and trailer he'd seen parked along the highway. That might have been her bike, he thought. But he didn't want to alarm Sheila. Not yet anyway. Instead he said, "I'll get Tizzard to start looking out for her."

"Thanks," said Sheila. "Any word on Eddie yet?"

"I haven't heard anything new, but I'll ask him about it when I see him tomorrow."

"We're all going to miss him," Sheila said. Windflower just nodded at this last remark. It was still a little too painful for him to talk about. Sheila reached out and took his hand in hers.

"What's new at the Council?" asked Windflower, trying to move the conversation to safer and less emotional grounds.

"Well, Francis Tibbo made it official today. He's going to run for the mayor's job again!"

"That officious little prig," started Windflower, but Sheila cut him off.

"Stay out of the politics, Sergeant," she cautioned. "The RCMP has to stay neutral in this race. You have to work with whoever gets elected."

"That doesn't mean I don't have an opinion."

"I appreciate the support, but I can fight my own political battles, thank you very much," said Sheila. "I'm not worried about Francis Tibbo. I'm not even worried about getting elected again. We've already got things moving in the right direction."

This time Windflower simply nodded his agreement. It was clear from the coat of fresh paint on the aging properties on the wharf to the popular new programming at the museum that things were headed in the right direction.

Sheila got up. "If you really want to help, you can do the dishes while I make us some tea."

"Finally, something I'm allowed to do." Windflower smiled. Sheila laughed and threw a dishcloth at him while she put on the kettle to boil.

"Let's watch a movie tonight," she said as she went to the fridge to look for something.

"Okay." Windflower had his hands in a sink full of soapy water and his eyes firmly fixed on her activities. When she pulled a small cardboard box out of the refrigerator he almost started to glow.

Sheila pretended to ignore him as she took their dessert out of the box, cut it into two pieces and put it along with her tea pot onto a small tray. "See you in the living room."

Windflower finished the chore in record time and was soon sitting next to Sheila on the couch with half of his dessert, the fabulous chocolate peanut butter cheesecake from the Mug-Up Café, already gone. He barely breathed as he finished it off. "Mmmmmm," was his only response.

Sheila laughed at his post-meal antics as she looked for a movie on T.V. "Let's watch 'To Kill a Mockingbird'," she said. "I just picked up the new Harper Lee book and I'd like to see the old movie before I dig into the new story."

"That would be great. "I love that movie. Atticus Finch has always been a hero of mine."

"I love Scout," said Sheila. "This was one of my favourite books growing up."

"Me too. Although I hear the new story is a bit more revealing of the racist attitudes that existed back then."

"That was always the reality. In some ways, the new book may be closer to the truth. I'm glad we had a kinder version of that truth when we were kids. It doesn't make it any easier to take, just the same."

"Let's just enjoy the movie. It's been a long week. We both deserve a break. And it's good to know that at least in the movies there's a possibility of a happy ending."

The pair snuggled up on the couch and totally enjoyed both the classic film and their time together. When the movie was over Windflower went back to his house for the final walk of the evening with Lady. Once again she was very pleased to see him and bounded out the door when he held it open for her. They did the extended loop that led them down near the brook where Lady had a good, long drink and then they darted around the perimeter of the wharf.

Chapter Four

There were no lights on at the Mug-Up Café. It stayed open long enough to provide a light supper for people who were going to the summer theatre festival and then the owners, Moira and Herb Stoodley who were friends of Windflower and Sheila, would close the café for the night. Windflower would come over and see Herb in the morning. If there was any news in Grand Bank worth retelling and even some that wasn't, Herb would know it. Windflower and Lady walked by the RCMP detachment building and while the lights were on, there were no cars out front. That meant whoever was on the overnight shift was probably out on a call. Windflower could find out about that in the morning too.

One last turn up the hill and around Seaview Drive, and then Lady led Windflower home. She hoped he was staying for the night, but after he refreshed her water and filled her bowl with food he patted her on the head and wished her goodnight. He walked back to Sheila's just as the full moon was rising over the Atlantic Ocean.

The moon always reminded him of his grandparents and he said a silent goodnight to Grandmother Moon who was watching over him. Sheila was getting out of the bath when Windflower came upstairs.

"It's all yours," she said.

Windflower smiled and soon after was sliding into the still hot bath. He had brought along his book. It was another Brunetti mystery by Donna Leon. This one was called "Falling in Love", and once again featured the glamorous and sometimes impetuous opera singer, Flavia Petrelli, along with Commissario Brunetti and his colleagues at the Venetian police department. He loved the writing, the setting, and most of all the foods that were standards in all Leon's books. He spent a lovely twenty minutes soaking and reading. He had planned to read a little more when he got to bed. But Sheila had other plans. That was certainly fine with Windflower.

In the morning Windflower was awake at first light. He kissed Sheila on the forehead as she slept and crept out of the bedroom. The first thing he noticed was the fog. Fog was the frequent companion of the people of Grand Bank. It seemed like the fog was ready to drop in, like an unwelcome guest, at any time during the day or night. The good news was that even though most days started off foggy, it usually 'burnt-off' later in the morning. Windflower hoped that would be the case today.

He drove home and said hello to Lady, who seemed determined to do her business, fog or no fog. He let her out in the back yard and put on a pot of coffee. A few minutes later, he let her in and enjoyed her company and a half cup of coffee. After a quick shower he grabbed his RCMP hoodie and Lady's leash. Then they were out the door and into the car. He drove out towards one of his, and Lady's favourite places, the L'Anse-aux-Loup T.

But first he had a little work to do. He wanted to take a quick look at the area where he'd seen the motorcycle yesterday. As he came over the hill towards Grand Beach he could see the bike and trailer were still there. It looked like it hadn't moved since last night. As he got closer he could see someone else had noticed the solitary motorcycle. There was a piece of bright yellow RCMP tape draped over the handlebars. Must have been the patrol from last night, he thought. He could find out more when he got to the office later. One thing he did notice was that the motorcycle had an Ontario license plate. Maybe the bike belonged to Sheila's cousin Carol. That was easy to check too.

That left Windflower free to go ahead with his plans to go to the T. That was quite fine with Lady. As soon as they got to the narrow spit of land between two bodies of water she flashed out of the car and headed down the beach. Windflower could come if he wanted, but she was determined to sniff and poke every bush and rock along the way. Windflower loved watching her here. She was obviously delighted with the scene and the scents and the constant wind blowing through her thick coat. Just as she had her routines, he had his rituals as well.

He walked along peacefully behind Lady and found a large rock on the beach to sit on. He watched the fog drifting back into the ocean and the island starting to reappear in the distance. This felt like a special and almost sacred place where the land met the immense and powerful ocean. He took his smudging kit out of his bag and filled a bowl with his sacred herbs, added a touch of moss to help create a quick flame and lit his medicine. As it smoked, he took an eagle feather from his bag and used it to guide the smoke over his head and his heart and under his feet.

After he had cleansed his body and mind and spirit, he offered up prayers for his ancestors whose guidance he still sought. He also prayed for the people in his world to give them strength to carry out their roles and responsibilities. Finally, he gave thanks for all the four-legged creatures that were sharing this journey with him, especially Lady, who just by being there was bringing him joy and happiness. As if on cue, Lady appeared at his feet to remind him it was time to go back.

He drove back quietly and at peace after such a beautiful start to his day. He got Lady fresh food and water and changed into his regular uniform. Then he filled his coffee mug with the last of his coffee, grabbed a banana off the top of the fridge, and drove to the Grand Bank RCMP Detachment to begin his morning at work.

Chapter Five

When he arrived, he noticed Tizzard's Jeep parked out in front. Inside he found his young Corporal engaged in his favourite activity, eating.

"Want a muffin?" asked Tizzard, passing Windflower the second-to-last one of the package. "Partridge berry," he mumbled.

Windflower nodded his thanks and took a bite of the soft, sweet pastry. It was all fat and sugar and white flour with a few tart partridge berries to try and level off the unhealthiness of the snack. It didn't do much on that end, but Windflower had to admit it was pretty tasty. Tizzard finished off the last of the muffins and put the plastic container in the garbage. "That was sum good, b'y." he said. "Another thing I'll never get again," he added with a sigh.

"Did you get any news on your posting?" asked Windflower.

"I'm going to Headquarters. They want me right away. I told them I needed a few days to get things in order down here. I think I'm going to be working in the international section. I always wanted to travel the world."

"That sounds very exciting, but don't make any sudden moves

out of here just yet. I'm going to talk to Quigley about it later today. I'm hoping for a reprieve, even if it's only for a few months."

"Okay," said Tizzard. "I think Evanchuk got some news too."

"That's just great. Where's she going?"

"You'll have to talk to her," said Tizzard. "By the way, we found a motorcycle out near Grand Beach," said Tizzard. "Frost tagged it last night."

"I saw it on the way in. It's got an Ontario license plate. Did Frost run it yet?"

"You can ask him yourself. Here he comes now." Tizzard pointed out the window at a cruiser being parked at the front of the building.

Constable Harry Frost was the newest member of the RCMP contingent in Grand Bank. He had been stationed with the regional drug task force before this assignment and was happy to be back on a regular beat, even if that meant an occasional overnighter. He also liked Tizzard and Windflower. That was evident from his wide smile when he saw both men in the lunchroom at the back of the building.

"Morning, Sarge," he said. "Corporal."

"Good morning. How was your shift?"

"It was good. I don't mind the overnighters. It beats waiting around on a stakeout. That's for sure."

"Yeah, I kind of like the all-nighters too. It gives me time to think."

"That's good," said Tizzard. "Because I've got you on the slate for tomorrow night. If that's okay with you?"

"Fine with me," said Windflower, then turning to Frost. "Tizzard told me you tagged the bike last night. Did you see anything in the area?"

"Nope, quiet as a church," said Frost. "There are not too many people up around there during the week. I don't think anybody lives there full-time anymore. It's mostly cabins."

"They're usually there on the weekends," said Tizzard. "But I'm going over there later this morning to see if anyone is around."

"Did you run the plates yet?" asked Windflower.

"I left a note to ask Betsy to do that when she comes in," Frost said. "Anyway, I have to go. I'm bagged."

"See ya," said Tizzard as Frost headed home.

"I think I might know who owns that motorcycle. It might be Sheila's cousin, Carol. She was on her way here for a visit. I saw someone who looked like her at Goobies. Check and see if anyone saw a woman motorcycle rider. Tall, blond, pony tail. She'd be hard to miss."

"Got it," said Tizzard.

"And aren't you on tonight? What are you doing here now?" he asked.

"I'll get a nap later before my shift," said Tizzard. "I'll be fine. Don't worry."

"I always worry about you, Corporal. Let me know if you find anything."

Windflower went to his office, and started in on the accumulation of paperwork that Betsy Molloy, his admin person, had so neatly arranged and collated for him. Things he had to sign were in a file on top, followed by things to action, things to notice and finally things to read when he had some time. Even with Betsy's excellent system Windflower was always falling behind. He had just finished his signing file when Betsy poked her head into his office doorway.

"Good morning, Sergeant," said Betsy. "I'm glad you're back. Is that file for me?" she asked, pointing to the signing file.

"It is," said Windflower, passing her the file. "Good morning to you too, Betsy. It's great to be back."

"Do you have anything for me this morning?"

"Constable Frost left a note for you on your desk, asking for a plate check on a motorcycle that was left parked out on the highway. Can you let me know what you find out?"

"Certainly," said Betsy. "I'll do it first thing."

"Thanks, Betsy." Windflower tucked himself back into his piles of paperwork.

It wasn't long before Betsy was back in his doorway. "The motorcycle is registered to a Carol Jackson from Smooth Rock Falls in Ontario, sir. I made a copy of her license photo." She handed him the photocopy.

Even in the harshness of a driver's license picture, it was clear Carol Jackson was a beautiful woman. Windflower was staring intently at the photograph when Betsy broke in. "Such a pretty girl," Betsy said. "I hope nothing bad has happened to her."

"I hope so, too," said Windflower.

"If you want I can dig up some more information about her. Sometimes people post details about their travels and trips on Facebook and other social media."

"That might be helpful," said Windflower. Betsy went away to do her social media check-up. He started to think about what the possibilities might be, almost none of them good, when Tizzard came into his office.

"Time for a bite?" he asked and answered at the same time.

Windflower laughed and shook his head at the always-hungry Corporal. They left and walked the short distance together to the Mug-Up Café.

Chapter Six

The café was crowded, stuffy and warm so Windflower and Tizzard ordered a coffee and a raisin tea biscuit to eat at the small table outside.

"So, what'd you find out?" asked Windflower.

"Not too much," said Tizzard, as Marie the waitress came out with their mugs of coffee. "Like we thought, there aren't too many people around out there during the week. The only guy I found to talk to said he tries to keep the T.V. on loud enough to drown out any noise from the highway."

"That's not very helpful. We've got confirmation on the owner though. Her name is Carol Jackson. Betsy is doing a Facebook check on her right now. She's Sheila's cousin. Do you know her?"

"Nope," said Tizzard. "Where's she from?"

"Northern Ontario," Windflower said. "A little place called Smooth Rock Falls. I drove through there one time. It's a beautiful small town with a paper mill. Probably shut down now like all the rest up there."

Marie came to deliver their hot raisin biscuits and there was a pause in the conversation while both men opened their steaming snacks and applied the contents of two small butter containers.

"What's next?" asked Tizzard, about three bites later, as he scraped the last few crumbs from his plate. "Is Carol Jackson a missing person yet?"

"I don't know. Guess I should talk to Sheila first. She was expecting Carol to come visit. She might be able to give us some more to go on. I'll see if she's around at the town office."

"Cool." Tizzard yawned and stretched. "If it's okay with you, I'm going to take a few hours off. I'll be back around 5 for the late show."

"Okay." Windflower was quite content to sit and enjoy the nice summer day. He could relax now that the fog had been banished, at least temporarily. His quiet reverie was only disturbed when Herb Stoodley came to pick up their dishes.

"Penny for your thoughts, Winston," said Herb. "You look like you were a million miles away."

"Good morning, Herb. I'm trying to enjoy this brief interlude of nice weather."

"Good plan. As soon as Moira lets me get rid of this apron, I'm out of here too. I have a date with a fishing pole and a few fat brook trout. You should come along."

Windflower laughed. "Maybe another time, Herb. Seems I can't shake my uniform as easily as you."

"Okay, your loss," said Stoodley with a laugh of his own. "But if I get some, how about you and Sheila coming over on the weekend? I want to try them out on the new barbecue I got."

"Sounds good to me. But I'll have to double check with Sheila. What about if you don't catch any?"

"Never fear," said Stoodley. "I've got a few in the freezer."

Windflower shook hands with Stoodley and left to walk back to his office. When he arrived, Betsy was waiting for him with a sheaf of paper.

"These are printouts from Carol Jackson's Facebook page," said

Betsy, looking particularly proud of her efforts. "As you can see, she kept a kind of diary here, posting pictures and talking about her next stop along the way." She paused to allow Windflower to look at the pictures. He scanned most of them quickly, but paused when he came to the last set of pictures. There were no captions provided to identify who was in the pictures but Windflower could see right away the Bacchus insignia on a jacket on the front of the person with Carol Jackson.

"Here's the last entry," said Betsy. "It's from yesterday morning. There's a picture of the sunrise and a caption from the woman that reads: 'Last sunrise before I see my peeps in Grand Bank'."

Windflower paused as if to say something to Betsy, and then hesitated again before simply thanking Betsy for her good work. Betsy could see something was bothering her boss. But she had learned long ago to leave him alone when he got like that. Sooner, rather than later, he would tell her what she needed to know. She turned and went back to her desk at the front of the building.

Well, a few things were becoming clearer, but this whole situation was getting a heck of a lot murkier. The clarity was that Carol Jackson had intended to be in Grand Bank by now and for whatever reason she was not. The involvement of the Bacchus crew in this situation was not a good omen either, he thought. Whether these two things were connected was yet to be seen. Someone who might be able to shed a little more light on the matter, however, was easily at hand.

Windflower grabbed his hat again, told Betsy he was gone for lunch and drove over to the Grand Bank Town Office to see Sheila. He was pretty sure Sheila knew something more about Carol Jackson that she hadn't shared with Windflower yet. That puzzled him a little, since they were so tight. But being a police officer often meant that people, even those closest to you, sometimes held back just a little bit. Enough thinking already. Let Sheila speak for herself.

Chapter Seven

Sheila was doing exactly that when Windflower poked his head into her office. She waved him in with a nod as she held the phone in one hand and furiously scribbled notes with the other. "Okay," she said. "That's good. I'll have something to you by the end of the week. Thanks for your help."

She hung up the phone and completed her notes. "That was the person from the Newfoundland and Labrador Arts Council. If we can get them our proposal by the end of the week there's a good chance the Memories Project will be funded for next year."

"Congratulations. I always thought bringing together the old sea captains' families to tell their stories was a great idea. It'd be a perfect fit for the museum."

"Yeah. They've got the music series going well so this can build on the audience they've started to create over there. But first, the paperwork."

"Ah yes. I know the joys of paperwork quite well."

"Is it time for lunch already?" said Sheila. "It's such a great day. Let's grab something at Sobey's and go for a walk."

"We can do that. But I'm actually here on official police business. We found Carol Jackson's motorcycle on the road out near Grand Beach. But there's no sign of her."

"Oh my God." Sheila looked shocked. "What happened to her?"

"We don't know yet. But is there anything we should know about Carol you haven't been telling me?"

"This might take a while." Sheila sighed. "Can we still have lunch and a walk while you complete your interrogation?"

"Absolutely. My car's out front."

Sheila and Windflower were quiet on the way to the supermarket. When they arrived, Sheila went in while Windflower stayed behind in the car. She came out smiling with a plastic bag and two bottles of water.

"What's in the bag?" asked Windflower.

"I refuse to answer because you may think I am trying to bribe a police officer," said Sheila. Then growing more serious she added, "Let's have our lunch and we'll talk along the walk if that's okay."

"That's perfect."

They drove to the Grand Bank Clinic and parked the car right next to the pathway that travelled down by the brook. Sheila took their lunch and the water while Windflower got a blanket from the trunk of the car. They walked to the dam that controlled the rushing waters from the river above and found a place to sit on the grass. Windflower spread out the blanket and Sheila opened her bag and laid out their lunch.

Windflower was very pleased with her choices. She had a small baguette, a wedge of brie, a small container of olives, a bag of grapes and a salad bag.

"Wonderful," he proclaimed, as Sheila tore him off a large piece of bread and sliced the brie with a plastic knife she had also picked up at the store. The pair said little as they enjoyed the sunshine and most of the fruit and salad. Sheila packed up the rest and put it back into the plastic bag.

"Come on," she said to Windflower as she stood up. "Let me tell you what I know about Carol."

Windflower followed behind Sheila as she walked up closer to the dam. "We were about the same age so we hung around together a lot when we were young. We were best friends, but Carol was always a bit on the wild side growing up. She never got into a lot of trouble, mostly because there wasn't that much trouble to get into around here. She was always the first one to try things, like smoking cigarettes. She would also hang around with the older guys all the time."

She took Windflower's hand as she led them up the path towards the lookout. "I was terrified of getting into any kind of trouble. My parents would have been apoplectic. But they liked Carol, and she could get away with anything around them. She even came over to my house one night when she was only about twelve, and she was so drunk she couldn't stand up. I snuck her into my room."

"What about Carol's parents?" inquired Windflower.

"That was part of the problem," said Sheila. "Carol's father was a drunk and he drifted in and out of the family home. He'd go to Wabush to work in the mines for a few months and then come home and drink until his money was all gone. Carol told me he also beat my Aunt Bernice on a regular basis. Eventually the police got involved but things were different back then and he kept getting kicked out and moving back in. When Carol was about fourteen my aunt finally had enough. She moved the whole family, without my uncle, to St. John's. I have no idea where my uncle went. Soon after Carol and her mother left, he was gone and nobody around here has ever seen him again. Somebody said he was living up in Toronto and others think he's dead."

"What about Carol?"

"Eventually her mother got remarried and Carol moved with them to various mining communities in Northern Ontario. Timmins, Sudbury," said Sheila. "Carol would call me every couple of months, usually after she'd been drinking. When she was seventeen she called me from Toronto. She'd met a guy who had a motorcycle and was living with him in the city. It wasn't hard to predict how that relationship would work out and as we now know it only led Carol into more problems. Much more serious problems."

"Drugs?" he prodded.

"Oh, yeah. Then the calls from Carol started getting more frantic. At one point I had to ask her not to call. But of course that didn't stop her. Next was rehab, more than a few times. There were also some shoplifting, possession charges. She did a few months in jail here and there. I lost contact with her for a little while. About ten years ago she called me again. She said she was clean and wanted to come for a visit. I was kind of scared, but I couldn't say no. She was as close as I had to a sister."

"So she came to Grand Bank?"

"Yes," Sheila replied. "She showed up with her motorcycle and her long blond hair. Every guy around here fell in love with her immediately."

"She is kind of cute. But definitely not my type," he quickly added.

"Carol is a charmer, but she was still pretty messed up. She told me she'd gotten mixed up with some bad people in a motor-cycle gang. She owed them a lot of money and was hoping they'd lose track of her if she came this way. But I guess they found her somehow. Two guys showed up one day and that was the last I saw of her."

Sheila paused to wipe away a few tears. "She called me from time to time but was always kind of evasive. It was like she was in trouble but trying to keep me out of it by not telling me too much. Then she called again about a month ago, sounding really scared. I thought about telling you but I figured that could wait until she got here. What do you think has happened to her?"

"I don't know. But we'll start looking for her. If she's around here, we'll find her. The first step would be for you to file a missing persons report on her. Why don't you come back with me now and I'll get Betsy to help you with the report?"

Sheila didn't say anything but buried her head in Windflower's arms instead. When she stopped crying and shaking, he gently took her hand in his and led her back to his RCMP cruiser. A few minutes later they were sitting together in front of Betsy's desk at the detachment office.

Chapter Eight

"Okay, let's get this up on the system, Betsy," said Windflower, after Sheila had provided all of the necessary information for Carol Jackson's missing persons report. "Send it over to Regional HQ and ask the media relations people to post it too. Get them to put it on social media as well."

"They automatically post on Facebook and Twitter," replied the assistant. "I'll send it over and get them to confirm when they've got it up and running."

"Thanks, Betsy. I'll take Sheila back to her office and I'll be right back."

Sheila nodded at Betsy and joined Windflower as he walked out to the car. "I'm really worried about her. I hope you can find her. Let me know if you hear anything, okay?"

"Okay," said Windflower as he drove her back to the Town Office. "By the way, I saw Herb Stoodley this morning. He invited us over for dinner this weekend."

"That would be nice," Sheila said, but Windflower could feel and see her spirits were down.

"We'll find her," said Windflower as they arrived at Sheila's destination. "The RCMP always get their man or woman."

Sheila smiled weakly and squeezed Windflower's hand just as weakly. She gave him a peck on the cheek and left him to return to work.

When Windflower got back, Tizzard was already back on the job and eating again, of course. This time he had a large submarine sandwich, and was reviewing the information Betsy had printed off about their missing person.

"It's funny that her bike is there, but there's no other sign of her, don't you think?" he asked Tizzard.

"It is strange. She's not likely out of gas. I saw her at the gas station at Goobies. Maybe it's broken down. But even if that's the case, where did she go?"

"Well, we could check on whether the motorcycle is running. I'll get Paul Herridge from the garage to come out with me to pick it up. He's a whiz with bikes and we have to bring it back here anyway. We can't just leave it out there."

"Good idea. Can you get prints off it too before you move it and take a look in the saddlebags and the trailer?"

"Sure." Tizzard folded up the paper wrapping of the few shreds of lettuce that remained from his sandwich. "I'll go and see if Paul is around."

Windflower went back to his still considerable pile of paperwork and was making good progress when Betsy beeped him from the front. "Inspector Quigley on line 2," she said.

"Thanks, Betsy," said Windflower as he picked up the phone. "Afternoon, Inspector. What can I do for you today?"

"That's certainly the attitude I want to hear from the troops," said Inspector Ron Quigley. "How was your time on the west coast, Winston?"

"It was good, Ron," said Windflower. The two men had been in the ranks together for too long to have to use formal titles in conversation. "I was happy to see the backs of that Bacchus crew though. They were nothing but trouble."

"Yeah, I guess the bad odour they stirred up keeps lingering. We heard two local bikers from Marystown, Avalon Riders, got patched over while their bosses were here for the weekend. That means Bacchus intends to formally set up shop down here. That's not good for any of us. I thought I should give you the info, even if it's bad news," Quigley said.

"We knew they were bringing some of the local guys on board. But we couldn't get close enough to them to see exactly what was going on. How'd you get that intel?"

"We had a guy on the inside. Anyway that wasn't your job. It sounds like you had your hands full just trying to stop the bikers from looting and pillaging the area."

"And preventing some of the local heroes from ending up too battered and bruised. Speaking of crime prevention, it's going to be difficult to keep the peace around here without any RCMP officers. Can you do anything to slow down the transfer process?"

"Both transfers have already been booked," said Quigley. "Evanchuk has to be out by the end of the week and Tizzard is scheduled to report to HQ in a week."

"Have you got any in-transfers yet?" asked Windflower. "We can't run the shop with only me and Frost."

"I'm working on it, but sorry, nothing confirmed. There are cutbacks everywhere. We're down a man here, too, so I can't even send someone on relief. I guess you're going to have to go on reduced service."

"Geez, Ron. That means we'll have to shut down the overnight shift and go on emergency call. You know how popular that will be."

"Sorry, Sergeant," said Quigley. "You'll have to make do until we figure something out. Anyway, I have to go."

With that, Windflower was left pondering how to deal with this, and how he was going to break the news to the Town about the reduced level of service. The last time they had to stop the regular overnight patrol, the Town Council had gone bananas. This time was not likely going to be any different, and it would be Mayor Sheila Hillier who would be doing the yelling. The more he thought about it, the less he liked his options.

He decided he might as well get it over with. He walked out to the front and told Betsy he needed to go to the Town Office. He practiced his lines to Sheila on the short drive over. When he got there the receptionist told him Sheila was out at a meeting. As he was about to leave, the Town Manager, Les Warren, walked by the desk.

"Hey, Winston. What are you doing here? Something I can help you with?"

Windflower was about to say no, when he thought about it again and said, "I was going to talk to Mayor Hillier, but maybe you're the right person to talk to. Have you got a few minutes?"

"Sure, come on in." Warren led Windflower to his office and pointed to the small conference table. "Have a seat."

"Thanks." Windflower sat. "So I guess I've got a bit of short-term bad news. You might have heard that Eddie Tizzard is getting transferred out."

"I did. That's too bad for Eddie. It's also been good for us to have a local guy on staff over at your place."

"Yeah, we're all going to miss him. We're also going to lose Evanchuk. She's going this weekend. And Tizzard by the end of next week." He paused, waiting for a reaction from Les Warren, but the Town Manager merely listened. "Our problem is we can't get a replacement in right away because of cutbacks. So, we're going to be down two men, or a man and a woman officer."

"What are you going to do?" asked Warren.

"We're going to have to shut down the overnight shift and go to emergency call," said Windflower.

"That's going to be a problem," said Warren, now starting to understand why the RCMP officer wanted to talk to him. "Council certainly won't be happy about this."

"Happy about what?" said Sheila as she walked into the Town Manager's office. "Hi, Sergeant, Mary at the front told me you were back here. What's going on?"

Windflower glanced quickly at Les Warren but he was pretending to look for something under a pile of papers on his desk. He gulped and said, "I was explaining our situation at the detachment to Les. I actually came to see you, but you were out. And I saw Les at the front."

Windflower was now fumbling with his words and Warren was trying to disappear under his desk. Sheila's eyes did not move from their fix on Windflower. He continued. "As I was telling Les, Evanchuk is getting transferred this weekend and Tizzard will be gone by the end of next week. I tried to get an extension, but so far I've been unsuccessful."

"What about replacements?" Sheila asked.

"They're coming, but I don't know when. I guess Marystown is short too because of funding cutbacks. In the interim we'll have to make do with what we have here."

"I see," said Sheila. "How will you manage?"

Windflower gulped again. "We're going to have to shut down the overnight shift and go to emergency call."

"That is unacceptable," said Sheila. "We are paying for a full police service, not a part-time one. We have a contract. I expect the RCMP to live up to it. All of it. So I suggest you get back on the phone to Inspector Quigley and give him our response. That's totally unacceptable and if he can't or won't do something about it, I'll be talking to his boss. You can let Les know what his response is. I'm giving you two days to fix this and then I'm taking it to Council."

With that, Sheila was gone, leaving Windflower and Les Warren in a sort of stunned silence. Neither man said a word and Windflower left the Town Office building as quietly and as quickly as he could.

Chapter Nine

Windflower thought about calling Sheila, but it reminded him of an old buddy of his who had said if you were out drinking you might as well not call to say you were going to be late, since that meant you would only get yelled at twice. Might as well wait until you got home to face the music. Windflower gave himself the same advice and decided to go for a run instead. He dropped by his house and picked up Lady along the way. That turned out to be a good decision. At least one female in his life was happy with him.

The fog was starting to blow back in from the Atlantic. In fact, you could hardly see the Cape that usually towered over Grand Bank. It was still up there, somewhere. You just couldn't see it through the thickening mist. Lady didn't care where they went so Windflower drove them back up to the trail behind the clinic. Lady was delighted to get out of the car the instant Windflower parked and opened the door. She ran around the car a couple of times to express her pure elation. Then she started exploring the nearby area, which was full of outdoor smells including the recent presence of other dogs.

In another month or so, this area would be a prime blueberry picking spot for the locals. It seemed to be one of the first places where the berries would ripen, but because it was so close to town they were also picked long before Windflower showed up with his bucket. He didn't mind. It gave him a good excuse for a longer hike up the trail towards the transmission tower where the blueberries were more plentiful and the people scarcer. In any case, there were only bushes and small white clusters so far this year. That was okay with Windflower and especially Lady who had already started up the trail.

Windflower ran to catch up, but Lady seemed intent on getting ahead. She disappeared around a corner before Windflower could get there. He couldn't see her, but soon he heard her and when he came around the bend he could see the reason why. Lady was barking as loud as she could at a fairly large black bear that was now standing on its hind legs and howling almost as loud as the dog. This is not good, not good at all, thought Windflower.

And worse, the bear had noticed his presence. It turned its attention from Lady to the Mountie. Windflower had been around a few bears in his lifetime, mostly when he was a kid in Pink Lake. He knew better than to run, which was certainly his first instinct. Instead he tried to raise himself up to his full height and started waving his arms and yelling at the bear. The bear was startled by this response, and if he had been by himself, the bear might have taken that as fair warning and moved off.

But at the same time as Windflower was yelling, Lady decided to do her part by yapping even louder and then starting to nip at the bear's heels. The bear was not impressed. All Windflower saw was a blur of black and brown as the bear slapped at the collie. Lady flew through the air for a few seconds in a kind of suspended animation, and then landed with a thud in the bushes. The bear started to follow. Windflower pulled out his service pistol.

The first shot got the bear's attention. The second shot sent it scampering back up the trail and into a thickly wooded area.

As the bear was fleeing, Windflower saw the reason for the bear's intensity. Scrambling behind his mother was a small black bear. The smaller bear gave one quick glance at Windflower to check him out, but a swift cuff by Mama Bear to the back of its head got it back on track with his mother.

"So that's what's going on," Windflower said out loud. His experience with bears was that they almost always avoided humans, except when people stood in between them and food, or in order to protect their young.

As soon as the pair of bears had disappeared, Windflower ran to Lady's side. She was lying close to where she had fallen. She wasn't bleeding, which was a good sign. But she was moaning. That meant she was in pain and had likely broken something. He picked up his dog and as gently as he could, hurried back to his car. He put Lady in the back and covered her with a blanket.

"Betsy," said Windflower, when the phone answered at the RCMP office. "I'm on my way to the vet in Marystown. Could you contact Media Relations and get them to put out a bear warning for the area near the trail behind the clinic?"

"Are you okay?" asked Betsy, sounding worried.

"I'm fine. But Lady's had an accident. I need to get her checked out. Also, can you get someone to go back up to the trail and put a notice about the bear at the entrance?" Then thinking about his earlier conversations, he added. "Can you also call the Town Office as well and let them know?"

"Will do, sir," said Betsy.

"Thanks, Betsy."

Windflower drove the half hour to Marystown at just above the speed limit. Inside he was trying to justify going as fast as he really wanted, but glancing back at Lady he could see she was hurt but not in immediate danger. At least he hoped not. He turned into the veterinary clinic on Harris Drive in Marystown. Lady was still gently moaning. He lifted her up along with the blanket and brought her inside.

The receptionist came out from behind her desk as soon as she saw him. "Mrs. Molloy called and said you were coming," she said. "I'll get Doctor Brinston for you."

Moments later the vet appeared and came over quickly to Windflower and Lady. "What happened?" he asked.

"Lady and I came between a mama bear and her cub. Lady tried to help, but she got a pretty good whack from Mama Bear for her efforts."

"Help me bring her in back and I'll take a look at her," said the vet.

He did some poking and probing of Lady, who moaned a little more and pulled back when he touched her chest area. After the examination he gave her a small biscuit as a treat, but Lady was too uncomfortable to even pay attention to that, and just sighed at the veterinarian.

"What do you think, Doc?" asked Windflower.

"She's in lot of pain," said Brinston. "But it's hard to tell whether she has anything broken or it's just bruised. I think we should get an x-ray and check that out. But first we should give her some painkillers. Is that okay with you?"

"Sure. But can you get x-rays done on a dog here?"

"I've had an x-ray machine for the last ten years," said the veterinarian. "People will spare no expense to ensure that their pets have good health care."

"Absolutely," said Windflower quickly, not wanting the vet to think he was too cheap to look after his dog. "Whatever Lady needs she can have."

The vet laughed. "You better be careful with that offer. I once had a lady ask if I could get contact lenses for her cat with glaucoma."

This time Windflower laughed. But he wasn't really sure if the vet was serious or not, so he didn't say anything else.

The veterinarian went to his pharmaceutical cabinet and loaded up a syringe with what Windflower assumed was the painkiller.

"Let's sedate her first. That way she won't mind the x-ray so much." He held up the long needle and looked at Windflower. "You can wait outside if you want."

Windflower hesitated and the vet added, "She's going to be okay. After I give her this shot she won't know that any of the rest of us are in the world." Windflower gave Lady one more pat on the head and turned to walk away. He could hear Lady give one long and loud moan, but resisted the urge to turn back, and went to the reception area.

He was sitting outside waiting and thinking that this must be what it was like when one of your children was in hospital when his phone rang. He looked at the number as he walked outside to take the call. It was Sheila.

"Winston, I heard about Lady and the bear. Is she okay?"

What about me, thought Windflower, and how did Sheila hear about this so quickly? But he didn't ask these questions and took a safer course. "I'm at the animal clinic in Marystown. Lady's in a lot of pain and it looks like she might have some broken ribs. The vet is doing x-rays right now."

"Are you okay?" asked Sheila.

Finally, thought Windflower to himself.

"Betsy called over to pass along the bear warning and I was there when she called," she added.

"I'm okay. It was a bit exciting, that's for sure."

Maybe now he could get some sympathy of his own. But that was not to be.

"I'm glad you're not hurt. But I am not happy about how today unfolded," continued Sheila. "It feels like you were trying to go around me and talk to Les. You knew I wouldn't like the news."

"I did go to talk to you, but you weren't there," said Windflower, offering up his best excuse.

"Les is a great Town Manager, but Council makes the decisions in Grand Bank and I am their representative. I am the liaison between the Town and the RCMP. Les Warren works for us. If there are going to be any suggested changes to our agreed-upon contract, I am the one that you, as the senior officer in Grand Bank, should be talking to."

"I can talk to Ron Quigley and see if there is anything else he can do," said Windflower, trying to shift the conversation back to friendlier ground. "I'm not happy about this situation either."

"I've already got a call into Inspector Quigley. Anyway, I've got to go. Let me know if there's any more news about Lady."

"I will. Will I see you later?" he asked gingerly.

"I've got a committee meeting and then I thought I'd have an early night. Let's talk tomorrow."

"Okay," said Windflower, although it wasn't at all. After he hung up he went back inside and pondered his life. One of his closest female companions was sedated and didn't know he was in the world and the other didn't care if he existed. This really wasn't okay at all.

Chapter Ten

Windflower went back inside to wait for news about Lady. He didn't have to wait long. Brinston came out from the back a few minutes later.

"So far, so good," said the vet. "It doesn't look like anything is broken, but given the tenderness in the chest area, it's clear she's been bruised and shaken up. I've bandaged her up tight and that will help. We'll know by tomorrow if she needs anything else, but I think she might be okay after a good night's sleep. I suggest you leave her here tonight."

"Sure. Can I see her before I go?"

"Come on back. She's out cold."

Windflower followed the veterinarian to a quiet area in the back where Lady lay sleeping on a rug in a cage in one corner of the room. Windflower went to her and patted her head. He could see the swath of bandages that the veterinarian had wrapped around her. She looked a bit like a furry mummy, having a good sleep.

"She'll be okay here for tonight," said the vet. "I have a bed in my office and I stay here whenever we have an overnight patient.

We have a baby monitor in here so I can hear if she wakes up. But I don't think she will."

"Thanks, Doc. I'll be back in the morning."

Windflower drove back to Grand Bank slowly as he thought about Lady and the joy she'd brought into his life. It was great having a dog again. He hoped she'd be okay. Well, he'd done as much as he could to help her today. Hopefully, she was now on the mend. He stopped at the supermarket along the way home and picked up a barbecued chicken, a baguette and a salad bag. That would be supper tonight and a couple of days of lunches too.

When he got home, he cut off half of the chicken breast, sliced off a big chunk of bread that he smothered in butter, and filled the rest of his plate with salad and some cherry tomatoes he found in the fridge. He ate as slowly as he could, which wasn't very slow, rinsed his plate and made a large pot of tea. Might as well enjoy the evening, he thought. He put his teapot on the living room table, turned on the Blue Jays game and picked up his Brunetti book.

He liked this book by Donna Leon, but was getting a little bit irritated by the fact that she seemed to skim over the meals in this story, instead of describing them in the great detail Windflower savoured. The food was still there, like involtini with fresh asparagus and fish dishes such as merluzzo con spinaci, but Windflower felt a little cheated when neither the author nor the diners in the book paid too much attention to what they were eating. The story itself was riveting, however, and Windflower spent a couple of relaxing hours stretched out on the couch with his book and his baseball game.

He took his book to bed with him, feeling a bit sad and even lonelier when he jumped under the covers. He and Sheila did spend a few nights apart from time to time, but usually because one of them had work commitments, and almost always by mutual consent. He didn't even have his dog with him. He tried to read but he realized he was simply too tired. He turned off the light and seconds later he was fast asleep.

But not for long. The first thing he heard was Eddie Tizzard yelling. "We've got a fire!!" Windflower didn't know how he got there but the next thing he knew he was chasing Tizzard down his driveway. He caught up to him as his Corporal was gunning his Jeep away from Windflower's house.

"Where's the fire?" he yelled at Tizzard.

"It's over on Seaview Drive," the other man shouted back. "I've called the Fire Department."

When they got to the old white house on Seaview Drive, there were flames licking out from underneath the eaves, and a steady stream of thick black smoke rising into the sky. The house had long been both neglected and abandoned, and was already suffering from the bitter offshore winds and weather. What hadn't been damaged by the elements was being destroyed through neglect and petty vandalism. There were visible holes in the clapboard, and several broken windows. And now this.

Windflower and Tizzard ran from door to door waking up people and getting them out of the nearby houses. They set up a perimeter at each end of the street, but that didn't keep the neighbourhood gawkers from trying to get as close as possible. Windflower radioed Constable Evanchuk to come and join them when she returned from her rounds of the local highway. She and Tizzard could provide a human barrier that would keep the onlookers out of the way and as safe as possible.

Windflower could hear the sirens of the Grand Bank Volunteer Fire Department growing closer when he heard one of the locals yell, "There's somebody in there." Windflower turned and saw a shadowy figure waving frantically from the far side of the second floor. At the same time the flames from the fire shot high into the night sky. A crash shook the street and provoked a collective gasp from the growing crowd. The truss of the roof collapsed into the fire. Windflower pushed the line of bystanders back a few more feet as the wind blew a hot breeze of sparks into his face. Even in this tumultuous uproar, he thought he heard a voice crying for help, and then nothing else.

He woke up and looked around him. He felt as though he had really been in a fire. He was sweaty and hot and a bit overwhelmed. Relieved to realize that it was a dream, just a dream, but a terrifying dream. He tried to go back to sleep but simply could not shake the image of the person in the second floor window from his mind. Still disturbed, he got up and had a long shower. That at least relaxed him enough to get back to sleep, and he didn't stir again until his alarm went off in the morning.

Chapter Eleven

He was still bothered by the dream in the morning. What did that dream mean? He knew from experience that dreams were often messages from your subconscious that you needed to pay attention to something. But what? He decided to let that sit for a little while as he began his day. Sometimes the answers came that way too.

He did his prayers and meditations slowly and deliberately this morning, allowing the smoke from his smudge bowl to linger a little longer. He prayed for Lady that she would be okay, and for him and Sheila to find a good path together. He also asked for help and guidance from his ancestors, that they would show him direction, even if they weren't with him in this world. Finally, he prayed for the mama bear and her cub that had showed up on his journey. Bears were powerful creatures, symbols of strength in his Cree culture, and he asked for some of that strength from his four-legged friend.

Half an hour later he was showered and shaved and ready for another day at work. When he arrived at the RCMP detachment, Tizzard was already there, this time with a package of croissants and a large chunk of cheddar cheese.

"Morning, Boss," said Tizzard. "Breakfast?"

"Thanks, Eddie," said Windflower, filling his coffee mug and grabbing a pastry. "Did you hear about the bear?"

"Yeah. How's Lady doing?"

"Lady is at the vet's in Marystown. I think she's going to be okay. But doesn't anybody care about me?" asked Windflower.

Tizzard looked at him as if it was a trick question and said, "Sure, but we can see you're okay. Now that Lady saved your life again."

Windflower shook his head and cut off a piece of cheese to lay on top of his buttered croissant. "What's going on with the missing young lady?"

"Oh, I'm glad you reminded me. First of all, the motorcycle is fine. Paul sparked it up and checked everything. And lots of gas like you said. He also opened the trailer. Not much there. Some cans of food, rope and a small tarp. But you have to see what I found in the saddlebags when I brought them back," said Tizzard.

"What?"

"Come back to the evidence locker and I'll show you." Tizzard led the way to the locked cabinet near the entrance to the garage. "Look inside," he said.

Windflower dialed the combination and opened the locker. Inside on the top shelf was a large plastic bag containing wads of Canadian one hundred dollar bills. "How much is there?"

"I counted sixty thousand dollars. Not only that, but there's a set of electronic scales and a cocaine purity testing kit." He held up another baggie containing a package with five small vials.

"How did you know what it was?" Windflower asked.

"It says so, right on the back," said Tizzard turning it over. When Windflower looked at him like he was crazy, he added. "I looked it up on the Internet. You can get home testing kits for everything now. You can test your drugs all by yourself. This one says it's guaranteed accurate, and you can get a full result with only 20 mgs of cocaine."

Windflower shook his head again. "This sure does look like a drug buy. I'll talk to Quigley this morning."

Tizzard nodded his okay and the two men went back to finish their breakfast. They were interrupted by a loud shout from the front entrance. "Anybody in 'ere?" the voice boomed. Windflower went out to investigate.

"Ah, Windflower," said the man with the big voice. "I'm 'ere on official police business," he continued.

"Then you're in the right place, Mister Tibbo. What can we do for you today?"

"Well, I'm 'ere about da moose," said Francis Tibbo. "As Deputy Mayor of Grand Bank I am demanding you take action to deal with da situation round 'ere."

Tizzard had come in from the back room and was standing behind Windflower. Windflower could feel him trying to stifle a laugh.

"Dis is no laughin' matter," said Tibbo. "My missus was coming 'ome last night when a big bloody moose jumped up outta the ditch and tried to attack her car."

"Was she hurt?" asked Windflower.

"She was badly disturbed," said Tibbo.

"Was there any damage to her vehicle?" asked Windflower.

"I told ya dat the moose tried to attack her, but I guess 'e missed," said Tibbo.

"So you're here to report a near-moose collision," said Windflower as Tizzard covered his face and walked away.

"I'm 'ere to report a dangerous situation." By this time Tibbo was growing red in the face. "You're supposed to be protectin' us, aren't ya? Well, start doing some protectin' from da moose. If someone dies around 'ere it'll be on your 'ead." With that, Tibbo marched out of the office and left Windflower shaking his head for about the third time that morning.

Tizzard came out and started to speak, but Windflower held up his hand. "Don't start. Just don't start."

Tizzard wisely held his comments to himself and went back to his croissants. Windflower refilled his coffee and went to his office. What else could happen today? He didn't have to wait long to find out. He had just sat down when his phone rang.

Chapter Twelve

"Good morning, Winston," came Ron Quigley's friendly voice over the receiver.

"Good morning, Ron. I'm glad you called. I was thinking about calling you."

"I already talked to the mayor, if that's what you're talking about," said Quigley. "She's not very happy with either of us by the sound of it."

"Nope. I tried to run a little interference through the Town Manager, but that didn't help. Might have made matters worse."

"I guess it's not surprising, but there's not too much we can do about it, at least in the short term. But that's not what I'm calling you about. Although, what I'm going to tell you will have an impact over there, if you agree."

"Agree to what?" asked Windflower.

"Two bodies were discovered last night. They were found in the forest, near the park where the Bacchus guys were hanging out in Bishops Falls. A man and a woman, hands tied behind their backs and shot in the back of the head. Nobody knows about this yet. There'll be a statement issued later this morning out of Grand Falls," said Quigley.

"Sounds like an execution," said Windflower.

"I want you to go over and lead the investigation. They'll be coordinating this from Halifax, but I want my own man on the ground."

"But what about everything here?"

"Tizzard can stay there until we get this thing cleared up. If there are any problems I'll go over to Grand Bank myself," said Quigley. "When can you go?"

"I can go later today. I've got a few things to clear up first. But we've also got a situation here." Windflower explained the missing female biker and Tizzard's surprise discovery.

"Okay, leave that with me. I'll follow up with Tizzard. Okay?" asked Quigley. "One more thing, Winston. We've got a guy in with the local bikers in Grand Falls. I'll put the word out for him to get in contact with you."

"Is he local or from the mainland?"

"Robert French from Bathurst in New Brunswick, I think. He's a big guy, hard to miss. He fits right in with the bikers. He doesn't report here, but I get some info from him on our local guys from time to time."

"Oh, by the way, did you hear about my bear encounter?" asked Windflower.

"I heard Lady saved your butt. Again," said Quigley. "Call me when you're out there, okay?"

"All right." Windflower still felt a little hard done by when it came to his near-death experience with Mama Bear. Lady, he thought. I wonder how she is. He picked up the phone and called the animal clinic in Marystown. The vet was with a patient, but the receptionist reported Lady was in good spirits this morning, had been for a short walk outside, and even eaten a little food. She was still being sedated so she was asleep right now. The receptionist took Windflower's number and promised to pass along the message that he had called.

That's one down, he thought. Now for the harder one. He called Sheila's cell phone but only got her voice mail. He left a message telling her he had to go out of town and asking her to call. Betsy came in to say good morning. Windflower gave her an update about his activities and the now obligatory report on Lady's condition. He asked her to send Tizzard in to see him.

"Well, I've got good news and bad news," he said to Tizzard. "The good news is that your transfer has been delayed, for a few days anyway."

"That is good news. What's the bad news?"

"I'm going back out to Central on a job. Inspector Quigley is going to be taking over responsibility for this area while I'm gone. I told him about the cash and the other stuff you found."

"That's not bad news. I like the Inspector. Not as much as you, of course," Tizzard added as a quick correction to his initial reaction.

"Sure. I still want you to keep me in the loop on everything, okay Corporal?"

"Okay. Any news on Lady?"

"The most talked-about dog in Grand Bank history had a good night and is resting peacefully in Marystown. I'm going to drop by and see her on my way out. Would you be able to look after her while I'm away?"

"I'd love to," said Tizzard. "As soon as I get the word I'll go pick her up."

"Thanks, Eddie. I'll give you an update after I talk to Doc Brinston." After Tizzard left Windflower closed up his computer and started choosing supplies to take with him. He drove back to his house and packed a small suitcase with a few changes of clothing and toiletries. He threw his book in on top and was closing the bag when he heard Sheila calling out his name.

"Hi Sheila," he said, when she came into the bedroom.

"I got your message," said Sheila. "Can we talk before you head out?"

"Sure. I was going to make some coffee. Do you want some?"

"That would be great." Sheila walked back out to the kitchen with Windflower. "I'm sorry if I was short with you yesterday. But I felt that you were trying to go around me, and I just can't have that. I have a job to do as mayor and I need you to fully respect my role in this community. This is really important to me."

"I did go to see you first." Windflower turned on the percolator and sat down at the kitchen table across from Sheila. "But I do admit that when I saw Les, I thought it would be easier than having to bring the bad news to you. So I take responsibility for my actions, and I'm sorry if you feel in any way that I do not respect you or support you as mayor."

"I accept your apology, Sergeant. I still think the decision to reduce service sucks and I've already told your Inspector that. But I forgive you."

"Ron told me that you spoke to him. He said you were pretty steamed. I'm not sure there's anything he can do, but in the short term he's going to spend a little time over here."

"That might help, as least with public perception. But Council is still going to go crazy about this. Especially Francis Tibbo."

"Tibbo was in to see me this morning. He wants the RCMP to do something about the moose."

"We all want you to do something about the moose," added Sheila. "What are you going to do?"

"I think I'll refer that one upstairs. Way above my pay grade," he added with a laugh.

Sheila laughed too. "I suspect it will be on the agenda at the meeting this morning. But once they hear about the decrease in service, that will take up all the space, even for Francis Tibbo."

Windflower got them both a cup of coffee.

"Thanks," said Sheila. "Is there anything new about Carol?"

"Not much," he said. He paused briefly to refocus and think about what he could tell Sheila. "Her motorcycle wasn't broken down or anything, but there's still no sign of her. We've put out a province-wide search notice and usually that prompts somebody to come forward with information."

"I hope that's soon. I'm worried about her."

Windflower thought of saying not to worry, but realized that might be a mistake. "So far there's no indication of anything bad happening. And Tizzard is on the case. If she's still around here, he'll find her."

"And how's Lady?" asked Sheila.

"I'm going to drop by and see her on my way out. She had a good night at the clinic and it sounds like she's doing well. I'll call you after I know more."

"I'm glad she's okay. She's a great little dog. And I'm glad you're okay too. You're a good man, Winston Windflower. You've got to trust me a little more. I don't bite, you know."

"Thanks, Sheila. I'm starting to figure out what Shakespeare was talking about when he said 'women speak two languages - one of which is verbal'."

Sheila laughed again and came to put her arms around Windflower. She hugged him close and he gladly returned the favour. "I love you, Winston."

"I love you too, Sheila. If you're finished your coffee, I'll walk you to your car, ma'am."

"Thank you kindly, Sergeant." Windflower waved as Sheila drove off, and then packed up his car for the first leg of his journey.

Chapter Thirteen

The ride to Marystown was clear and smooth, the way Windflower hoped the rest of his day would go. But that appeared unlikely because just as he was starting to enjoy the morning drive and his topped-up thermos of coffee, he saw them on the side of the highway. It was Mama Bear and her cub ambling along the road, and heading into the woods near the turnoff to Garnish.

Windflower radioed into the Grand Bank Detachment.

"Windflower here on Route 210 near the Garnish exit. Reporting a large female black bear and a cub moving from the side of the highway into a wooded area. Do you copy?"

"Copy," came a female voice Windflower recognized as Betsy even over the crackle of the radio. "Will report to Corporal Tizzard. Any more instructions? Over."

"Thanks, Betsy. Please advise Tizzard to contact Wildlife Control. And advise Garnish Town Office. Over."

"Confirmed. Over."

"Over and out."

Mama and her cub were scavenging for food. They were likely

tired of their regular shoots and leaves, and since there were few berries ripe enough yet, they might be looking for other options. He hoped they hadn't gotten an appetite for human-type food because that would be a problem for both the bears and the locals. Back home, they'd had a few bears that had become garbage eaters. That became more than a nuisance and was perceived as a threat by some on the band council who forced a decision to try and eliminate the problem.

The situation was usually treated more humanely in the south, but there was a big danger, mostly to the bears, when people thought they were encroaching on their territory. At best, the bears could be relocated back into a wilder or more remote area. At worst, well, Windflower didn't want to think about the worst. In fact, he didn't want to think at all. So he tuned in to the classical music station on the radio and settled into the smooth waves of Chopin's nocturnes. He was still floating along when he passed the 'Welcome to Marystown' sign at the edge of town.

He passed by the always-crowded Tim Hortons and through the one busy intersection to the veterinarian's office. The reception-ist greeted him with a smile and led him back to the cage where Lady was sleeping. When he came close to her, she stirred and tried to get up. He was careful not to touch the area where she was bandaged. While she was still groggy from her medication, she did seem pleased to see Windflower. She quickly relaxed into his gentle rubbing motion on her rump. Windflower didn't even notice the veterinarian come into the room until he spoke.

"She's going to be okay. I'm pretty sure nothing's broken and a few more days of rest and painkillers and she should be back to normal."

"That's good news, Doc. When can she go home?" asked Wind-flower.

"I think she'd probably do better with another night here, if that's okay with you. She seems comfortable and won't move around as much here. That would be good for her healing."

"Okay. I'm going out of town, but I have a back-up. I'll let him know and he can come over tomorrow to pick her up."

"Great. You can take her out back for a little walk if you want. Not too far though. The slower she goes right now, the better."

"Thanks again, Doc." Windflower nudged Lady to her feet. Despite being a little unsteady she seemed happy to be up. The pair walked out the back door and into a grassy area overlooking the water. Lady did a perfunctory stoop and sniff inspection, had a quick pee and indicated to Windflower she had completed her tasks. Windflower took her back inside, where she was quite content to curl up again in her temporary home.

On his way out Windflower asked for and received his bill from the receptionist. He was slightly surprised by the total: almost $700.00. But that did include room and board for his favourite canine. Truth be told, Windflower would have paid anything to have his Lady be okay. He paid the bill, and stopped in at Tim Hortons for a coffee for the road and to make his phone calls. He made one to Ron Quigley's office and left a message that he was on his way to Grand Falls and another to Tizzard to confirm his attention to the bear situation, and to make arrangements for Lady. His last call was to Sheila, ostensibly to tell her about Lady, but really just to reconnect. This was going to be his wife, after all.

Driving up to the Trans Canada Highway was almost always a peaceful and reflective time for Windflower. Today was no exception. He loved the solitary isolation and the lack of human presence. Except for this thin ribbon of highway, there was little evidence of people ever having lived here. It reminded him of the vast expanses of bush and water and nature that he had grown up with in Northern Alberta. Even though the trees were smaller and the hills much shorter than back home, he loved the feeling that he was alone here with Mother Earth.

Too fast the scenery changed from barrens to blacktop as he approached Goobies and the turnoff onto the Trans Canada. He filled up the gas tank, grabbed a turkey with dressing sandwich and was soon back on the road towards Grand Falls. Along the way he passed the majestic views of the ocean off Clarenville, and then back through Terra Nova National Park. Windflower loved driving through the park. Even though he didn't have time to stop today, he did spend a few moments recollecting the many fond memories he'd had here with both Lady and Sheila.

After Terra Nova, the highway swung back near the coast again and through the flatlands on the Gambo River. Then it drifted back inland through the airport town of Gander. He was meeting his contacts at the Grand Falls RCMP Detachment but he had to pass through Bishops Falls first. This was where the Bacchus gang had been hanging out, and where the two bodies had been discovered. Might as well take a look, he thought, as he turned off the TCH into the small town of Bishops Falls.

Windflower had been to Bishops Falls a few times before his latest excursion with the bike patrol. He had stayed in a nearby cabin with his old buddy Bill Ford. The two of them had spent a wonderful weekend salmon fishing on the Exploits River. Some of the best salmon fishing in the world was around this area, and Ford knew a couple of prime spots where they each managed to hook and catch a couple of Atlantic salmon. It was fun and relaxing to enjoy the fly-fishing-only atmosphere. That was matched only by frying up some of the salmon every night for their dinner.

But this was not to be a fun visit, thought Windflower, as he drove through Bishops Falls and parked his vehicle on the perimeter of Fallsview Municipal Park. There was a lone Mountie on site near the area that had been marked off by bright yellow police tape. He waved hello and walked over to the Constable who was playing with his cellphone. He didn't notice Windflower's appearance until the other man got almost up to his car.

The Mountie, who was supposed to be on sentry duty fumbled with his phone when he saw Windflower, dropping it to the ground in the realization that he'd been caught out. Windflower smiled and said, "I'm Windflower. Are you in charge of the crime scene?"

"I'm Daniels," said the Constable. "Yes, Sergeant, I was just ..."

Windflower cut him off. "I'm going to have a quick look around. I won't disturb anything."

Before Daniels could say or do anything else, Windflower stepped under the police tape and walked down by the dam and power station. There was a salmon ladder here he seemed to recall, but it was too late in the season for many Atlantic salmon to be making the journey back home to spawn in the river. He walked over near the area where the grass had been well trampled down, probably the place they had carried the bodies out from. He peered into the woods but didn't go all the way in. He didn't want or need to see the scene to imagine what had happened and could only hope that all of the evidence had been collected already.

Windflower went a little farther towards the water where he remembered there was a magnificent view of the falls. He spent a few more moments taking in the spectacle before heading back to his car. He had wanted, maybe needed, a brief glimpse of the natural beauty that he remembered from his previous visits to Bishops Falls, in order to cleanse him a little before he had to enter the dark world of death and murder.

He nodded his goodbyes to Daniels, who at least now looked like he was paying attention. Although Windflower suspected that would only last until he'd driven off. On his way out of the park he saw the white forensics van pulling in. He waved to the officer and he pulled over.

"Windflower, how's it going b'y?" said another RCMP officer getting out on the passenger side.

"Hey, Brownie. You guys just getting here?"

"Yeah," said Brown. "I guess there are problems everywhere. This one sounds pretty awful though. What are you doing here so far from home?"

"I'm helping out the locals. If you're around later, let's go for a beer."

"Sounds good," said the forensics team leader. Then pointing to his crew unloading its equipment said, "I guess I better get at it. See you later."

"Good luck," said Windflower, happy to have professionals on the scene. He didn't have a lot of faith in the young RCMP officer back there. Anyway, that wasn't his problem. His problem awaited him down the road at the Grand Falls Detachment. First of all, he had to fight his way through the crush of media people who had stationed themselves in the narrow doorway of the building.

Chapter Fourteen

They gathered around Windflower like wild dogs to fresh meat, and started yelling questions at him while their cameras were filming what they hoped would be his response. But his only reaction was to smile glumly and push his way through.

The receptionist at the RCMP office forced a smile at Windflower as he came in the door and stood to greet him. "Good afternoon, Sergeant Windflower, and welcome back to Grand Falls. Sorry about the circus, they've been perched there since the first media release went out this morning. We've got a Super coming down from Halifax to meet with them at 3 p.m. Usually, we'd handle it ourselves, but because the bikers are involved, they want to send in the big brass."

"Thanks, Lynn. Good to see you too. Is the boss around?"

"Just a second. I'll get him," The woman pushed the intercom button. "Sergeant Windflower is here."

"Thank you," came a voice back over the intercom. Seconds later a tall blond Mountie came walking out to meet Windflower.

"Good to see you, Winston." Corporal Lars Lundquist held out a big, meaty hand that resembled a bear paw to Windflower.

"Same here, Lars. Although I wish we were here for a bit of salmon fishing, instead of this other stuff. "

"Me, too. We've set up a command centre in back. Come on back and I'll show you what we have so far."

The local officers, led by Lundquist, had taken over the storage area in the back of the building and converted it to a make-shift centre where they had placed all of the evidence collected to date on a number of tables. Windflower was impressed. There were various pictures of the deceased and of the surrounding area where they had been killed. He recognized the location at the park right away, but it sure seemed a lot colder and less friendly than before. There were also a number of see-through plastic evidence bags with clothing and personal effects that Windflower scanned and noted. Most chilling of all were at least a dozen shell casings.

"Good job," he said to Lundquist. "Who were the victims?"

"The man was Todd Lundrigan and the woman was Stella Louise Winslow. Both were well-known to us and to the criminal justice system. He was 29 and affiliated with the Outlaws. She, on the other hand, was 25 and used to be the girlfriend and live-in partner of one of the full-patch Bacchus guys."

"Were they still a couple?" Windflower looked in his element. "I knew both crews were operating in Grand Falls, but I thought they had a non-competition agreement, not a coming together like that."

"We don't know. That's one of a long list of questions we don't have answers to yet."

"Recent trouble between them?"

"You know, we've had both these gangs here for a long time, but we haven't had even a good dust-up for the last five years I've been here. They may have been headquartered here, but it's like they didn't want to soil their own nest."

"Anyway, I'd like a full profile on them. Everything you know and anything anybody wants to tell us. Can you do that?"

"Sure," Lundquist said. "It's all hands on deck until we get this sorted out. We've even got a reprieve from the cuts to deal with it. So you've got me and Daniels, full-time."

"I met Daniels out at the park on the way in. I'd prefer to deal with you, if that's okay."

Lundquist laughed. "Yeah, he may not have the full attention span necessary for a long career on the Force," he said.

Windflower smiled back. "What about other evidence from the scene? Any witnesses, anybody hear or see anything?"

"Just what you see here. We did the best we could, but forensics is still on their way. They should be here soon. We tried to keep the scene as secure as possible."

"I saw Brownie and the crew on the way in. Witnesses?" he asked again.

"Nothing yet, but it is a popular place for young people. They hang around in their cars, and do what they usually do when they are hanging around in cars," said Lundquist. "I've got Daniels assigned to start poking around and asking questions later tonight when more people are more likely to show up."

"Is there anything from the coroner yet?" asked Windflower.

"That's a bit of a problem," said Lundquist. "We haven't got anybody in that official role, so one of the doctors at the hospital is looking into it for us. So far, nothing on time of death, or even final cause, but as you can see from the pictures, they were clearly shot in the back of the head."

"Who found the bodies?" asked Windflower.

"A guy heading out for some salmon fishing on the river," said Lundquist. "A tourist from the States. He's still around if you want to talk to him. He's staying at the same hotel as you, I think."

Windflower was about to ask for the man's name when he heard the ruckus from outside that could only mean the big cheese from Halifax had arrived. Windflower followed Lundquist out to the boardroom where a podium with a microphone had been set up. The first person he saw was a familiar face, Superintendent

Wally Majesky. He had worked for Majesky at the Halifax Airport. Majesky was an Inspector then, and led a very successful team that almost completely shut down a gang operating a smuggling ring at the airport. Everybody involved got a promotion out of that job. It was where Windflower got his Sergeant's stripes. Obviously, Majesky had done okay too.

Windflower liked Majesky. He was one of the good guys in his books. He had been the perfect leader in Windflower's mind: fair, consistent, and loyal. He always had your back. Majesky liked Windflower too, and that was evident from the broad smile that crossed his face when he saw him across the room. Majesky had the full throng of media people surrounding him, but he managed to break away by promising to come back for the formal press conference in fifteen minutes.

"Lynn," he said to the receptionist who had accompanied him into the room and was trying to fend off the reporters, "Can you help these folks get set up? I have to talk to these other officers for a few minutes and I'll be right back."

The receptionist didn't need any more encouragement to start pushing the media people back into place, and was soon organizing all of them into their appropriate spots for the press conference.

"She's a natural leader," said Majesky to Lundquist.

"Can we talk for a few minutes?" He reached out his hand to Windflower. "Good to see you, Windflower. Are you going to be leading this investigation from here?"

"Yes, sir. Good to see you again, too, sir."

They followed Lundquist back to the evidence area where he gave the Superintendent a similar run-through like the one he'd given to Windflower. "So, nothing new?" Majesky asked.

"No, sir," said Lundquist. "We're going to start interviewing people in the area tonight and forensics is at the scene right now."

"It's Corporal Ted Brown and his crew. They're very good, thorough."

"Good," said Majesky. "Let's go feed some meat to the wolves.

I want you to stand beside me, Windflower. You don't have to say anything. But I want them to go to you if they have any questions later. It's better than them going after Lundquist here."

Lundquist looked relieved. Windflower nodded and followed the Superintendent out into the boardroom that was now well-lit and wired for sound.

Majesky read an opening statement, repeating the talking points from the media release that had been issued that morning. Then he opened the floor to questions. A few asked for more specifics, and the RCMP Superintendent had to admit they had little information collected so far. Not surprisingly, the reporters wanted to know if the outlaw motorcycle gangs were involved in these murders. "Too early to say," said the Superintendent. "This investigation is just getting underway. Our forensics team is combing the area right now and we are interviewing all possible witnesses to these horrible crimes."

"Should the public be worried about a biker war?" shouted one reporter from a national T.V. network who had come into town just for this story.

"People should always be vigilant," said Majesky. "But there's no reason for panic. We don't have all the information yet and there's no reason for wild speculation at this time," he said with a stern glare in the offending reporter's direction. "We have good police protection with our local RCMP detachment, and we have brought in Sergeant Winston Windflower, the best investigator in the province, to lead our team."

He pointed at Windflower who smiled, took a step forward, and nodded in the media's direction, blinking a little in the lights.

"He's just arrived so he doesn't have any new information to provide yet. But as soon as he does, he'll be happy to answer your questions." Windflower nodded once more and the RCMP Superintendent added. "We are asking for the public's cooperation and support in this investigation. If you saw or heard anything unusual at or around Fallsview Municipal Park in the last few days, please contact Sergeant Windflower or the Grand Falls RCMP as soon as possible."

Then, even as the reporters continued to yell questions, Majesky led the two other Mounties to the back room.

"That's always the hardest one," said the Superintendent. "You don't have anything to give them, but you still have to stand there and try and reassure the public that everything is going to be okay."

"I thought you did great, sir," said Windflower, as Lundquist nodded his agreement.

"Well, it's all over to you now," said Majesky. "We'll give the vultures a few minutes to pack up and then I'm heading back. I'm going to stay in Deer Lake tonight, and then back home tomorrow morning. How are things going with you, Windflower? I saw Guy Simard a few weeks ago. He said you were getting married."

"I am sir. I'm looking forward to seeing Guy again. We had good times working together back in Halifax."

"We did indeed," said Majesky. "Where's the back door to this place, Lundquist? I told my guy to park the getaway car back there."

"Right this way, sir," said Lundquist.

"If there's anything you need from me, you know where I am," said Majesky to Windflower as he followed the other RCMP officer out. "I want to know how this investigation unfolds every step of the way. Is that clear, Sergeant?"

"Perfectly, sir," said Windflower.

"Remember, someone saw, heard or knows something about what happened at the park. There's never been a perfect crime that someone hasn't witnessed or wanted to tell somebody about." With that, Majesky was gone and Windflower was left to ponder his next steps. By the time Lundquist got back, he had decided at least that much.

"So where do we start?" asked Lundquist.

"Let's go see your acting coroner. They can usually tell us things about dead people that the deceased are unable to provide. And right now, we can use all the information we can get."

Chapter Fifteen

The Central Newfoundland Regional Health Centre was not new, but the medical facility that served the people of Grand Falls and surrounding areas had been refurbished and renovated in the past couple of years. That was good, since like most other hospitals of its kind it was over 50 years old and starting to show its age. But Windflower liked the place anyway. There were large grassy grounds to walk around, and a nice place to have a picnic on the few fine days they got each season.

Lundquist drove while Windflower took in the sights of a busy little municipality going about its business. Like the hospital, the town had rebuilt itself from the devastating impact of the closing of the town's main employer, a pulp and paper mill, a few years back. It still had over 13,000 people, which was a tribute to its determination to forge a future in these uncertain times. It had plenty of amenities and opportunities for its citizens. It also had an underside that Windflower was about to discover as well.

Lundquist drove around the back of the building and parked in the area reserved for emergency and police vehicles. He and

Windflower entered through the ambulance entrance and were waved in by the security guard on duty. Lundquist made a phone call from the security desk to get their contact to meet them. Windflower followed Lundquist down the rabbit warren of rooms until they came to an older section of the building that was obviously not being used for regular patients.

Inside one of these rooms they met a young-looking doctor who Lundquist introduced as Doctor Lonnie Stock. Stock reached out his hand to Windflower and led them into another area of the hospital that, if anything, was even older and more rundown.

"It's not much, but it's quiet and cool and we can do what we need to do without being interrupted," said Stock. "Let me pull out the files on our deceased." He ruffled through the papers in the first file. "Lundrigan was overweight and a smoker, but in surprisingly good health for his lifestyle. His liver is a little distended, probably from alcohol consumption. Otherwise, he could have lived a long time if those bullets hadn't found the back of his head."

Windflower smiled wryly. What is it with these guys who like forensic medicine, he thought? Just like Doc Sanjay back home, they all had this weird sense of humour about the dead.

"How many bullets did you find?" asked Windflower.

"We took three out of Lundrigan and four from Winslow. She was in pretty good shape too," said Doctor Stock and then after a pause added, "She and her baby were doing well."

"She was pregnant?" asked Lundquist.

"Yes. I'd say about four months," said Stock. "The fetus was struck by one of the other bullets that hit Ms. Winslow, through her back and out again through her stomach. You might want these," he said, handing Windflower the tagged and bagged bullets removed from the victims. "There are more bullets inside them, including in the fetus, but we just took out the ones that were easily accessible."

"Have you sent the blood for testing?" asked Windflower.

"Not yet, but I can," said Stock.

"Can you also get a blood sample from the baby as well?" asked Windflower. When Lundquist looked at him strangely he added, "It might help to know who the father was."

"Sure," said Doctor Stock. "I haven't done many of these things before. That's good to know about the blood tests. What should I be looking for?"

"Drugs, prescription and otherwise, as well as anything out of the ordinary. You never know what can help you in an investigation, especially a murder case."

"No problem," said the doctor. "We can probably get that done overnight. Should I call you, Corporal?"

"No, call Sergeant Windflower," said the other policeman. "He's in charge of this case now."

The two RCMP officers shook hands again with the doctor and wound their way back to their car. When they drove back to the detachment, there was no sign of the media crush from a while ago. Daniels was back from his sentry duty at the crime scene, and having what looked like a pleasant chat with the receptionist. He almost jumped to attention when he saw Lundquist and Windflower come in.

"What's going on out at the park?" asked Lundquist.

"The forensics people told me they would look after things now. I'm going back out there in a couple of hours to start talking to people. Fitzpatrick is already going door to door in the surrounding neighbourhood to see if anyone saw or heard anything unusual. I'll do the same with the young people once they start showing up this evening."

"Good," said Lundquist. "What's next?"

"I'd like to have a look at all the files on both deceased as well as any intel you have on the local bikers. And I guess we should talk to the ex-boyfriend. Is he still around?"

"Joey Snow," said Lundquist. "Yeah, he's around. Goes by the nickname of Joe Blow. You can probably guess why. He's like the unofficial main guy for Bacchus. He was away for a bit in Renous, but has been back here, causing trouble again, for the last few months."

"Let's bring him in tomorrow morning for a chat," said Windflower.

"Can you look after that?" Lundquist asked Daniels.

"With pleasure," said Daniels. "They've got a hangout in Grenfell Heights. He's usually out around there most days. If not, I'll track him down."

"Great. Now, if you'll get me those files and a cup of coffee, I'll be all set."

Lundquist got Windflower his coffee and minutes later Lynn, the receptionist, came into the makeshift command centre with a stack of files. Windflower scanned the files quickly and took a few notes, but realized he was getting both hungry and a little tired. He said goodnight to Lundquist, and went over to the hotel to drop off his bags and check in.

Chapter Sixteen

It felt like a long day already by the time Windflower got to his hotel room. Even though it was not even dark, all he wanted was to go to bed. He fought that urge by having an alternating hot and cold shower. It didn't just wake him up, it was an old muscle relaxing strategy he'd learned years ago. Fifteen minutes later, he not only felt alive again, he also realized he was very hungry. He changed into his civvies and decided to go for take-out.

There was a great Chinese take-out place in Grand Falls. It reminded him of being out west, on the prairies in Saskatchewan and Alberta. Every small town had a Chinese restaurant. The original operators of those establishments likely came over to work on the railroad. When that work was done and they wanted to settle down, they opened small restaurants. Windflower wondered what had brought a Chinese family to Grand Falls. He was pondering that very question when he pulled up to the restaurant door and saw the forensics van parked in front.

He almost bumped into Brown who was coming out with a box-load of food, paper plates and plastic utensils.

"I hope you left some for me, Ted," said Windflower.

"Winston. I guess it's no surprise to see you here. Best Chinese food outside of St. John's. Just picking up some stuff for the crew. We'll go 'til dark and then start again as soon as it's light in the morning."

"You find anything yet?" Windflower asked.

"We found tracks from an ATV," said Brown. "And a number of footprints. It's hard to tell who's who though, because we have to separate out the locals and the paramedics and the deceased, from whoever else was there."

"How many people do you think were there initially?"

"I'd guess at least two, but it could be more. There are prints that look a little different on both sides of where the ATV was parked. It'll take some time to sort all this out. We'll have more in the morning,"

"Thanks. I'll let you go have supper."

"Okay," said Brown. "Hey, are you at the Grand Falls Hotel? Maybe we can get together for a drink later?"

"That sounds great," Windflower replied with a smile. "Give me a call."

Brown went off with his box of Chinese food for the troops. Windflower went into the restaurant and took a quick look at the dinner buffet, but decided to order some take-out from the menu instead. He knew from past experience that simple was always better when it came to ordering any take-out food. He selected Combo #3 with an egg roll, beef with vegetables and almonds, sweet and sour chicken balls and chicken fried rice. In twenty minutes, he was back in his hotel room with his food and a large tea from Tim Hortons.

After he finished his meal, he turned on the television and saw a repeat of the news highlights. Much to his surprise, there was Superintendent Majesky talking and he could see himself standing in the background, looking quite serious. That was the look he was going for, he thought, feeling particularly pleased with himself. He was trying to find the ballgame when his cellphone rang.

"Hi, Winston, just checking in to see if you miss me. I miss you, a lot."

"Hi, Sheila. I miss you too. Things are crazy busy out here."

"I saw you on the news," said Sheila. "You looked good, serious, but good. Who is that good-looking Inspector?"

"That's Superintendent Wally Majesky. He was my boss at the Halifax airport."

"So he must know Guy Simard too?" asked Sheila.

"Yeah, we were all on the same crew. Guy will probably tell you a few stories about that time if he gets a chance. I was young and innocent then."

"You may have been young, but you have never been innocent," said Sheila, laughing. "How long do you think you'll be out in Grand Falls? I'm only asking because I can cancel dinner with Herb and Moira on the weekend if you want."

"I don't know yet. But let's leave the dinner on for now. Even if I have to come back out here, I think I'll want a day or two at home."

"That would be great," said Sheila. "Give me a call later tonight if you get a chance. I miss you," she said again. "Love you, Winston."

"I love you too," said Windflower.

Windflower gave up on the T.V. and picked up his book. But he was more tired than he thought and fell asleep. He woke to the jarring ring, ring, ring of his hotel room phone.

"Windflower," he answered groggily.

"It's me, Ted," said Brown. "Me and the boys are in the bar. Coming for a drink?"

"I'll be there in fifteen minutes. Save me a seat."

The bar was in a building behind the hotel. It was crowded for a Wednesday night. When Windflower got there, Brown explained it was Ladies Night. There was a band warming up in one corner and even though the night was advertised for the gentler sex, most of the audience was male, loud and getting drunk by the sounds of it. Windflower knew that Ladies Night was sometimes the worst night of the week for trouble because the bar often had drinks at reduced prices for both sexes. And the men attracted to this evening were also often disappointed when more of them than the ladies decided to show up. So they got drunk, and then some of them got mean.

It was not really his kind of place, but he wanted to connect with Brown and his guys. Windflower was reintroduced to the forensics team and ordered a round when the waitress came by. He sipped his beer and watched the evening at the bar develop. Before the band started up, there was a mild commotion at one of the tables. One of the more inebriated customers decided to get a little too close to one of the servers. She screamed and Dixon, one of Brown's men, walked over and stepped in between them. The server was grateful, but the customer was not, especially when he was physically escorted off the premises by the security staff.

Neither Windflower, Brown nor Dixon thought too much more about this. They had another round of beer but once the band started playing, the loud music convinced them it was time to go.

Windflower, Brown and the other three forensics guys walked outside to get a breath of air. When they came out they could see there was a ruckus going on in the parking lot. Dixon was the first one over to investigate. That was a mistake. The customer who had been ejected earlier was in the middle of the fight. He saw Dixon and turned his attention on him.

"You bastard. Why don't you mind your own business for a change?"

Dixon turned to walk away and the man continued. "You're a big man inside. Are you too chicken to be a man out here? Maybe you're a pig. Are you a pig?"

Dixon made his second mistake. He turned around and started back towards the man who was yelling at him. "What did you say?" he asked. Brown yelled at him to come back and Dixon turned to comply. When he did, the loud man behind him ran towards him.

"Watch out. He's got something in his hands."

The drunk had grabbed a crowbar from his car and was swinging it towards Dixon. Now there was no choice for the other Mounties but to intervene, but when they did they noticed they weren't alone in the parking lot. Across the way from them were a dozen or so guys standing next to their motorcycles. When Windflower and his guys moved, so did they. Not only that, but so too did the people who were in the initial fight.

Brown tried to diffuse the situation by saying, "We don't want any trouble." But by then it was too late. Soon it was a pitched battle between the locals and the RCMP officers. They didn't know they were fighting Mounties, but Windflower wasn't sure that would make any difference. He had one beefy guy hanging off his back, one holding his arms and a third starting to swing. Windflower managed to duck the first punch but someone caught him in the back, with what felt like a metal bar. That guy was moving in to give him a few more whacks when someone grabbed his arms and pulled him off. It was Brown, who had managed to shake his guy and saw that Windflower needed help.

Windflower tried to get to his feet but his back was killing him. As one more possible assailant was moving in for the kill, he saw another big guy, this time one of theirs, give his attacker a slam in the back of the head. Windflower got to his feet and heard the sirens. He was still in a lot of pain as he watched almost everybody, including the man who was going to attack him, scramble away. To his surprise, his new protector did not run with the crowd who saw the RCMP cruisers arrive. Instead, he whispered to Windflower, "Hit me."

"What?" Windflower was confused.

"Take a swing at me," the other man said. "Do it!"

Windflower leaned back and took a hefty cut at the man. He missed, but the other man ducked and pretended to go down in a clump. He was still lying there when Daniels and another local RCMP officer finally pulled into the parking lot. "Put me in the car," the man on the ground hissed to Windflower.

"What?" asked Windflower again.

"Arrest me," said the man. "Just do it."

So Windflower did. He got a set of handcuffs from Daniels, cuffed his prisoner and put him in the back seat. He got into the front with Daniels.

"Take us to the detachment," he said. "Back entrance."

Chapter Seventeen

"Put him in the quietest cell you have," Windflower ordered when they got back to the detachment. "Away from everybody else."

"Are you okay?" asked Daniels, seeing Windflower crouch over.

"I will be." Windflower followed the constable into the jail. Daniels put the prisoner in a cell and took off his handcuffs.

"You can leave us here." Daniels nodded in compliance and went out to the other part of the building.

"Robert French." The man in the cell held out his hand through the bars to shake Windflower's. "I'm hoping you're Windflower. I got word you might be around."

"Nice to meet you. Winston Windflower. Thanks for your help back there."

"You got a pretty good chop in the back," remarked French. "How's it feeling?"

"Sore. I don't think anything is broken, but it sure hurts," he added, bending over.

"Wait 'til tomorrow. So what were you guys doing getting involved in a scrap in the parking lot?"

"We had a young chap who probably overstepped his welcome in Grand Falls. Those are the forensics guys. I'm in from Grand Bank to be the local lead on the murder investigation."

"I saw you here last weekend. I've been embedded with this crew for over a year now. This was a bit of a risk, but it looked like you needed some help."

"Yeah, thanks again. I hope we didn't blow your cover."

"Nah, it'll be fine. I'll stay here tonight and you can let me out tomorrow. I wanted to talk to you anyway. We were on the edge of a big drug deal, when all hell broke loose."

"So, do you know what happened around the murders?" Windflower was hoping for insight.

"There's a couple of conflicting stories. Some people think it was Joe Blow getting back at his old lady. Others say it was about getting rid of a possible rival. All of that might be true, but with Bacchus, it's always about business. Money."

"We're going to talk to Snow tomorrow. What can you tell me about him?"

"He looks and talks like a country hick, but that's an act to fool people. He didn't rise to the top of the food chain here without being ruthless and a good businessman. Don't forget that his bosses are all about business. If you can make them money, they'll stick with you. And Joe Blow has made them a ton of money."

Windflower nodded. "Thanks for this. How can we stay in touch?"

"I'll call you if I hear any more," French spoke confidently. "Don't worry. I'll find you."

"I bet you can. I'll tell the guy out front to let you out in the morning. I have to go home and soak my back."

"Good luck." French then laid back on the bunk and settled in for the night.

Windflower went out and bid good night to Daniels. He borrowed a bottle of Tylenol and took two quickly with a glass of water. By the time he got back to his hotel room they had kicked in and he felt sore but a little numb. He ran a hot bath and soaked for as long as he could stay awake. Then he stumbled from the bathroom and crawled into bed. Soon he was soundly and solidly asleep.

Two hours later he was wide awake again. It might have been the throbbing in his back that woke him, but that's not what kept Windflower awake. He went to the bathroom, got some water and two more painkillers and tried to get his breathing back to normal. Finally, after a few more moments of panting and sweating his heart rate lowered and he felt almost normal. He realized he'd had another dream, or a version of the same dream he'd just had: the fire dream.

In tonight's dream, he was back at the house on Seaview Drive. Once again he watched as the person on the second floor of the building waved and seemed to cry out for help. But this time the dream continued. Tizzard ran into the house to try and save the person in the fire. Windflower could almost feel the heat on his face as he saw Tizzard appear in the window. Then suddenly the flames leapt higher and the whole building collapsed in on itself.

Windflower sat and waited for the Tylenol to kick in. He also tried breathing a little more slowly. First, physical relief came, followed by a dulling of his emotions. He didn't want to, but he forced himself to think about the dream and what it meant. He knew that dreams always meant something, always carried a message. What did the fire mean and why was Tizzard in the dream, and even more importantly, was Tizzard in some kind of danger?

Maybe it was the lateness of the hour or maybe it was the combination of both pain and painkillers, but Windflower couldn't figure this one out. The best he could do was to make a plan to call somebody who might be able to help him do just that. He could call his Uncle Frank back home in Pink Lake. Frank was a dream weaver and he had helped Windflower make sense of his dreams before. Once he made the commitment to phone his uncle, he was able to get back to sleep. He didn't stir again until the morning light peeked through his hotel room window.

Chapter Eighteen

Windflower's back made him feel like he was about eighty, but he managed to get up, have a cold shower and then a hot bath. Soaking in the bath certainly helped, along with a cup of coffee that he made with the supplies in his room, and gave him hope he might actually be able to walk again. He was pretty sure it was just bruised, but he decided to get it checked out later if he had a chance.

When he looked out the window, he could see there was a wooded area past the parking lot at the back of the hotel. It was overcast, but free of the fog he'd grown accustomed to. He finished his coffee, grabbed his smudge kit and went for a slow wander in the woods. He walked for a few minutes and then when he thought he heard water running, he went a little farther. He was happy that he did, because he found a path that led right to a little brook. He sat quietly at the edge, allowing the water to calm his mind and his spirit.

Then he took out his medicine pouch and poured a small amount into his smudge bowl. He placed a little moss on top and soon there was a steady thin stream of white smoke coming from his bowl. He performed his smudge with a little difficulty because of his back, but it felt really good to slow down and just breathe.

After smudging, he said his usual prayers for his ancestors and for the people and animals who were with him on this journey. He said a special prayer of gratitude for having Sheila in his life and another one for Tizzard, to make sure he was okay. Just in case.

By the time he got back to his hotel room, the skies were starting to clear but the pain in his back was not. He took two more Tylenol tablets and had a hot shower. That helped, not a lot, but enough to get him moving again. He slowly made his way to the hotel lobby and found the breakfast buffet. He didn't eat much, some fruit and oatmeal with nuts and raisins. But he knew better than to not eat and take painkillers. That would be even worse than not eating at all.

He was finishing his breakfast when his cell phone rang. He went outside to take the call.

"Good morning, Boss. How's life in the big town of Grand Falls?"

"Good morning, Eddie. Other than a back that's killing me, things are good. What's new on the home front?"

"Well, that's too bad about your back. I thought you'd want to know. Lady is coming home today. I talked to the clinic last night and they said to come by any time. I'm going to head over there right now."

"That's good news. Did they say how she's doing?"

"The girl I spoke to said she was starting to get a little restless. She said that was one of the signs Lady was ready to come home. She'll have some medication to take, but I'll get that too while I'm over there."

"Thanks, Eddie, that's super."

"No problem. I'm going to keep her over here with me at the office so I can keep an eye on her. She likes hanging around here. I also wanted to tell you we got a tip last night about Carol Jackson.

Somebody heard the missing person report on the radio and called in. They said they picked up a female hitchhiker on the highway. They dropped her off at the Frenchman's Cove exit."

"That's interesting too."

"Yeah, I'm going to check out that area on the way to Marystown. See if anybody saw anything," Tizzard sounded pleased with himself.

"Check out the park, too. She might have enough stuff with her to camp out."

"Will do."

"Okay, thanks." Windflower was about to hang up when he added. "Are you okay, I mean is everything okay with you, Eddie?"

"I'm great, Boss. Never better. Why'd you ask?"

"No reason. Just checking. Anyway, I'll talk to you later."

He went back in to get another cup of coffee and when he got to the breakfast room, Brown and his crew were sitting down to breakfast.

"Morning, Winston. How's your back?" Brown inquired while sipping on his coffee.

"It's okay. A little sore, but I've been worse."

"Care to join us?"

"Nah, I have to get to work." As they were speaking, Dixon, the younger Mountie who had been involved in the initial confrontation at the bar, came up to Windflower.

"Sorry about last night." Dixon looked sheepish. "I didn't mean to cause all that trouble."

"Well, apart from my back, there's no real damage done. You might want to be a bit more careful when you pick your spots to intervene, though. Especially when you're from out of town." Windflower gave a wave to Brown and the other Forensic guys at the table before leaving to go to the RCMP detachment.

He was driving over there when he passed by the hospital. Just then, his back gave him a quick twinge of pain that made him wince. I guess that's as good a sign as any, he thought, and he pulled into the hospital parking lot. He went around the back again to the emergency entrance and walked into the admissions area. There was nobody else around that early in the morning. A nurse checked him in and told him to take a seat. He was expecting to have to wait for a while, but was surprised when soon afterwards Doctor Stock, the guy who was filling in as temporary coroner, came out from behind the swinging doors.

"Sergeant Windflower what are you doing here?"

"I've got a bit of a problem with my back. I was hoping somebody could have a look at it."

"Sure." The doctor smiled. "That's what we're here for. Come on back and we'll take a look." He got Windflower to take off his shirt and started examining him.

"Ow." Windflower exhaled when the doctor touched a particularly sore region of his lower back.

"Yeah, I'm not surprised it's a little tender down there. It's still a bit swollen and starting to bruise up pretty good. What the heck happened to you, anyway?"

"I got hit with a metal bar." Windflower grimaced through the pain. "You should see the other guy."

"That's a good one," said Stock, smiling wider than before. "You might have a bit of internal bruising around your kidneys, but I actually think you're going to be okay. Nothing broken. You'll have a fair amount of pain for the next few days though. I recommend lots of rest. But I suspect you're not going to do that, are you?"

Windflower shook his head.

"In that case, I suggest alternating cold showers with lots of warm baths to help relieve the swelling and some meds for the pain. What are you taking now?"

"Tylenol."

"They'll be good enough for the pain. But it might start to tighten up later. I'm going to give you some muscle relaxants to take at night." He went to a cabinet and pulled out a package and handed it to Windflower. "If you can relax and go to sleep, then that's when you'll get the most healing. Okay?"

"Okay, Doc."

"If the pain gets any worse, come back and see me. Otherwise you're good to go. As a matter of fact, if you have a chance, come back to see me at the end of the day. I can take another look at you and I also should have the blood tests back from the lab."

"Thanks again, Doc. I'll see you later."

Windflower walked gingerly out to his cruiser and was ready to leave when his cell phone rang again.

"Windflower here"

"Hello, my little rabbit." There was a soft voice on the end of the line. "It's your Auntie Marie."

"Auntie, how are you? It's so nice to hear your voice."

"I am well, Winston. I take my time a little more now since I had my stroke, but I am so looking forward to your wedding. You have a wonderful woman, and I can't wait to see the beautiful children you will make together."

Windflower laughed. "One step at a time, Auntie. And how is Uncle Frank?"

"Frank is well. He is the main reason I am calling you. He got it in his mind he would like to come there a little early for the wedding. He said he wanted some time to visit with his friends."

"That would be fine. When is he planning to come?"

"He's on his way now. He got a ride to Edmonton and will probably be in Newfoundland by tonight."

"Oh. But I'm out of town right now."

"He said to tell you not to worry. He already has a key from the last time he visited." Auntie Marie chuckled.

Windflower was silent for a few minutes as he processed this latest information. Then he gently asked the real question that was on his mind. "Is Uncle Frank drinking right now?"

"He hasn't had a drop in a few months now. He's quite proud of himself. He's even gone back to his dream work. I've never seen him happier or healthier."

"That's great news. I've been having a terrible dream lately. I was going to call and talk to him about it."

"There are no terrible dreams," said Auntie Marie. "Some of them we may not wish to hear, and sometimes we are afraid. But dreams are still messages from our inner selves and our allies. We must never ignore our dreams, because we may be missing something very important."

"Thank you, Auntie. I almost forgot that you were also a dream interpreter. Tell me, what is the significance of fire in our dreams?"

"The fire is at the centre of our medicine wheel. It is the place we gather around to share our teachings. It is at the core of our selves and our being. When we see fire in our dreams, it could mean many things: things that may be very close to your heart, to your core beliefs. I am sorry, but I cannot help you with your dream over the phone. You have to do this in person. Maybe Frank can help you. I have a question for you as well, Nephew. Why didn't you tell me about Mama Bear and her cub?" asked his aunt.

"What? How did you know about that?"

"Even old people have dreams too," said Auntie Marie. "What do you think the significance of her showing up in your life is?"

"I don't know. Do you?"

"It's not up to me to say what role your allies play in your life. That's up to you," said his aunt. Then hearing nothing from Windflower in reply she added. "Another thing to talk to your uncle about."

"Thank you, again, Auntie. I'll look after Uncle Frank"

"I know you will. But look after that lovely lady of yours. And your back too."

"My back? How'd you know about that?" he asked.

"Please ask Frank to call me when you see him," said Auntie Marie. "And I'll see you at the wedding. Bye, Winston."

"Goodbye, Auntie," said Windflower. That was one special lady, he thought. One very special lady.

Chapter Nineteen

He was still thinking about his Auntie Marie, and his Uncle Frank too, when he pulled into the parking lot at the Grand Falls RCMP office. He watched with some amusement as Daniels and a female Constable tried to push and pull and cajole and coax a short, stocky man into the detachment ahead of them. He wasn't simply resisting, as much as he was actively defying them from accomplishing their mission. But once they got him moving towards the door the motion propelled him forward. Windflower opened the door, to the relief of the two RCMP officers. The object of their attention was not happy at all about this latest turn of events and unleashed a barrage of curses and evil incantations, many of which Windflower had never heard before.

"I'm assuming that was Snow," said Windflower when Daniels and his partner returned to the front.

"That would be him," said Daniels. "He's quite the prince, isn't he? He likes to pretend he's above the law here, and basically that's true. If we catch him with something small, the bosses tell us to wait for something big. And when it's something big, he lawyers up right away. And they've got really good lawyers."

"That must make it tough," said Windflower.

"Yeah, but that's the game around here," said Daniels. "Anyway, Sarge, this is Megan Fitzpatrick. Fitz, this is Sergeant Winston Windflower. He's the prime on the murders I've been telling you about."

"Nice to meet you Sergeant," said Fitzpatrick. "You were here on the weekend too, weren't you? I would have said hello but I was too busy giving the bikers a tour of the area."

"Good to meet you, too," said Windflower.

"Do you want us to bring Snow out, or would you rather talk to him in there?" asked Daniels, pointing to the cell.

"I think I'll go back and talk to him. He might be more cooperative while he's still locked up."

"Maybe," said Daniels. "But he's already yelling for his attorney."

"I don't mind a bit of yelling. We're just looking to have a little chat."

Windflower walked down the corridor and picked up a chair along the way. It was easy to find Snow. He was indeed yelling and between the curses Windflower thought he actually did hear the word attorney. But he would pretend not to hear that, at least not right away.

He stopped in front of the cell containing Snow and placed his chair on the floor so that he could directly face him. He sat down and said, "Good morning. How are you today?"

"Who the hell are you?" asked Snow.

"That's not very nice," said Windflower.

"I wants my lawyer," said Snow.

"We only want to ask you a few questions," said Windflower.

"I got nuttin to say to you guys," exclaimed Snow. "You got no reason to hold me. I knows my rights."

"I bet you do," said Windflower coldly. "But one way or another you and I are going to have a chat and then we'll see what happens after that. We can do this the easy way or the hard way. Your choice."

"Listen, doofus. I don't know who you are, but pretty soon you are going to find out who I am." Snow stood up inside the cell and raised himself up. Windflower could see that while Snow wasn't very tall, he was big. His muscles bulged against his jean jacket and he had the barrel chest of a street fighter that Windflower once knew back in Vancouver, a guy who loved to fight and almost never lost. He pushed himself up against the bars and said, "I can make it worth your while."

"You know what. I'm going to pretend I didn't hear that, 'cause if I did, I'd have to charge you with trying to influence an officer of the law. Besides, I don't think you want to cooperate just yet. Maybe I'll leave you in here to think about it for a while." Windflower finished speaking, picked up his chair and walked back down the hall.

He left Joey Snow screaming at the top of his lungs as he walked down the hallway. He couldn't make this situation last for long, but it sure felt good for now. As he shut the metal door separating the cells from the rest of the building, Snow's yelling became muted. By the time he reached the front, you could almost forget that the most dangerous man in town was back there.

He spent an hour going back through the files on the two murder victims. They had a long record of interaction with the justice system, and mostly they were the ones causing the trouble. But Windflower noted that the woman, Stella Winslow, had also been the complainant in a number of assault claims, including two against the prisoner in the back, one Joey Snow. He guessed that relationship wasn't a lot of fun.

Lundquist came in to see him with a cup of coffee. "I heard you had a bit of trouble at the bar last night." he began.

"Wrong place, wrong time. Thanks for the coffee."

"I heard you met Frenchie last night too," said Lundquist. When Windflower looked at him cautiously he added. "I'm the only one here who knows. He comes to me to send and receive messages. I guess he saved your bacon, by the sound of it."

"Yeah, I took a pretty good shot in the back. He bailed me out, for sure. I dropped by the hospital this morning. The doctor gave me some muscle relaxants that I can't wait to try out tonight. By the way, he said he might have some results from the blood tests later today. Can you pick them up?"

"Sure," said Lundquist. "So what's the plan with our friend out back? I expect to see his lawyer show up anytime now."

"I'll go see if he's ready to talk to us without screaming. Why don't you come with me? You can play good cop and I'll be the bad guy," said Windflower.

"Sounds good," said Lundquist. "I don't often get to be the good guy around here. Why don't I get Daniels and Fitzpatrick to bring him into the small conference room?"

A few minutes later Windflower and Lundquist walked into the interview room, where a very agitated prisoner was barely sitting still in a chair at the table. The two RCMP officers sat beside each other and directly across from Snow. Snow sat there with his massive arms crossed and a look on his face that gave a glimpse of the violence he might be capable of delivering.

Windflower ignored the man's attempt at intimidation and started his interrogation. "I'm Sergeant Winston Windflower. We're investigating two murders in this town. We would like your cooperation to find out what happened. If you answer our questions you can go. If not, we will hold you as a suspect in these murders."

"I got nuttin to say," and then looking at his watch, added, "I'd say you got about half an hour before my lawyer gets here."

"Good. Let's not waste time then. So what was your relationship with Stella Winslow? Wasn't she your girlfriend?"

"Ex-girlfriend," said Snow, unable to stay quiet at the mention of the woman.

"What about Todd Lundrigan?" asked Windflower.

This time Snow grimaced, but did not respond.

"Did you beat Stella up because she was going to leave you?"

asked Windflower.

At the last comment Snow couldn't help himself, and jumped up and tried to grab Windflower. The police officer was too quick and deftly moved back from the table. He smiled at Snow and said to Lundquist. "I think our prisoner tried to assault an officer of the law. I'm going to write up the charges. Will you look after him?"

Lundquist nodded and motioned to Snow to sit down. Windflower left the pair and could hear Snow yelling at his fellow officer, something about "crazy and stupid", and a whole lot more from his vocabulary of profanities. He could also hear Lundquist trying to calm Snow down. This dialogue was still going on as Windflower continued down the hallway and went to refresh his coffee.

Snow had been right about one thing. When Windflower went to the front he was met by the receptionist, Lynn, who informed him that Snow's lawyer had arrived. Windflower walked to the foyer to meet him.

"Good morning Sergeant. I'm Jeremy Earle. I'm the attorney for Joseph Snow. I believe you have my client in custody," said the lawyer.

Windflower was a little surprised, not by the lawyer's appearance which was the standard medium to high end suit, an Italian briefcase, which probably contained a Mont Blanc pen, and a legal note pad, but by his age. Jeremy Earle was in his mid-sixties, kind of old, Windflower thought, to be the lawyer for the bikers. But then again, lawyers often followed the money, and he suspected that with Snow and his crew, there was always need for a lawyer.

"Good morning, I'm Sergeant Winston Windflower. I am the lead investigator into a double homicide. You may have heard about it," said Windflower, offering his hand to the lawyer.

"I have heard about it. That's a terrible business," said Earle, as he shook Windflower's hand. "But you're not suggesting my client had anything to do with it, are you?"

"We want to ask him some questions. He was in a relationship with the woman who was killed. He didn't seem very sorry about her passing when I first talked to him. In fact, he threatened me, and we are considering attempted assault charges in that regard."

"I'm sure my client will be more cooperative, now that I'm here. And if you agree to overlook his over-enthusiasm, I can also ignore the fact that he is being held here under duress, and without the presence of his lawyer, which I am confident he has already requested."

This guy is good, thought Windflower. "Let's see what your client has to say for himself then. But we need him to answer our questions."

"I'd like a few moments alone with my client," said Earle. "I'm sure we'll find a way to resolve this situation quickly."

Windflower walked back to the cells with the lawyer. Lundquist came out of the interview room and joined him in the corridor while Earle went in to see the prisoner.

"How did that go?" asked Windflower.

"It was interesting," said Lundquist. "We don't like each other, at all. But I guess I'm kind of the devil he knows. And you're just the devil. He had a very severe and intense reaction to you. I think he's afraid of you, and that's weird, because usually Snow is not afraid of anybody."

"Must be my charm. Did you get anything out of him?"

"He's actually upset about the woman," said Lundquist. "I have the feeling that he loved her, at least as much as he is capable of loving anybody."

"That's interesting. I didn't think he had the capacity for any feelings beyond pain." He was about to say more when they heard a knock from inside the interview room. "I guess we're on."

The two Mounties went back into the room where the lawyer was sitting beside his client. Snow still had his arms folded across his chest, but now had a slight grin to go along with his attitude.

"My client is prepared to entertain your questions now," said Earle. "However I will caution you to remain within the confines of this particular investigation. I have cautioned him to refuse to answer any questions that fall outside of that matter. Is that agreeable?"

"Certainly. What was your relationship to the late Stella Winslow?"

"She was my ex-girlfriend," said Snow.

"When was the last time you spoke with her?" asked Windflower.

"Probably a week or so ago. I saw her at Tim Hortons. Didn't say much, just nodded," said Snow.

"Where were you on Saturday night?" asked Windflower, thinking he might be able to catch Snow out in a lie.

"I was at the clubhouse," said Snow. "All night."

"Any witnesses to collaborate that?" asked Windflower.

"Ten of my best friends," said Snow with a laugh. "And a couple of girls, dancers if you know what I mean." Another laugh.

Windflower didn't laugh. Instead, he leaned across the table and said sternly, "Did you kill Todd Lundrigan and Stella Winslow?"

Snow leaned back in and said, "No."

"Do you know who did?" asked Windflower.

"No," said Snow and turning to his lawyer, he asked, "Are we done now?"

"I think he's answered your questions," said the lawyer. "Can we leave now?"

"I guess so. But we request that your client remain in town, at least for the next few days in case there are any follow up questions."

"Agreed," said Earle. He and Snow got up and Lundquist opened the door.

As they were leaving Windflower stood up too and looked Snow right in the eye. "Did you know she was pregnant?"

Snow looked startled and then began to reach for Windflower. His lawyer grabbed his arm and pushed him out the door. Snow continued to stare back at Windflower all the way down the hall.

"He didn't know, did he?" asked Lundquist.

"I don't think he did. I'm not sure what that means, but nope, I don't think he knew."

Chapter Twenty

After the interview with Snow and his legal beagle, Windflower decided to make the trip out to Bishops Falls to check in with Brown and the forensics team. It was a pleasant late summer morning, and the sun had warmed things up enough for Windflower to have the windows open as he drove along the highway. He stopped and picked up a box of donuts at the Tim Hortons as a greeting gift. Then he drove through Bishops Falls to the park. He parked next to the forensics van and carried his box of goodies with him as he walked towards the crime scene.

Brown saw him coming and waved him over. "I see you brought snacks. That's great," he said, grabbing one for himself and calling his team over.

"We're making good progress here," he said to Windflower. "It looks like they were driven here on an ATV," said Brown, pointing to an area leading into the woods. "We've got photos and imprints of the tracks. We can match the make of the ATV if not the exact vehicle. And judging by the footprints, there were at least two other people, likely males by the size of the prints, along with the two victims."

"Any sign of a struggle?" asked Windflower.

"It's hard to tell because the bush is beaten down pretty good. But I'd say not. There's not a lot of blood, except for near where the victim's bodies were found. They were either tied up before they got here, or maybe they were drugged," said Brown.

"That's good. Anything else?"

"Just that there were a lot of shots. We must have picked up a dozen casings."

"And that's not including the ones that were inside. What about time of death?"

"Not my area of expertise," said Brown. "But if it were anytime before midnight, you would think someone would have heard all those shots."

"Agreed. So are you guys out of here soon?"

"Hopefully, right after lunch," said Brown. "We have to go to Whitbourne. They want us to have a look at an accident scene. Usually the traffic guys can handle them, but this one was a head-on collision in broad daylight. They want to know if we can see anything they couldn't."

"Good luck. E-mail me a copy of your report, will you?"

"Will do," said Brown. "Are the rest of these for us?" he asked looking at the donuts.

"Help yourself. I have to watch my girlish figure." Brown was laughing as he walked back to the crime scene with the remaining donuts. Windflower was smiling too as he headed back to Grand Falls.

When he got back, he met Lundquist leaving the office. "I'm going over to see the doctor at the hospital. He says he's got some news for us."

"Can you ask him for estimated times of death on the victims? Also, did Daniels pick up anything from his questioning at the park last night?" asked Windflower.

"Okay," said Lundquist. "I don't think Daniels got anything, but you can check with him when he gets back from lunch. He said something about being interrupted to break up a bar fight or something."

Windflower smiled again and waved goodbye to Lundquist. That reminded him. Lunch, he thought. It's lunchtime and I'm not even hungry. It might be the pain or the Tylenol. It was certainly time for more of them. He got two tablets, went to the lunchroom and poured himself a glass of water to wash them down. Maybe it was in his head, but as soon as the two pills went down he felt better.

At the front the receptionist greeted him with a stack of messages. Windflower scanned them quickly. "All from the media?" he asked.

"Yes," said Lynn. "Except for the one from Superintendent Majesky."

"Okay, I'll call him back right away," said Windflower.

"What should I tell the media when they call back?" asked Lynn, knowing those calls were inevitable.

"Tell them the investigation is ongoing, but that we might have something to tell them tomorrow," said Windflower.

The receptionist looked happy as she walked away. At least one person is pleased with me, thought Windflower. Now let's see if I can make that two. He called the number on the pink message slip.

"Majesky," was what Windflower heard next.

"Superintendent, it's Windflower."

"How's it going over there?" asked Majesky. "What have you found out?"

"It's slow going, but a couple of things. It looks like an ATV was involved in bringing the couple and their killers in. Maybe two people directly involved. It appears to be an execution of some sort. The female victim is the ex-partner of the head Bacchus guy in town and she was pregnant, about three months or so."

"Pregnant, do we know who the daddy is?" asked Majesky.

"We're getting a sample from the deceased fetus. So we can start ruling people out based on that. There are also a lot of footprints at the site. That becomes a challenge to try and make a match."

"That only helps after you have a suspect," said the Superintendent. "I'm guessing you are probably still getting a lot of media attention."

"Yeah, tons. I'm putting them off for now, but I think we should say something before the weekend, while it's still fresh in people's minds. Maybe ask for the public's help in finding the ATV."

"That's not bad," said Majesky. "You'll have to handle the media on your own this time. There's no way I can get back over again so soon."

"I can do that," said Windflower, although he really didn't want to. "We don't have a lot to give them, but it's probably better to say something before they start making things up."

"You've done this before. I knew you'd be the right man for this job. Let me know how it goes."

Windflower felt a little dizzy after talking to the Superintendent, so he went back and got some water and a banana. He realized he wasn't only shaky; he was nervous as well. He could do the media part of the job but it was probably his least favourite. The water calmed him a little and the banana gave him a jolt of fruit sugars to balance him out. He had just gone back to reviewing the files on the victims when his cell phone rang.

Chapter Twenty-one

"Hi, Winston. How are you?"

"I'm fine, Sheila. Sorry I didn't get a chance to call you last night. I was busy and we had a bit of an incident. I hurt my back," said Windflower.

"Oh, are you all right?" asked Sheila, sounding worried.

"I will be. I saw the doctor and he gave me some muscle relaxants. Somebody hit me with a metal bar."

"That must have hurt," said Sheila. "You're obviously hanging around the wrong people."

"That would be true. It's kind of part of the job though. So what's new with you?"

"Busy, but not crazy. I miss you. Is there any chance of you coming home soon?"

"I miss you too," added Windflower. "Let me see what I can do. I'm still trying to come for the weekend. I'll have to come back right afterwards, but it would be good to see you."

"That would be good," replied Sheila. "I saw Moira Stoodley and she reminded me they've invited us over on Saturday night."

"Oh yeah, I was looking forward to that. Well, I'll let you know later today if I think I can come back. By the way, how is the issue around policing going at the Council?"

"That's not good. I don't think we should talk about it right now. People are upset and quite frankly, so am I. We've got a meeting scheduled with Inspector Quigley for tomorrow morning. He can tell you how that goes."

"Okay," said Windflower, wishing he could have that last question back. "Tizzard is going to pick up Lady today. The reports are she's made great improvements," he added, hoping to steer the conversation back to more friendly terrain.

"That's great," said Sheila, but Windflower could tell she didn't fall for his ruse. "Let me know about the weekend, and take care of your back, okay?"

"Okay. Bye, Sheila. I love you," he said.

"Me too," said Sheila as the phone went dead. She loves me but is still not happy with me, thought Windflower. I guess it's not my day to please everybody. Again.

He didn't have much more time to think before Lundquist came into his office carrying a manila folder. "Report from our temporary coroner."

"Have you read it?" asked Windflower.

"I talked briefly to the doctor and scanned the report," said Lundquist. "Have a look."

Windflower opened the file. It was on the letterhead of the Grand Falls Regional Hospital Corporation. The heading was 'Preliminary Medical Report into the Deaths of T. Lundrigan and S. Winslow'.

The report was on a form with sections on the demographics of the deceased, places to note next of kin, addresses, and other information. Windflower skipped right to the parts he wanted.

"Cause of death," he said out loud. "Death by gunshot, .357 Magnum caliber bullets removed from both deceased." Then he went to the place and estimated time of death section. "Fallsview

Municipal Park, Bishops Falls, Newfoundland and Labrador. Time of death is estimated at approximately 11:30 p.m."

"That's good to know," said Lundquist. "It's pretty likely somebody would have heard all those shots."

"Absolutely. Make sure Daniels does a full round of interviews in the area and checks back in at the location tonight."

"Will do," said Lundquist. "I've got both him and Fitzpatrick on it."

Windflower continued reading. He came to the section that was headed: 'Medical History and Other Significant Conditions'. Under this, he saw that Lundrigan had an enlarged liver. That usually meant an issue with alcohol, thought Windflower. And then he read out loud again, "Winslow was second trimester pregnant."

"What about the blood tests?" he asked Lundquist.

"It's on the last page," said Lundquist. "That's what I talked to the doctor about. Look right there." He pointed to the section entitled 'Other Observations'.

Windflower read the section, which noted the presence of alcohol and marijuana in both deceased. The report also noted high levels of Benzodiazepines. "So they may have been drugged," said Windflower.

"That's what the Doc said," Lundquist responded. "But he also said something very interesting. He did a blood sample of the fetus. While he doesn't know who the father is, he does know who it is not."

"It's not Lundrigan's baby," said Windflower.

"Blood types don't match," said Lundquist. "I'm not sure what that means, but it may mean something."

"These things always mean something. We have to figure out what exactly that might be, and what if anything it has to do with these two people getting killed."

Lundquist left Windflower with the report and he spent a few more minutes seeing if he couldn't derive anything else from the medical examiner's report. He was still poring through the document when his cell phone rang again.

"Hey, Boss, it's me," said Tizzard when Windflower opened the phone.

"Tizzard, do we have any news about Lady?" asked Windflower.

"I have a collie who is very pleased with herself, sitting in the back seat right now. I'm stopped at that little lookout on the Garnish turnoff," said Tizzard. "She was very happy to see me, and even happier to get out of the animal hospital. I let her out a few minutes ago and she must have run around the car half a dozen times."

"I'd say she's feeling better, by the sounds of it," said Windflower.

"Yeah, I'd say so. We also got another lead on Carol Jackson. When I was in the park in Frenchman's Cove, one of the locals told me that he saw her. It's pretty easy to spot somebody who isn't from around here. He said she spent a night in the park, but got picked up this morning by a man in a blue van. He didn't get a good look at the guy, but he said the van had a sign on it. Something to do with plumbing and heating."

"Did he say which way they were going?" asked Windflower.

"Just that they were headed back out towards the highway. I called Marystown and asked them to put out a note on the van, and to pass it up the line to Swift Current and Goobies. If they're going to the TCH, we might be able to spot them along the way. I'm going to be doing some checking here on plumbing and heating companies. There can't be too many," said Tizzard.

"Okay, let me know how that goes. Have you seen Quigley over there yet?"

"Not yet, and I'm a bit worried. I told Carrie, I mean Evanchuk, that I would drive her to the airport in St. John's on Saturday, but that only leaves Frost to look after everything," said Tizzard.

"I think the Inspector is going to be over there tomorrow morning for a meeting with the Council. But maybe I'll give him a call. I was hoping to be back for the weekend and I could do half a shift on Saturday and maybe Sunday if that would help."

"That would be great," said Tizzard. "I'll let you know if any-thing turns up on Carol Jackson in the meantime."

"Oh, and can you also be on the lookout for my Uncle Frank? Apparently he's coming for an early visit before the wedding."

"It'll be great to see Uncle Frank again," said Tizzard. "He's the life of the party."

"That's what I'm afraid of. Bye, Eddie."

"See ya, Sarge," said Tizzard as he hung up.

Chapter Twenty-two

Windflower went back to his review of the files and the coroner's report, but his head wasn't really into it. His back was bothering him, and after checking with Lynn and telling her he could be reached by cell phone, and doing the same with Lundquist, he drove back to his hotel. He ran a hot bath and spent as long as he could in there, soaking his aching back. Then he took one of the muscle relaxants and decided to lie down. It will only be for a few minutes, he told himself, long enough for the medication to kick in.

How long he slept he wasn't really sure. But his sleep was deep and long. So deep that he had a dream of when he was back in Pink Lake as a young boy of about twelve. He was on a vision quest with his grandfather, an Elder and former Chief of his nation. They had spent two days already in the forest, without any food and without any shelter, except for the canopy of trees in the deep woods. They were on a journey to find Windflower's animal allies, the spirits from the animal world who would be by his side throughout his life. During the previous few days, a number of them had showed up. A fox, many squirrels and a rabbit that not only came to visit, but stayed with the pair all throughout one night, waiting for them to wake, and only then scampering back into the woods.

Grandfather told him to be patient and more allies would come, but Windflower started to be afraid, to doubt himself and his abilities, to think he was going insane. But his Elder's strong voice steadied him and reminded him it was only the "Weesa-geechak", the Cree name for the 'Trickster' who was trying to lure him into that crazy world. He wasn't happy about it, but he had to listen to his Elder. Finally, on the third day while his grandfather still slept beside him, he had his moment of great awakening. It felt like he was awake and still asleep at the same time when the bear appeared.

It was a large black bear. Windflower was terribly frightened. He could not move or even speak. It was like he was frozen to the spot. The bear came right up to him and sniffed him as if to check him out for a possible meal. The breath of the bear was sour and hot on his face, like a wind from near an oil well. He fully expected the bear to knock him over and eat him. He struggled to rise from his sleeping place and run. But the creature reached over and held him down. As he did, Windflower felt the connection between him and the bear, like he could hear the bear speaking to him without using any words, and he could talk back.

He spent a few moments in this silent communion with the bear, until finally the creature raised itself up on its hind legs. It wants to show me how powerful it is, thought Windflower. Then just as quickly the bear reached back down and gently touched the young boy's head with a paw. To show that power is not always in how big or strong you are, Windflower felt the bear saying to him. He got out of his sleeping bag and stood to say goodbye to the bear who by now was rambling back into the woods.

"Grandfather, Grandfather, wake up," said Windflower, finally able to speak out loud again.

"What is it, my son?" asked Grandfather.

"I had a visit from a bear and he was so big and he told me all these things," said Windflower.

"I know," said Grandfather.

"You know. Why didn't you say or do something?" asked Windflower.

"I know because I already saw this unfold in my dream world," said Grandfather. "Your vision quest is over. You have found your main ally in the world. A very strong and powerful ally; that if you allow him, will help you throughout all of your time in this world."

The dream had surprised and shocked Windflower a little, but then he realized that this was more than just his imagination, it was a memory dream. Those were the ones where your subconscious wanted you to travel back in time, in order to retrieve something from your past that you would need today. At least that's what his Uncle Frank, the family expert on dreams, had told him. Now he was really looking forward to seeing his uncle.

Windflower lay there for a few moments after waking, noticing that the pain in his back had greatly subsided, but also that his head felt clearer than it had all day as well. The power of a little sleep, he thought. And maybe the dream too. He checked the clock on his bedside table and was surprised to see it was still only 8:30 p.m. He ordered a club sandwich from room service along with a large pot of tea. He was ready for a quiet night at home, in his home away from home.

He was halfway through his sandwich when the phone in his hotel room started to jangle, in that way only hotel phones seemed to ring. He walked over and picked it up.

"Windflower," he said.

"Superintendent Majesky says you are doing a great job. And if my boss is happy, then I'm happy too," said Ron Quigley.

"Inspector. What can I do for you?"

"A couple of things," said Quigley. "But first, how's life in Grand Falls?"

"Well, the investigation is creeping along and I managed to

have some direct contact with some of the more unsavoury locals, and my back is killing me. Other than that, I'm doing great," said Windflower.

"I wanted to get some intel from you before the Council meeting tomorrow morning. I'm on the hot seat at 10 a.m."

"I heard. I talked to Sheila today. She's not happy and she's probably the most reasonable of the bunch. I think you better have a plan that gets the full policing program back up to speed quickly, or it will be out of your hands and over your head."

"That's going to be tough," said Quigley. "These cutbacks are coming directly from HQ in Ottawa, and when I asked why, they told me it was political. Apparently they are trying to restrain spending so that the Minister can look good."

"What about the safety of the public, and of our officers who are going to be in danger because of short-staffing?" asked Windflower.

"Way above my pay grade," said Quigley. "I'm a spear carrier like everybody else. I don't guess you can influence the mayor in any way on this issue? I hear you have connections."

"I'd kind of like all of my body parts to stay in their present condition and location. I will give you a tip though. Watch out for the Deputy Mayor, Francis Tibbo. He's a bit of a loon. He was in my office the other day demanding that we deal with the moose situation because his wife had a near miss."

"That's good to know. Speaking of moose, we've had two more collisions just outside of town. You think people could slow down a little, especially at night when you can't really see anything in the fog," said Quigley.

"I know. One thing that puzzles me is that these accidents always seem to happen around the same area, don't they? In our patch you can almost predict there will be moose sightings and an eventual incident around Grand Beach and the Garnish turnoff. There are a few exceptions, but surely we should be able to do something about preventing the inevitable."

"You're not talking about fencing or those moose sensors, are you?" asked Quigley. "They seem to have been a colossal waste of money."

"No, something simpler than that. We could have a sign that says 'Moose Danger Next 10 kilometers'."

"They already do that," said Quigley. "It doesn't seem to make a lot of difference."

"Agreed. But what about if we added a deterrent as well? We could reduce the maximum speed for that area to 50 k's an hour and do some monitoring, hand out a few tickets until people get the message."

"You know what? That might work. We'd have to get the Province on board, as well as the municipalities, but it might be worth a shot. Let me think about that," said Quigley. "The other thing I wanted to ask is if you could come back for the weekend as a backup. I'm going to try and spend a bit of time in Grand Bank next week, but I can't this weekend."

"I can probably sneak away for the weekend. I'll have to run it by Majesky, but I think it will be okay."

"Great," said Quigley. "Talk to you soon,"

Well, that worked out pretty well, thought Windflower. I get to go home and Quigley thinks I'm doing him a favour. Not bad at all.

Chapter Twenty-three

Windflower finished his dinner and watched T.V. for a little while, but was back in bed again not long after. His sleep was rough and fitful and sometime after 1 a.m. he took another muscle relaxant. That got him all the way to daylight. No more dreams, and as he gingerly started to move around, he realized he also had about half the pain and a great deal more mobility. Thank goodness for doctors and muscle relaxants.

He made a cup of coffee in his room and opened the blinds. He already knew what to expect. He'd heard the rain coming down as soon as he woke. Oh well, a little rain wouldn't hurt him. He finished his coffee, pulled on his hoodie and hat, and went out the back door of the hotel towards the woods and the little brook.

Except it was not a little brook any more. The rain overnight had swelled the waters so that it was fast, deep and almost up to the banks on both sides. This couldn't be good in spring, he thought, as the rising waters would have to go somewhere. But for him and for today, there was little to worry about, except maybe getting his boots wet.

He took out his supplies and carefully mixed up his smudge mixture, being careful not to let it all fall on the ground. He lit his bowl and waved it slowly over his head, across his heart and under both of his feet, guiding the smoke with the eagle feather that Grandfather had given him so many years ago. He thought about him as he smudged, and was grateful for the many things he had learned from that man. He was long gone, as were Windflower's parents, but he always felt he could call on Grandfather for help if he needed it. And that he would be there.

Windflower completed his smudging and stood silently in the rain for a few more minutes. He watched the waters rush by and felt a sense of calmness and cleansing as it passed. He also did something he had not done for a long time. He asked his allies to come, especially Bear, his main ally. He asked them to watch over him and to keep him safe and he offered his thanks for the many times they had also been with him on his journey. After his short prayers, he packed up all his supplies and walked quietly back to the hotel. He shaved and took one more hot bath, this one much shorter, packed up all his clothes in the hopes that he was checking out today, and went downstairs to the dining room.

He was hungry this morning, so he had a little bit of everything on the buffet table. Some scrambled eggs, a couple of sausages, a scoop of beans and even a piece of French toast. He grabbed a raisin bran muffin and a banana along with more coffee to wash it all down. He took his time and savoured both the food and the drastic improvement in his back. Before it was pure and constant pain, now it was a steady twinge with the occasional spike. He could definitely handle this.

After breakfast, he drove to the RCMP office. When he arrived he checked his messages. The ever-efficient Lynn had created a temporary slot for him along with a smiley face. Efficient and sweet too, thought Windflower. There was a pile of media requests along with a note from Constable Fitzpatrick. It read "Did interviews with Daniels last night. We found someone who saw two men driving an ATV, a new orange Honda, with a trailer on the back, on the road to the park in Bishops Falls, around 10 p.m. on the night of the murders."

Now that's welcome news, thought Windflower as he went to the makeshift command centre in the back. How many new orange ATV's are sold around Grand Falls? He was still pondering this and his note when Lundquist walked in.

"Good morning," said Lundquist. "Something interesting?"

Windflower showed him the note. "Can you check out Honda ATV sales, orange ones, in the last couple of months?"

"That's easy enough to do. We only have a couple of dealers in town. But let me check something first. I think we had a break-in at one of the dealers back in May," said Lundquist.

He came back shortly afterwards with a file. "Here it is," he said. "On May 17th, three Honda ATV's were reported stolen at the GF Goodtime Centre. As I recall, two of them were subsequently recovered weeks later, abandoned and burnt at a quarry outside of town."

"I'm guessing nobody was ever charged with this," said Windflower.

"Nope," said Lundquist. "But we all suspected it was the bikers. We couldn't catch them and the stolen property together. There's a lot of bush out there."

"Okay, at least we have a few things to follow up on now. I'll talk to Fitzpatrick and Daniels when they get in about the witness last night if you would start checking out the usual spots where the bikers stash their stolen booty. I'm also going to arrange a media briefing for this afternoon so that we can ask for the public's help as well. It finally feels like we're moving," said Windflower.

"Good," said Lundquist. "I'm going out to do my tour of the bikers' favourite places. All of them dark and dingy and dirty."

"Thanks. I'm going to try Majesky."

He called Majesky's number but was only able to leave a message. He thought he might as well call Tizzard while he was waiting.

"Morning, Sarge," said Tizzard when he answered the phone. "I was going to call you later."

"Great minds think alike, but fools seldom differ," said Windflower.

"Are you quoting Shakespeare this early in the morning?" asked Tizzard wearily

"No, not Shakespeare, and I was actually giving you a compliment for a change. Never mind. It looks like I may be able to come this weekend. Quigley is busy, and he asked me to fill in. I have to check with the big boss in Halifax, but I think it'll be okay."

"That's good news," said Tizzard. "I've got some news too. I found the van. It belongs to a plumber, Wes Huntington. I talked to him this morning. He was over in Garnish doing a job and picked up Carol Jackson along the road. He dropped her off at a cabin up at the back of Molliers. I'm on my way out there now."

"Great. Call me when you know what's going on. And how's my dog?"

"Lady is great. But I think she misses you. When we come into the detachment, she always goes into your office and lies on the floor underneath your desk," said Tizzard. "She'll be happy to see you."

"I'll be happy to see her too. Call me," he said as he hung up. He'd be glad to see Tizzard too. Even though they didn't know how to say it or show it, they both cared a lot about each other. And he would get to see Sheila too, thought Windflower. This is shaping up to be a great weekend.

Chapter Twenty-four

Superintendent Majesky phoned back shortly afterwards. Windflower gave him an update about what had happened so far and told him what he planned for the media conference. "It's a way to keep them happy, plus we could use their help right now. We think someone must have seen or heard something on the evening of the murders."

"Maybe they're scared to come forward," said Majesky. "Why don't we sweeten the pot? Make it easier for them."

"What do you mean?" asked Windflower.

"We've got some money from Crime Stoppers to offer a reward from time to time. This might be a good time," said Majesky. "Offer $500 to anyone who can help us find the missing ATV. And another $500 to anyone who offers information that leads to an arrest. That will give the media a hook to run with all weekend, and might encourage people who saw something else to come out of the woods as well."

"That's a great idea. It's a lot of money for around here, and it will certainly get people talking."

"They're already talking," said Majesky. "But they may be afraid of the bikers, for good reason. We need to give them an incentive to talk to us. I'll get the Media Relations people to put out the notice if you can look after the local people. And let me know how it goes."

"One more thing, sir. Inspector Quigley has asked me to cover off back in Grand Bank this weekend. Would that be okay?"

"I already approved it when Quigley called me," said Majesky. "By the way, Windflower, have you been in contact with our guy on the ground, French?"

"I have, sir. He helped me out in a scrape."

"Did he look okay?" asked Majesky.

"He looked like a biker to me. Do you want me to do something?"

"Just keep your eyes open," said Majesky. With that, he was gone.

That was weird, thought Windflower. But he was only asked to keep his eyes open. He could certainly do that. The other thing he could do would be to start looking forward to his weekend. It would be so good to go home for a few days, sleep in his own bed, see Shelia. And Lady too! He would call her with the good news later this morning after he got everything organized with Lynn for the media conference. He walked over to the receptionist's desk.

"Good morning, Lynn. And how are you this fine wet morning?"

"I'm well, Sergeant," said the receptionist. "But it looks like another indoor weekend at the trailer. I could relax and read my book or just listen to the rain all day. The kids however, need some entertainment. I guess we'll bring some movies and games."

"Yeah, it's not as much fun in the rain. I'm going to need your help to organize a media conference this afternoon. I need you to call back all the local media who have been phoning about the murder investigation and get them to come at 2 p.m. I will draft a statement, and if you wouldn't mind proofreading it and making copies to hand out, that would be great. I'll get Corporal

Lundquist to set up the room."

"No problem," said Lynn. "I'd be happy to help. I find the day goes so much faster when you're busy."

"Me too," said Windflower, happy again to find an admin person with the perfect attitude to work in an RCMP office. He left the receptionist to do her work and went looking for Constable Fitzpatrick.

"Morning, Sarge," said Fitzpatrick, when she saw Windflower come into the lunchroom.

"Good morning, Constable. Thanks for the note from last night," he said. "I wanted to follow up with you on that."

"Sure," she said. "Coffee?"

"Great. Black, please."

Fitzpatrick poured him a cup, passed it to him and re-filled her own. She pulled out her notebook. "What do you want to know?"

"Tell me how you found the witness, and what he or she had to say," said Windflower.

"Daniels and I were canvassing the main road before the turnoff to the park. At one house near the end, we found a man who said he was out walking his dog on the night of the murders. He saw the ATV. He didn't think much of it because there was always somebody coming or going from the park. He remembered this one because he said the men driving the ATV had ski masks on. He thought that was very strange for the middle of summer. At this point he went and got his missus who confirmed he had told her about the strange men in the masks," said Fitzpatrick.

"Wasn't there a trailer?" asked Windflower.

"Yes," said Fitzpatrick, looking at her notes. "The witness said the ATV was towing a small home-made trailer and it was covered with a tarp."

"Good work. Keep at the canvass. We now have an estimated time of death at around 11:30 p.m., so somebody may have heard all those shots."

"We usually make a run up there every night, sometime after

midnight. By then, the young kids are gone and the few older ones are hanging out in their cars. But there's somebody there every night, guaranteed," said Fitzpatrick. "So far they've been ignoring us or taking off when they see the cop cars show up."

"We're going to offer a reward for information. That might get their attention," said Windflower.

"Yeah," said Fitzpatrick. "Plus it's Friday night. That means a lot more people. Maybe Daniels and I will park the car and go down there in our civvies? See if we can't shake this up."

"Good thinking. If you find out anything, let Corporal Lundquist know. I'll be away for the weekend."

Fitzpatrick nodded her agreement. Windflower went back to the work area to take another look at the files and the medical report. His back, which had been so good all morning, had started to tighten up again. He stood and tried to stretch but knew he needed to do a little more. A walk was what he really needed. He went to the front and told Lynn he would be out for a few minutes and walked out the door.

One of the nicest things about living and working in Newfoundland was that you were never too far away from nature. The central part of the province was no different, except that you weren't as close to the ocean. But there were many rivers and streams and lakes, which Newfoundlanders almost always called ponds. The mighty Exploits River was never too far away, and it reminded him of the powerful rivers in Northern Alberta where he grew up.

He could go and tramp around the woods forever and never get bored or tired. It was part of his DNA. Sheila was the same way, and that was one of the reasons they got along so well. They could have the biggest fight over the smallest thing, as couples often do. But a long walk in the woods, together or by themselves was often enough to bring them back to sanity, and back to the person they loved. Today's walk would not be one of those, as the light rain turned into a downpour just as Windflower was getting started.

He got back to the RCMP detachment, dripping wet, but

feeling better about himself, and his lot in life. Even his back had improved. He hung up his wet hat and coat and went to his temporary office. Thinking about Sheila on his short walk reminded him to call her. He picked up his phone and dialed her cell phone.

Chapter Twenty-five

"Oh, hi, Winston," said Sheila. "The Council meeting just broke up."

"How did it go?" asked Windflower, a little tentatively.

"It was a strange meeting," said Sheila. "At first it was very tense, because your Inspector was trying to give us some bureaucratic gobbledygook. Then it went weird when Francis Tibbo went after the RCMP for their handling of the moose issue. But that turned out okay when Quigley said they were going to be studying special measures for our area on a trial basis. Something about reducing speed limits in high risk areas. It sounded really intelligent and scientific."

Windflower gulped hard, but decided to swallow his pride and the fact that reducing the speed limits was his idea. Instead, he simply asked about the rest of the meeting. "What about the police service issues?" he asked, self-censoring his additional commentary about that being the real reason for the meeting.

"Inspector Quigley apologized for not having consulted us before the decision was made to reduce service, and he agreed to have a permanent solution within a month," said Sheila. "In the meantime, he agreed to my suggestion of providing a highway run every night and a twice-weekly patrol through town on irregular nights, so that potential criminals will not know when they'll show up. That seemed to satisfy the majority of Council, so I'm happy."

"I'm happy too," said Windflower, although he still wished he could have a piece of credit for the moose idea. "I'm even happier that I'm coming home this weekend."

"Great," said Sheila. "When will you get here?"

"I have a press conference in an hour, and then I hope to be on the road soon after. That should get me into Grand Bank before dark."

"That would be good. Watch out for the moose," said Sheila. "You slow down like your Inspector suggested."

Once again Windflower bit his tongue. That's going to leave a mark, he thought. "I'll see you tonight."

"Bye, Winston," said Sheila. "I'll tell Moira and Herb we're on for dinner tomorrow night."

"Bye, Sheila," said Windflower.

He only had an hour before the media event, so he raced to freshen up and check out of his hotel. He wanted to look good in front of the cameras, but he also wanted to get out of there as soon as possible afterwards. He grabbed a candy bar in the gift shop on the way out. Not the best lunch, but enough energy to get him through the next hour or so.

When he got back to the detachment, the parking lot was half-full and more media were arriving. There were three T.V. stations and a couple of radio outlets in attendance. The local newspaper would be the last to arrive. Must be a slow news day, he thought. Then he realized that around here, this was the news. He walked into the detachment and motioned to Lynn to follow him. She was handing out the notices to the media as they arrived, but she gave her stack of paper to Daniels, who was standing next to her, and followed Windflower.

"How many are here?' he asked when they got to the command centre.

"There's nine registered already, but six more have confirmed. They all want personal interviews, but I told them you would only be making a statement and taking a few questions," said Lynn. "I hope that was all right."

Windflower would have kissed her on the spot, but since that would not be appropriate, he simply said, "That was perfect."

He sent Lynn out to bring all the remaining attendees into the briefing room. He spent a few minutes re-reading the statement to get comfortable and to calm his nerves. Right at 2 p.m., he walked into the glare of lights and the noise of the room where the media were waiting. A few cameras flashed, but mostly the room grew deadly quiet as Windflower walked to the podium.

He was nervous, but read the statement in a slow and steady voice. At the end, he asked for questions. The questions were tough but predictable and focused on what the RCMP knew now, and when the police would know more. Finally, one of the reporters asked about the purpose of the reward, and Windflower knew that this was the one he cared about most. He thanked the reporter for the question, and then staring directly into the cameras he spoke. "We need your help in finding the people who committed these horrible crimes in your community. We are offering a reward of $500 if you have any information that can lead us to find this ATV," he said, holding up a picture of the model of the off-road vehicle that Lynn had thoughtfully prepared to go along with the handout.

"These murders have shaken our community and we need your help. If you saw or heard anything on the evening of these murders, in or around Fallsview Municipal Park, please come forward to accept your reward."

There were seemingly endless questions and Windflower stood there answering them to the best of his ability until the media crowd thinned out. Then seeing her opportunity, Lynn reached over, grabbed his arm and led him out to the back room.

"You were fabulous," she said.

"Thanks for all your help, and for getting me out of there," said Windflower.

"Yeah, you've got the media touch," said Lundquist. "I always freeze up."

"It takes practice. Anyway, I'm glad that's over. I'm going to head out. Do you have time for a coffee along the way?"

"I'm a cop," said Lundquist. "Anytime is coffee time."

Lundquist followed Windflower over to the Tim Hortons. Windflower bought a sandwich and coffee for himself and another coffee for Lundquist. They sat at a corner table and watched the steady stream of traffic in the coffee shop and going through the busy drive-through.

"Every cop's dream," said Lundquist. Windflower looked confused. "To own a Tim Hortons."

"Yeah," said Windflower between bites of his grilled cheese sandwich. "Although once you get away from coffee for a few days, you realize how unhealthy it is to be pumped up on caffeine all the time."

"I know what you mean," said Lundquist. "I can feel myself vibrating by the end of my shift. But it does keep me awake, especially on the night shifts. Did you talk to Fitzpatrick and Daniels?"

"I spoke with Fitzpatrick. She was helpful and keen to get back looking for information. She and Daniels are going to the park incognito tonight."

"It should be a good night for it," said Lundquist. "Friday night is party night around here. Plus, the reward money will get people's attention. I didn't see the ATV in any of the usual dumping spots, but I'll bet the five hundred bucks will turn up something."

Windflower finished his sandwich and stood to leave. "Okay, I'm off," he said. "You have my number if anything develops. I'll be working on both days this weekend so give me a call anytime. And I'll be back here for sure by Monday morning."

"Sounds good," said Lundquist. "Enjoy your drive. And watch

out for the moose."

Windflower smiled and got into his car. He waved goodbye to Lundquist and pulled out onto the Trans Canada Highway heading east. The rain slowed to a mist and by the time he got to Gander, there were signs of a break in the dark and gray skies. He took that as an omen of good things to come, and settled back into his seat as he continued along the highway. The traffic was light all along the way and he enjoyed the quiet company of the silence as he moved towards his destination. A little before he got to Goobies, his cell phone rang. He pulled over to the shoulder of the road to take the call.

Chapter Twenty-six

"Hey, Boss, it's me," said Tizzard. "I'm at the detachment and I've got somebody in the back cell."

"Carol Jackson?" asked Windflower.

"Yes, indeed," said Tizzard. "I found her in that cabin out at Molliers. She was in rough shape. Looked like she hadn't eaten, or washed in days. I got Carrie, I mean Evanchuk, to go with her while she showered, and I picked up some soup for her at the Mug-Up."

"What did she say when you found her?" asked Windflower.

"She said, I'm glad it's you," said Tizzard. "I don't think she meant me, she meant the RCMP."

"I suspect you're right, Eddie. It probably also means somebody else might be looking for her. How is she now?"

"She seems fine. The last time I checked, she was sleeping like a baby back there."

"Okay. I'm on my way back. I'll drop in along the way to see her."

"Good," said Tizzard. "I'll stay here until you get here. Evanchuk is going to stay overnight. By the way, you have a guest at your house."

"Uncle Frank. Is he behaving himself?"

"I think so," said Tizzard. "He's having a good time, anyway. When I went by your house earlier, all the lights were on and you could hear the music from the road."

"Okay. I'll see you in a few hours."

Windflower loved his Uncle Frank. But he sure could be a pain in the behind sometimes. Let's hope he's not back on the sauce, Windflower thought. If that happens, then all bets are off when it comes to what Frank might or might not do. All he could hope for now was the best, and get ready for the worst. With this less than pleasant thought, he continued his drive towards Goobies and the road to Grand Bank and home.

He stopped at the gas station long enough to get gas and to call Sheila and tell her he was on his way. He couldn't reach her, but left a message. He hoped that not only would she pick it up, but that she might have supper on as well. That changed Windflower's mood considerably, as did the clearing skies that were revealing a beautiful pink sky ahead of the sunset.

He put on the classical music station again and was pleased to hear 'Spring' from Vivaldi's 'Four Seasons'. It was light and lively and the perfect musical accompaniment to the pleasant curves of the highway. He passed through Swift Current quickly. Before he knew it, he was past the Terrenceville turn-off as well. Soon, he was coming into more familiar terrain approaching Marystown.

In the near-dark, the Marystown shipyard was an imposing sight. They were working on another module for the offshore oil rigs and it looked like a spaceship ready for take-off. The deep water port was always impressive to Windflower as a small town boy from Northern Alberta. It gave him a sense of the power and vastness of the Atlantic Ocean. He drove through the centre of town and even though he really wanted another coffee, he resisted the urge and passed longingly by the crowded Tim Hortons. He could make it through the last leg of the journey without caffeine.

It was starting to get almost completely dark now, and Windflower put his high beam lights on whenever there was no other traffic. That allowed him to see the sides of the highway as well as far ahead. That was useful to spot any animals, especially moose on the road. To be sure, he slowed down and locked his car into cruise control so he wouldn't inadvertently speed up. That was good because as soon as he came to the first Garnish exit, he saw a big female moose on the right hand shoulder. He slowed even more, and as he approached, the moose ambled off into the woods.

It happened again at the second Garnish turn-off. This time a moose was on the far side of the highway, but decided to walk across right in front of Windflower. He was going slowly enough to stop and watch her cross. She seemed to be ignorant of the fact that he and his RCMP cruiser were there. I guess I didn't know it was a moose crossing, thought Windflower. There should have been a sign. Exactly.

By the time he started getting closer to Grand Bank, Windflower was barely crawling along. That was good too, since right at the road to Grand Beach was the third moose of the evening. This time it was a bull, probably looking for the females. Although it wasn't mating or rutting season, some young males still liked to hang out with the older females. Whatever the case, this moose didn't move or blink an eye when Windflower passed him on the side of the highway. He looked like he was waiting for something. Maybe he was waiting for Francis Tibbo's missus, thought Windflower.

He was still laughing to himself about that when he pulled into the parking lot at the Grand Bank RCMP Detachment. The lights were on and Tizzard's Jeep was parked out in front.

"What's so funny?" asked Tizzard.

"Francis Tibbo," said Windflower.

"Well, I actually find him a bit mean, but I can go for funny. How was your ride down?"

"Three moose. One on either end of Garnish and the other at Grand Beach."

"They're always there," said Tizzard.

"My point exactly," said Windflower. Tizzard looked puzzled and just nodded. "How's our guest?"

"She seems fine," said Tizzard. "She woke up from her nap a little while ago and asked if there was anything else to eat. I made her a couple of sandwiches."

"Has she said anything else?" asked Windflower.

"No," said Tizzard. "I told her you were coming and would talk to her. She seemed fine with that, relaxed almost. By the way, Boss, under which statute exactly are we holding her? I know we found the money and the scales, but without anything else that's not illegal is it?"

"Could be another case of 'protective custody'," said Windflower with a wink to his younger companion. "Let's see what she has to say."

Windflower walked down the hallway to the back cell with Tizzard at his heels.

"Hello, I'm Sergeant Winston Windflower. We have a few questions for you."

"Okay," said the woman. "We can do that, or I can tell you what I'm doing here."

"That would be even better," said Windflower.

"First of all, I hope you have my Harley," she said.

"We do. It's out back."

"Good," she said. "I work for you guys," she added.

"For the RCMP?" blurted out Tizzard, unable to contain himself.

"I'm under contract with the RCMP Outlaw Gang Unit," said Jackson.

"Why didn't you tell me that?" asked Tizzard.

"You didn't ask me." said the woman. "I needed a place to hide out and this," she said, waving her hands in the air, "is the perfect spot for that."

"What are you hiding from?" asked Windflower.

Carol Jackson looked at him and said, "I'll need to talk to somebody higher than you, with all due respect, Sergeant. Call Majesky, he'll tell you what you need to know."

"Superintendent Majesky?" asked Windflower.

"That's the contact name I was given, if I needed it," said Jackson. "Can you do that?"

"I can. I'll call and leave a message. Once I get a hold of the Superintendent, I'll let you know. In the meantime, we'd like to continue to provide you with our hospitality, if that's okay with you."

"Fine with me," said the woman. "I haven't slept for days."

Windflower and Tizzard turned around and walked out to the front of the building.

"That was weird, Boss," said Tizzard. "Is she telling the truth?"

"We're going to find out," said Windflower as he picked up his cell phone to call Majesky. "No answer," he said to Tizzard as the message kicked in. "Superintendent, it's Windflower. I'm in Grand Bank. We're holding a woman by the name of Carol Jackson. She had your name as a contact. Can you call me? Thanks."

"What's next?" asked Tizzard.

"We wait. I'll let you know if I hear anything, but I've got an appointment with some home-cooked food and my own bed."

"And your Uncle Frank," said Tizzard.

"Thanks for reminding me. Where's my dog, by the way?"

"I saw Sheila earlier. She suggested I bring Lady over there," said Tizzard. "She'll be glad to see you."

"I hope so," said Windflower, wondering if Tizzard meant Sheila or Lady. He hoped both. "See you tomorrow."

Chapter Twenty-seven

It was a short drive to Sheila's house. Windflower was happy to see that all of the lights were on in the old house where Sheila had grown up. Like Windflower, she too had lost both of her parents when she was still quite young, but she also bore the loss of her husband, Bart, a few years ago. They hadn't been married long, but had been quite happy together. Bart was working as a heavy equipment mechanic in Alberta when he was killed in an industrial accident. They were planning to build a new home together, but of course, that never happened.

Instead, Sheila put part of her energy into restoring and renewing her old family homestead. The other main way of dealing with her grief came from building the Mug-Up Café into a thriving and successful business. She had given that up and transferred the café to Moira Stoodley after she and Windflower got together, first as friends, and now in a romantic relationship. Today, she focused on being a good mayor for the Town of Grand Bank, and in becoming the future wife and partner of the RCMP officer who was coming in her back door.

"Winston, I'm so glad you're home. I always worry about you out on the highway at nighttime." She gave him a big hug to welcome him home.

"No worries," said Windflower and he bent to kiss her. And no need to worry her any more by telling her about his moose visitations. Then Lady came bounding out of the living room and almost bowled them both over. She didn't just stop and say hello. She proceeded to make three complete laps of the whole first floor of the house, stopping each time to get petted by the pair in the kitchen.

"I think someone else is glad to see you," said Sheila as Lady finally settled down in between them. She almost purred when they both rubbed and patted her.

"What's that delicious smell?" asked Windflower.

"It's a salmon casserole," said Sheila. "Pour us a glass of wine, and if you're hungry, I'll dish up."

"I'm so hungry," said Windflower, "I could eat a ..." He almost said moose, but didn't want to rekindle that discussion. So he simply added, "a lot."

He got the white wine out of the fridge and poured them both a glass. Sheila put the salad on the table first. Windflower could smell Sheila's special homemade raspberry vinaigrette on the mixed greens. Then she put the salmon casserole on a pot holder on the table. It was topped with golden brown bread crumbs. When Sheila put the slotted spoon into the dish it released a puff of steam and spices that almost made Windflower go weak at the knees.

She scooped up a large portion for him and a smaller portion for herself, along with a double spoonful of steamed broccoli. Windflower was in food heaven as he tasted the chunks of salmon and potato in the creamy sauce. He was silently engaged in his task and didn't come up for air until he passed his plate over to Sheila for seconds.

"That is sum good, b'y," he said. "What is that flavouring you used?"

"That's tarragon," said Sheila. "It goes well with the salmon, doesn't it?"

"It is fabulous," said Windflower, already lost in his second round of dinner. When he finished he got up and went over to Sheila. "Thank you, my love. That was a great dinner," and he gave her a kiss on the forehead.

"You'll have to do better than that to thank me properly," said Sheila.

"No problem, ma'am. I am at your service."

"Good," said Sheila. "You can start by cleaning up while I get tea and dessert organized."

Windflower happily went about the task of cleaning the plates and stacking the dishwasher while Sheila made a pot of tea. Minutes later Windflower walked out to the living room where Sheila was sitting with their tea and dessert. Windflower's eyes lit up when he saw that it was his all-time favourite, chocolate peanut butter cheesecake. He sat beside Sheila and tried to eat his dessert as slowly as he could, but it still disappeared far too quickly.

When it was gone Windflower reached over and gave Sheila a deep kiss, a very deep kiss.

"That's more what I had in mind," said Sheila as she reached back in to return the favour.

"Let me go and take Lady out for the final time, and I have to drop by my house for a minute. But I promise you, I won't be long."

Sheila smiled as Windflower grabbed Lady and her leash for the short ride home. When they got there the lights were on, but it looked like nobody was home. He threw his bag into the hallway and he and Lady went off on a short, but very brisk walk. Lady showed very little effect of her injuries and seemed quite happy to show off the fact that her master was back home. She could have gone on longer, but Windflower had other commitments. He got Lady a couple of Milk Bone dog biscuits and refilled her food and water.

It was evident his uncle had been there. There were dirty dishes in the sink and on the kitchen table, and the spare bedroom was a jumble of clothes and bedding. Windflower closed the door on this mess and spent a few minutes cleaning up the kitchen. At least there were no signs of drinking, he thought, and no dirty ashtrays to clean up. Uncle Frank had learnt a few of the rules and that was something to be grateful for. He'd talk to him again in the morning, when he saw him, about being a better and cleaner house guest.

Windflower patted Lady good night and walked back to Sheila's. The sky had cleared and the moon shone brightly out over the Atlantic Ocean. When he got to Sheila's all of the lights on the main floor except one were off. He opened the door and called out his hello.

"Come on up," said Sheila.

Windflower went quickly and happily up the stairs.

Chapter Twenty-eight

It was wonderful to get acquainted again with Sheila in an intimate way. Afterwards, Windflower fell fast asleep. His next recollection was waking up again in his dream, the fire dream. This time the fire was still raging inside the old house in Grand Bank, but what happened next surprised and shocked him. As the roof started to give way, he looked up and saw Tizzard standing in the second floor window, holding the other person in his arms. Windflower tried to scream to tell him to get out, but nothing would come out of his mouth.

It was too late. The roof collapsed and the last thing Windflower remembered was seeing the look of terror in Tizzard's eyes as he and the person he was carrying were engulfed in the flames. Windflower woke with a start and sat upright in the bed. He got up, went to the bathroom and washed his face with a cool towel. Slowly, his breath came back to normal. He crawled back into bed with Sheila and held her until sleep finally overtook him again.

He woke early, a little after the sun had risen, which was good, since he had a lot to do today. He snuck quietly out of the bedroom and was out the door and on his way home shortly afterwards. There was a morning chill in the air, but you could feel it being warmed away by the sun already. It was going to be a hot day, thought Windflower. He walked slowly through the little town that he had grown to love and back over to his own house. In a few months, after the wedding, he would give up this little piece of personal freedom and move in with Sheila. He looked forward to that, but also knew he should appreciate this time alone before it was gone.

Lady greeted him at the door in her usual state of happiness. Soon, both of them were walking along the back roads towards the beach. There was no one but them and the sea gulls out this morning. That was fine with Lady. She seemed to like having Windflower all to herself. They took the long way back through town and near the wharf, which was also having a sleepy morning. Soon all types of boats and fishermen and walkers and gawkers would be wandering around. But for now, it was just Windflower and his dog.

When they got back, Windflower gave Lady her treats and went into his bedroom to organize his laundry. He could hear that Uncle Frank had made it home. The snores emanating from the spare bedroom were a dead giveaway. Windflower tried to be considerate as he put on a pot of coffee while he tidied up a little. He filled his thermos with coffee, grabbed a banana and his Donna Leon book, and drove up to the laundromat.

People kept telling him to get a washing machine, but Windflower actually liked going to the laundromat. He put in his washes, filled the machines with quarters from a roll in his bag and laid out his banana and coffee on the table. He got his book out and for the next forty-five minutes was perfectly content with his morning joe and the company of Commissario Brunetti. When the wash was done, he flipped the wet clothes into the dryers and sat down again in peaceful solitude.

After folding and putting away his newly cleaned laundry he

drove back home. When he arrived, his Uncle Frank was up and sitting at his kitchen table with a cup of coffee in his hands.

"Thanks for the coffee, Winston," said Uncle Frank.

"Good to see you. When did you arrive?"

"I came in on the taxi yesterday afternoon," said his uncle. "I decided to come a little early before the wedding. It will give me a chance to visit with my friends before your Auntie arrives."

"The wedding is still months away," said Windflower.

"If you don't want me here, I have other places to stay," said Uncle Frank, just a little grumpily.

"Stay, stay. You know you are welcome here any time. I'm not here much anyway. But keep things tidy, okay?"

"Okay, Winston, if you insist, then I'll stay."

Windflower was going to say that's not what he said, but why bother? Instead he said, "Don't forget to call Auntie Marie. She's worried about you."

"I'll call her later today," said Uncle Frank. "I'm starving. I'm going to cook up some eggs and blood pudding I got at Warrens yesterday. Do you want some?"

"No thank you, Uncle. I have to go to Sheila's and then in to work. But I would like to talk to you later. I have some dreams I'm trying to figure out."

"What about the bear?" asked Uncle Frank.

"How did you know?" Windflower started to say and then stopped. "That too," he said with a laugh, and went out the door.

Chapter Twenty-nine

On his way to Sheila's, Windflower remembered Carol Jackson and two other important things. One was that he hadn't told Sheila she'd been found. That was interesting, because he told Sheila almost everything. But maybe he wasn't sure yet if Jackson was one of the good guys, or on the other side. Maybe he was protecting Sheila. Whatever the reason, it was interesting, he thought. The second thing was a bit more pressing. He'd left his phone back at Sheila's and hadn't checked for messages from Majesky before he went to bed last night. That he could fix right away.

He found his cell phone on top of the fridge and scanned quickly for messages. One new voice mail, 10:35 p.m. last night. "Shoot," he said out loud. He dialed his mail-box and listened to the message. It was from Majesky. "Call me," was all it said.

Windflower could hear Sheila moving around upstairs and called out. "I'll put on some coffee. I have to make a quick call, and I'll be up soon."

"Okay," Sheila called back.

Windflower walked outside and dialed Majesky's number.

"Good morning, sir," he said as soon as the Superintendent answered.

"Where the hell have you been?" asked Majesky, clearly not pleased with Windflower.

"Sorry, sir, I guess my phone was off last night," he said. "Plus, I was tired from driving back from Grand Falls."

"Never mind the crap," said Majesky. "When I call, I want you to be there. Understood?"

"Yes, sir," said Windflower.

"I checked with HQ and can confirm that Carol Jackson is a civilian freelancer with the Biker Task force," said the Superintendent. "There are some complications, however. Did you recover any money in her possession?"

"Yes, sir. We recovered $60,000 in cash and some scales and drug testing equipment that were in her saddlebags."

"That's good, since it's apparently our money," said Majesky. "I don't have all the details, but I guess she was going to make a drug buy while she was in the province. They can't figure out at HQ what went wrong, but my suspicions are that it's connected to the troubles in Grand Falls."

"So what do you want me to do?" asked Windflower. "I don't really have anything to hold her on."

"Don't worry about that for now. HQ wants you to interview her and report back to me. Find out what her story is and see if you can't make any connections to the murders," said Majesky. "Talk to her this morning and then call me back, okay?"

"Okay," said Windflower. He had many more questions to ask the Superintendent, but Majesky was gone. He closed his phone and went back inside.

"Where's my coffee?" called Sheila when she heard him come back in.

"Coming right up," said Windflower as he got two cups and brought them up to Sheila.

"When were you going to tell me about Carol?" asked Sheila, as she sipped her coffee.

"How did you know she was here?" asked Windflower.

"I saw Eddie bring her into the RCMP office. We just said hi. Can you tell me what's going on?" Sheila asked.

"We don't actually know yet. I'm sorry I didn't speak to you about it. I guess I was a bit preoccupied last night. I didn't even take a call from my big boss. He's mad with me today too."

"I'm not mad," said Sheila. "I know you have your police work and sometimes it's confidential. I don't want any secrets between us, okay?"

"Okay. I'm going to talk to Carol later this morning. Maybe I can tell you more afterwards. Now, I'm starving. Do you want some breakfast?"

"That's what I've been missing in my life," said Sheila. "I love a man who can cook."

"You relax and I'll get things going," said Windflower.

Half an hour later he was walking back upstairs with a breakfast tray. Two omelets with cheese and mushrooms, a small basket of molasses raisin toast, partridge berry jam and a fresh carafe of coffee. Windflower sat on the side of the bed while Sheila was propped up on her pillows. The two shared good company and a great breakfast until it was time for Windflower to go to work.

"I'll give you a call later," said Windflower as he kissed Sheila gently on the forehead.

"We should go over to the Stoodleys around 5," said Sheila. "I hear he's got a treat for you."

"I hope it's those trout he was telling me about. I get hungry just thinking about them," said Windflower.

"You just ate breakfast," said Sheila with a laugh.

"Always plan ahead, especially when it comes to food," said Windflower.

"Bye, Winston," said Sheila, shaking her head at her crazy man.

Windflower drove to the RCMP offices, where once again Tizzard's Jeep was out in front. This time he was not alone. Constable

Carrie Evanchuk was there, but dressed in civilian clothes. Windflower remembered she was leaving today. Tizzard was driving her into St. John's to catch her flight to Ottawa and her new assignment.

"Wow, last day in Grand Bank. We are going to miss you, you know?"

"I'm going to miss Grand Bank," said Evanchuk. "This was my first posting and I'm glad it was here with you and Eddie, I mean Corporal Tizzard."

"Somebody taking my name in vain?" asked Tizzard as he came out of the lunchroom, wiping crumbs off the front of his shirt.

Both Windflower and Evanchuk laughed. "We all love you, Eddie," said Windflower jokingly. Surprisingly, at least to Windflower, Evanchuk didn't laugh at his small attempt at humour.

"How's our guest?" asked Windflower.

"She seems fine," said Evanchuk. "I checked on her a few times during the night, but it looks like she slept right through. I got us some breakfast. There may be some left, unless Corporal Tizzard has finished it off."

Tizzard looked guilty as charged but Windflower eased that situation by saying, "I already ate at home. What time do you have to leave?"

"I guess we'll head out around noon," said Tizzard. "Is that okay?" he asked, looking at Evanchuk.

"Sounds good," she said.

"Okay. I'm going to talk to Jackson."

"We'll hold the fort 'til you're done," said Tizzard.

Chapter Thirty

Windflower walked down the corridor to the cell at the back of the building. Carol Jackson had been lying on her bunk, but rose to her feet when she heard Windflower approaching.

She was a good-looking lady, thought Windflower, after she'd had a little sleep. She'd obviously had another shower this morning, since her long dirty blond hair looked still damp. She also put out an elfish charm, he thought, when she smiled at him. She had that look of 'I'm just a little girl, I'm helpless, what can a big man like you do to help me?' He bet she had gotten an awful lot of what she wanted in life with that look.

He smiled back, but had become too cynical in his years of police work to fall for that false charm. That only worked on fools and drunks, preferably ones who were both at the same time.

"Good morning," he said. "It looks like you slept well."

"I did. Now can I get my bike and get out of here?" she asked.

"Well, I've got a few questions first, and then we'll see what happens after that," said Windflower as he picked up a plastic chair out of one of the other cells and sat down directly in front of her.

"Where should I begin?" asked Jackson, a little coyly.

"Let's not beat around the bush. It's been a long week and I have a very low tolerance for bull at this point. Your personal freedom depends on telling me the truth."

"Didn't you talk to the Outlaw Gang people? They could have told you what was going on," said Jackson.

"They have confirmed you were on a project with them. But obviously something went wrong, didn't it?" said Windflower, his voice rising. He forced himself to calm down and continued. "To start off with, tell me how you got involved in this, and what you were supposed to be doing on the island."

The woman didn't bat an eye at Windflower's attempt to push her. She's probably dealt with much tougher and rougher people than me, thought Windflower. He decided to add a little sugar to see if he couldn't get this particular fly to come into his web. "Listen, I am your one and only get-out-of-this-jail card. I want to help you, but the guys upstairs want me to vet your story before any of that can happen."

"I've been involved with bikers my whole life," said Jackson. "Most of it on the other side. I was married to a Choice guy and when that scene blew up I ran for cover. He wasn't so lucky, or so fast. But sooner or later these guys catch up to you, or you run back to them. It's crazy, but it's the only life I know. I got pinched a few times, the last one as a mule bringing stuff in from the States. That's when the Task Force scooped me up. They got me into rehab and afterwards offered me this deal: I could work for you or I could do at least ten years as a guest of the Crown."

Windflower simply nodded, encouraging her to continue.

"This was supposed to be my last gig. After this I was getting a new ID and relocation, somewhere peaceful and quiet," she said. When Windflower laughed she said, "What's so funny? I can do small town. I lived in this god-forsaken place for twelve years."

"Okay," said Windflower quietly.

"I was here to do a buy with Bacchus and Joey Blow. He was

running a multi-million-dollar operation right out of some shack in the woods. Bacchus was shipping stuff in through the airports at Gander and Deer Lake, and then the local guys were repackaging it and sending it back across the ferry to Southern Ontario. I was going to buy a sample, and then use that to get inside with Joey Blow. Once that happened, the sting would be on and I'd get my free pass to Pleasant Valley," said Jackson.

"What did happen?" asked Windflower.

"I don't know for sure. My contact didn't show up for the meet and then I decided to come here to see my cousin, Sheila Hillier. You know her?"

"Yeah, I know her," said Windflower, not willing to reveal anything else yet. "That's when I saw you in Goobies."

"Yes," said Jackson. "The other thing is, I put a call in to somebody who was supposed to be working on the inside. But he didn't answer or call me back. So I figured the best thing to do was to get out of sight as quickly as I could."

"Why didn't you report in then?" asked Windflower.

"I don't know," said Jackson. "I figured my best move was to get out of town and lay low. I was heading to Grand Bank when I heard about the murders in Grand Falls. The names hadn't been released, but they were talking about possible biker involvement. I stopped in Marystown to get a coffee. I was actually going to stay at the motel for the night. But I think I got spotted by some local guys. That's when I decided to run."

"Local biker guys?" asked Windflower.

"Yeah," said Jackson. "I forget what they used to be called. But some of them just got patched over to Bacchus. When I saw them, I took off. They started to follow me so I ran like hell out of there. I parked the bike on the side of the road in Grand Beach and then I hitchhiked the other way. I stayed for a while in the park at Frenchman's Cove until I felt it was safe to come out again."

"Weren't you worried about leaving the money with your motorcycle?" Windflower asked.

"It wasn't my money," said Jackson. "Besides, I watched until it got dark to see if the guys were still following me. When they didn't show I figured they were gone. I also thought that sooner or later you guys would show up and find my bike and the money."

"I still can't figure out why you didn't just turn yourself in, here or in Marystown," said Windflower.

"You don't know who you can trust in this line of work," said Jackson. "I wasn't going to take the chance that somehow all of this wouldn't get laid on me."

"That's a very interesting story," said Windflower.

"It's the truth. A girl like me wouldn't lie, now would I?" she said as she batted her eyes at Windflower and moved to press her breasts together and up against the bars of the cell.

"It's not up to me," said Windflower, ignoring her flirting. "I'll make the call and see what they say. You sit here for now. And you probably should know this as well, Sheila Hillier is my fiancée." With that, Windflower put his chair back in the nearby cell and walked back down the hallway.

"So how did that go?" asked Tizzard when Windflower came into the front area of the office.

"She's got a very interesting story to tell. I'm not sure I believe I have all the information yet, but I think I'm getting there. Anyway, I've got to call Majesky in Halifax. You're still here for an hour or so, right?"

"Right," said Tizzard. "Carrie's gone to pick up her bags."

"Is there anything you want to tell me?" asked Windflower.

"What do you mean?" asked Tizzard, trying to appear nonchalant.

"You and Carrie," said Windflower.

"Well," said Tizzard, pausing to think out his words before he spoke. "That wouldn't be appropriate for someone supervising someone else, now would it?"

"But if she's not here, there's no conflict. I get it," said Windflower.

"Get what?" asked Evanchuk walking in through the door.

Windflower couldn't resist throwing a little Shakespeare into the mix. "'But love is blind, and lovers cannot see the pretty follies that themselves commit; for, if they could, Cupid himself would blush'."

"What?" asked Evanchuk, now looking particularly puzzled. Tizzard gave her a quick look as if to say he'd explain everything later.

"Never mind. I have to go home and get Lady, and then make my call. Will you guys stay here until I get back?"

"Yes," said Tizzard and Evanchuk, simultaneously.

Young love, Windflower thought as he got into his car and drove back home to get Lady. At least he wouldn't have to watch it flower and bloom and maybe even crash on his watch. There were always things to be grateful for.

Chapter Thirty-one

As always, Lady bounced to the door when she heard Windflower come in. She ran to get petted and then ran some more, just because she felt like it. She finally settled down when Windflower gave her a treat. There was no sign of Uncle Frank and thankfully no sign of his breakfast either. It looked like he had washed, dried, and put away all his dishes and wiped the stove and countertop too. Windflower was pleased, and impressed. This might work out after all.

He grabbed Lady's leash and off they went for a walk. The sun was really starting to heat things up. Windflower was glad to leave his jacket behind and walk along in his shirt sleeves. Lady was just glad for the walk. They walked through town, past the Salvation Army Citadel, and all the way to the brook. There was the usual variety of ducks and sea birds in the narrow channel. At first, they thought Windflower might be bringing them an early lunch. But when they saw the dog, they paddled quickly in the other direction.

Lady had a quick drink from the brook and tugged Windflower

along the shore towards the wharf. He and Lady walked past the old fishing stages to a place where a congregation of men had gathered around two wooden benches. In the middle of the circle was Uncle Frank, and judging by the laughter of the men around him, he was spinning a great yarn. Windflower waved to his uncle and the other men and kept walking along. He didn't want to get caught up in one of Uncle Frank's stories. It would likely be long and it might even be about him.

Instead, he smiled and continued his walk with Lady. They went up past the old B & B that had been restored and was once again offering special lunches and dinner. It was a favourite spot for Sheila and Windflower, who were fans of its unique French cuisine with a distinct Newfoundland twist. When he turned the corner, he realized they were coming onto Seaview Drive and the old house that had been on fire in his dreams. He walked slowly by, half expecting to see flames coming out of the building, but seeing nothing but a house slowly dying from neglect.

Soon they were home. Lady was pleased when, instead of putting her in the house, Windflower opened the back door of his cruiser. She jumped in and was ready to go, whenever he was. She had hoped for a bit of an outdoor adventure, but those hopes were dashed when Windflower pulled up in front of the Grand Bank RCMP Detachment. One more thing to do first though. He pulled out his phone and called Superintendent Majesky's number.

"Majesky," the voice said at the other end of the line.

"I've talked to Jackson," said Windflower. He gave his superior officer a rundown of their conversation.

"What do you think?" asked Majesky after Windflower finished his summary.

"She's got quite a story to tell. It all sounds legit, but it also feels like there are missing pieces," said Windflower.

"Like what?" asked the other man.

"Like why she was running away and why she left all that money sitting by the side of the road. And I still can't figure out what happened in Grand Falls. All she said was that when things screwed up, her connection, our guy, wasn't available," said Windflower.

"Is she talking about French?" asked Majesky.

"I guess so. It might have been a missed connection."

"It may have been," said the Superintendent. "Or something else. The only one who might know is French. Arrange to have him picked up and then ask him what the heck's going on."

"Under what pretense should we arrest him, sir?" asked Windflower.

"He's masquerading as an outlaw biker," said Majesky. "He must be doing something wrong. One more question, Windflower. Do you believe her story?"

"She is a very convincing witness. But somehow I'm not quite convinced, at least not yet."

"Let me know when you get French and what he has to say," said Majesky. "In the meantime, keep Jackson there."

"What should I tell her, sir?" asked Windflower.

"Tell her to sit tight. She's safe where she is. For now."

Windflower closed his phone and put it in his pocket. "Come on, Lady," he said as he let her out of the back seat. "Time to go to work."

Tizzard and Evanchuk were sitting near the reception desk when he came in. Lady immediately ran to Tizzard.

"She's looking for food," said Tizzard.

"Probably at the right place," said Evanchuk. All three of them laughed.

"So I guess we're off," said Tizzard. "Frost will be in later to relieve you. If you need him to, he can stay overnight."

"Thanks," said Windflower. He went over to shake Evanchuk's hand, but she had other plans and was soon wrapped around him. He conceded and hugged her back.

"Good luck," said Windflower.

"Thank you, Sergeant," said Evanchuk. Tizzard simply waved goodbye and picked up one of her bags. Windflower watched them get into Tizzard's Jeep and drive away. He was pleased Evanchuk had been given such a great opportunity for her career, but he was sorry to see her go. And by the looks of it, Tizzard might be even sorrier.

Chapter Thirty-two

He got Lady set up with fresh food and water in his office. She had already taken up occupancy under his desk. Then he went down the corridor to see Carol Jackson.

"Are you here to let me out?" she asked.

"Not yet. My instructions were to hold you for now. I think the term, 'you'd be safer here', was used."

"Could be worse, I guess," said Jackson.

"It certainly could be. You might as well have an afternoon nap. That's my plan," he said as he walked away.

But before his nap time, Windflower had a phone call to make. He went to his office and called the RCMP Detachment in Grand Falls.

"RCMP," came the answer.

"Lundquist. You're the man I was looking for. How are things in the big city of Grand Falls-Windsor?"

"Things are relatively quiet," said Lundquist. "We've got a couple of drunks still here from last night. Both want to charge the other with assault, but neither remembers enough for that to happen."

Windflower laughed. "I need you to do something. We need to bring in French. Find some excuse and bring him in. Hold him until I get back on Sunday night. Tell him Windflower wants to talk to him. He'll understand," said Windflower.

"No problem," said Lundquist. "I'll see Daniels and Fitzpatrick soon. They worked late last night on the canvass. Hopefully they'll have something to report. The other thing is that I went to the funeral for the girl this morning. Guess who was there?"

"Who?" asked Windflower.

"Joey Blow," said Lundquist. "Sitting at the back, crying his eyes out. I heard him muttering about getting whoever did this to her."

"Now, that's interesting. Kind of suggests that he didn't do it. At least not her."

"You never know with these guys," said Lundquist. "But that is the impression I had too."

"Anyway, I have to go. Let me know when you get French."

His last mission completed, there were no more barriers to Windflower and his long-awaited nap. He locked the front door and did one more check on Carol Jackson. She had apparently taken his advice and was curled up in her cell. He opened another cell a few yards away and with Lady as his very willing companion, lay on the bunk for a mid-afternoon snooze.

Windflower and Lady slept together quietly and solidly. He couldn't believe his eyes when he checked his phone and saw it had been almost three hours. He checked in again with Jackson who was now propped up on the bunk in her cell, reading one of the magazines that Evanchuk had brought in. Windflower missed Evanchuk already.

He made a pot of coffee and grabbed a couple of Tizzard's Purity Cream Crackers out of the cupboard. He crumbled up one of the crackers and put it in Lady's bowl for a treat. She was soon happily engaged in crunching the cracker between her teeth while Windflower buttered his biscuits and sliced off a piece of cheese to round out his snack. When the coffee was ready, he went in to see Jackson and brought her a cup.

"Do you want it?" he asked. "It's black."

"Yeah," said Jackson. Windflower opened the door and passed in her coffee. She took the cup silently as Windflower locked the cell and went back to the front. He sat at his desk, played with the papers on his desk, and ate his snack. Just before 4 p.m., his phone rang.

"Windflower," he answered.

"We've got some information from the canvass," said Lundquist. "Fitz and Daniels found a couple of people who heard the shots."

"That's good," said Windflower.

"It gets even better," said Lundquist. "There's a witness who saw the two men leaving the park on the ATV. And one of them took off their ski mask. Our witness got a look at him."

"Did they recognize him?" asked Windflower.

"No, but he gave us enough of a description that we think we can help make a positive ID. He's in the back right now taking a look at pictures. We're pretty sure it's one of the bikers," said Lundquist. "But we have quite a few around here, as you know."

"I know. Any sign of French?"

"Not yet," said Lundquist. "But we did get a tip on our ATV. Somebody said they saw one out by the mill smelter. I'm going out now to have a look at it."

"More good news. Good work, Lars. Keep me posted."

Constable Harry Frost had come in while Windflower was on the phone. When Windflower came out, he and Lady were playing on the floor.

"Having fun?" asked Windflower.

"I so miss my dog," said Frost. "You're lucky to have such a great dog."

"Yeah," said Windflower, "Say, do you mind if I leave her here with you? I've got to run home and get changed. We're going out for dinner."

"No problem," said Frost. "I'd like the company."

"Super. I'll be back to see you and pick up Lady later. There are cold plates in the fridge for you and our guest out back."

"I'll pass on the cold plate. I never got what people saw in cold plates. Two scoops of mystery salads and two slices of mystery meat," said Frost. "I brought my own lunch from home."

"It should be quiet. If you need me, you know how to get me," said Windflower.

"We'll be fine," said Frost as Windflower patted Lady and went out to his car. It was still a beautiful day and Windflower rolled down the window to get a few more breaths of this warm summer air. He could hear the music coming from his house as soon as he pulled into his driveway. Uncle Frank, thought Windflower and he was right. Uncle Frank had the stereo blasting country music very loudly, and was providing his own vocal accompaniment from the kitchen where he was cooking up something.

"Hi Uncle," said Windflower, and then much more loudly, "Uncle!"

"Oh, Winston, it's you," said his Uncle Frank. "I'll turn the music down."

"That's better," said Uncle Frank, and Windflower's ears certainly agreed. "I was making up a batch of chili. I'm going over to Jarge's to play cards and I'm bringing supper. It's almost done if you want a taste."

"No thanks, Uncle. I'm going for supper with Sheila. I have to get a shower and clean up first. I was hoping maybe you and I could have some time tomorrow morning. Maybe go for a walk up the trail."

"Sure," said Uncle Frank. "Is that where you saw the bear?"

"Yes. Although I'm starting to get some more insight into what that was about."

"It's related to your vision quest," said Uncle Frank. "Maybe your allies are trying to give you a message too."

"Yeah. I had another dream and I remember the vision quest

with Grandfather now. It's funny how we forget some things that were so important in our lives."

"It could be dangerous too," said his uncle. "Sometimes our allies are sending us warnings we need to pay attention to as well."

Windflower nodded his agreement. "It will be good to talk tomorrow. Thank you, Uncle."

Chapter Thirty-three

Freshly showered and shaved, with a nicely starched white shirt over his jeans, Windflower was ready for his dinner date with Sheila. He said goodbye to Uncle Frank, and drove because he would need his car later to check in on Frost and Carol Jackson.

"Hi, Sheila, I'm here," he called as he came into the kitchen.

"Be right there," said Sheila. Moments later she appeared, wearing a short flowery dress and a single set of pearls around her neck. She had her hair up, the way Windflower liked it, highlighted with a tinge of crimson. One solitary ringlet curled over her forehead.

"You look absolutely gorgeous," said Windflower.

"Thank you," said Sheila. "You clean up pretty nicely too."

She grabbed a white cashmere sweater for later and took Windflower's proffered arm for the short walk to the Stoodleys. It seemed like most of Grand Bank was out this early Saturday evening as well. They were walking along enjoying the sunshine while it lasted. Everywhere was that fabulous aroma of burning meat on the barbecue. Windflower was with his girl and he was in heaven.

The walk took a little longer than planned because Mayor Sheila had to stop and talk with her constituents along the way. Windflower didn't mind, but he was glad he'd had a few crackers and cheese. The various smells from the barbecues along their path were driving him crazy. Soon they were at the Stoodleys, a fabulous old house that was clinging to the side of the cliffs overlooking the islands off the southeast coast.

Moira Stoodley greeted them at the door and got them each a drink. White wine for Sheila, and a Black Horse beer for Windflower. He didn't need to be told where to find Herb Stoodley; he could smell the barbecue as soon as Moira opened the door. He took his beer out to see Herb while Sheila went to help Moira make the salad.

"Evening, Herb. That smells so good."

"Oh, hi Winston, I see you got a beer," said Herb Stoodley. "I'm trying a new recipe. It's from one of Moira's magazines, Canadian Living, I think."

"That's where I get my recipes too. I've only ever cooked fish on the barbecue using tin foil. What are you doing here?"

"You know I always did the same. But fish is actually meant to be grilled, as long as you can cook it fast and make sure it doesn't stick. These trout here are almost done. I put on the lemon potatoes about twenty-five minutes ago and they should be ready as well," said Stoodley, turning over the potatoes that were now golden brown on both sides.

"Did you marinate the trout before you put them on the barbecue?" asked Windflower as he eyed the browning fish on the grill.

"A little soy sauce, lemon juice, some oil and a dash of rosemary," said Stoodley. "You only have to marinate these beauties for about an hour and then use the rest of the marinade for basting. One more shot of basting and we'll be ready to go." He applied a thin coating of sauce and closed the barbecue cover.

"How'd you make the potatoes?" Windflower asked, trying not to drool as he let the beautiful aromas waft over him.

"Easy as pie," said Stoodley. "Cut your potatoes into wedges and toss them in a bowl with some olive oil, salt and pepper and a heavy dose of grated lemon rind. Then grease up the grill and you're ready to go. And so are we." He took the trout and potatoes off the barbecue and put them on a platter. "Let's eat," he said.

As usual, Windflower did not have to be asked twice. Moira poured everyone a glass of chilled white wine and passed around the salad while Herb dished up a nice fat trout and a couple of potato wedges for each of them. The foursome sat around the big dining room table, happily engaged in the beautiful dinner and in reconnecting with one another.

Herb Stoodley was a retired Crown Attorney and always had plenty of funny stories to tell about the good guys, and not so good guys from his past. He and Windflower shared a love of the law and Shakespeare. That made for a good friendship, along with the fact they both also loved to cook and loved to eat even more.

Moira Stoodley and Sheila were also close. Moira had helped run the Mug-Up Café after Sheila's terrible car accident. She later bought the business when Sheila decided she needed a change of pace and career.

Windflower didn't say much during dinner, except to compliment Moira on the green salad with fresh strawberries and a tangy balsamic vinegar kick. He nodded his pleasure to Herb as he passed his plate twice to get more trout.

"I'm going to try making this myself," Windflower pronounced as he finished off the last of his share of the barbecued trout.

"I'm looking forward to that," said Sheila.

"You'll have to come out with me to catch them," said Herb. "I found another great spot for trout fishing near Molliers. Why don't you come with me this week?"

"I'd love to, Herb, but I've got to go back to Grand Falls. I'll tell you about it later. It's not the stuff for a dinner conversation," said Windflower.

"Did Carol Jackson ever show up?" asked Moira. When both

Sheila and Windflower reacted with mild shocks of confusion, she added. "I knew you'd been talking about it," she said to Sheila.

"Carol has a bit of a situation going on, as usual," said Sheila. "That's kind of the story of her life." Windflower remained silent, but smiled at Sheila to acknowledge her helpfulness in moving past a tricky situation.

Moira Stoodley took that cue as well and said, "You cooked, so we clean. Why don't you guys go out on the deck and we'll get coffee and dessert going?"

Chapter Thirty-four

Windflower and Herb Stoodley took the last of their wine and went outside. It was a wonderful evening and you could see just about forever as they gazed out into the Atlantic Ocean. You could even see a few of the smaller islands, like Greens Island, where fishermen once had their summer fishing grounds. Today, there were very few fishermen, and no one visiting these islands but an occasional mariner from the States, families of harp seals, and a wide assortment of gulls and turrs and other sea birds.

It was a quiet, peaceful place to be, and both men relaxed for a few minutes as their swollen bellies subsided. Finally, Windflower broke the silence.

"So I'm investigating a double homicide. Grand Falls is becoming the murder capital of Newfoundland."

"Bikers?" asked Stoodley.

"Yeah, they're still all over the place, maggoty is a word that comes to mind," said Windflower.

"Great Newfoundland word," said Stoodley. "But for all their bravado, these guys are just cowards dressed up as bullies."

"But they can sure cause havoc in their path. 'Hell is empty and all the devils are here'."

"I know what you mean," said Stoodley. "We didn't have many outlaw bikers back in my early days with the Crown. I guess there wasn't enough money around here to make it worth their while. Once the drug scene grew and the offshore economy blew everything up, you started to see more of them."

"Well right now they're moving in big time, and even attracting some local talent to supplement their own goons. Including a few right here in Marystown," said Windflower.

"'Lawless are they that make their wills the law,'" said Stoodley, as Moira and Sheila were coming out with the dessert and coffee tray.

"Are you guys talking Shakespeare again?" asked Moira. "It's like they have their own secret language," she said to Sheila.

"'The lady doth protest too much, me thinks,'" responded Herb.

"'A fool thinks himself wise, but a wise man knows himself to be a fool,'" piped in Sheila.

"That's good," said Herb Stoodley.

"I think it's time for dessert," said Windflower, who had been anxiously eyeing the tray ever since it had arrived outside. Everyone laughed at his singleness of purpose when it came to his food, particularly his dessert opportunities.

"I've got lemon meringue pie and coconut cream cheesecake," said Moira.

"I'll try the pie first," said Windflower. The others all laughed. Windflower couldn't see what was so funny. He took his slice of pie greedily from Moira and tasted a forkful.

"This is amazing," said Windflower. The lemon meringue pie was perfect. The meringue was stiff but crystallized in his mouth. The lemon filling was tart and sweet at the same time. The crust was, as Windflower described it, "Perfect." It didn't take long for him to finish his pie. He handed his plate back to Moira for his second choice.

"I'll have a small piece of the cheesecake," he said to Moira.

The other three were still on their first dessert when Wind-flower dipped his fork into the cheesecake. The coconut cream cheesecake was also very, very good. It had a perfectly whipped cream on top of a layer of delicate yet solid cheesecake with a strong essence of coconut infused throughout. "Ah," said Wind-flower.

"It looks like you approve," said Moira. "This is all Beulah's handiwork. She does all the cheesecakes and pies for the café. I can sell as many as she can make."

"Is that the Beulah who used to clean houses?" asked Sheila.

"She still does some of that too, since she gave up housekeeping for Marge Breton," said Moira.

"Is Marge Breton gone?" asked Windflower.

"Yes," said Moira. "She really wasn't the same since Harvey got killed and her son went to prison."

"It's a hard thing to say, but nobody misses Harvey Breton," said Herb Stoodley. "He was a bad man who only made the people around him worse."

"I kind of feel sorry for Marge, though. She had a hard life with that man."

"I heard she moved to New Brunswick so she could visit her son in jail," said Sheila. "At least Beulah stayed with us."

"Amen to that," said Windflower, thinking about asking for another piece of dessert, but forced himself to resist. "That lemon meringue pie may have been the best I've ever tasted. And even though I'm a chocolate peanut butter cheesecake man, I wouldn't turn down that coconut cream."

"I bet you wouldn't," said Sheila with a laugh.

Chapter Thirty-five

The foursome shared more laughs together and then they got out the cards for a few hands of cribbage. Windflower and Herb were partners against their lady companions and got severely beaten. In fact, they were skunked in one hand and double-skunked in the next. They managed to squeak out a win in the middle and then lost the next, again quite badly. The sun was setting as they finished their last game, and they paused to watch the red sun drop like a rock into the horizon. Soon afterwards, the stars began to show and a sliver of moon rose in the eastern sky. It was a magnificent and awe-inspiring sight, and the dinner party watched in silent wonder as the night-time sky was revealed.

Moira picked up the tray and Sheila helped her carry the left-over dessert back to the kitchen. Windflower and Herb Stoodley stayed outside for a few more minutes.

"I'm reading another great book by Donna Leon," said Windflower.

"Is it another Brunetti mystery?" asked Herb.

"Yes. The opera singer, Flavia is back. This time she's singing

Tosca."

"I love Tosca," said Herb. "It's a classic tale of love and betrayal and murder. Everything a perfect opera should be. The music is heartbreakingly beautiful. I particularly like the arias in Tosca. Each one is a highlight. Tosca is my favourite opera."

"Have you ever seen it live?" asked Windflower.

"It is still on my bucket list," said Stoodley. "But I listen to the music regularly. Religiously is the word Moira would use. She's not a classical music person. How about you?"

"I'm learning to appreciate it more. There is a calmness I feel when I listen to some of it. Peaceful even."

"Why don't I lend you my Tosca CD?" asked Herb. "You have to listen to the whole thing in order to get the true feeling of any opera."

"That would be great. Are you sure you can bear being without it?"

"I think I can trust the police, although not Scarpia in Tosca," said Stoodley.

"What was wrong with Scarpia?" asked Windflower.

"Scarpia was the head of the secret police," said Herb. "He was not a nice man, maybe more cruel to his friends than to his enemies. Come with me and I'll get you that CD."

Windflower followed Stoodley into his den where his music collection was located.

"Wow," said Windflower as he surveyed the racks of records and CDs that completely filled the room. "This is incredible," he said.

"It took a long time," said Stoodley. "Especially since I had to replace all the vinyl with CDs. But there's nowhere to hear live classical music anywhere around here so I've tried to create a little library to enjoy as much as I can. I didn't know you liked the classics, or I would have shared it with you before."

"I didn't know I liked it either. But I'd be happy to learn more about it. If you're willing to help me," he added.

"Absolutely," said Herb, as he passed Windflower the compact disk. "'If music be the food of love, play on'."

"What are you guys gabbing about?" asked Sheila as she came into the den to fetch Windflower.

"Classical music," said Windflower, feeling pretty proud of himself.

"Good," said Sheila. "Maybe you can teach me something too."

"Well, if you play your cards right," said Windflower.

"I didn't think you would want to bring up cards again so soon," said Sheila. "After the beat down that Moira and I put on you two."

"Ouch," said Stoodley. "But remember, 'revenge is sweet and not fattening'."

"That's not Shakespeare," said Sheila. "Even I know that."

"Nope," said Stoodley. "Alfred Hitchcock." He laughed as Sheila and Windflower broke up laughing too.

Sheila led the way out and Windflower followed. Moira met them at the entrance with a small white cardboard box. "I've put a piece of each in here for you," she said to Windflower.

Windflower could have kissed her and in fact did give her a peck on the cheek, along with a big hug. "Thank you so much," he said as Sheila did the same to Herb Stoodley. The two men shook hands and the Stoodleys waved them goodbye as they walked away and towards home.

"They are such a nice couple," said Sheila as she nestled in closely beside Windflower.

"I agree," he said. "They are kind and considerate and all around good people."

"Winston?" asked Sheila as they walked along. "Would it be all right if I saw Carol for a few minutes? It seems really strange to have someone you were so close with be alone in a jail cell in your own hometown. I won't give away any state secrets."

"I guess so. Frost is on duty and if everything is okay over there, I don't see why not. I can take Lady out for a walk while you talk to Carol. It will have to be through the bars though. I can't let her out, even for you."

"Okay," said Sheila. "I can live with that. Thank you, Sergeant."

"You are most welcome, ma'am," said Windflower as they arrived at her house. "Your chariot awaits," he said and opened the cruiser door.

Chapter Thirty-six

Frost was sitting in Windflower's office with his feet up on the desk when he and Sheila came in. "Oh, sorry, Boss. I didn't hear you come in," said Frost.

"It's a good thing we weren't here to break out the prisoner," said Windflower as Lady came out quickly from beneath his desk to greet him. "Mayor Hillier would like a few minutes with Carol Jackson. If that's okay with you."

"Yes, sir, certainly ma'am, right this way," said Frost as he led Sheila down the hallway. Windflower put on Lady's leash and took her outside. They walked the back streets of Grand Bank as it was getting ready to shut down for the evening. A few T.V.'s flickered in the darkness, but most residents appeared to be home and settled in for the night. The moon was still shining, but when Windflower looked up he could see dark clouds racing across the sky. The fog lingered on the horizon, like an unwelcome house guest determined to try and come in.

Lady led Windflower for a full circuit tonight. He was glad for the walk both for his legs and his back, which was finally returning to normal. It was also good to get a few minutes of thinking time. He had a lot going on up there right now and not too much of it made sense. By the time they got back to the detachment, he felt the pressure relieved and finally was ready to relax.

Of course, his cell phone rang.

"It's me, Winston," said Lundquist. "I thought you should know we identified the biker who was seen at the park. His name is William Morris, aka the Moose. He's got a long record and a very mean streak. He is known as an enforcer within the crew out here. Anybody gets out of line gets a visit from the Moose. Fitz and Daniels are out looking for him now."

"What about French?" asked Windflower.

"Nothing yet," said Lundquist. "But if he's around, our guys will find him. Also, I managed to get some prints from the ATV. Looks like at least two sets. I'll put them into the system and see what pops up."

"Okay. Anything else?"

"Not for now. I'll call if there are any more developments," said Lundquist.

"Thanks," said Windflower and closed his phone. Sheila and Frost were coming out of the back. "Thank you, Constable," said Sheila.

"You're welcome," said Frost.

"See you in the morning," said Windflower. He put Lady in the back seat and drove back to Sheila's house. She was quiet all the way home and Windflower didn't see any need to interrupt her thinking. He got Lady some water and food, and soon she was lying on her makeshift bed in the corner of the kitchen with her head down and her eyes already closing.

Windflower could hear the bath running upstairs and passed a few minutes reading Sheila's magazines on the couch. He didn't get the fashion ones, but he loved the magazines with pictures and recipes. He was deep into how to make a three-level vegetarian lasagna when Sheila called him upstairs.

"It was hard to see Carol in there like that," she said.

"It must be tough," said Windflower.

"She's changed so much too," said Sheila. "I've seen her in bad places before; times when she's been using drugs, or strung out. But this is a much different Carol than I've seen before."

"What do you mean?" asked Windflower.

"It's difficult to explain," Sheila said. "It's like she's harder now, like she's got a protective shell up to protect herself even from me. Is she in a lot of trouble?"

"I don't know yet. We're still trying to figure that out."

"Well, I still love her, even if she isn't very lovable right now. Do you think I could bring her over a few magazines?" asked Sheila.

"I'm sure that would be fine, but you'll have to go through the duty officer. I can't show any favouritism, even for you," said Windflower.

"I understand," said Sheila. "Thank you."

"Oh, and can I have a recipe out of one of them first?" asked Windflower. "I found a great recipe for vegetarian lasagna."

"Sure. Now go have your bath," said Sheila, smiling. "Then come to bed. I really need a hug tonight."

Me too, thought Windflower. Me too.

Chapter Thirty-seven

In the morning Windflower struggled to get awake. He reached over beside him, but Sheila was gone. He got up, stretched and looked out the window. He could hardly see across the street. The fog that had been threatening to visit looked like it had moved in, permanently. At least it wasn't raining, he thought, as he went to the bathroom. When he came out, he could hear Sheila and the radio in the kitchen below. He put on his bathrobe and wandered downstairs.

Sheila was busy at the stove, and with the radio playing she didn't hear him creep up from behind her. He grabbed her and started nuzzling her neck.

"That's very nice," she said. "But if you want breakfast, you better let me go."

Windflower laughed and bent to pet Lady, who had snuggled up between them. "Maybe I'll have better luck with you," he said to the dog who was happy for any type of attention. It was clear she'd already been out that morning because after Windflower petted her, she was quite content to sit beside them. And to wait for any food scraps that might intentionally or inadvertently come her way.

"Thank you for getting up this morning and for taking Lady out," said Windflower, pouring himself a cup of coffee. "It's good to have a lie-in for a change."

"You're welcome," said Sheila. "If you want to sit down, this is almost ready."

As usual, Windflower was ready too. Sheila put a plate in front of him with fresh fruit, a large waffle with strawberries and whipped cream, and three slices of turkey bacon. Windflower would have preferred real bacon, but Sheila was slowly eliminating processed pork products from their diet. In any case, he was more than happy to dig in.

Sheila finished making her waffle and sat beside him at the table. They listened to the Weekend Arts Magazine on CBC radio and enjoyed each other's company and their wonderful breakfast. Afterwards, Windflower insisted on cleaning up while Sheila went to soak in the bath. He went up to see her before he left, and promised to call on the way to Grand Falls later in the day.

Windflower and Lady drove to the RCMP detachment to check in. Frost was gone, but Tizzard had replaced him, almost in the same position as last night, feet up on Windflower's desk. Lady ran in to greet Tizzard, who was happy to share the remnants of a muffin with her.

"You spoil her, you know," said Windflower.

"You have to treat a lady right," said Tizzard. "That's what my Dad told me."

"So is everything okay here?" asked Windflower, pointing to the back.

"Other than listening to her complain about how bored she is, things are good," said Tizzard. "When are you going back to Grand Falls?"

"After lunch. I've got to get my stuff and see Uncle Frank for a few minutes."

"Okay," said Tizzard, grabbing another muffin from the package. "I'll be here."

Windflower was ready to leave when his cell phone rang. He sat down and answered it.

"Windflower," he said.

"We found the Moose," said Lundquist. "Out behind the Walmart on Cromer Ave."

"Dead?" asked Windflower.

"Shot to death," said Lundquist. "Casings all over the ground. We've got the area sealed off and we're going over the scene inch by inch. This one looks pretty straight-forward from a forensics point of view. There's a ton of blood. We're taking samples to make sure it's all his."

"And French?" asked Windflower.

"Nothing," said Lundquist. "Are you coming back here?"

"I'll be back late this afternoon, early evening," said Windflower.

"Good," said Lundquist. "We're already getting calls from the media. They want to know if it's a gang war. And who knows, maybe it is."

"Tell them we'll have a statement later. I'll talk to Majesky and get back to you."

"Trouble?" asked Tizzard as Windflower closed up his phone.

"Another biker dead," said Windflower.

He called Majesky's number and gave him the latest news.

After Majesky yelled for a few minutes about things getting out of control and a few choice words about the missing French, he finally slowed down long enough to breathe and to give Windflower some direction.

"We'll have to get some additional resources in there," said Majesky. "Who knows where this thing is going? I'll talk to Quigley and get back to you. As far as the media goes, you'll have to handle it again by yourself. There's no way I can get back over there. Call a media conference for the morning."

"What will I tell them?" asked Windflower.

"We're going to tell everybody we have the situation under control and that we have some leads we're following up on," said Majesky. "You'll also need to talk to the mayor. Lundquist can set that up. Bring him in and give him as much as you can. Ask for his help in settling everybody down and reassuring the public."

"Okay," said Windflower, feeling like it wasn't very okay at all.

"You can do this," said Majesky. "This is just public relations. Give the media a little bit of meat so they have something to print and show. And let the local politicians in so that they think they are part of the solution. They will do the rest for you. Trust me."

Windflower didn't feel like he had much choice, so he simply replied, "Yes, sir," as his cell phone went silent.

"Anything I can do?" asked Tizzard.

"No. I'm going to see Uncle Frank."

Chapter Thirty-eight

Even Lady seemed to feel sorry for Windflower. She pushed up against him in that way dogs do when they want your attention. When Windflower reached absentmindedly to pet her, she rubbed her head against his fingers, as if to tell him that she thought it was going to be okay. Windflower gave her an extra pat for her sentiment, and drove to his house to see his uncle.

Uncle Frank was up and sitting at the kitchen table playing solitaire when Windflower arrived. "Good morning, Nephew," said Uncle Frank. "Are you ready for our little talk?"

"Let's go up to Farmers Hill," said Windflower as his uncle rose and followed him to the cruiser. The morning was still dark and gray and thick with fog, but Uncle Frank's spirits were bright, even cheery. He whistled a little tune to himself as they drove along. Windflower was starting to warm up, despite the weather and the problems that seemed to be mounting inside his head and within his police work.

"Here we go," he said to his uncle as they pulled up into the parking lot behind the clinic.

"Jarge told me that one time this was all gardens up here," said Uncle Frank.

"You can still see the fencing for some of them," said Windflower, pointing to a few fragments of wood that lay half-buried beneath the overgrowth of alders and wild rose bushes. Lady dove underneath one particular pile and emerged with half a bush still clinging to her back end. Both men laughed as Windflower removed the offending shrub.

"Thank you for coming with me today, Uncle," said Windflower.

"You are welcome, my son," said Uncle Frank. "It's good to be outdoors, even if the fog hides the sun. You can feel the power of Mother Earth in this place. Let's go down by the water. I want to feel that energy running beside me as we speak."

Windflower led them down a narrow pathway to the river. They stood on the shoreline and looked downstream towards the dam. Lady, of course, took the opportunity to have a drink from the flowing water.

"So you remember your vision quest," said Uncle Frank.

"I do. It was such an exciting time in my life. I felt very special to be out alone in the forest with Grandfather."

"You were pretty excited when you came back too," said Uncle Frank. "I thought you were going to pee your pants when you were telling us about it."

Windflower laughed at his uncle's recollection of those days, then paused and thought for a few moments. "It feels like I have drifted away a little bit," he said finally.

"Maybe," said Uncle Frank. "But sometimes the road runs crooked too. The challenge is to stay on a good path, even when it twists and turns. Along the way our allies will show up to tell us when we are moving in the right direction. That is what has happened to you."

"I have always known that Bear is my ally. He has been inside of me. I can feel his strength. It's hard sometimes because I am so far away from home and there aren't too many bears in this part of the world. Why does Mama Bear show up now and with her cub?"

"Strength comes in many forms and many sizes," said Uncle Frank. "Now that you are an adult, you may need a different kind of strength in order to grow into your time in the West, the time of responsibility and caring for others, maybe even children."

"That makes sense. But where do I find that new kind of strength?"

"Ah," said his uncle. "You already have it inside of you. You just need to unlock the door and let it out."

"So how do I do that?" asked Windflower.

"I am a man and I do not understand some things," said Uncle Frank. "I am not the right person to answer that question."

"Auntie Marie?" asked Windflower.

"Maybe," said Uncle Frank. "But maybe someone even closer."

Sheila, thought Windflower, but he stayed silent.

"You already know who to ask, just as you already know the answer," said Uncle Frank. "Now tell me about your dreams."

Windflower told his uncle about the house on fire and how each dream had revealed a little more. "The last time I saw Tizzard in the second floor window. He was holding somebody in his arms. It was terrifying," said Windflower, sounding a little shocked from the retelling of the dream.

"Fire is a powerful symbol," said Uncle Frank. "It is a gift from Creator and the heavens to help us poor creatures stay warm in the cold, dark earth. Sometimes in our dreams, as in life, it is a sign of cleansing and renewal. Just as lightning strikes will cause fires in the bush to clear up the deadwood and allow new growth, that kind of fire will bring us new energy and life. But that doesn't sound like the fire in your dream."

"No. It made me nervous and afraid."

"Hmmm," said his uncle. "Having a house on fire in your dream is also very interesting. A house might represent your family in a dream and if it is on fire, then maybe someone in your family is in danger. Or that something is unsettled inside your own home, your heart or spirit."

"I do feel like my life is at a crossroad. I'm getting married and many changes are coming. All of them good, but it is still change, something different. I'm not even sure which direction to take in my career."

"Allow yourself to feel all of those things," said Uncle Frank. "Serenity is not only having calm waters, but a sense that you will make it to shore, no matter how stormy the seas may become."

"What about seeing Tizzard in my dream?" he asked.

"Someone you care about may or may not be making a difficult decision too," said his uncle. "One thing is for certain. Unless we ask the question, we will never find the answer."

Windflower paused again to think about his uncle's words.

"Remember our teaching, 'Love one another and help one another'," his uncle said. "You are a good man, Winston. Follow the goodness in your heart and listen to your allies and you will be okay."

"Thank you, Uncle," said Windflower and he went over to the older man to give him a long hug. Lady got in on the action too by squeezing herself in between them.

"Let's go back," said Uncle Frank. "The b'y's will be wondering what I got up to. Which of course is nutting b'y," he said with a laugh. "I love these Newfies."

Chapter Thirty-nine

Windflower dropped Uncle Frank and Lady off at his house and went to say goodbye to Sheila. She was tidying up the living room when he came by. She had her hair tied up in a bandana and was wearing a sweatshirt and old jeans, but when Windflower saw her, he still thought she was the most beautiful woman he knew.

"How'd it go with Uncle Frank?" she asked.

"I'm not sure exactly what he said, but I feel better, calmer, after I talk to him," said Windflower.

"Maybe that's because you trust him," said Sheila. "He loves you and cares about you, and wants you to be happy. Like me."

"I know. Thank you, Sheila. I'm going to start trusting you a little more too," he said, coming closer to hold her tightly.

"Now be careful on the highway," said Sheila. "Especially with the fog. You know what the moose are like. I can't wait until we get the speed limit reduced, like Inspector Quigley suggested."

Windflower thought of saying something, but once again rejected that idea. "Me too," was all he ultimately responded. "Me too."

Sheila walked out to the driveway to give him one last kiss and then he was off to the RCMP detachment to check in on Tizzard and Carol Jackson before he left for Grand Falls. His cell phone rang as he pulled into the parking lot.

"We've got the scene all roped off, but it's becoming a bit of a media circus over there," said Lundquist after Windflower answered.

"I talked to Majesky. He's going to see what he can do about getting some more resources. He also wants us to call a media conference for tomorrow morning. Can you call Lynn in and get her to work with PR to set that up? Also, can you call the mayor and see if he can meet me tonight?" asked Windflower.

"Sure," said Lundquist. "The news about the media conference will help a little. At least we have something to say instead of no comment. I'll call Lynn and track down the mayor. We got one positive on the prints from the ATV," he added. "It's the Moose. But we can't identify the other set."

"Send it to HQ. They have a bigger database. Plus, they go outside the regular system. Is there any news about French? Majesky is freaking out about that."

"Nope," said Lundquist. "Either he's hiding out, or he's skipped out of town. Maybe we should expand the search area?"

"Okay. When Lynn comes in, get her to put it up on the system. Also, put a watch on at the airports and ferry terminals."

"Will do," said Lundquist. "It will be pretty hard for a biker like him to be inconspicuous."

"Unless he changes his appearance. I'll ask Majesky for a clean photo of him. I'm on my way in a few minutes. See you tonight."

Windflower walked into the office. Tizzard was again sitting at his desk, leafing through the paperwork in his in-basket.

"Oh, sorry, Boss, I was looking for something," said Tizzard.

"Be my guest, Corporal. You can have all of it, if you want," said Windflower with a laugh. Tizzard laughed too, but they didn't get a chance to continue their conversation because Windflower's cell phone went off again.

"You got the media set up?" asked Majesky.

"We're working on it. Lundquist and the admin will set it up and I've asked him to call the mayor."

"What about French?" asked the Superintendent.

"Nothing. Maybe he's doing a runner. We're moving to check the airports and the ferry. Can we get a clean photo of him?"

"I'll send that down to Grand Falls," said Majesky.

"It also looks like we've got a print match with the dead guy, and the ATV from the first murder scene," said Windflower.

"What's that mean?" asked Majesky.

"We don't know yet, but there might be a connection," said Windflower.

"Might be is not good enough," barked Majesky. "We need to be sure."

"Still working on it. While I have you, what should we do about Carol Jackson?"

"Let her sit, for now," said Majesky. "Call me when you have better news."

"We have to keep her for now," Windflower said to Tizzard after he got off the phone.

"Okay," said Tizzard. "I guess I'll have a bag of overtime after we're done with this. Maybe I'll take a vacation before I transfer out."

"Don't go anywhere until we get sorted out here. I'll go to Quigley again if need be."

"Okay, Boss, don't worry," said Tizzard. "I'll have to get Frost to pick up some more groceries though. It's hungry sitting around here."

Windflower laughed. "I know your appetite is okay, but is everything else good with you? Anything bothering you?"

Tizzard looked at Windflower for a moment, as if he was going to speak, then hesitated. "Things are good, Boss. Good."

"If you need to talk about anything, I'm here, okay, Eddie? Not only as your boss, but as your friend. Okay?"

Tizzard simply smiled and said, "Okay, thanks."

Chapter Forty

Windflower turned and waved goodbye back to Tizzard. He got into his cruiser and pointed it towards the highway. It almost knew what to do on its own. The drive to Goobies was foggy, but uneventful. He gassed up and grabbed a coffee and a turkey and dressing sandwich from the cooler. As he was getting in the car, he remembered the CD he'd borrowed from Herb Stoodley.

He put the CD into the player and was surprised to hear a short narration about the opera before the music came on. The storyline of Tosca was fascinating. Windflower knew it was a tragedy and that there was a police officer in it, but little more. This should be good, he thought.

He listened to the narrator talk about the three acts of the opera. The story takes place in Rome in 1800 and there is chaos as the Republic collapses and the political system reverts to the royalty. Scarpia, the head of the secret police, is having a wonderful time arresting republicans and throwing them in jail.

There is great drama as two republicans break out of jail, one of them the boyfriend of the title character, the singer Tosca. Scarpia tricks Tosca into revealing the location of her lover and Scarpia gives chase.

Act II gets even better, thought Windflower, as he listened to the intrigue that followed, culminating in Tosca stabbing Scarpia when he tries to force himself on her in exchange for her boyfriend's freedom. Even more drama was to be found in Act III when the secret police finally catch up with Tosca, after her lover is shot by a firing squad. When they try and arrest her for Scarpia's murder, she jumps off the castle of Sant'Angelo and kills herself.

Windflower was trying to take all of this in when the music finally began. Soon he was lost in the music as it rose and fell with the drama of the story. He particularly liked the solos, the arias, like the light-hearted recondita armonia (hidden harmony) in Act I and the two other arias that both were so chillingly beautiful Windflower felt goosebumps on his arms as he listened. Wow, he thought, that's why people love opera.

After the CD had finished, Windflower basked in its afterglow and hardly noticed when the fog lifted and the sun peeked out from behind the clouds. It was almost like he had been in a dream, while still awake and driving, when he saw the sign announcing the turnoff to the Gander International Airport. That meant he only had an hour to go and rather than stop for a break he motored through. He was about to go to the RCMP detachment when he saw the sign for the Cromer Avenue exit and the big Walmart sitting just past the turnoff. Might as well check out the latest crime scene.

There were two media trucks on location and one reporter was giving what looked to be a live update from outside the yellow police tape. Windflower saw Constable Fitzpatrick standing next to her car and called her over.

"Hi, Sergeant," said Fitzpatrick. "Welcome back."

"It looks like you've got the scene secure. That's good. I'm going to have a look around. Make sure these guys over there don't come too close," he said, pointing to the media people.

Fitzpatrick nodded and Windflower stepped under the police tape. He walked right over to an area that had been marked off with numbered chalk circles indicating where the officers had found bullet casings, and a large chalk silhouette that had obviously been where the body was discovered. That was more evident when Windflower got closer because there was a large dark red stain on the pavement inside the silhouette.

He was about to head back towards the police line when a bird flew by. He stopped to look up at the bird and when he did he saw what looked like a security camera on the side of the building. He called Fitzpatrick over.

"Look up there," he said, pointing to the side of the Walmart building.

"Closed circuit T. V.?" asked Fitzpatrick.

"Security camera, for sure. Talk to the manager and ask for the tapes for the last twenty-four hours. I'll stay here while you talk to him."

Fitzpatrick went into the building and soon afterwards came back with a box containing a number of DVD tapes. "Got 'em," she said triumphantly.

"Good work. Maybe this is the break we need."

He put the tapes in the car and drove to the detachment, where more media vehicles were parked outside and another reporter was doing a live shot. He waited until she had finished and then walked into the office.

The scene inside was almost as chaotic as outside. Lundquist was on the phone and the receptionist was trying to fend off two more reporters who were hounding her for information. She was calm and cool as she deflected their questions and smiled to Windflower. He smiled back and gave her a thumbs-up as he walked to the command centre. Daniels was there along with two new RCMP officers. Daniels came over and introduced the new men.

"Sergeant Windflower, this is Smithson and Ezekial. They got here from Stephenville today," he said.

"Good to have you on board. Do you have a T. V. and player?" he asked Daniels, as he laid the box with the tapes on the table.

"It's on a cart," said Daniels. "I think it's in the media room. I'll go get it."

Lundquist came in while Windflower was waiting. "I see you met the infantry," he said. Then speaking to the new officers he said, "Can you go and relieve Fitzpatrick at the Walmart? Then tell her to go out to Grenfell Heights and New Bay Road. We've got a report of a motorcycle out there. Get her to check it out. Okay?"

"Okay," both men mumbled together, looking confused. "Where's the Walmart?" one of them finally asked.

"Go back on the highway from here and take the Cromer Avenue exit," said Lundquist. "You can't miss it."

"Newbies," said Lundquist to Windflower after the new officers left on their mission.

"I understand. It's good to have help but they don't know the area. At least you'll have a few more bodies to put on the street. More police presence is always reassuring, especially for the local politicians. Speaking of which, is the mayor coming by?"

"Lynn talked to him. Should be here anytime now," said Lundquist.

Daniels came into the room with the T. V. cart. He plugged it into the wall and turned it on. Windflower passed him one of the tapes.

"Security tapes from Walmart," said Windflower.

"You know I thought about that," said Lundquist. "I figured Walmart would have security. I didn't get a chance to get around to doing it yet."

"No worries. Let's see what we've got." He loaded the first tape into the video player. The date/time in the top right corner read from the day before. In the grainy black and white replay there were cars and people moving around from time to time. Windflower sped through this tape and picked up another one. This one started from about 6 p.m. and as Windflower moved quickly through it, the number of cars and people dwindled as the night time came closer.

Soon it was dark except for the street lamps in the parking lot and the light from what Windflower figured might be a few spotlights on the side of the building. There was little sign of movement now, and he was about to give up hope of seeing anything as he scrolled through, when Daniels who was standing nearby, yelled, "There's something moving."

Chapter Forty-one

Windflower paused and rewound the tape, this time going through much more slowly. He stopped the tape when a car came into view. You could barely see inside the vehicle, but it looked like the car was full of passengers, front and back. The car went out of sight but as Windflower patiently inched the tape forward, the car came back into view, and people spilled out of the vehicle.

"That's the Moose," said Lundquist, pointing to one man who was being held by two others. "I can tell by that baseball cap he's wearing," pointing to a skull-and-crossbones leather cap on the man that was being held. A shorter man came up to these other three men and stood in front of them. He was clearly talking to the one identified as the Moose and was waving his arms around.

"I think he's got a gun," said Windflower. Then he ran the tape forward as slowly as he could. It was shadowy, but you could still see the two men holding the Moose let him go and back away. It was a guess, but Windflower conjectured the bigger man was asking the smaller one not to shoot him. It didn't seem to work because the next thing you saw was a flare of bullets coming out of the gun, and the Moose crumpling to the ground. Then the shooter stood over him for a few seconds before turning around towards the car.

It was just for a moment, but the second man's face became more clearly visible, even in the half-light. It was Joey Snow.

All of the Mounties held their breath at this revelation. Windflower let the tape continue to roll as the car left the parking lot and out of sight.

"We'll need to pick up Snow. As a matter of fact, let's pick up all his friends, every single one of these outlaw bikers. We can use the new anti-gang laws to charge them with belonging to a criminal organization to start with. But let's get them all off the street for now."

"They're likely at the clubhouse," said Lundquist. "We can't go out there tonight. It's too dangerous."

"No, let's go over there early tomorrow morning when it gets light. We'll take everybody who's here, all loaded up. What do you have in the arsenal?"

"We got lots," said Lundquist. "Two semis and a few brand-new long range rifles with scopes, plus some noise and tear gas canisters. And enough vests for everybody."

"Okay. Who's the local judge you use?" asked Windflower.

"It's Judge Sinnott," said Lundquist. "You want a warrant?"

"Yeah. Tell him we're looking for weapons related to the murder investigations and that we have a strong suspicion there are drugs on the premises."

"I'll make the call," said Lundquist.

"Good. Get the warrant and organize all the equipment. Have everybody here and ready to go at 6 o'clock sharp," said Windflower.

Lundquist nodded and went off to phone the judge. As he was leaving the room, the receptionist came in. "Mayor Loder is here," she said.

"Would you bring him in here, please, Lynn," said Windflower.

Lynn smiled and walked back out. She returned seconds later with Mayor Harris Loder. He was an older man with a thick shock of white hair and a warm smile as he offered his hand to Windflower.

"Harris Loder," said the mayor.

"I'm Sergeant Winston Windflower. Thank you for coming in. Please have a seat. It's a little disorganized in here, but this is our temporary command centre."

"Do you have everything you need?" asked Mayor Loder. "Because if you need anything I'd be happy to help. I have to tell you that people are pretty shook up around here. This is a quiet town, especially since the mill shut down a few years back. Most people are like me, getting too old to deal with all this," he said, waving his arms around him.

"I understand. This is a difficult time for everybody. But it's really important that people stay calm and don't panic. It looks bad now, but it will get better. And we also need people, your people, to help us. Already we've gotten tips that have led to important evidence being discovered and we need that cooperation to continue."

"People are scared," said the mayor. "Three murders in a week and criminals riding around their neighbourhoods all hours of the day and night. All kinds of drugs on the streets. We're worried we're going to lose our kids to some of this. Some are already gone."

Windflower nodded in agreement with the mayor and to show his support. "I'm not the politician here, you are," he said. "But this might be a turning point for this town. If we get it right. I'm not saying we will get rid of all the bikers, and all the drugs and all the problems right away. But this is a chance to get the community on board and once that happens, you will see results."

"That's a fine speech, Sergeant. Does that mean you have a plan to back this up?" asked Loder.

"First, we cut off the head of the snake. Then we deal with some of the cockroaches. After that, my suggestion would be an

202 • Mike Martin

increased police presence and a community policing plan."

"All of that sounds good, too," said Mayor Loder. "Where are you getting all these additional resources?"

Windflower smiled. "I think you and I should talk to Superintendent Majesky. He's the man controlling the purse strings."

Now it was the mayor's turn to smile. "That's very good," he said. "Now tell me more about that snake and the cockroaches."

"Tomorrow morning we'll hit them," he said. "Then I'd like you to come to the media conference to show your support."

"You got it," said Loder. "Maybe you're right. Maybe these tragedies can be the wake-up call this community needs."

The two men shook hands again and Windflower walked the mayor out to the front. Loder got nabbed by one of the media people for a comment on his way out.

"Well, the police are doing everything they can to find the people responsible for these tragic events. We have to support them and trust that they know what they're doing. And anybody who has any information that could help them should give them a call right away," said the mayor.

"Can you give us any more information after your briefing with the RCMP?" asked the reporter as a follow-up.

"There will be a press conference tomorrow morning. They'll have more information to provide at that time," said Loder. He said goodnight to the reporter and smiled at Windflower as he left the building.

Chapter Forty-two

Windflower walked into the back and got Daniels to run through the tapes again. He wanted to make sure they didn't miss anything. He had Daniels take notes and mark the important time periods on each tape. This information was then put into the evidence log and the tapes were secured in the evidence locker.

"We're confirmed for 10 a.m. tomorrow morning," said Lynn as she came into the room. "Big crowd as usual."

"Thanks, Lynn."

"If you don't need me anymore I'm going home now," she said. "But I'll be here early. Corporal Lundquist asked me to come in by 6."

"That would be fine, Lynn. See you tomorrow."

After the receptionist left, Windflower took off too. He went to his hotel and checked in. He took a quick look at the dinner menu and ordered a hamburger and a pot of tea from room service. While he was waiting for his food, he called Sheila.

"Winston, it's nice to hear your voice. I miss you already," said Sheila.

"Me too. How was your day?"

"I didn't do too much, some cleaning and laundry. It was a cloudy, foggy old day. It felt good to just sit around in my jammies for most of the day," said Sheila.

"Did you go see Carol again?" asked Windflower.

"I got back from there a little while ago," said Sheila. "I brought a pot of pea soup over. Thought she and Eddie might like a change from the take-out he's been feeding her."

"That was nice. How is Tizzard?"

"He wasn't there," said Sheila with a laugh. "But Harry Frost was happy for the soup. I think Carol was too. Although, she's pretty low right now."

"Did she say anything to you?" asked Windflower.

"No, but I used to know Carol. There's something really wrong going on with her. I told her that if she wanted to talk I'd be here."

"That was another nice thing to do," said Windflower.

"Thank you, Winston. I know you're a nice person too. That's why I love you. Maybe you should let that niceness out a little bit more," said Sheila.

"I'm a cop. I don't usually deal with nice people."

"Even more important that you model that good behaviour then," said Sheila. "You can catch more flies with honey than vinegar."

"True," said Windflower as he heard a knock on the door. "I think my dinner is here. Good night, my love. 'Parting is such sweet sorrow, that I shall say good night 'til it be morrow'".

Sheila laughed again. "Good night, Winston. I love you."

Windflower opened the door and took the tray from the room service person. He ate his hamburger hungrily, and probably a little too quickly. He got a little heartburn from eating it so fast, but blamed that on the extra jalapenos he had ordered. He drank a cup of tea and tried to watch some T.V., but was too tired. He had a quick bath and not long after was in bed, and solidly asleep very quickly afterwards.

It was still dark when he found himself being roused. Those nasty little jalapenos, he thought, having their revenge. It may have been the hot peppers that stirred him, but he soon realized he wasn't awake, he was dreaming. In this dream he was once again walking through the forest. Only this time, it seemed like the forest near Grand Falls and not back home. He was moving along a path towards the river when he saw a bear, a large bear, on the path ahead. Then he saw another bear, a baby bear standing behind the first.

His first inclination was to run, but once again his knowledge overcame his instincts. He started to back up slowly, to show that he was no threat to the bear and her cub. He was inching backwards when he stumbled on a branch that was strewn across the path. Before he could get up, the large bear raced towards him and stood on her hind legs. He struggled to get to his feet but as he did the bear reached over and pushed him back to the ground.

Now he was trapped and felt very afraid. But instead of moving to attack him as he anticipated, the bear reached up with one paw and somehow pulled the front of her head back to reveal a human face. Windflower lay on the ground, completely dumbfounded. The person or bear who was now standing in front of him was his mother. How could this be possible, he wondered? Then it came to him slowly that he was in a dream. The woman bear spoke:

"Hello, Winston," she said.

"Hello," said Windflower.

"Don't you recognize me?" she asked.

"You look like my mother," said Windflower.

"Good," said the woman bear. "I am here to bring you a message from your mother. She is worried about you. She says she is sorry she had to leave you so young, before she could give you all the emotional teachings that you needed. She says you are missing some knowledge about yourself and the world. She misses you."

"I miss her too," said Windflower.

"She says you have the strength of the bear but you still need a woman's heart to guide you. That physical strength alone will not be enough on your journey," said the woman bear.

"How do I do that?" asked Windflower.

"Look for the opportunities to practice kindness and trust the female guides you have been given," said the woman bear. Then just as quickly her head turned around and she was once again a full bear. She and her cub turned from Windflower as he lay on the ground and walked slowly into the river where they started to swim, but quickly sank, as if to the bottom of the flowing river.

Windflower ran after them quickly but all that remained was a large, spreading ripple on the water. He touched the water with his hand and woke up.

Chapter Forty-three

It was still early, but that was a good thing. He needed to be up and super alert this morning. He thought about coffee to help him do that, and then rejected that option. This was not a day to be over-caffeinated. Calm and focused, without the edge, was what he was going for. He dressed quickly in the near dark, and walked out the back door of the hotel to do his morning routine. He smudged carefully and efficiently. His prayers took a little longer because he wanted to be sure to acknowledge all of his allies, and to pray for all of the people who might face danger this morning.

He picked up an orange in the breakfast room, and peeled and ate it as he went outside. The sun was beginning to poke its nose over the pink horizon when he walked to his car. More blood red than pink, he thought. A sign of something, but what? Probably more rain on the way, he concluded. The first few drops came on his windshield as he pulled into the RCMP parking lot.

It was already busy when he went inside. Lundquist was handing out weapons and bullet-proof vests to the young RCMP officers. There was a taste of adrenalin in the air, mixed with a heavy dose of tension. Lynn handed him a cup of coffee and offered him a homemade muffin from a tin. Windflower took both, and had a bite of the muffin.

"Very good," he said to the receptionist. "Lemon cranberry, my favourite. Did you make these?" Lynn nodded yes, and smiled as she walked around to offer the other officers some of her breakfast treats.

Windflower took a moment to enjoy his muffin and to have a few sips of coffee before nodding to Lundquist to join him in the back. The other Mountie saw his cue and followed him into the command centre.

"I want you to give the background briefing. Do you have all the details on the location?"

"Daniels and I went through it last night," said Lundquist. "We have some photos that we blew up and can share. We've been at this location before. There's a back door that they think is secret, but we've seen them use it before."

"That's good to know. They will have weapons inside. Any idea how much firepower they have?"

"High-powered rifles and handguns for sure. But a pretty good bet they have some automatic weapons as well," said Lundquist. "There have been reports of them having target practice, or just shooting up the place. The only real question is whether they have explosives. We've had some construction site robberies in the area."

"More good news," said Windflower, a little sarcastically. "The most important thing today is that we keep everybody safe. Are your guys okay?"

"I don't know much about the new people. But Fitz and Daniels are solid," said Lundquist.

"Okay, they stay with you and I'll take the others. What are their names again?" asked Windflower.

"Smithson and Ezekial," said Lundquist, looking at the paper in his hand. "Sam Smithson and Morgan Ezekial."

"I'll keep them with me at the front, while you take the back entrance, okay?" asked Windflower.

"Okay," said Lundquist. "Oh, this is for you," he said, handing him a vest. "I've got the canister launcher in my car."

"I'll take that, along with a Colt," said Windflower, pulling his vest on over his jacket. "Let's bring them in."

Lundquist was back shortly afterwards and passed Windflower his weapon. He fingered the coldness of the Colt C7, an automatic rifle that was more appropriate as a weapon of war, rather than policing, but a very effective one nonetheless. He hadn't used one in a while, not since his time on the drug squad at the Halifax Airport. He took a moment to re-familiarize himself with it, since once you started using this fully automatic model, things happened quickly, very quickly.

The other Mounties soon joined them. Windflower nodded to Lundquist and he went through the briefing including handing around the blown-up pictures from the clubhouse. "The front door is fortified steel and there are bars on all the windows," said Lundquist. "It's not an easy place to get into. But we do have this. Show them Daniels."

Constable Daniels went over to a corner and, with some effort, picked up what looked like a massive steel beam. "A battering ram," said Daniels. "We've been dying to use this."

"That's good. It might come in handy, but I'd prefer it if they came out on their own. How many people do we think are inside?" asked Windflower.

"Hard to say," said Lundquist. "Could be anywhere from a couple to a dozen."

"I guess we'll find out soon enough. I'm going to the front, and I want you two to come with me," he said, pointing to Smithson and Ezekial. "We will try and get them to open up voluntarily. If not, we fire one of these in through the window," he continued, picking up the canister launcher from Lundquist.

"Is that tear gas?" asked Smithson.

"We have gas and noise grenades," said Lundquist. "In case we need to get their attention."

A little nervous laughter followed that last comment. Windflower brought the mood back to serious very quickly with what he said next. "Our main job this morning is not to get hurt. Follow my lead in front and Lundquist in back, and we should be okay. All our weapons should be ready for use, safety off as soon as we get to the location. But no one fires until I give the order. Is that clear?"

All of the Mounties nodded at this last statement.

"Are we ready?" Windflower asked Lundquist.

"Yes, sir," said Lundquist.

All six Mounties walked silently to the waiting cruisers. Windflower and Lundquist drove together while the other foursome came in pairs as well. There was a steady but light rain falling now and the sun had disappeared behind a wall of grayness. If anything, it appeared darker now than when Windflower first arrived at the office this morning. That kind of matched the two RCMP officers' moods as they silently drove along in Lundquist's vehicle.

They arrived at the laneway to the clubhouse first and waited until the other cruisers got there. Once everyone was at the location they got out of their vehicles and unloaded their weaponry. Windflower carried the rifle in his hands and had the canister launcher on a strap over his shoulder. He took out one of each canister and handed them to Ezekial to hold, along with a bag containing the remaining canisters.

The clubhouse was a one-story cinder block building with two small windows on the front and as Lundquist had described, a fortified door at what looked like the main entrance. Lundquist pointed up at the side of the building and whispered "Security cameras." Windflower shrugged. They couldn't do much about that. Pretty soon everybody inside would know they were there anyway.

He motioned to Lundquist, who took a circular route along the perimeter, with Fitzpatrick and Daniels to take up their position at the back. Windflower heard a crackle on his walkie-talkie a few minutes later. "We're ready," said Lundquist.

Windflower whispered back. "We're going to say hello. Weapons ready."

He moved forward towards the front door with the other two RCMP officers on his flanks. All three men had their weapons ready, but pointed to the ground. When he got close enough he raised his weapon and pounded on the door with the butt of his rifle.

"RCMP," he shouted. "Open up."

He thought he heard rustling from inside the building and shouted again.

"RCMP. Open up." There was no response.

He looked at Ezekial and pointed to the noise grenade. He took the launcher off his back and loaded the grenade.

"RCMP. Open up," he shouted one more time. When he heard nothing else he took the butt of his rifle and smashed one of the windows. He pointed the launcher in the window and fired. "Boom!!" went the noise grenade as it exploded and reverberated inside the building. It was deafening from the outside, so Windflower could only imagine how loud it must have been inside the clubhouse. Then he heard a commotion from the back of the building.

"Got 'em," Lundquist said over the receiver. Windflower and his two fellow officers at the front raced around to the back of the building. There they found Lundquist, Fitzpatrick and Daniels standing behind five men who were pushed up against the back wall of the building. All of them seemed to be in some distress from the noise grenade.

"Everybody on the ground," ordered Windflower. "Now," he shouted, when they didn't move quickly enough. One of them turned around to face him. It was Snow. He started to snarl something at Windflower, but Windflower was having none of it.

212 • Mike Martin

"Take him and put him in the cruiser," he said to Ezekial. The younger officer spun Snow around and quickly put him in handcuffs. He marched him back to the front and into one of the waiting cruisers.

"You take the rest," he said to Fitzpatrick and Daniels. "Two each per cruiser. We'll get all these guys back and get them processed. You do the search with Smithson," he said to Lundquist.

Lundquist nodded his agreement, and went inside with Smithson to begin the search. Windflower followed the other officers to the cruisers. They put the prisoners in the back of the police cars and Windflower jumped in with Fitzpatrick. He looked at the pair of bikers in the back, breathed a long sigh of relief, and smiled at the female constable beside him.

"That went well," he said, as much to himself as anybody else. "Not too bad at all."

Chapter Forty-four

"I checked out that motorcycle," said Fitzpatrick as they drove to the detachment. "Don't know for sure, but I'm thinking it's French's. Took some prints, but there's no immediate match."

"Anything in the saddlebags?" asked Windflower.

"No, sir," said Fitzpatrick. "It's very strange for a biker to leave his bike. What do you think it means?"

"Could be anything. If it's French's, it could be because something happened to him. Or he could be doing a runner and wanted to leave that piece behind."

Fitzpatrick pulled her cruiser up to the back door of the RCMP building, where Ezekial was already pushing and pulling a belligerent Joey Snow in through the door. He made one final push until Snow was securely inside. He put Snow into the first open cell and slammed and locked the door behind him. Windflower left Fitzpatrick to watch the two prisoners in her cruiser, and went to help process and search Snow. That wasn't easy either but they managed to search him and empty his pockets.

Windflower took all of Snow's personal belongings and went

214 • Mike Martin

to get an evidence envelope. It would all need to be catalogued and recorded, but for now Windflower was curious as to what a lead outlaw biker would have in his pants and jean jacket. There was a package of cigarettes and a lighter, some rolling papers, but no weed or other drugs, a gold money clip with a wad of bills, a couple of thousand dollars by a quick estimate. And a set of keys on a Bacchus key chain.

Windflower took a moment to have a look at the keys. There were some motorcycle and car keys, along with what looked like house or apartment keys. Maybe even the keys to the clubhouse, Windflower thought. But his eyes were drawn to one particular key, a large rectangular key with the number 40 etched into it. He was still looking at the key when he heard Fitzpatrick prodding and coaxing the first of her two prisoners into the next open cell. He put the key in his pocket and went to help her.

The next hour was all about getting the prisoners secured and processed. By the time they were finished, they were all exhausted, both from the work and the adrenalin rush that had diminished since the morning. The three younger RCMP officers all went for coffee at Tim Hortons, but Windflower was quite content to sit in the back by himself and sip a cup of tea. He took a few moments to be grateful that the morning had gone well. Then he drafted up some notes for the press release that he handed to Lynn for typing and copying.

He was beginning to unwind when Mayor Loder arrived. As much as he would have preferred to have more time to collect himself, he took a few moments to connect with the mayor. They made a little small talk, the mayor telling him about growing up in the area and Windflower sharing a bit about elk hunting in Alberta. It was actually quite pleasant and he was enjoying himself when Lynn came in to tell him that the media had arrived and everything was ready for the media conference.

Windflower and the mayor walked into the room together. The mayor stood behind him as he read out the prepared statement.

First, he identified the dead man as William Morris Spearns, also known as the Moose, a known and full-patch member of the Bacchus Motorcycle Club. Then he described the raid this morning at the biker's clubhouse. He also noted that they had a number of people in custody for questioning as a result of their investigation. Finally, he asked for the public's assistance in coming forward with any information they might have to assist in the investigation.

Then he introduced the mayor.

"Ladies and Gentlemen, Mayor Harris Loder would like to add a few words."

The mayor stepped up to the microphone.

"Morning," he said, clearing his throat. "These are difficult days for our community. Three sudden deaths, murders, all in one week. Many of us are in shock. Some of us are afraid in our own homes. We will get over the shock, and I have all the confidence in the world that the RCMP and officers like Sergeant Windflower here, will find the people who did this and put them behind bars where they belong. But we also have to do our part, as citizens and as a community." He paused for a break.

"For far too long we've allowed a few hoods on motorcycles to run this place, to terrorize us and to subvert our young people with drugs, and dressing it up as some kind of fancy outlaw business. They are punks and criminals. They have been allowed to operate here because we have been afraid, individually and collectively. I will take responsibility for our inaction as a Council, and commit to you today, that this ends immediately. We will be working closely with our partners here at the RCMP, and with our youth agencies and social service people to stamp out these cockroaches and take back our community.

I will be meeting with Council this afternoon to start talking about how we make this our number one priority. I ask you, the citizens of Grand Falls-Windsor to join me in this initiative. You can do that by calling the RCMP with any information you have, anything you may have seen or heard, over the last week. Maybe you have been afraid to do before, and that's okay. But now is the time to step up and step forward. Let's take back our town."

The mayor stepped back from the microphone and shook Windflower's hand. As he was doing this one of the newspaper reporters started clapping. Before long, everyone in the room, all of the media people and all of the RCMP officers who were watching, joined in. "Great job," Windflower whispered in Loder's ear.

"Any questions?" he asked the media.

Chapter Forty-five

Half an hour later, Windflower and Harris Loder were sitting in the back drinking coffee and sharing the last of Lynn's homemade muffins. Lundquist came into the room with Daniels and Smithson, all of them carrying boxes. The mayor took his cue from their arrival, shook hands with Windflower again, and left to go back to his duties.

"This what you found?" asked Windflower.

"First go," said Lundquist. "I'm going to go back later and have another poke around. But yeah. About $8,000 in cash, a couple of ounces of weed and another bag we figure is cocaine, and various pills and scales, drug paraphernalia."

"That's not their stash," said Windflower.

"No," said Lundquist. "That's why I'm going back over there. They must have a supply somewhere. We know they're running quantities through here. The drug guys told us that."

"Just not in their clubhouse," said Windflower.

"There's also a couple of shotguns and three of these," he said, pulling a plastic bag containing a handgun out of one of the boxes.

"They are fully automatic MAC 10 machine pistols, each capable of firing about thirty bullets in less than ten seconds."

"Sheesh. I'm glad we didn't have a shoot-out with these. Check them out against the casings found at the Walmart."

"And, this one," Lundquist said, holding up a bag containing a .357 Magnum revolver.

"Get that one tested too. It looks like the same caliber as the murder weapon from the park."

"It's loaded, too," said Lundquist. "We'll check the bullets for a match as well."

"Good job. But we still need to find their stash. Let me know if you find anything when you go back over."

It had been such a hectic morning that Windflower needed to go outside and get a breath of air. It was still raining, but he didn't mind. He walked around the back of the RCMP detachment and was soon strolling in the nearby forest. The tree canopy provided a great umbrella and he only got dripped on, rather than being soaked. He wouldn't have cared one way or the other. He took his time and wandered around, not doing anything more than reconnecting with nature and with himself.

He was on his way back to the office when his cell phone rang. It was Sheila.

"Good morning, my love," said Windflower.

"Good morning, Winston," said Sheila. "I was driving to work when I heard you on the radio. You were great and that mayor is fabulous. That's what I want to be like."

"You already are. Mayor Loder is a special guy. I think he's going to turn this community around, like you're doing in Grand Bank."

"Oh, thank you, Winston," said Sheila. "I also wanted to let you know that I went to see Carol again at the jail. I think she's ready to open up."

"What do you mean?" asked Windflower.

"She started talking to me about some of the trouble she's in. But I told her she had to talk to the police. That there was no point telling me. I can't do anything about it. I suggested she talk to you."

"And she agreed?" asked Windflower.

"Not in so many words, but I think she will, if you take the right approach," said Sheila.

"That's very interesting. Would you consider coming along with me, as her friend, not as my partner, but as her friend?"

"I could do that," said Sheila. "I really care about Carol. She obviously needs help."

"No promises. But I'll talk to her. Let me get a few things straightened out here first and I'll get back to you. And thank you, Sheila. You're the best."

"I know," said Sheila. "Call me."

Windflower went back inside and hung up his jacket to dry. Lynn was on the telephone, but motioned him over to see her. She hung up the phone and handed him a message slip and a fax. The phone message was from Majesky.

"He seemed very… excited, to speak with you," said Lynn. "That fax just came in. It's addressed to Corporal Lundquist, but it's marked urgent."

"Thank you, Lynn. I'm going to call the Superintendent right now," said Windflower. He walked to the back reading the fax as he went along. It was from RCMP HQ Forensic Science and Investigation Services. He scanned the document quickly. 'In response to your request we have identified the fingerprints you provided as belonging to RCMP Contractor Robert French. Operation and location currently unknown'. There was more, but that was all he needed for now. He went back to the front and handed the fax back to Lynn. "Give this to Lundquist as soon as he gets back. Tell him to see me."

He called Majesky's number from the secure phone in the command centre.

"Majesky," came the gruff response.

"Superintendent, it's Windflower. There have been some developments."

"I hope it's good news," said Majesky. "So far you've brought your share of the other stuff."

"I'm not sure it's good news, but we think that Joey Snow killed the other biker, the Moose guy. We've got him in the shop along with a few of his buddies. We raided their house this morning. We didn't get much, so we're still looking for their stash. French is still missing but we've got confirmation on his prints from a vehicle at the initial crime scene. We think he's done a runner."

'I saw the note on the board on that. Any intel coming in on him yet?" asked Majesky.

"No, sir. But now that we've confirmed his prints at the murder scene, I want permission to release his civilian photo."

Majesky paused and then said, "Okay. But don't identify him as connected to us. Anything else?"

"Carol Jackson looks like she's ready to talk," said Windflower.

"So talk to her," said Majesky.

"That's a bit of a problem. She's still in Grand Bank. I can't spare a day to go back and forth. Things are starting to break here."

"I'll send the chopper," said Majesky. "Somebody will call you. And while I have you, who the hell is Harris Loder, and why is he calling me?"

"That would be the mayor of Grand Falls-Windsor. I think he wants to talk to you about community policing. He's a good guy."

"I bet he is," said Majesky. "When you find French, put him in isolation. Nobody talks to him until I get there. Got it?"

"Got it. Thank you," he added. But Majesky was gone before he could hear that last comment.

Chapter Forty-six

About an hour later, Lundquist came into the room. He carried the fax in his hand. "It's French?"

Windflower shrugged. "Yeah, and now he may be rogue. At the very least he's AWOL. We need to get his civilian photo and put it on the board. Can you get Lynn to look after that?"

"Okay," said Lundquist.

"And we don't identify him publicly as having any connections to us," said Windflower.

"Not a problem there," said Lundquist. "I'll do the checks on the bike prints myself. Nobody else needs to know. They all assume it's Frenchie, the biker, anyway."

"Thanks. You know what? We might as well check all the prints from the park scene as well."

"Yeah," said Lundquist. "By the way, I left Daniels and Smithson out at the clubhouse. Told them to scour the place. That'll keep them out of trouble for a while. Like to grab a sandwich?"

"That would be good. Although I have to eat light. I'm going for a chopper ride later."

Lundquist drove them over to the nearby Subway. He ordered the foot-long steak and cheese and true to his promise Windflower had the six-inch version. The two Mounties stood in line to wait for their sandwiches and when they were fully loaded and ready, they moved down the line to the cash. "I'll get this," said Windflower and he reached into his back pocket for his wallet. When the bill rang up to a quarter over the dollar he reached again into his pants, this time to look for change.

He pulled out a handful of miscellaneous change and picked out a quarter to hand to the cashier. But he also found the key that he pocketed that morning from Joey Blow's possessions. He laid the key on the tray with the two sandwiches and carried it to the table where Lundquist was waiting. He handed Lundquist his sandwich and picked up the key again.

"Where'd you get that?" asked Lundquist. "It looks like a key from a locker at the storage centre."

"What?" said Windflower. "You know what this is?"

"Let me see it again," said Lundquist. Windflower passed over the key, and Lundquist reached into his own pocket to fish out his own set of keys. There jingling on the end was an almost exact match for the key that Windflower had found. Except that Lundquist's had a different number. "I have a locker in that new storage centre out in the industrial park," said Lundquist. "I have a small apartment, so I need the space for my stuff. I also put my snowmobile out there during the summer."

"How often do you go out there?" asked Windflower.

"Like, never," said Lundquist, biting into his sandwich. "Maybe once a year. It's cheap, long-term storage. You lock things up and then forget about them. If it wasn't for the snowmobile, I wouldn't be out there until it was time to move. So where'd you get the key?"

"Out of Joey Blow's pocket," said Windflower. He was about to suggest they go over and check out the locker, but his cell phone rang.

"Windflower," he answered.

"Sergeant Windflower, this is Corporal Ted Reid. I'm the chopper pilot. I was told to pick you up and take you to Grand Bank. When will you be ready to go?"

"Whenever you are," said Windflower.

"I'll be there in about two hours," said Reid. "Meet me at the helipad at the hospital."

"Okay," said Windflower, and he closed his phone. "That was my ride," he said to Lundquist. "I want to go have a look at the storage locker, but first we should talk to Snow and at least do an initial questioning on the others. I suspect the lawyers will be circulating around soon."

"Like buzzards you mean?' asked Lundquist.

"Exactly," said Windflower. The two men finished their sandwiches and went back to the detachment. Windflower's suspicions proved correct. There were three lawyers sitting in the small reception area, including Jeremy Earle.

"Sergeant Windflower, good to see you again," said Earle. "I understand you have my client, and these fine gentlemen with me are also inquiring about theirs. Are there charges pending or can we expect an early release?"

Windflower forced himself to smile. "Gentlemen. We are under a bit of pressure here today with media requests and simultaneous investigations. We are still in the initial processing phase with your clients. You are welcome to stay, but I would suggest that you might want to come back in a couple of hours. We should have more news for you by then."

Earle smiled again and nodded to his fellow attorneys. "Thank you, Sergeant. We'll be back later." With that, the trio of lawyers were gone.

"That was smooth," said Lundquist.

"They're just part of the system. On the wrong side, but still part of the wheels of justice. No point in upsetting them unnecessarily. So we have a couple of hours to work with. See what you can pick up for outstanding charges on the other bikers. I'm going to see if Snow has anything to say before his mouthpiece gets back. And can you talk to the judge again? See if he won't amend our original warrant to include the storage locker as well."

Lundquist went to ask Lynn to start pulling files on the bikers they had in custody. Windflower went to talk to Joey Snow. Before he did, he went to the evidence locker and found Snow's possessions. He pulled out the biker's pack of cigarettes and lighter.

Snow was lying on his bed when Windflower came by. He hardly moved, just sneered.

"Let's take a walk," said Windflower as he unlocked the jail cell. He wanted to talk to Snow away from the prying eyes and ears of his confederates.

"Where are we going?" asked Snow.

Windflower held up the cigarettes. Snow smiled and walked out through the open door. "I'm getting a fresh air break," he said very loudly so that his friends in the nearby cells could hear him. They laughed and cheered even more loudly.

When they got outside, Windflower directed Snow to a small gazebo near the back of the building. There was a picnic bench inside. Windflower put the pack of cigarettes and the lighter on the table and sat down across from Snow. Snow picked up the cigarettes and lit one, inhaling deeply and then exhaling. He smoked about half of the cigarette before speaking. "I'm not telling you anything. You're wasting your time with this good cop shtick. But thanks for the smokes anyway."

"That must have been a shock. To find out she was pregnant. You must have really loved her," said Windflower.

Snow stared at him, almost glaring, almost ready to pop, thought Windflower. Snow didn't say a word. He finished his cigarette, threw the butt on the ground and lit another one.

"Is that why you killed him?" asked Windflower. "Because he killed your girl?"

Snow didn't move and he didn't blink. He sat there and smoked his cigarette. But Windflower could see him thinking, processing, hopefully getting ready to react.

"What about the other guy? Can't find him?" asked Windflower. "Maybe he's too smart for you."

That was enough for Snow. He threw his cigarette on the ground and stood up. "Nobody around here is smarter than me," he said.

"How about French?" said Windflower.

"Another loser," said Snow. "Don't worry. He got what was coming to him. Like all of them who try and screw around Joey Blow," he said, waving his arms around.

"You killed him too?" asked Windflower.

"Listen," said Snow, standing up to try and poke his finger in Windflower's chest. "I look after people and I 'specially look after people who try and mess with me. I'm done out here. Take me back. My lawyer will be here soon."

Windflower took Snow back inside and put him back into his cell. His fellow bikers cheered his return.

"We're charging you with the murder of William Morris. We have you on tape," said Windflower, loudly enough for the others to hear.

"That's why we have lawyers," said Snow, also quite loudly. His friends cheered that comment too.

Windflower walked back down the hallway as the bikers were making jokes and laughing. He glanced back to see Snow back on his bunk, lying there looking like he didn't have a care in the world. And maybe he didn't, thought Windflower.

Lundquist met him at the command centre. "I've got Fitz and Daniels doing the interviews. Here's the list of pending charges," he said, handing over a file folder with four sheets of paper, one each for Snow's fellow bikers.

Windflower scanned the sheets quickly. It had the usual list: breach of probation for hanging around the other bikers, possession of stolen property, missed court appearances. "Not much here," he said. "Nope," said Lundquist. "Just enough to hold them until their lawyers get back and get in front of a judge. That won't happen 'til tomorrow. So we've got a few hours to come up with more."

"I told Snow we're charging him for Morris. He didn't seem too worried," said Windflower.

"Yeah, but at least we've got him on tape," said Lundquist.

"True. But I've seen lawyers twist the truth, even when it's on tape. I'd be happier if we had more. Like a witness."

"It's none of these guys," said Lundquist, pointing to the back. "If we could find French that might help."

"Snow said something about dealing with French. I wonder what that means."

"Maybe French is still around here somewhere. Dead or alive," said Lundquist.

Windflower checked his watch. "I've got another hour. Did you talk to the judge about the storage locker?"

"I did. Let's take a run out there now," said Lundquist.

Chapter Forty-seven

Windflower rode with Lundquist the short distance to the Grand Falls Industrial Park where the storage lockers were located. They were near the back of the park at the end of an unpaved road. There were four sections of large green and red trimmed silver lockers, each about ten feet high. They went first to Lundquist's locker where he showed off his new snowmobile.

"You could get a lot of stuff in here," said Windflower, amazed at how far back the space went.

"All of my life, plus my baby here," said Lundquist, patting his snowmobile. "Let's go check out your key."

They walked to the section marked 30-40 and found number 40 at the very end of the row. Before he got there, Windflower looked up and around. He could see a video surveillance camera on the light standard above them. But he could also see that this particular camera had been smashed, or maybe even shot at. In any case it looked inoperable. Something to check later.

Windflower pushed his number 40 key into the slot at that locker. The lock clicked and he pushed the door open. He reached around on the wall, found the light switch and turned it on. You could smell the weed right away. Large burlap sacks of it, stinking like a hundred skunks had made their home in the locker. In another corner was a stack of boxes, like orange crates, with packages of white powder inside. Then Windflower thought he heard a noise. More like a moan, he thought. It was coming from the back of the storage locker.

Windflower walked to the back of the locker and started to pull up a large, thick, Oriental-type rug. Lundquist came to help him. What they found underneath shocked and surprised both men. It was French, barely conscious and barely alive. There were spatters of blood everywhere, and a large brown circle on his right leg. He was ashen pale, gray, and seemingly unaware of their presence. His lips were blue, almost purple.

"Looks like he's been shot. But he's still alive. Pulse is very faint," he added, as he felt the injured man's wrist. "Call for an ambulance." He covered the man again with the rug.

Lundquist ran outside and called emergency while Windflower stood over French's trembling body.

"His body is in complete shock. But judging by the small amount of blood here he may be lucky, as strange as that seems," said Windflower when Lundquist came back. When the other man seemed confused he added, "If he was shot, which I think he was, then he probably still has a few more slugs in him. Exit wounds make a bigger hole and cause much more bleeding. He'd be dead by now."

They could hear the sirens approaching in the distance. "We need to act quickly. First, we have to secure this scene, but as quietly as we can. We want Snow to think this place is still safe. It looks like his drug stash," he said, pointing at the bags and crates. "If possible, we want Snow to come back here and catch him at the location. Then we get the drugs and him together."

"I'll get my guys to monitor undercover," said Lundquist. "They can use my locker as HQ."

"Good. I'll go with the ambulance to the hospital. That way we can make sure we can get him treated without a lot of attention. You hold things together here. I'll be back tonight."

The sirens grew closer and soon the paramedics were lifting a nearly dead French onto a stretcher and into the back of the ambulance. Windflower jumped in and rode along with one of the attendants until they roared into the hospital's emergency entrance. The paramedics wheeled the body to the door and were met by the emergency attendants. "Gunshot," said one of the paramedics. "He's in shock and lost a lot of blood."

The doctor on duty was a young Asian woman. Windflower saw her tag, Dr. V. Lim. He followed her along with the gurney as it was rushed into one of the emergency treatment rooms. The doctor barked out a few orders and soon French was hooked up to an IV and several monitors. She glared at Windflower until he realized he shouldn't be there, and left.

On his way out, he was met by one of the nurses who asked him if he could identify the patient. "John Doe," he said. Then he asked if Doctor Stock was on today. The nurse nodded and paged "Doctor Stock to Emergency to meet a visitor."

"Thank you," said Windflower and he sat in the waiting room to catch his breath and wait for Stock.

He didn't have to wait very long. "Sergeant Windflower, how's your back?"

"It's much better. Almost as good as new. But I'm here on another mission today. Can we talk somewhere private?"

"Sure," said the doctor and he led Windflower into one of the examination rooms. He sat on the bed and gestured for Windflower to take the chair.

"We brought in a person with gunshot wounds," said Windflower.

"There seems to be a lot of that going around," said Stock.

"This is a person of interest in some of the other murders. We would like to keep his identify secret and his presence here as quiet as possible. We're also going to need to have security on him, assuming he survives."

"We can do that," said the doctor. "Let me get an update on his condition."

Five minutes later the doctor came into the examination room where Windflower was waiting.

"He might make it," said Stock. "The preliminary examination shows he still has at least one and maybe two bullets still in his leg. He is suffering from extreme shock, maybe stage three."

"How many stages are there?" asked Windflower.

"When you hit stage four, you die," said the doctor. "He must have been in excellent physical shape and I suspect he must have been covered up somehow. Otherwise he wouldn't be here."

"He had an old rug wrapped around him. So what's the prognosis?"

"Well, we still may lose him," said Stock. "But we'll start pumping antibiotics into him and see if we can't pull him back. Doctor Lim says he will almost certainly lose that leg where he was shot. Somehow the blood clotted, but it also cut off circulation."

"Okay," said Windflower. Then they both heard a great roaring noise outside the window.

"I think that's my ride," said Windflower, as the helicopter circled above and landed on the square marked with an **H** in a large circle at the back of the building.

"You get all the excitement," said Stock. Windflower shook the doctor's hand and went out to meet the helicopter pilot.

Chapter Forty-eight

The helicopter's blades were still slowing when Windflower saw the pilot getting out of the machine. He walked towards Windflower and came into the hospital.

"Corporal Ted Reid," said the pilot. "Are you Sergeant Windflower?"

"I am. I've got to make a couple of calls and then I'm ready to go."

"Great," said the other Mountie. "I'm going to see if I can get a cup of coffee."

Windflower walked outside where the helicopter had finally shut down. He went to a quiet spot and called Majesky.

"We've got French," said Windflower when Majesky answered. "He's been shot, but it looks like he might make it. We also found Snow's stash."

"Can you keep French out of the spotlight?" asked Majesky.

"I think so. We've got him registered as anonymous at the hospital and they'll help us with that. We're also going to have security here to keep an eye on things."

"Okay," said Majesky. "Are you going to talk to Carol Jackson?"

"I'm on my way. The chopper is here and we should be on the way soon."

"Let me know what she says," said the Superintendent and hung up.

"You're welcome," Windflower said to the now-dead phone.

His next phone call was to Grand Bank. He phoned the detachment office and got Betsy Molloy.

"Sergeant, how nice to hear from you. Are you well? How are things in Grand Falls?" asked Betsy.

Windflower had to smile at Betsy's gentle kindness and mild manners. Rather than burden her bright day with all of the crazy and even gory stuff going on in his life, he simply said, "Things are fine, Betsy. I miss you and Grand Bank, but things are very nice in Grand Falls. Can I speak to Corporal Tizzard please?"

Tizzard was soon on the line. "Boss, how are you? I hear you're coming for a visit."

"How did you know that?" Windflower asked.

"Inspector Quigley told me," said Tizzard. "Said you were coming in on the chopper. We're all excited here."

"I bet you are. I will be there in a couple of hours. Can you get hold of Sheila and arrange for her to be at the detachment when I get there? And can you pick me up at the clinic?"

"Will do," said Tizzard.

"See you then," said Windflower as he saw Ted Reid come out of the building holding two cups. "Thought you might want one too," said the helicopter pilot.

"Thanks," said Windflower, but as he walked behind Reid to the helicopter he wondered if the chopper had cup holders, or if he could even hold the coffee as they took off up into the sky.

Both of those questions were answered to Windflower's great relief.

The AS 350B3 helicopter was a far better ride than the loud and rickety helicopters that Windflower had been on in the past. Most of those were industrial workhorses that were mostly used for firefighting and taking men to remote logging camps. Windflower had taken a few trips on these when he worked on the highway patrol in rural British Columbia and had dreaded a repeat experience. By comparison, this was the lap of luxury, he thought, as he placed his coffee in the cup holder in front of him.

The chopper moved into the air almost effortlessly and he gave the pilot the thumbs up as they rose up past the low-lying clouds and into the blue skies beyond. Soon after they levelled off and were sailing along at quite a nice clip.

"How long will it take?" asked Windflower, surprised at first that he didn't have to shout inside this helicopter. Some of the other improvements obviously included better soundproofing for the cabin.

"About two hours," said Reid. "We'll fly at about two hundred clicks an hour and cut across land to avoid the traffic," he added with a laugh.

"How high are we now?" asked Windflower.

"We're at about 4,000 feet right now, still climbing slowly til we reach about 6,000," said the pilot. "With any luck, the cloud cover should break and we'll get a chance to see a bit more of the country."

Windflower smiled and sipped his coffee. There was peace and tranquility, flying along above the clouds below. He always had the sensation when he was flying of almost being a bird in flight. He hoped that the clouds would part so he could see the terrain below, but at least for now he had a bird's eye view of the world. After about an hour, he got his wish. He had been starting to doze off when Reid gave him a gentle nudge.

"We'll never run out of water around here," said the pilot, pointing down.

Windflower looked down and could see what he meant. The whole countryside was dotted with lakes and ponds and rivers and brooks, breaking the forest and rocky hills up into what seemed to be quiet little oases. He thought that anywhere around here would be a great place to get dropped off and wander around for a few days. You certainly wouldn't run out of water. The two men seemed to relax into watching this calming scene unfold below them and before he knew it, Windflower could feel the pilot begin his descent into the Burin Peninsula.

He felt this, but couldn't see a thing. They passed down into the heavy cloud bank below them and after that went right into a thick fog. Windflower looked a little concerned at the lack of visibility, but the pilot seemed to know what he was doing. He saw Windflower's concern and smiled over at him.

"I'm going to let the controls guide me in," said Reid. "Don't worry, I've done this before. Many times. Usually we get called on prisoner transfer or medivacs and often the weather is much worse. Especially in the winter when the wind picks up. That's the real danger for birds like this. But there's hardly a breeze today. We'll be fine." And they were.

It seemed to Windflower that Grand Bank rose out of a giant fog bank to appear before them. The helicopter sliced easily through the fog and before he knew it he could see the town growing larger below them. He saw the **H** on the circle below and knew they were near the town's clinic. He could even see Tizzard's Jeep parked in the lot nearby. About a minute later they were on the ground and Windflower was climbing into the vehicle as Tizzard opened the back door to let Reid jump in.

"Tizzard, this is Reid. Can you look after him while I do my interview?" asked Windflower.

"No problem," said Tizzard. "I'll take him to the Mug-Up. Welcome to Grand Bank," he said to the other Mountie.

"Thanks," said Reid. "I love the Mug-Up. Do they still have the cheesecake?"

"Absolutely," said Tizzard as they approached the Grand Bank RCMP Detachment. "Here's your stop," he said to Windflower. "Frost is ready to help setting up the interview. Inspector Quigley and Mayor Hillier are in your office."

"Thanks. Why don't you bring Reid back here when you're done over there? I'm thinking it'll take about an hour or so. Okay?"

Both men nodded and Reid got into the front with Tizzard. They were already talking about what kind of cheesecake they were going to get as they drove away.

Chapter Forty-nine

Betsy greeted him with a warm smile as he came in the door. "Good afternoon, Sergeant," she said. "I meant to ask you before, how's Lynn doing in Grand Falls?"

"She's great. She's very good at her job, like you," he added.

Now Betsy was beaming. "We went to some training together a few years back. We stay in touch. She said you were very professional."

"That's good to know," said Windflower as he passed by her desk and went into his office where Sheila and Quigley were sharing a laugh and a cup of coffee.

"Good afternoon Madam Mayor, Inspector," said Windflower.

"You've risen in the world," said Quigley. "Private helicopter and everything. Let's chat before you head back. I'm assuming you'd like to talk to Sheila before you speak with Carol Jackson. Frost will bring her to the interview room. I'll be watching on the other side." Quigley took his coffee and went to find Frost.

After Quigley left, Sheila got up and closed the door. "I know we're supposed to be all professional, but I need a hug," she said.

"I could use one of those too right now. It's been crazy the last few days."

"Sounds like it," said Sheila, finally loosening her tight grasp around Windflower's waist. "When do you think you'll be done out in Grand Falls?"

"Not sure yet. But it feels like things may be breaking. Let's hope they break our way. Are you ready?"

Sheila nodded and the pair walked down the hallway to the interview room. Windflower knocked on the door, which was opened by Frost. The other policeman moved aside to let Windflower and Sheila in and then closed the door behind them. Carol Jackson was sitting on one side of the long table, facing a mirror on the other side. Sheila went and sat beside her. Windflower pulled up a chair and sat across from Jackson with his back to the mirror, behind which Inspector Quigley would be monitoring the interview.

"I understand you have something to say," said Windflower.

"What kind of protection can you offer me?" asked Jackson.

"We usually protect the innocent," said Windflower.

"I guess I don't know if I can trust you," said Jackson. Then looking at Sheila she added, "I probably don't have any choice, do I?"

"No. The only commitment I can make to you is that I will listen to what you have to say, and I will report that to my superiors."

"Does that include whoever is behind the glass there?" asked Jackson.

"Don't worry about that. It looks to me like you're on the wrong side of the glass any way you want to look at it. Why don't you tell me what's going on here?"

Carol Jackson took a deep breath and looked again at Sheila. Sheila smiled and reached over to squeeze her hand. "Okay. I'm going to tell you what I know. In return I want protection from the Bacchus guys. Can you do that?"

"As long as you're inside, we can do that. So, talk."

"I've had connections with the bikers for a long time," said Jackson. "My old man was 'Choice' and I fell into the drugs and the lifestyle. I made a ton of bad choices. But you know what, after Rocky died, I cleaned myself up and tried to go straight. I even came down here for a while. Remember, cuz?" she asked Sheila.

"I remember," said Sheila, smiling at her again.

"Then I got pulled back into the drugs. And before I knew it, I was back in the 'life'. Running, dealing and stealing. I met Frenchie when I was still up North. I didn't know he was undercover at the time. I just thought he was hot," said Jackson, with a laugh. "I started riding around with him and we had a lot of fun. I might have even fallen in love with him." She paused, and Windflower thought she was going to cry.

But she didn't. Instead, she started talking again. "It's kind of the story of my life, you know? Some people lie so much that you think you can't believe anyone. Then you let your guard down and…" Now she started to cry. Windflower just let her, and when Sheila went to offer her a Kleenex, he indicated she should leave Carol alone. He'd learnt that sometimes people needed to get things out, and it was best to give them the space to do just that.

Carol stopped crying after a few moments, wiped her eyes and continued. "I thought we could have a life together. Maybe a crazy idea, but that's what I thought. Then one night he told me. I was shocked. I couldn't believe he was working with 'the man'. Then he shocked me again. He told me he was going to be transferred to the east coast to try and infiltrate Bacchus. He made me promise not to tell and I don't know why, but I didn't tell anybody. Not 'til today."

Windflower was listening intently as Carol Jackson told her story. "So far you haven't told us anything we don't know," he said. "Other than the fact that you apparently knew French."

"There's more," said Jackson. "Much more. Frenchie stayed in touch with me, called me every few weeks. Then he made me an offer. He brought me into the program with you guys. I told him I wouldn't do anything up North. I was too close to too many people and they would figure it out right away. He suggested I come down there and help him make a sting."

"But something went wrong," said Windflower.

"No, actually things went great," said Jackson. "I came three times and we picked off a couple of guys along the way. I would set up the buy and he would tip off the drug guys. I dealt with a cop called Pomeroy."

Windflower knew Pomeroy from some previous cases in his area. He was the head of the drug unit in the Region. But he didn't tell Jackson that or say anything else. He waited for her to continue.

"Then came the biggest shock of all. Frenchie told me he wanted to sting Bacchus and take off. He'd seen their stash. He said there were kilos of cocaine. My job was to set up an initial buy with Snow, and then one more time afterwards we'd make the big sting. Then, we'd take off for Mexico and retire. That was the plan."

"So what happened?" asked Windflower.

"I don't know," said Jackson. "I rode into town and was supposed to meet up with Frenchie. But he didn't show up. I stayed around as long as I could and then I panicked and took off. I was planning to come here and hang out with Sheila until things settled down."

"But that didn't work out either," said Windflower.

"No," said Jackson. "I was on my way here when I saw those bikers in Marystown. I thought they might have heard what was going on and so I ran for it, like I told you before. I ditched my bike and hid out. I wasn't really sure what happened and until I knew what they and you knew, I was going to sit it out. So what did happen to Frenchie?"

Windflower ignored the last question. "I think we should stay focused on you for now. For starters, I'm going to need you to make a statement, outlining everything you told us here today. Then I'll take it upstairs and see what they say. Anything else?"

Carol Jackson shook her head no and started to cry again. This time Windflower didn't interfere when Sheila offered her a Kleenex and a hug. He opened the door to the interview room and called Frost in. "Please escort Miss Jackson back to her cell," he said. "Mayor Hillier will stay with her for a few minutes."

Sheila smiled faintly at him as she helped the other woman get to her feet. The pair walked along with Frost back to Jackson's cell.

Chapter Fifty

Ron Quigley came into the room shortly after Sheila and Carol Jackson left.

"What do you think?" asked Quigley.

"I think we got a piece of the story. How big a piece, I'm not sure yet. We'll have to do some checking. And I'd sure like to hear French's version of events."

"Me, too," said Quigley. "What's his status?"

"Not good. He was shot in the leg and left to die. I'm surprised that he was still alive when we found him. Even if he comes around I'm not sure how much he'll have left."

"Well, I guess we go with what we have," said Quigley. "I'm going to see if I can't find Pomeroy. He might be able to give us some information about Jackson and French."

"I'm going to call Majesky to give him an update," said Windflower. Quigley left to make his call and Windflower dialed the Inspector's number in Halifax.

"What did Jackson have to say?" asked Majesky once Windflower got through.

"She says French was planning to scam Bacchus and take off with their drugs," said Windflower.

"Do you believe her?" asked Majesky.

"Until we can talk to French, that's the only information we have so far. Inspector Quigley is going to talk to Pomeroy and the drug squad. I think that some of what Jackson is telling us is the truth. I'm not sure it's all the truth," replied Windflower.

"That's the best you can do?" asked Majesky.

"It is for now. What do you want us to do with Jackson?"

"Bring her back with you to Grand Falls for now," said Majesky. "Let's see what happens with French and what Pomeroy has to say."

"It's getting a bit crowded out there," said Windflower.

"Deal with it," said Majesky, and he was gone before Windflower could reply.

Windflower put his phone back in his pocket and went back to his office where Quigley was sitting at his desk. "Okay," he heard Quigley say. "I'll tell him."

"Tell him what?" asked Windflower.

"Pomeroy is in Deer Lake. He's going over to Grand Falls tonight. He'll see you there," said Quigley. "What did Majesky say?"

Windflower rolled his eyes. "He said to deal with it. And to take Carol Jackson with me to Grand Falls."

"Hey, Boss," said Tizzard as he poked his head into Windflower's office. "Brought you a sandwich from the Mug-Up." He handed Windflower a paper bag. "Reid's in the back having a catnap. He said to give him a shout when you're ready to go."

"Thanks," said Windflower. He opened the bag and took out the cellophane-wrapped ham and cheese sandwich. He took a bite and savoured it for a minute. "Sorry," he said to Quigley. "I'm starved."

"No worries," said Quigley. "I'm going to stay here for a few days to help out. I'm also working with the Council on the moose idea,"

My idea, thought Windflower, but again he stayed quiet and

munched on his sandwich. "Good luck with that," he finally added after he finished. "I better say goodbye to Sheila and get Jackson ready to go," said Windflower.

"Okay, I'll let you get to it," said Quigley as he left.

Windflower crumpled up his paper bag and wrappings and threw them in the garbage. He found Frost sitting on a chair in the hallway to the cells. Sheila was on another chair in front of Carol Jackson's cell.

"We need to get her belongings together," said Windflower to Frost. "She's being transferred to Grand Falls. Can you also ask Betsy to get the paperwork ready?"

Frost went off to carry out these tasks and Windflower walked down to talk to Jackson and Sheila.

"I've been instructed to transfer you to Grand Falls," he said to Jackson. "Constable Frost will help you get all your stuff ready."

"What's going to happen to me?" asked Jackson.

"I don't know yet. For now, my orders are to bring you to Grand Falls. You'll be held there until a decision is made. But that's not mine to make. I'll leave you to say goodbye," he said to Sheila.

Along the way he passed by Ted Reid, peacefully curled up like a baby, sleeping in an open cell. Windflower looked in at the bunk and the sleeping man longingly. What came to mind was the poet, Robert Frost … 'The woods are lovely, dark and deep, But I have promises to keep, And miles to go before I sleep, And miles to go before I sleep'.

Windflower and Sheila had a few quiet moments together while Frost got everything ready for Carol Jackson's departure. They didn't say much, but he was able to hold Sheila while she had what Windflower would describe as a bit of a cry.

"Will she be okay?" asked Sheila.

"She will be safe with us. If her story holds up, I suspect they'll offer her some sort of arrangement. If not…" his voice trailed off. He gave Sheila one last hug, a long and tight one, just to make sure she knew how much he loved her.

246 • Mike Martin

"When will you be back?" she asked.

"Soon, I hope. Maybe by the weekend. I miss my own bed."

"I miss you in it," said Sheila. "Bye, Winston. I love you."

"Bye, Sheila. Love you, too," said Windflower.

Chapter Fifty-one

Betsy came by with the transfer papers as Reid was coming out of the back. "That was good," he said to Windflower.

"How can you sleep for only a few minutes like that?" asked Windflower. "If that was me, I'd be out for the night."

"You learn to get a few winks when you can in this job," said Reid. "We're often called out on short notice and you never know how long you'll be. We have limits on how much we can fly in a twenty-four-hour period, but no restrictions on how much we can wait around."

"So, are you ready to go again?" asked Windflower. "We have another passenger."

Reid nodded as Frost came out with Carol Jackson in cuffs and leg irons. He also carried a knapsack that Windflower presumed was hers.

"Is this really necessary?" asked Jackson, pointing to the restraints.

"Standard operating procedure," said Windflower picking up the bag and taking her by the arm. Outside, Tizzard was waiting and he opened the doors of the Jeep to let Windflower and the woman get into the back seat. Reid got into the front with Tizzard.

"One second," said Windflower and he ran back inside to say goodbye to Quigley. The Inspector was on the phone but he paused his conversation to talk to Windflower. "Can you call Grand Falls and tell them we're bringing Jackson?'

"Will do. Let me know what happens," said Quigley. "And if you need anything, give me a call."

"Can I come home now?" asked Windflower, only half-jokingly. "See you, Ron."

Minutes later the trio bound for Grand Falls were loaded up in the helicopter. They waved goodbye to Tizzard and were on their way. Carol Jackson was in the back seat of the four-seat chopper, handcuffed to her armrest and looking like she felt sorry for herself. Windflower didn't have a whole lot of sympathy for her. It wasn't clear yet how much trouble she was in, but whatever it was, it looked like it was mostly her own choosing, if not all her doing.

The evening was getting dusky as they lifted off and soon the sun started to sink into the western horizon. Before it did, the sky seemed to catch fire and it burned like forever in shades of red and orange before it faded to blue and purple and darkness. They rose towards their cruising altitude, passing through the layers of puffy clouds until they finally broke through into the starlit sky. It was like moving close to heaven, thought Windflower, and both men were silent as the majesty of the nighttime skies was revealed.

As they started to level off, Windflower felt the steady hum of the engine begin to lull him to sleep. He could not resist and before he knew it he was lost to this world and into a deep slumber. The next thing he remembered was Reid nudging him awake. When he opened his eyes and looked down he could see lights below him.

"Grand Falls?" he asked.

"Next stop," said Reid.

Windflower could see a cruiser on the ground next to the

hospital with its lights flashing. When they landed and the rotors slowed, he led Carol Jackson out of the helicopter and to the waiting police car. Fitzpatrick opened the back door and guided the woman into her seat.

"We have to take her to the hotel," said Fitzpatrick. "There's no room at the RCMP Inn."

"Will you stay with her?" asked Windflower. The female constable nodded and got back into the cruiser. "Drop me off over there first," said Windflower. A few minutes later he was walking into the Grand Falls RCMP Detachment.

There was a lot of activity at the RCMP offices this evening. Lundquist was directing people to different activities, and when Windflower walked down the hallway he could see that the cells were all still occupied.

He went back into the command centre as the two new RCMP officers were leaving. "They're going to start the stakeout," said Lundquist. "Daniels is out there now and he'll come back in to hold the fort here. Apparently Smithson is a bit of techie whiz so he's going to see what he can set up at the industrial park."

"Good. I see all our buddies are still in back."

"Yeah, we've got new charges ready for a couple of them and breaches for the other two. Plus, of course, Snow. The Crown is coming especially to charge him. Their lawyers are not happy about any of this, but c'est la vie."

"Did the Crown talk about bail for Snow?" asked Windflower.

"I thought you might talk to him about it in the morning," said Lundquist.

"Excellent. We could probably have him held, but I'm thinking that if he got out we could try and connect him with the stash at the locker. Here's the key to go back into his possession envelope."

"Okay. I'll put it back. You know we could try and slip a GPS tracker on him. Maybe on the bottom of his shoe," said Lundquist.

"That's very good. You've got to love technology, don't you?"

"Yeah, people use them to track their kids, even their pets now," said Lundquist. "Very useful for our purposes."

As Windflower and Lundquist were talking, another Mountie came into the room.

"Pomeroy," said Windflower.

"Windflower," replied the other man.

"You guys know each other?" Windflower asked. Both men nodded, but he could tell from Lundquist's body language that there was little amity between them. Nobody liked the drug guys. They tended to want to take over whatever operation they were involved with, and because of their high profile and the money involved, they usually succeeded.

"I'm going to check on that GPS tracker," said Lundquist, excusing himself.

"How's French doing?" asked Pomeroy.

"I don't know. He was in pretty bad shape when we brought him in. Touch and go."

"I also hear you got Carol Jackson," said Pomeroy. "Where is she now?"

"She's at the hotel under guard. She was one of yours?"

"Yeah, she was working with French," said Pomeroy. "She'd been here a few times before and was getting closer to Snow. We also thought we had Lundrigan turning our way, but all of that seems like it's gone now."

"Maybe not. But that's interesting about Lundrigan. That might have something to do with why he was killed."

"Do we know who did that yet?" asked Pomeroy.

"It looks like a guy named the Moose and French may have been involved. And we have Snow on tape shooting the Moose. Now French is laid up too."

"You seem to know an awful lot," said Pomeroy. Maybe even sounding a little resentful, thought Windflower. That was another disappointing characteristic of the drug squad. They always wanted to take credit, unless things went badly.

"Why don't you tell me what you know?" asked Windflower.

"We've got Snow in the back and we've found a stash of drugs. It's in a storage locker out at the industrial park. Sacks of weed and kilos of cocaine. We're putting together a plan to get him and his stash. You want in or not?"

The piece about the drug stash and kilos of cocaine clearly got Pomeroy's attention.

"Okay. So the Outlaw Gang Unit had been running French here for a while when we were plugged in. At first it was just for intel, and then he suggested bringing in Jackson to make a few buys. All good, and we picked up a couple of small fish coming and going. Then he suggested this major buy," said Pomeroy.

"The sixty grand," said Windflower.

"Yeah, we got approval from Majesky and started to set it up. We knew that Bacchus and Snow were the eastern connection and that the mainland big boys were shipping drugs in here. We needed to get close enough to figure out their pattern and routes. The idea was Jackson would make the initial buy, French would be able to find the stash, and we could move in later to clean it up," said the drug squad guy.

"Then it started to unravel," said Windflower.

Pomeroy sighed and said, "Yeah. First, we hear about the murders at the park, and then Jackson was gone with our money. And we couldn't find French. People upstairs were not happy."

"I bet. Jackson says French was doing a double sting."

"Maybe," said Pomeroy. "But my head is still spinning. I thought we had a handle on this, but when the bikers are involved, anything can, and often does, happen."

"So we won't have the full story until we talk to French. If we ever do get to talk to French," said Windflower.

"Sounds like it," said Pomeroy, sighing again. "But let's get Snow and the stash if we can. I've got two guys in Deer Lake I can bring over to help."

"Okay. Bring them over and tell them to report to Lundquist. He's coordinating the stakeout. Snow is due in court tomorrow morning. We're hoping to slip him a get out of jail card. When he bites, we'll start tracking him and sooner, rather than later, we hope he will lead us back to the stash."

Pomeroy nodded his agreement and walked out of the command centre to make arrangements to bring his people over from Deer Lake. Windflower thought about trying to do something else, but his brain and his body were fried. All he wanted now was a bath and somewhere soft to lie down. He said goodnight to Lundquist, and waved goodbye to the other cops circulating around the detachment.

He drove to the hotel and went to the restaurant. He had a bowl of pea soup and fish and chips. Neither were great, but they filled the hole in his stomach. Then he kind of stumbled his way back to his room, ran a bath and nearly fell asleep in it. He roused himself enough to crawl into bed. Without even thinking about the crazy day that had just happened, he dropped off, and didn't know where he was until a few slivers of light sneaked in through his hotel room window and woke him in the morning.

Chapter Fifty-two

It wasn't just light. It was sunny and bright when Windflower opened the curtains wide. He had slept like a log. So solidly, in fact, that his back was bothering him from lying in the same position all night. But that was a small price to pay for how good he felt inside, especially inside his head. He didn't have any more clarity than when he went to bed, but somehow a good night's sleep helped you to feel better about your situation, whatever that situation was. At least it did for Windflower this morning.

He made a cup of coffee and drank it while listening to the birds serenading the morning. Then he picked up his smudge kit and walked out the back door of the hotel. This time he shifted direction and walked away from the path that led to the river. He followed another path through the woods until it started to climb towards a nearby hill. He continued up to the top and was very pleased he had made this decision.

It was not a very high hill but it still afforded a magnificent view of the main town site and the river below. He especially liked following the river's current with his eyes as it twisted and turned its way down through the valley. It felt like he was a bird, overlooking his territory. As he had this thought, a large bird flew by overhead. It was a bald eagle, not rare, but unusual for these parts.

The bird looked massive and its wing span stretched out at least six feet. It was dark brown with white feathers on its head. As he watched, the eagle dove down towards the river, probably looking for breakfast. Shortly afterwards, he could see the eagle clutching a fish, maybe a trout or a small salmon, in its large talons.

Feeling particularly blessed by this morning visit, he laid out his smudge kit and filled his bowl. Soon the smoke was circulating around him, filling him with the energy of the morning. He gave thanks for his ally, the eagle, who had come into his world. It reminded him of Grandfather, who had passed on the gift of the eagle feather he was using this morning. In his prayers he asked his ally to help him see as far and as long as the eagle could, up to seven times farther than any human.

He prayed for courage and strength to carry out his role in the community. He also asked for wisdom to know the right steps to take for himself and to be able to guide and lead others. Finally, he prayed for a kind heart, and to have compassion and kindness as his companions, even when things were tough. Especially when things were tough. He asked for all of these things for himself and for those he loved. At the end, before he came back down the hill, he gave thanks for the morning and for his allies. He laid down a little tobacco to honour his eagle ally and his grandfather. Now he was fully ready to begin his day.

He walked slowly back to his room to enjoy the morning and all of the life around him. He showered and shaved, and headed downstairs for breakfast. He was hungry this morning, and filled his plate from the breakfast buffet. He had finished his fruit, scrambled eggs, sausages and two pieces of French toast, and was seriously contemplating seconds when he saw Fitzpatrick come into the breakfast room. She had a tray and was filling up two plates from the buffet.

Windflower waved to her, and when she had completed her selections she came over to see him.

"Eating for two this morning?" he jokingly asked.

"I feel like the baby sitter," said Fitzpatrick. "She's still asleep. I checked on her before I came down. But we're having early breakfast this morning. At least I get to decide that."

"It's always a little boring. Like ninety-five percent of all police work. But it has to be done. I'll check with Lundquist to see if you can't get a pass, at least for a few hours."

"That would be great. Thanks, Sarge." Fitzpatrick took her food-laden tray and went back to her escort assignment. It looked like she had a little jump in her step after her conversation with Windflower. Hope springs eternal, thought Windflower. Or maybe even, 'True hope is swift and flies with swallows wings'. Can't go wrong with the Bard. How good was this: a bald eagle to greet him, a full cooked breakfast and an opportunity to use a Shakespeare quote first thing in the morning. It might just be a perfect day. And then he thought of everything that might lie ahead.

A little less elated, but still determined, Windflower drove over to the RCMP offices. He was surprised to see Smithson and Ezekial already there. They were busily engaged in taking equipment out of a white panel truck. They weren't in the usual uniforms. Instead, they were wearing blue coveralls and had tool belts hanging off their hips.

"Morning, Sarge," said Ezekial as he carried a large monitor into the detachment, followed by Smithson who was lugging what looked like switches and a bale of wire. "We're setting up a remote centre so people here can see what's happening out at the industrial park," said Smithson.

"Who's out there now?" asked Windflower.

"Daniels is holding the fort until we get this organized," said Smithson. "We were out there all last night. We talked to the park management and got them to route their feed into Lundquist's locker and we fixed the camera over by the other locker. When we're done we'll have a four-way screen to monitor everything that comes into the industrial park or near the bikers' locker."

"So you're the cable repair guys?" asked Windflower, pointing to the coveralls.

"Technical support, sir, at your service," said Smithson. "I'm also going to set up a monitor so that you can follow Snow's progress on a local map."

"You can do that?" asked Windflower.

"Absolutely," said Smithson. "It's built right into the GPS computer program. It will find us and then show us every move the GPS and the person wearing it makes, down to the house and street level."

"Good stuff," said Windflower, then realizing that Smithson would stay and talk to him about technology and electronics all day if he wanted, added, "I'll let you get back to it, then."

He still hadn't made it inside when Lundquist pulled up in the parking lot beside him. "Jump in," he said. "I got a call from Doctor Stock at the hospital. French is in bad shape. But he's awake. Let's go."

Windflower didn't have to wait long and Lundquist raced his police car to the hospital, pulling up in the emergency parking zone. The pair got out and ran into the reception area. The nurse on duty paged Stock. Moments later he was there to guide them into the Intensive Care Unit. They put on gloves and masks and hurried past the security guard into the unit.

French was the only patient in the ICU and he was attached to several tubes and monitors. "He's still pretty heavily sedated, but he comes in and out of consciousness," said the doctor. "We had to amputate his leg. He doesn't know it and couldn't probably feel it anyway, which is likely a good thing. The blood loss was surprisingly minimal but the after-effects of the shock have damaged some of his internal organs and weakened his heart. None of those things are good, and his prognosis is poor at best," said the doctor.

"But you said he had periods of consciousness?" asked

Windflower.

"Yes," said Stock. "As far as I can tell, he has a few moments of lucidity as his medication starts to wear off. I heard him asking the nurse where he was."

"You think he will have another moment anytime soon?" asked Windflower.

"He's on a timed dosage," said the doctor. "If this chart is right, he's due for another shot of morphine in about ten minutes. That's when the pain starts waking him up."

Lundquist and Windflower watched the almost lifeless French lying in the bed. It was hard to imagine he would actually emerge from that state. But after about five minutes they could see French's body start to twitch a little bit. After another five minutes Windflower thought he heard a moan.

Chapter Fifty-three

"French. Can you hear me? French, wake up."

The man in the hospital bed shifted a very tiny bit and moaned again, this time a little louder than before. Windflower could see the light start to blink red on the I.V. He turned towards the doctor. "Can you slow that down for a minute?" he asked.

Stock didn't look very happy with this request and almost glared at Windflower. "You got one minute," he said, reaching up to turn off the I.V. He stared at his watch.

"French, French, it's Windflower. Can you hear me?"

"Whah...?" croaked French, starting to writhe in pain, but clearly becoming more alert.

"We need to know about you and Carol Jackson. Can you tell us anything?"

"Hurts so much," moaned French. "Please, give me something."

The doctor pretended not to hear and kept staring at his watch. "Twenty seconds," he said.

"Tell us about you and Carol and we'll give you something for the pain," said Windflower.

"Carol's the one. Carol made him shoot them," said French. "Carol's the one."

"Carol's the one what?" yelled Windflower.

"Time's up," said Stock and he reached up and turned on the I.V. The light blinked red to green and within seconds French's face started to relax and less than a minute later he was out of it again.

"We'll need identification and info on next of kin," said the doctor.

"I'll make the call. He's not going to make it, is he?" asked Windflower.

"Not very likely," said Stock. "The morphine is helping him deal with the pain but it's also weakening his heart, which was already damaged from the trauma and the shock. There's not a whole lot we can do."

"Thanks, Doc," said Windflower. He and Lundquist left the ICU. They dropped their gloves and masks in the bin on the way out. Windflower called Majesky as soon as they got outside the building, but only managed to get his machine.

"Superintendent, it's Windflower. French is not doing well. In fact, the doctor thinks he may not make it. We will need to give them full contact information and next of kin. Can your office please provide that to the Grand Falls Regional Hospital? My contact is Doctor Lonnie Stock. Thanks."

Lundquist and Windflower drove back to the detachment in silence. When they arrived, Smithson and Ezekial were getting into their van to go back to the industrial park. Windflower flagged them down.

"Is it all set up?" he asked.

"Yes, Sergeant," said Smithson. "We've got both monitors set up in the command centre, one tracking the GPS and the other with the split screens of the park and the locker."

"Good. I need one of you to go relieve Fitzpatrick at the hotel. She's watching a prisoner, Carol Jackson."

"I can go," said Ezekial. He jumped out of the van and went

inside to get keys for a vehicle.

"Will you be okay out there by yourself?" he asked the other young Mountie.

"I'm good," said Smithson. "It's mostly sitting around anyway." He drove off in the van.

"That looks like the Crown Attorney's car," said Lundquist, pointing to a white Chevrolet with a Government of Newfoundland and Labrador sticker on it. "Probably wants to talk to us about this morning."

Windflower and Lundquist went inside, where the receptionist was bringing the Crown Attorney a cup of coffee in Lundquist's office. "Good morning gentlemen," said Lynn. "Can I get you one too?" she asked.

"Thanks, Lynn, that would be great," said Windflower.

"Me, too," said Lundquist. "Good morning, Paul. Paul Fowler, this is Sergeant Winston Windflower. He's the prime on the murders."

"Morning," said Fowler and he stood to shake Windflower's hand. "Quite a mess we've got here in Grand Falls, isn't it, Sergeant?"

"Yeah, that sums it up pretty good," said Windflower.

"I was hoping to get a nice quiet posting so I could ease into retirement," said Fowler, who had a growing edge of gray around a close, almost brush-cut hairstyle. "Instead we get this," he said waving a large, thick file around.

"It's a lot for one small community. But we are making some progress. Did Lars tell you about our plan?"

"Roughly," said Fowler. "I have some concerns about letting Snow out, even on a large surety."

"We do too. But we will be monitoring his every move. And we have the potential to make a large drug seizure, and to directly connect Snow with it. That would really put a dent in their operations."

"Okay," said Fowler. "I'm going to ask for two hundred thousand in bonds and twice a day reporting. Make sure nothing goes wrong with this. Or all us of us will be in it, pretty freaking deep." he added.

Lundquist looked at Windflower a little anxiously. "We'll be okay," said Windflower. He rose and shook the Crown Attorney's hand. Lundquist stayed behind to go through the other cases with Fowler, while Windflower walked to the command centre in back. Lynn came in with his coffee.

"Thank you, Lynn. By the way, Betsy Molloy says hello."

"Betsy is such a sweetheart," said Lynn. "We had such a nice time together when we did that training. I wish we could do more of that."

"I could talk to Inspector Quigley about that. What kind of training would you like?"

"Really?" said the receptionist. "Let me check with a few people and I'll let you know. Thanks again." She went away smiling.

Windflower was smiling too. Until the phone on his desk started ringing and he picked it up. "Windflower," he answered.

"Sarge, it's Ezekial. Jackson is gone."

"Where's Fitzpatrick?" he asked.

"She's lying on the bed, passed out," said Ezekial. "I tried to wake her but it kind of looks like she's been drugged or something."

Chapter Fifty-four

"Is her car in the parking lot?" asked Windflower.

"I didn't see it on the way in. Let me run out and check," said Ezekial. A long minute later a breathless Ezekial said, "Nope, not there. I checked Fitz's pockets. No keys."

For the first time in a very long time Windflower wanted to curse. Long, loudly, and very profanely. He wanted to curse Ezekial for bringing him this news. Even more, he wanted to curse Fitzpatrick, who couldn't get one simple task done. He wanted to curse his luck, the heavens and all of the bikers who walked like scum on the earth and brought so much misery. He wanted to curse so badly. But he didn't. Because it wouldn't help, and because that wasn't the man he was, or the man he wanted to be.

Instead, Windflower said, "Make sure Fitzpatrick is okay and then come back when you can."

After he hung up he walked over and closed the door. Then he did what he was allowed to do. He yelled. He yelled at the top of his lungs, so loudly that the prisoners in the back grew very, very quiet. So loudly that everyone in the building who wasn't locked up ran to the command centre. But the door was locked and all they could hear was Windflower, or some madman, yelling inside. When he finally opened the door, they all jumped back.

Finally, Lundquist asked him if he was okay.

"I will be. In fact, I feel better already."

He told Lundquist what had happened and got him to work with Lynn to set up an emergency bulletin. Pomeroy showed up along with his officers from the drug squad. Windflower sent them out to tour through town in different directions and then to head both east and west on the highway. He called Quigley in Grand Bank and asked him to divert resources from Gander and all points west to help find Jackson.

Fifteen minutes later, Pomeroy reported back in. They'd found Fitzpatrick's cruiser in a parking lot at the back of the shopping mall. The trunk was open, which Windflower knew wasn't a good sign. It probably meant that Jackson had Fitzpatrick's weapon. And it also meant that she likely had another vehicle.

"Turn on your siren to get everybody's attention and find out if she's got somebody's car. Move as fast as you can, and call it in when you have something."

He went out to the front to give Lynn the added information to pass along. "Call Inspector Quigley in Grand Bank, too," he said. "Tell him Jackson likely has another vehicle and to put the watch on the airports and the ferries in Port-aux-Basques and Argentia."

Lynn nodded and started punching in the information.

"I've got to go to the courthouse," said Lundquist. "Luckily, I arranged for the bailiffs to pick up our guys out back. I just saw the van go by. I'll let you know what happens. Sorry about one of my people screwing up."

"It's not your fault. People make mistakes. All we can do is keep moving forward and do a good job from here on."

"Thanks," said Lundquist, and he went to meet the prisoner's van at the back door of the detachment.

Windflower searched his brain for a Shakespeare quote on

mistakes. That often helped him to get through thorny situations. It was a bit of a mind trick to take attention off a problem in order to start focusing on the solution. He couldn't think of one. But he did remember one from George Bernard Shaw. 'A life spent making mistakes is not only more honorable, but more useful than a life spent doing nothing'. That would just have to do.

He didn't have time for much more thinking because the calls started coming and didn't stop. First up was Majesky. Unfortunately for Windflower, the Superintendent was not a member in the no-cursing club. In fact, Windflower thought that some of his coarse language was quite colourful, and interesting, especially the combinations of different animals and variations of human waste products. Majesky seemed particularly incensed that Carol Jackson had gotten out of custody, and he threatened Windflower with personal recriminations and discipline if they didn't find her. And fast.

"We're working on it, sir," said Windflower.

"Call me when you have her," said Majesky and Windflower's ears were still ringing from his superior's strong suggestions when his cell phone rang. It was Sheila.

"Good morning, Sheila," said Windflower when he heard her voice. "It is good to hear a friendly voice."

Sheila laughed. "I guess things are not going as well as you'd like out there."

"You could say that," said Windflower, not quite laughing but at least smiling again. "The latest bit of misfortune is that Carol is gone."

"Gone where?" asked Sheila. "You mean she's missing? How did that happen?"

"Let's not talk about that right now. She managed to escape custody and is now on the loose, likely armed and if not exactly dangerous, then certainly unpredictable."

"She is that," said Sheila. "It's hard to know what to believe when Carol starts telling a story. I'm not sure even she knows the truth anymore. I remember one time when she said she was done with men and the next thing she called me from a guy's place in Rocky Harbour, telling me she might spend the winter there."

"What did you say? She spent some time in Rocky Harbour? Do you remember the guy's name?"

"I'm pretty sure it was Rocky Harbour. She said she loved riding around the park on her bike. The guy's name, I think, was Piercey. Tony Piercey," said Sheila.

"Thank you, my love. I'm going to run and check out that lead you gave me," said Windflower.

"Wait," said Sheila. "When are you coming home? When will I see you for more than a few minutes?"

"Maybe by the weekend. Love you, talk soon."

Before he could do anything with this new information, the phone on his desk rang again.

"It's Pomeroy. We've got a car reported stolen from the parking lot. A white Chevy Impala, Newfoundland license."

"Give me the plate number," said Windflower. He wrote it on a slip of paper. "Are your guys still out on the road?"

"Yeah, one guy just called me from Gander, nothing there. The other is on his way west. Expect to hear from him soon," said Pomeroy.

"Okay. I'll put the plate number out on the system. Why don't you call the guy going east back and both of you come back here? Let the guy going west continue to Deer Lake and stay put there for now. Jackson may be heading north, up to Gros Morne."

"Will do," said Pomeroy.

Windflower ran to the front to give Lynn the message about the stolen plate number. "Can you add that the escapee is likely armed as well? Thanks, Lynn."

Then he called Ron Quigley in Grand Bank. "Ron, I need you to check out this guy, Tony Piercey in Rocky Harbour. Sheila says he's an ex of Carol Jackson. She may be headed there."

"Okay," said Quigley. "I'll call Peter Gagne in Rocky Harbour. If anybody does, he'll know Piercey."

"Let me know," said Windflower.

"Will do," said Quigley. "Hey, I just saw the update flash up on my screen. White Impala. That makes it easier. You guys are good."

"Technology and good admin people. Let's hope we can get some luck to go along with that. Ciao, Ron."

Chapter Fifty-five

Things slowed down around the office long enough for Windflower to catch his breath and clear his head a little. But it seemed like there were too many balls in the air. He went back to the command centre and went to the whiteboard that had been leaning unused against one of the walls.

He started writing names on the board. The list included French, Carol Jackson, Joey Snow, Todd Lundrigan, Stella Winslow, and the Moose. Three of whom were dead, and one almost dead. Two of whom were in custody and both, for different reasons, were about to be free from police custody.

He was still writing and thinking when Ezekial and a very groggy Fitzpatrick came into the room.

"What happened?" he asked Fitzpatrick.

"I'm not really sure," said the female constable. "I guess she must have put something in my orange juice. I could feel myself fading quickly, but there was nothing I could do about it. I guess she must have had the stuff in her cosmetic bag. I should have checked it, been more careful."

"Maybe. But we probably should have caught it in Grand Bank when we had her there too. We all make mistakes. The important thing about them is to learn from them, and never repeat them. Got it?"

"Got it," said Fitzpatrick, relieved that she didn't get yelled at.

"I expect Corporal Lundquist will do a full review of this event. So there may be discipline coming from that. But for now, go home and sleep off whatever is in your system. We'll need you back here as soon as you can. Dismissed."

Fitzpatrick nodded and left the room quietly. Ezekial was just as quiet standing by the side. "You stay here. We're going to need a plan to make sure there are no more screw-ups. We're also going to need coffee and donuts. Go to Tim's and get us a box of donuts and I'll make us some fresh coffee." He threw ten bucks at the young constable and went to the lunchroom to make the coffee.

While he was pouring the water into the machine, Pomeroy came in with another RCMP officer. "This is Wilson," he said. "Part of my crew. Tyler is the guy still on the road. This is Sergeant Windflower, Wilson."

"Pleased to meet you," said Wilson.

"Same here. I'm getting the fuel ready for a brainstorming session," said Windflower, pointing to the coffee maker.

"Have you got the donuts too?" asked Pomeroy.

"You've done this before," said Windflower, with one of his first smiles of the morning. "They're on their way. As soon as Lundquist gets back, we'll get going."

Once the coffee had perked, Windflower poured each man a cup and they went back to the command centre. Ezekial was coming in with the box of donuts when one of the monitors started beeping. All of the Mounties walked over to see the monitor start to glow as well. Soon the screen was lit with a map of the local area and a blinking red dot in the middle of it.

"That's the GPS. That means Joey Snow is out of jail."

"That would be correct," said Lundquist, walking into the room.

"He and two of his compatriots are walking the streets again, most likely heading back to their clubhouse for a little celebration. The other two are going the other direction, to the pen in St. John's. Did I just hear a beep?"

"It sounds and looks like the GPS tracker is working. Let's double check with Smithson to make sure everything is okay on his end. And then we're having a brainstormer," said Windflower.

"I see you've got the supplies," said Lundquist. "Let me talk to Smithson and then I'll get a cup. Save me a Boston Cream."

Lundquist walked back in again a few minutes later with a cup of coffee in his hand. "Smithson's good. He says all the cameras are operational, and the GPS is doing fine. He says if you check the screen, you'll see that Snow is at the clubhouse location."

Once again, all of the Mounties crowded around the screen and Windflower could easily confirm that the GPS tracker signal was solid and holding from the Bacchus clubhouse. "Good," he pronounced. "Let's see where we are. Do you remember the ground rules for brainstorming?"

"There are no rules," the other Mounties chorused back.

"And no bad questions," said Windflower.

"Right now, we're waiting for Snow to make a move to grab his stash," Windflower said. "And then we grab him."

"We're all set up at the industrial park," said Lundquist. "Daniels and Smithson were both at my locker when I went out there to take a look. The cameras are all in place and working, and Smithson even made sure that the camera areas are lit as well. So we'll have eyes in the dark too."

"What happens if Snow takes off his shoes or the GPS breaks down?" asked Wilson.

"Good question. I guess we should have a back-up for that. Pomeroy, why don't you guys set up outside the clubhouse when we're done here? That way, you can spot Snow or his guys if they leave, and also be there to follow."

Pomeroy looked to his fellow drug squad officer and nodded to

Windflower. "Okay," he said.

"We're also in a bit of a waiting mode on Carol Jackson too," said Windflower.

"There was no sign of her from here to Gander," said Wilson. "She might have gotten off the highway along the way."

"I don't think so," said Lundquist. "She would be trying to put distance between her and Grand Falls. She would be moving somewhere safe, or out of the province."

"My thinking exactly. You may not all know this, but we think she's driving a white Chevy Impala she stole from the shopping centre. And I got a tip about an ex-boyfriend in Rocky Harbour. I've asked Inspector Quigley to check that one out for us. Plus, we've already moved to seal the airports and the ferry terminals."

"I guess I should give you an update on what we know as well," said Pomeroy.

"That would be good," said Windflower, grabbing a donut from the box.

"We've been active in this area for a while now. French was working with us as an informer with Snow and his gang. And we were trying to get inside the Outlaws with Lundrigan. That work has been going on for about a year. Carol Jackson came on the scene a few months ago, and we have been able to make a couple of dents in their armour. We were in the process of making a major buy we hoped would lead us directly to Snow when all of this crap broke loose."

"What can you tell us about the Bacchus activities?" said Wind-flower. "Carol Jackson said something about using this area as a distribution point."

"Yeah," said Pomeroy. "We were starting to piece that together. Bacchus was using Snow and his crew here as a hub for the Atlantic region and a springboard into Ontario. The drugs, mostly cocaine and some weed, were coming up the coast and being dropped off all over the Maritimes. His guys would go pick it up and bring it here. They had some kind of depot where they would store it and ship it out as requested to the areas that ordered it. Kind of like a Walmart distribution centre."

"That might be what they were using the storage locker for. Although there's not the quantity you're talking about in there now."

"That's because we've been pinching them," said Pomeroy. "We think they are re-evaluating their strategy. Maybe even looking at moving out of here."

"That would be good," said Lundquist. "But why were they still doing the big run last weekend? That didn't look like moving out."

"Appearances can be deceiving," said Pomeroy. "We heard that the run was actually about handing over more patches and more autonomy to local guys, while squeezing Snow and his guys out."

"Like the guys in Marystown who were patched over," said Windflower.

"Or the local bikers in our area who got recruited as well," said Ezekial.

"How does all of that fit into the murders?" asked Lundquist.

"That's another great question. It's not clear to me exactly what happened. Who's telling the truth? Why were Lundrigan and the girl killed and who did it? Why did Snow shoot the Moose and did he shoot French too?"

"Let's start with Todd Lundrigan first," said Pomeroy. "Like I told you before, we were working on turning him. Maybe somebody found out about that?"

"Or maybe it was just Snow taking out a rival," said Lundquist. "There's no love lost between them or their compatriots in the Outlaws and Bacchus. It seems like every week one of their crew is getting stitched up at the hospital."

"Both of those things make sense. We also know the Moose and French were also there, and that likely one or both of them were involved in the shootings. But what about the girl, what was she doing there?" asked Windflower.

"She might just be Lundrigan's girlfriend," said Ezekial.

"True. But she wasn't carrying his baby. Whose baby was it, anyway?"

"Maybe wrong time and place for Stella Winslow?" said Lundquist.

"Could be. Although I'm thinking that somehow she might be a link in all of this. I just can't figure out how."

Chapter Fifty-six

"What about if the baby was French's?" asked Ezekial.

Windflower thought about saying that was a dumb question, but resisted the urge. Instead, he went to the board and drew a line between French and Stella Winslow. "Let's run with that for a minute. So French and this young lady are involved. We know that he and Carol Jackson have at least a working relationship. Maybe she wants more. They bring the Moose into the deal as a partner and then she sets up this side arrangement with Lundrigan, knowing that he'll bring Winslow along. Then she gets the Moose to shoot them both."

"Like French said at the hospital about Carol being the one and telling him to shoot them," said Lundquist.

"That could mean anything," said Pomeroy.

"I still think it was personal," said Lundquist. "Snow was crying at Winslow's funeral. I think he still loved her. Even after she left him. It was weird seeing such a hard nut bawling in public."

"Maybe. But we'll have to wait until we get Carol Jackson in order to confirm our theories on that side. Now turning our attention to the Moose, we know Snow shot him, but why?"

"It might have been simple betrayal," said Pomeroy. "That's enough to get you killed seven days a week with this crew."

"What about French? You have to think it was Snow, or his buddies," said Windflower.

"That one is pure gangland," said Pomeroy. "I've seen it once before. It was in New Brunswick with the 'Angels'. They found a guy who had ratted them out. So they shot him in the leg and left him to die. It's a brutal way to go."

Those last comments seemed to sober the group and dry up the conversation. "Okay, gentlemen. Thank you for your considerate offerings. I'm not sure we have all the answers, but I feel like we're at least pointed in the right direction. And all the donuts are gone," said Windflower, checking the now-empty box. "So, it's back to work."

The others went off to their tasks. Windflower hoped the day didn't drag on too long while he waited for news on Carol Jackson. He tried to read over the files again but couldn't concentrate. He was relieved when his cell phone rang. He could see from the number that it was Ron Quigley.

"Inspector, I hope you have good news for me," said Windflower.

"You know me," said Quigley. "Never want to disappoint the troops. I wish I could say we've found Carol Jackson, but not yet. I did however talk to Gagne in Rocky Harbour.

He does in fact know Tony Piercey. Quite well, in fact. Piercey has a long acquaintance with the RCMP in that community."

"Is Piercey there now?" asked Windflower.

"He was last night," said Quigley. "He spent the night as a guest of the RCMP Rocky Harbour Detachment. High as a kite and violent, according to Peter. He got out this morning. Peter's gone over to his place now to look for him."

The phone on Windflower's desk rang. "One second, Ron, my other line is ringing," said Windflower. When he picked it up, it was Pomeroy.

"Tyler called from Deer Lake. He found the Impala at the Deer Lake motel. He hasn't seen anybody around for a while and Jackson didn't check into the hotel," said Pomeroy.

"Tell him to stay there until we figure out what's going on. I'll call you back."

"We found Jackson's car in Deer Lake," Windflower said to Quigley when he picked up his cell phone again.

"Well, we're narrowing down the search area," said Quigley. "Here's Peter Gagne's cell phone number. You can talk to him directly. Let me know how it goes."

"Thanks, Ron," said Windflower as he hung up and dialed the number for the officer in Rocky Harbour.

"Gagne," came the voice over the phone.

"Peter, it's Winston Windflower. I hear you're trying to track down Tony Piercey."

"Windflower, good to hear from you," said Gagne. "I'm outside his house. No sign of him or his motorcycle. If his bike's not here, he's usually not either."

"Our suspect ditched her vehicle in Deer Lake earlier today. She knows Piercey and may be trying to reach him," said Windflower.

"This is a pretty small town," said Gagne. "But you know, Piercey also has a cabin up in Trout River," said Gagne. "I'll take a run up there later on to check it out."

"Be careful. She has an RCMP service weapon. And she may be desperate. I'm going to send our guy in Deer Lake, Tyler, up for support. Plus, he can check the highway on the way."

"Great, and thanks for the warning," said Gagne. "I'll bring back-up when we go to Trout River."

"Let me know as soon as you hear anything," said Windflower. After he hung up, he relayed the instructions to Tyler through Pomeroy. He could feel the noose tightening around Carol Jackson, but he also knew that an animal was most dangerous when it felt cornered. He didn't have a good feeling about this, not a good feeling at all.

Lundquist came in again as he was finishing up his calls. He had heard the anxiousness in Windflower's voice.

"News?" he asked.

"Jackson's car is confirmed in Deer Lake. We still think she's heading for Rocky Harbour or somewhere up north."

"That's good news, isn't it?" asked Lundquist.

"It's good to know where she is or might be. But she has Fitz-patrick's weapon. And I think she'd use it if she had to," said Wind-flower.

"Got it," said Lundquist. "If it helps, why don't you focus on Carol Jackson and I'll look after the stakeout? Everything is in place here anyway."

"Thanks, Lars. I might do that. For now, all we can do is wait."

Once again, Windflower didn't have to wait long. His cell phone rang. This time it was Superintendent Majesky.

Chapter Fifty-seven

"I talked to the hospital," said Majesky. "You were right. I guess French is not likely going to make it through the night. We'll need to let the media know there's been another shooting. I'll let Media Relations know about it and they can work with your girl down there to get something out."

"You mean Lynn, the administrative assistant," said Windflower, a little perturbed by the Super's casual sexism. "I won't have time to deal with the media. We've got an active stakeout on for Joey Snow and it looks like Carol Jackson's meeting up with an ex-boyfriend, somewhere around Rocky Harbour."

"Don't worry about the media," said Majesky. "I've ordered Quigley to come in and look after that. He's on his way there now. He can handle the media."

"Okay, but we better have something else to tell them other than we've had another shooting," said Windflower.

"I've given Quigley approval for an additional two officers for Grand Falls. Community policing," said Majesky. "That will give him something to tell the media, and should keep that mayor happy too. Tell me more about Jackson."

"We found the car she stole in Deer Lake and she's got an ex in Rocky Harbour, a biker type named Tony Piercey. He's well known to our guys. Has a place in town and a cabin around Trout River. The locals have eyes on both and I've got a guy heading up the highway from Deer Lake to link up with them. Plus, she's likely got a weapon she stole from the cruiser."

"We have to find Jackson," said Majesky. "She's the only one who can piece all of this together. I'm going to see where the chopper is and re-route it over there. If our guys find her, I want you to be the one who talks to her, before anybody else and certainly before anybody starts shooting. Is that clear?"

"Yes, sir," said Windflower. He went out to find Lundquist.

"What's up?" asked Lundquist.

"I talked to Majesky and he wants me to go out to Rocky Harbour if they find Jackson. So I guess I will take you up on the offer to look after the stakeout. Let's run through it again so we make sure we've got everything covered," said Windflower. Lundquist nodded, and the two men spent the next fifteen minutes walking through the possible scenarios, and making sure that they had a plan to cover all contingencies. When he was satisfied, Windflower patted him on the back and walked to the front to brief Lynn about the media release.

"Thanks, Lynn," said Windflower after he'd given her the information. "Inspector Quigley will be dealing with the media from here on. He should be here later today."

"Did I hear the Inspector is coming to pay us a visit?" asked Lundquist, who was passing by the front desk.

"He is indeed. And I hear he is bearing gifts." When both the receptionist and Lundquist looked surprised, he added. "A little bird told me the Grand Falls RCMP Detachment is getting two new officers for community policing."

"Wow, that's great news, and fast too," said Lundquist. "Good job, Sergeant."

"It's not me. That's a pretty powerful mayor you have. I just pointed him in the right direction. He's the one who made that happen."

"You know, if we can nail Snow for both the murder and the drugs, and we can have the resources we need for a real community policing program, we might be able to turn this town around," said Lundquist.

"I believe you can. But there's still a lot of work to do."

At this point, all that was left was to sit and wait for something to happen. This was always the hardest part of being a police officer, thought Windflower. You wanted to do something, anything, but now that the table had been set, you simply had to wait until the meal was served. In the case of the stakeout, they had to stay in place until Joey Snow made his move. And Windflower had to wait for news from Gagne out in Gros Morne.

After about an hour of this infernal waiting, Windflower went outside to get a breath of air. He was walking around the building when he heard it. It was the thump, thump, thumping sound of a helicopter coming closer. Somebody once described this as being like a severely unbalanced washing machine, but for Windflower it meant that his ride was here, if he needed one. And as things were to unfold, he did.

When he came in, Lynn was frantically waving to him to come and answer the line in the command centre. Windflower picked up the phone on her desk. He pushed the blinking red light. "Windflower," he said.

"It's Peter Gagne. We've located Tony Piercey and he's got a woman with him. They're at his cabin in Trout River. One of the locals saw him ride in with a girl on the back. Said it didn't look like anyone from around here. Looked like she was wearing one of Piercey's old leather jackets, blond hair."

"Do they know you're there?" asked Windflower.

"I don't think so," said Gagne.

"That's good. Let's keep it that way, if we can. What's your situation on the ground?"

"I've got two guys blocking off the roads, and your guy from Deer Lake is with me," said Gagne.

"Weapons?" asked Windflower.

"We've got our service pistols. But I've got another guy bringing a shotgun and a Colt from Rocky Harbour," said Gagne.

"Do not engage unless it is defensively. Jackson is armed and unpredictable. We don't want anybody getting hurt. We have to talk to Jackson. Is that clear?"

"Yes, sir," said Gagne.

"Okay. I've got a chopper here to give me a lift. Here's my cell phone number in case you need to reach me. I'm on my way. I'll call when I get close. Send Tyler to pick me up. And don't do anything until I get there. Okay?"

"Okay," said Gagne.

"Take me to the hospital," said Windflower to Lundquist. "I'm going to Trout River."

The men said little to each other on the short ride over. When they got there, Reid was standing alongside the helicopter that still had its rotor blades spinning.

"Call me if anything breaks here," said Windflower. He waved goodbye to Lundquist, jumped in the chopper and strapped in. Within minutes they were in the air and on the way west to Trout River in Gros Morne National Park.

Chapter Fifty-eight

The helicopter ride was smooth and as breathtaking as usual. They flew across central Newfoundland and headed north into the Long Range Mountains that lined the west coast leading up to what the locals called the Great Northern Peninsula. The majesty of Gros Morne National Park, a UNESCO World Heritage Site, was revealed before them as they descended. Windflower could see Western Brook Pond, actually a fjord created by glaciers that had crept down the mountains. After the glaciers melted, the land rebounded and the fjord was cut off from the sea, leaving the pristine blue pond that Windflower and Reid could clearly view from the chopper.

Farther on, as they crossed over Bonne Bay and approached Trout River, they could also see the Tablelands, one of the very few places on earth where you can see the earth's mantle, created when tectonic plates raised the earth and flipped it over. It was caused by a plate collision several hundred million years ago. Windflower always thought it might be what the earth looked like if you turned it inside out. It had a brown, almost rusty look to it from the iron in the rock, more like a barren desert than the rich green forests of Newfoundland. But this was no time to be playing tourist, thought Windflower, as the helicopter drifted down and came to a stop in the parking lot of the RCMP sub-office in Trout River.

Windflower shook hands with Reid, who was in the process of shutting down the helicopter. He ran to a nearby car where Tyler was waiting. The young officer put his foot on the gas and peeled out of the parking lot.

"There's been some action at the scene," said Tyler. "We tried to call, but I guess there was no service."

"What's going on?" asked Windflower.

"It started a few minutes ago. The guy came out of the house and must have spotted us. He ran back in and got a shotgun, start-ing waving it around. He's either crazy or high," said Tyler.

"Any sign of Jackson?" asked Windflower.

"Somebody said they saw the curtains move, and that there's somebody else inside. But no confirmation," said Tyler. "After the shots, everybody moved back down the road. Here they are now."

Windflower got out of the car and walked to the waiting cruis-ers. "Hey, Peter," he said to the officer who was walking towards him.

"Good to see you, too," said Gagne. "I'd rather you were coming to go hiking or fishing, but..."

"Yeah, me too. Tyler told me you've had some action."

"Piercey doesn't seem too pleased to see us," said Gagne. "He's volatile when he's sober, but I think he's cranked out on E or crystal meth or something. He was going bananas with the shotgun."

"Drugs?" asked Windflower.

"Yeah, long list of convictions, but mostly a guy with addictions and mental health issues. Unpredictable when he's drunk or high. Very unpredictable and dangerous."

"Is Carol Jackson inside?"

"We think so," said Gagne. "Somebody else is in there for sure."

"Okay, let's find out. Have you got a megaphone?"

"In the trunk," said Gagne and he walked to the back, opened the trunk and took out a large white megaphone with orange RCMP lettering across the side.

"Bring the Colt," said Windflower and he and Gagne walked up the narrow road towards the cabin. It was a one-story affair, more of a lean-to than a formal cabin with a stovepipe jutting out of the roof and a large window in the front. The curtains were pulled tightly, but Windflower could see them moving a little as they neared the cabin. About sixty feet away, the Mounties stopped and Windflower picked up the megaphone.

"Carol, Carol Jackson, it's Windflower. We need to talk."

The curtains fluttered and were pulled open. Windflower could see a man standing inside, peering out. Then the door of the cabin flew open and out came a screaming Tony Piercey. He still had a shotgun in his hands and was waving his arms around. Windflower could hear Gagne click his automatic rifle into firing position behind him. He put his hand up to indicate that Gagne should hold on, at least for now.

Piercey was still yelling and moving his arms around, but it became clear to Windflower that the man was more agitated than angry with them in particular. He had seen people in drug psychosis states before, and that was what this looked like. Piercey was still a threat, but not necessarily to them as much as he was to the whole world around him. They didn't even know if the gun he was brandishing was loaded. As long as he didn't point it at them… He glanced briefly at Gagne to see if he was reading the situation in the same way. Gagne nodded quickly to let him know he was.

"Carol, we know you're in there. You better get Piercey out of here before he gets shot. You know this is going nowhere."

Piercey looked kind of stunned at this latest interaction as if he couldn't figure out what was going on. Which he likely couldn't, thought Windflower. Then they heard a woman's voice calling out. Piercey looked around and started to head back into the cabin.

Gagne touched Windflower from behind to see if he wanted him to do anything; maybe to try and stop Piercey, but Windflower shook his head. Piercey went back inside and soon they could hear an animated conversation.

"I want him to get looked after," said the woman's voice from inside the cabin. "He's just stoned and crazy."

"Okay. Throw out the shotgun and your gun."

There was another discussion inside the cabin, this time more heated than before, but soon afterwards the shotgun came flying out of the cabin door and landed on the ground a few feet away, followed by the RCMP weapon.

"Send him out first," said Windflower. He also whispered to Gagne to call the rest of the RCMP officers to come up with them.

Tony Piercey came out first as requested and while he still had a wild look in his eyes, somehow Carol Jackson had calmed him down a little. Within seconds, Tyler and the other officers had him lying on the ground with his hands cuffed behind him.

A minute later, a drawn-looking Carol Jackson emerged from the cabin. Gagne grabbed her as soon as she came close enough and put her in handcuffs and laid her on the ground alongside Piercey. Windflower searched her pockets and frisked her thoroughly. Not exactly perfect protocol, but he was not taking any more chances with Jackson. He grabbed her purse and searched it while the other officers picked up the weapons. Windflower took the RCMP service pistol for himself.

Chapter Fifty-nine

"Somebody I know will be glad to have this back," he said to Gagne.

"I'll bet," said Gagne. Both men knew there was almost nothing worse than for an RCMP officer to lose his or her weapon. No, make it nothing worse. Fitzpatrick would certainly be grateful to get hers back.

"Good job, Peter," said Windflower.

"Thank you," said Gagne. "I was a little nervous when he came out with the shotgun, though."

"Yeah, but you held your cool. Like they taught us. I've got to make a call and see what the big boss wants me to do with her," he said, pointing to the prostrate female prisoner. "I'm assuming you know what to do with Piercey."

"Yeah," said Gagne. "After we clean this place up here and check his house in Rocky Harbour, we'll let him come down, and go from there. We'll offer him detox and treatment. But he's turned us down a dozen times on that. So we'll wait for the next time and lock him up again."

Windflower nodded his sympathy and picked up his cell phone

to call Superintendent Majesky.

"We got Jackson," he said when his superior officer answered. "What do you want me to do with her?"

"Send her back to Halifax with the chopper," said Majesky. "We'll take it over from here."

"There are still some loose ends we'd like to talk to her about," said Windflower.

"You'll have to do that without Jackson. We need her here," said Majesky. "And you should know: French didn't make it. We're making arrangements to have his body sent back home."

"Was he dirty?" asked Windflower, thinking he might as well ask.

"I don't know," said Majesky. "That's part of what we need to talk to Jackson about."

Windflower was quiet and the Superintendent could sense his discomfort. "Listen, there are still plenty of things that need to be tied up, here, and down there. French has been a private operative for us and we'll look after his family. But nobody outside the system can know about his role. It would compromise too many people. That's just the business we're in."

"Okay," he said, even though it wasn't. "I'll send her back with Reid and one of Pomeroy's guys."

Windflower found Tyler with the group of Mounties gathered around the prisoners near the cruisers at the end of the road. "I'm sending you to Halifax with Jackson," he said. "Let me have your keys."

Tyler handed over the keys to his police cruiser rather reluctantly. "Don't worry, I'll talk to your boss. Put her in the back."

Tyler took Carol Jackson and put her in the back of the car as requested. "We're off," said Windflower and he shook hands with Gagne and the other officers. "Thanks again for your help."

Tyler sat quietly beside Windflower as they drove back to the RCMP office.

"Stay here for a minute," said Windflower as he went inside.

Reid was sitting there with a cup of coffee. He poured a cup for Windflower.

"Thanks. We've got a package for you to deliver back to Halifax."

When Reid looked at him quizzically, he added, "A person of interest in the Grand Falls murders, Carol Jackson, and her escort."

Reid peered out through the window at Tyler and the cruiser and nodded. "How will you get back?"

"I'll take the cruiser. It's a bit of a drive, but I need the time to clear my head. It's been a little hectic."

"Okay," said Reid. "I'm ready whenever you are."

"Might as well get started. I'm going to send the kid in for a coffee. I want to talk to Jackson for a minute, then we're good to go." Reid nodded again and Windflower went outside.

"Go get a coffee before you take off," said Windflower. Tyler went inside, leaving him alone in the cruiser with Carol Jackson.

"I don't have to talk to you," said Jackson as Windflower sipped on his coffee.

"I know. We're sending you to Halifax to talk to the big boys." He could see Jackson smile to herself in the back seat.

"But I want to ask you a question anyway." Jackson didn't say anything so he continued. "What was French's role in all of this? Was he your partner or did he lead?"

"Like I said, I don't have to talk to you," said Jackson. "But," and she paused, "I don't follow anybody else's lead." She smiled again.

Windflower drained his coffee and went back inside to get Tyler. Reid was already climbing into the helicopter when Windflower helped Tyler get Jackson into the chopper and handcuffed to her seat. He went back and sat in the cruiser as the helicopter engine grew louder and the rotors spun faster until the aircraft lifted off the ground and into the now dark sky. He watched for a few more minutes until the blinking red lights disappeared into the darkness.

He drove back through Gros Morne National Park to Deer Lake, where he stopped for dinner at the Irving Big Stop. He made his phone calls to Grand Falls and talked to Lundquist, who told him they were still waiting on Snow to make his move. They were not expecting that to happen anytime soon, since more beer, supplies and people kept arriving at the biker's clubhouse. He also talked to Pomeroy and told him about Tyler's diversion. He wasn't happy about that, but Windflower told him to talk to Majesky if he had any complaints. He didn't feel like operating his usual friendly customer service section right now.

After his phone calls, he had a bowl of turkey soup and a grilled cheese sandwich for dinner. He needed some comfort food. He still had hours of driving ahead of him so he got an extra-large coffee to take with him, along with one of those large rocky road marshmallow cookies, pure sugar with a butterscotch flavouring. Perfect for helping someone stay awake.

He called Sheila, but was only able to leave a message. That was too bad. He would have liked to talk to a friendly voice, but maybe she would call back. Feeling a little low, but fully supplied with caffeine and sugar, he left Deer Lake and headed for Grand Falls.

The night was clear and the moon was rising on the horizon in the distance as he turned onto the highway. He still drove a little slowly and more carefully than usual. The area outside of Deer Lake was well known for moose. Windflower heard one local describe it as "magotty with em, b'y". That brought a smile to his face as he travelled along, determined to remain vigilant against the menace of the Trans Canada Highway.

Chapter Sixty

That was a good thing, since he saw his first moose just past the Springdale turnoff, his second before South Brook, and then his third in the ditch on the side of the road somewhere in the middle of nowhere. He was already creeping along when his cell phone rang. He pulled over to the side of the road to answer it when another moose popped up out of the bushes to greet him. He glanced at his phone. It was Sheila.

"Hello, Winston. I was worried about you. I heard you were driving back from Deer Lake. You know how much I worry about you and the moose at night," said Sheila.

"It is nice to hear your voice," said Windflower, choosing not to respond to the concerns that Sheila was raising. "I'm almost there. I'm near the Buchans exit," he said.

"Well, that's good," said Sheila. "You're almost home for the night. How did things go out there? Any news about Carol?"

"Things went as well as possible. Carol is safe. She is being shipped back to Halifax. They'll deal with her up there."

"Is she in a lot of trouble?" asked Sheila.

"Carol Jackson is always in a lot of trouble. But that's kind of the story of her life, isn't it?" said Windflower. "The problem with people like Carol is that they drag other people, good people, down with them."

"I guess you're right," said Sheila. "Anyway, I wanted to make sure you were okay and to tell you that I love you."

"That is the best thing I've heard all day. I love you too, Sheila Hillier. How's my little dog?"

"Lady is great," said Sheila. "But every time someone comes to the door she jumps up. She misses you. And I miss you too."

"I miss both of you too. Hopefully I'll see you soon,"

"Good night. Winston. And drive carefully. Okay?"

"I will. Good night, Sheila."

Windflower did drive very carefully for the next hour and safely made it back to Grand Falls. He thought about checking in at the detachment, but he didn't have it in him. He pointed his car towards the hotel and kind of glided into the parking lot. He forced himself to stay awake long enough for a quick hot shower, and then fell into bed.

His head hit the pillow and that was all he remembered until he heard the birds singing in the morning.

He made some coffee and took it with him to the back of the hotel. Outside it was dark and gray and gloomy and rainy. Pouring rain. Windflower ran back and grabbed his RCMP hoodie and ventured out anyway. He found a sheltered spot under a large tree and organized his smudge kit. Soon it was smoking and he passed the sacred smoke over his head and his heart. He needed a little healing for his own heart today.

It never felt good to be around violence or hurtful people and sometimes their energy would come into your heart too, if you weren't careful. That was one lesson his grandfather had taught him many years ago: to let go of bad energy so that the goodness of life would have room to come in. He also thought about his dreams and the messages about kindness and strength that he had received. One of the insights that he received this morning was about kindness, and the reminder that we have to be kind to ourselves in order to practice kindness with others.

He gave thanks for these insights and wisdom as he prayed for his family and friends, for his allies and his ancestors. He offered a special prayer this morning for Robert French, whose spirit was now on another journey. Before he left the canopy of the tree, he laid down a little tobacco to bring French blessings on his way. His prayers and smudging finished, he ran back to the hotel between the rain drops and organized himself for the day to come.

He was having breakfast at the hotel when he saw a familiar face coming into the dining room. He waved him over.

"Morning, Ron," said Windflower.

"Good morning, Winston," said Quigley. "What's good for breakfast?"

"It's all good, my friend. Grab a plate and sit down," said Windflower.

The two men shared a table and some light conversation as they enjoyed their breakfast together. Neither seemed anxious to start talking shop this early in the morning. Instead, they focused on the many hunting and fishing options available in this part of the province. Quigley was an especially keen salmon fisherman and they talked about various good fishing spots along the Exploits River. When their food ran out, they got one more cup of coffee and seemed finally ready to begin the day.

"I hear it was pretty exciting out in Trout River," said Quigley.

"We were lucky. It could have turned out much differently, much worse. Peter Gagne was good. He held his cool even as the guy was waving that shotgun around."

"I hear you were pretty calm under fire, too," said Quigley. "Good job."

"Thanks. So, are you all set for meet the press time today?" asked Windflower.

"We're never really ready for that, are we?" asked Quigley. "But

I'll do it. At least I have a bit of a carrot with the new community officers."

"Is Mayor Loder coming?" asked Windflower.

"I talked to him last night. He's a dynamo, isn't he?" said Quigley.

"I think he and the whole community have had it with the sleazebags who've been running wild around here. I don't blame them."

"Too bad about French," said Quigley. "It's always sad when you see someone go down like that."

"Yeah. I guess we'll never know how deep he was into this. Doesn't matter much now anyway."

"Not to him, that's for sure," said Quigley, draining his coffee. "Let's go to work."

Chapter Sixty-one

The two men drove separately to the Grand Falls RCMP Detachment, where there was already a T.V. satellite truck parked in the lot. Quigley smiled weakly at Windflower as they walked into the office. Quigley stopped to talk to the receptionist, who was waiting with phone messages from various media outlets. Windflower waved a quick hello and went back to the command centre.

Lundquist was sitting at the desk watching the monitors from the industrial park when Windflower came in.

"Pretty quiet over there this morning," said Lundquist pointing to the screen. "Although it does feel like the calm before the storm."

"What's going on at the clubhouse?" asked Windflower.

"That's pretty quiet too," said Lundquist. "There was quite a party going on there last night according to Pomeroy, but it seems like Snow has stayed put, at least for now."

"That likely means nobody will be stirring anytime soon," said Windflower.

"Maybe," said Lundquist. "But we stay vigilant, just in case. It sucks about French."

"Yeah," said Windflower.

"We gave the hearse an escort to the airport in Gander," said Lundquist. "Seemed like the least we could do."

"That was a good thing. He was working for us, at least part of the time. I'm not sure where exactly he falls on the good guy, bad guy line, but it's still a rough way to go out."

"My thinking exactly," said Windflower. "I can take over in here for a while. Why don't you go have a break?"

"Thanks, I appreciate it," said Lundquist.

Windflower was sitting in the command centre, almost blankly staring at the computer screen when Constable Fitzpatrick came in.

"Good morning, Sergeant," she said.

"Constable. I have something that belongs to you in my car. Here's the keys. It's in the trunk."

Fitzpatrick took the keys and went to the parking lot. When she returned she was wearing her service pistol on her hip. "Thank you, Sergeant. I also wanted to tell you I appreciate that you didn't scream at me yesterday. I might have deserved it. I know I screwed up, but I can beat myself up pretty badly without any help from anybody else," she said.

"I know that feeling. So what did you learn from your mistake? That's what's important," said Windflower.

"I think I learned to be more observant and to not allow myself to become complacent, especially when I'm on duty. I think I let my guard down a little bit around Carol Jackson. That was my biggest mistake," said the female constable.

"Well, for what it's worth, Carol Jackson has fooled many, many people. You are neither the first, nor certainly the last."

"Thank you again," said Fitzpatrick. "It may be worth the two-day suspension Corporal Lundquist gave me to learn that."

"You've just had experience. That is what a wise man said is 'the name that everyone gives to their mistakes'."

"Are you quoting Shakespeare this early in the morning?" asked a man's voice as he was coming into the room. Fitzpatrick nodded good morning to Mayor Loder and quickly left the room.

"Good morning, sir. It's never too early for the Bard, but that was actually Oscar Wilde."

"Wilde," said Mayor Loder. "He's one of my favorites. A bit cynical, but always on the mark. I love the one that goes, 'the only worse thing than being talked about is not being talked about.'"

"Great motto for a politician," said Windflower.

"I'm not really much of a politician," said the mayor. "I like to speak my mind too freely."

Windflower laughed. "Well, you got Majesky's attention and even more importantly you got him to share some additional resources. You've got to know how tough that is these days."

"I think the Superintendent made a calculated choice," said Mayor Loder. "As Wilde would have said, 'A man cannot be too careful in his choice of enemies'."

Windflower laughed again. "Let's go and see Inspector Quigley and get ready for the media."

Windflower and the mayor walked to the media briefing room, where Lynn was handing out copies of the statement that Inspector Ron Quigley stood ready to read. Mayor Loder and Windflower stood behind the podium where Quigley was beginning his remarks. Quigley was about halfway through his prepared statement when Lundquist burst into the back of the room. He was desperately trying to get Windflower's attention.

Windflower saw him frantically waving and walked quickly to join him. He hoped the people in the room wouldn't notice, but it was too late. All of the media had turned their attention away from Quigley who continued to read his statement. They were completely focused on Windflower.

"What is it?" whispered Windflower.

"Snow is on the move," said Lundquist as quietly as he could. But by now all eyes were on the back of the room. Quigley stopped reading long enough to see Windflower and Lundquist race out through the door and into their cars. The next thing everybody in the room heard was cars screeching out of the parking lot. First, they ran to the windows to see what was happening, and then they turned their attention back to Quigley.

"What's going on?" one of them yelled. "Is there something happening?" called another. Soon the room was erupting in shouted questions. Quigley initially froze. Then he realized that if he didn't do or say something all these media people would not just steamroll him, but stampede out of the room and chase the police cars that were rapidly departing the parking lot.

"There's been a development," he started to say and then a little louder said, "Ladies and gentlemen, we have an open and on-going investigation that is unfolding right as we speak this morning. If you will be patient, I will try and answer your immediate questions. And I will stay here with you and be available to respond and give you more information as we receive it."

That settled the media pack down and they began to ask questions. Quigley looked over at Mayor Loder who smiled back at him. You got them right where you want them, his look seemed to say.

Chapter Sixty-two

While Quigley was dealing with the media and keeping them from both following and getting in the way, Windflower and Lundquist were hurtling towards the industrial park. Lundquist was there first and parked off the front entrance behind the front row of storage lockers. He had Smithson on the radio when Windflower pulled up beside him.

"We're tracking Snow's GPS and he's approaching the area," they heard Smithson say over the car's radio. "We heard from Pomeroy there are two others in the car with Snow. He's trailing close behind them. Over."

"Is Pomeroy on this channel too?" asked Windflower. "Over."

"Affirmative. Over," came the reply back from Pomeroy.

"Okay. Lundquist and I are near the entrance. As soon as we see them pass, we will approach on foot. Pomeroy, you and your guy block off the front and back entrances to the park. Confirm. Over."

"Confirmed," came the reply. "Over."

"Smithson, you and Daniels take up position behind their

storage locker now. Do you have your portable? Over."

"Affirmative. Moving towards there now. Over."

"Car approaching. It's them. Move into positions. Over."

Windflower grabbed his walkie-talkie and he and Lundquist sprinted towards Snow's locker. They had just turned the corner when they saw the car parked out in front and Snow putting the key into the lock. They saw him push the door open and walk in, followed by his associates.

"Go. Go. Go," shouted Windflower. He took his service weapon out of his holster and ran towards the locker door with Lundquist right behind him.

"Snow, hands up. Come out with your hands up," shouted Windflower.

You could hear muffled voices from inside the locker, and then shouts from behind.

"On the ground. On the ground," was what Windflower and Lundquist heard next. When they got there, Snow and his buddies were lying face down on the ground with Smithson and Daniels looking very contentedly at the prone bikers. They heard a car pull up out front and Lundquist went to check.

"It's Pomeroy," he said. "They're already starting to catalogue the loot."

"Cuff 'em and put them in the cars," said Windflower. The younger Mounties happily complied.

As Snow was getting to his feet he snarled at Windflower. "You still don't know who I am, do ya, pig?"

All the other RCMP officers looked at Windflower to see his reaction. Windflower looked back at Snow, looked him up and down, and then smiled. "You are a criminal, Mister Snow. And you are under arrest. These fine officers here will escort you to your jail cell and I suspect that it will be a long time, a very long time, before you get out of one again. So enjoy your day, and the rest of your life in jail."

With that, Windflower spun around and headed inside the

locker, leaving Joey Snow sputtering and stammering and cursing his way into the nearby cruiser. Inside the locker, Pomeroy and his partner from the drug squad were still oohing and aahing at their find.

"Must be at least eighteen kilos of cocaine and a ton of weed," said Pomeroy. "That's about two million bucks worth on the street."

"Hey, Sarge, look at this," said the other drug squad guy, pulling another old carpet off a stack of metal cabinets in a corner of the locker.

"It's the motherlode," said Pomeroy. Inside the cabinets were pills of all size, colour and description. "Wow," he said as he unveiled rows and rows and rows of pills, tablets and powders.

"What have we got?" asked Windflower.

"Ecstasy, crystal meth, speed, probably PCP, and every type of opiate and pharmaceutical you can think of," said Pomeroy. "This will put a hole in their operations and their wallets. There must be another million dollars' worth of stuff here."

"Have you got a camera?" asked Windflower.

"Go get it from the car," said Pomeroy to the other officer.

"Get all the pictures you want and then leave everything here, intact," said Windflower.

Pomeroy started to object. Windflower cut him off. "You stay here and guard all of this, but I think the public deserves to see the fruits of our labour. You can even be on T.V. if you want."

For the first time Windflower could remember, Pomeroy actually smiled. "That won't be necessary. Good job, Windflower," he said, as he offered his hand to the other RCMP officer.

Windflower shook it firmly. "Good job to you guys, too," he said. "Now, I'm going to call Inspector Quigley and give him the good news."

Chapter Sixty-three

Inspector Quigley was indeed glad to hear the news that was coming from the stakeout in the industrial park.

"We'll be sending the prisoners back in the next fifteen minutes, if you want to alert your friends in the media," said Windflower.

"They'll be delighted to hear that news," said Quigley. "I've almost had to put them under arrest to keep them here. I also like your idea about letting them film the stash that you uncovered. When do you think that could happen?"

"Give us a couple of hours to scan the scene first. But we can let them have a look sometime after lunch."

"Good," said Quigley. "I'll set it up for around 2 p.m. And I'll send somebody over with some sandwiches for you."

"Well, thank you, Inspector. That'll keep the troops happy," said Windflower.

"That's my job," said Quigley. "And Winston, congratulations on a great job out here. We could not have had this success without you."

"Thank you, Ron. As long as you let me go home by the

weekend, all will be forgiven. And of course, you still have to fix our staffing problems."

"I know, I know," said Quigley. "All in due time, my friend. Patience. 'Wisely, and slow. They stumble that run fast'."

"Very good, Ron. You've been practicing. But remember: 'Talking isn't doing... and yet words are not deeds'."

"Fair enough, Winston. I'll see you a bit later with my new friends from the media."

The scene at the industrial park grew more hectic and crowded during the next couple of hours. Pomeroy and his assistant catalogued the drug stash and laid it out so that the media could get a good look at it. Daniels and Smithson, under the supervision of Lundquist, scoured the interior of the locker. Then they photographed and dusted the contents for fingerprints and other evidence.

Fitzpatrick arrived with two large plates of sandwiches and a large thermos of coffee. This was a welcome break for all of the RCMP officers, and they enjoyed their food and coffee until the first media vehicles began to arrive. Windflower had arranged for a string of yellow police tape to keep the media out of the locker, which was now a crime scene. When Quigley arrived shortly afterwards he explained they could let the cameras in one at a time, followed by the still photographers. Lundquist organized this while Quigley was setting up, just outside the locker.

The media people were buzzing as they were led inside to take a peek at the drugs that the RCMP officers had organized. Standing next to the pile was Pomeroy, along with his associate, Wilson, from the drug squad. Pomeroy was pleased to point out the various narcotics, opiates and pharmaceuticals to the T.V. camera operators and reporters, who were equally pleased to photograph and record the drug supply for the evening news.

Quigley introduced the mayor, who gave a short speech expressing his gratitude to the RCMP, and pledging the town's cooperation to creating a safe and healthy environment for all of its citizens. Quigley then spoke of the work of all the RCMP officers involved in this initiative. Especially those of "B" Division, Newfoundland and Labrador, and that of the Grand Falls Detachment, led by Corporal Lars Lundquist. He also noted the active participation of the Atlantic Drug Task Force and its coordinator Sergeant Robert Pomeroy.

"But I also want to acknowledge the true leader of this whole operation, Sergeant Winston Windflower of the Grand Bank Detachment, who was loaned to this project. His leadership and courage under fire is very much appreciated by both the Force and by the town of Grand Falls," said Quigley. As he finished speaking these words, Mayor Loder went over to Windflower and offered his handshake. This would be the front page picture in all the newspapers the next day. "Thank you, Sergeant," said the mayor.

"It was my pleasure to serve," said Windflower as all of the other RCMP officers, and most of the media applauded.

There was still a lot to do at the scene after the media spotlight had dimmed and Windflower spent the rest of the afternoon there helping out. He got back into the office around 4 p.m. and was absolutely beat. All he wanted right now was a long hot bath and a nap. But first, there was a debriefing with Quigley and the rest of the crew. They ran through all of the day's activities and divided up responsibilities for the next phase. Windflower's job was to work with the Crown Attorney to finalize the case against Snow and his gang members. That would mean one more day in beautiful Grand Falls, and then he could go home. That was fine with him.

"I want to thank you all again for your hard work," said Quigley as he was wrapping up the session. "I've also got approval from Superintendent Majesky to take you all out to dinner. I hear there's roast beef on tonight at the hotel. So, bring your partner and meet us there around six-thirty."

Windflower could have done without a commitment this evening, but he knew this was important for morale and team-building. At least he could get a nap in between. He was on his way out of the building when the receptionist flagged him down.

"Sergeant, have you got a sec?"

"Sure," said Windflower.

"Well, we've done some talking and we'd like to have some media and community relations training," said Lynn. "We already do some of that work, and we think we could do more if we had a bit of training."

"That sounds like a great idea. Let me go talk to the Inspector now."

Windflower walked back into the command centre where Quigley was talking to Lundquist. "Got a minute, Inspector?" he asked.

Lundquist left to check on the prisoners and to help Daniels get organized for the evening. Someone would have to stay and guard the fort and the crew in back. Daniels had drawn the short straw.

"Lynn and the other admin people are looking for some training. They're thinking a mini-conference with a focus on media and community relations. I told her I'd bring it forward. You should know that Betsy, and I bet, Louise in your office, are already onto this."

"I'll see what I can do," said Quigley.

"That would be good. Just remember that hell hath no fury like a woman or an admin person scorned," said Windflower.

"That's not Shakespeare," said Quigley.

"No, some obscure English poet, I think. But the sentiment fits, don't you think? And if I could make another suggestion, I might invite Lynn and her husband to dinner tonight. That might make your life easier too."

With that, Windflower left the command centre and headed back to the hotel. As he was leaving, he could see Quigley coming to the reception area for a chat with Lynn. Good man, he thought. You saved yourself and everybody else a whole lot of grief.

Chapter Sixty-four

A long soak in the tub helped. A lot. After that, Windflower closed the curtains in his room, turned off all the lights and crawled under the covers in his bed. He was out cold, almost instantly and fell into such a deep sleep that he didn't know where he was, or what that ringing noise was in his ears. Then he realized it was his cell phone.

"Windflower," he answered groggily.

"How's the hero of the hour?" asked Sheila. "I saw you on the news shaking hands with the mayor of Grand Falls."

"That's Harris Loder. Second-best mayor in the province."

"Good answer," said Sheila. "It sounds like you had a successful day out there."

"It went really well. We got a few of the bad guys, very bad guys in fact. And we certainly put a crimp into their business plan."

"That was a lot of drugs I saw on the T.V.," said Sheila. "Are all those drugs coming into this province?"

"Some of them. But most of it was being circulated back out. We had kind of a drug distribution centre happening out here."

"Wow," said Sheila. "Is that the end of it then?"

"Unfortunately, no. This is kind of like fighting wildfires in a very dry and windy season. You put one fire out, and it pops up somewhere else. But I think this community might get a break from the work we've done. As long as they're willing to work with us."

"I guess that's where the Mayor and Council come in," said Sheila.

"Yeah. And I think Mayor Loder is going to push them to make that happen."

"Good news all around then," said Sheila. "When are you coming home?"

"Probably the day after tomorrow. I've got to close some things off with the Crown, and then I'll very happily be coming home."

"More good news," said Sheila. "Oh, I saw Uncle Frank this morning. He said to say hi."

"Oh, and what's he been up to?" asked Windflower.

"I don't know," said Sheila. "He said he had an appointment with Eddie Tizzard. Wouldn't say any more."

"Now that's an interesting pair. I wonder what they're up to."

"I guess you'll have to ask them when you get back," said Sheila. "Anyway, I have to go. I've got a special committee meeting tonight. The safety inspectors want to close the theatre building. So we have to find some more money for renovations."

"Good luck with that. If I know you, you probably already have a plan. Or know where to get the money. That's the way I like my elected officials. Brainy and beautiful too."

Sheila laughed. "Always the charmer, Winston Windflower. But keep it up. Flattery will get you everywhere."

"That is my fervent hope. Bye, Sheila."

Windflower put on a clean shirt and his jeans and walked to the restaurant in the hotel. Quigley had arranged for a small private room for their group, and Windflower was one of the last to arrive. He met all the partners and spouses and got a special introduction to Lynn's husband.

"Bob, this is the nice Sergeant I was telling you about," said Lynn.

"Nice to meet you," said Windflower as he shook the man's hand. "Glad you could come."

Dinner was about to be served and Quigley had ordered carafes of red wine that everybody was sipping. While the soup was being served Quigley stood and offered a toast to the crew that had made this investigation so successful. Everyone drank and toasted each other. After the soup came a delicious salad with fresh greens and a tart vinaigrette dressing. Then came the main course: roast beef and Yorkshire pudding with ginger carrots, mashed potatoes, and tureens of gravy to pour over everything.

Windflower hadn't realized how hungry he was until he saw the large piece of roast beef on his plate. It looked perfect, with a slight ring of brown around the edges, moving pinker to bright red at its core. He was in heaven at the first bite.

He chatted with Lynn and her husband, Bob, throughout the meal. Or rather he and Bob listened to Lynn talk non-stop. He followed Bob's lead and smiled and nodded at everything she said.

He didn't think he could eat dessert, but that was until he saw what it was. Dessert that evening was a speciality of the house, a British bread and butter pudding. Windflower had eaten it one time before at the Stoodleys. Herb made it from an old family recipe in which slices of buttered bread are scattered with raisins, covered with an egg custard mixture and then baked in the oven. Stoodley's recipe added nutmeg and some other spices. The one tonight had some of those spices and a touch of vanilla, and was served with a large dollop of fresh cream. After that, Windflower was so full he could barely sip his coffee.

Some of the gang was headed to the bar at the other side of the hotel for Karaoke Night, but Windflower decided to take a pass on that. He wasn't much of a singer and his recollection of previous such events was that you had to be able to sing, or be very drunk, to fully appreciate the entertainment. He said he was going for a walk and Ron Quigley decided to join him.

"Man, I am so full," said Quigley as the two men went outside.

"Me, too. Stuffed."

They walked around the building and found one of the little paths that ran down towards the river. The moonlight on this clear evening made it easy to see their way. It was a warm night, even muggy, and Windflower noticed there was no wind, not even a breeze. That was unusual. One thing about Newfoundland weather is that it was entirely unpredictable. The other thing was that there was always a wind of some sort. Always. Yet tonight the air was still and calm.

"It's muggy," he said to Quigley.

"Yeah, sometimes it's like that out this way," said Quigley. 'It must be because we're so far inland. Usually in Newfoundland we're by the water. It's always windy in St. John's."

"Grand Bank too," said Windflower.

"Speaking of Grand Bank I have some news for you," said Quigley.

"Good news or bad news?" asked Windflower.

"Oh ye of little faith," said Quigley with a laugh. "I think I have a plan to keep Tizzard in the area. At least for a while."

"What does that mean?" asked Windflower.

"I've talked to Majesky and he's agreed to let me hire a second-in-command. We've always had one in Marystown and he will let me have Tizzard, on a six-month trial."

"That's great news for you, but how does it help me?" asked Windflower.

"Here's the deal," said Quigley. "Tizzard can stay in Grand Bank and come over when I need him, probably a day or so a week. Or when I want him for special projects. You can have him the rest of the time."

"Okay. I'll take it. But we're still down a man, or a woman."

"I'm going to transfer Smithson into Grand Bank," said Quigley.

"You get your man and I get somebody in the area who can help me figure out this blasted new computer system."

"That's not bad either. I could certainly use some help in that area as well. You're good at this stuff, Inspector Quigley."

Quigley laughed. "I'm not good, just a little lucky, my friend."

"Well, I hope your luck holds out," said Windflower.

Quigley laughed again. "'Good luck is often with the man who doesn't include it in his plans'."

This time it was Windflower's turn to laugh, and he clapped his friend on the back as they continued on their walk. They followed the path to the river and then turned back towards the hotel. When they reached the door, Windflower said goodnight and headed inside. Quigley continued on. He was going to join the revelries at the club. That was okay for him, Windflower thought. He had heard Quigley sing before. He was quite good. But Windflower was quite content to call it a night. He turned on the baseball game, but didn't last more than an inning before he felt his eyes start to close. He crawled under the covers again, and was soon fast and contentedly asleep.

Chapter Sixty-five

When he awoke, Windflower felt completely refreshed. That was good, he thought. No, it was better than good, it was great! He jumped out of bed and made a cup of coffee. He pulled open the curtains to check out the morning. It was a beautiful day and a grand day to be alive. He drank his coffee while watching the birds flirt with each other in a nearby tree.

He grabbed his medicines and smudge kit and found the same path that he and Quigley had followed the night before. For Windflower, this morning's ritual was all about gratitude. He gave thanks for the sun and the morning and for Mother Nature and the river, and for Sheila and their present and future life together. He offered thanks for the safe way in which everyone had come through the past few days and for Tizzard's continuation in Grand Bank. He thought about praying for another, longer extension. Instead, he smiled and resisted the urge.

He was still smiling when he got back to his room and drained the second cup of coffee. He cleaned up, dressed and walked to the dining room for breakfast. He must have still been smiling because

Ron Quigley smiled back at him from across the room.

"You look happy this morning," said Quigley.

"Gratitude. I like to show it. In fact, 'it's a sign of mediocrity when you demonstrate gratitude with moderation'."

"That's not Shakespeare, is it?" asked Quigley.

"Roberto Benigni. Let me get some food and I'll join you." A few minutes later he was back with a large plate of scrambled eggs, bacon and toast with jam. He and Quigley enjoyed the morning and their breakfast in the quiet comfort of friends.

"How was the karaoke last night?" asked Windflower when they had finished eating.

"It was fun," said Quigley. "I did my usual, Blue Suede Shoes, and then called it a night. The young guys were still going pretty strong when I left."

Windflower had heard Quigley's Elvis. It was actually pretty good. "Speaking of young guys… Have you talked to Tizzard yet?" Windflower asked.

"I talked to Smithson last night. He's pretty happy to go to Grand Bank, seemed excited about working with you. But I thought you might want to give Tizzard the news yourself."

"Thanks, Ron. I'll call him this morning. When are you heading back?" asked Windflower.

"I'm going to stop by the detachment and hit the road afterwards," said Quigley.

"Okay. I'm going to give Sheila a call and then I'll see you over there."

Quigley went to check out and Windflower headed to his room to make his call.

"Good morning, beautiful," said Windflower when Sheila answered the phone.

"If you could see me, you might not think that right at this moment," said Sheila. "I just got out of bed. But I take all compliments gladly. You seem in a good mood this morning."

"Why not?" asked Windflower. "I have a good life, a good job and most importantly the love of a good woman."

"Thank you. I think," said Sheila. "As long as you're part of mine, I'm happy and grateful too. But is there anything that you are especially happy about this morning?"

"Tizzard is going to be staying in Grand Bank, at least for a few more months, longer if I can swing it. And we've got a new guy coming in, a whiz with computers and technology," said Windflower.

"That's great news about Eddie. I'll make sure to congratulate him when I see him," said Sheila.

"Er, hang on for a little while on that. I got the news from Ron Quigley, but I haven't talked to Tizzard yet. He's next on my list."

"Anyway, that's all good news. Maybe the RCMP can get its operation back on a full schedule again too," said Sheila.

"Absolutely. We'll be out there patrolling the highways and byways and keeping the roads safe for man and moose."

"Speaking of moose, your Inspector and I have a plan ready for you to implement when you get back," said Sheila. "We've got the Highways people on board and the new reduced speed signs are being done up in Marystown at the new office there."

"That's great," said Windflower, still feeling a little bit perturbed. But he wasn't going to let it get in the way of enjoying this fine morning.

"We're thinking about calling the area where the pilot is taking place, Windflower Way," said Sheila.

"What?" asked Windflower.

"Ron told me it was your idea," said Sheila. "He said you were too modest to tell me yourself. I thought that was quite cute."

He was going for smart, even intelligent, but cute it was. He'd take it. "All in a day's work," he replied.

"Anyway, I hope you continue to have a wonderful day, Winston. I can't wait til you get home. Call me tonight if you get a chance," said Sheila.

"I will. Love you," said Windflower. This will be a wonderful day, he thought, as he put his things together and drove to the RCMP offices. It already is.

Quigley was saying goodbye to Lynn when Windflower came in. He said good morning to the receptionist, wished his Inspector a safe journey, and walked to the command centre at the back.

It was quiet so far this morning. The rest of the gang must have had a late night. Windflower picked up the phone and called Grand Bank.

"Good morning, Sergeant," said Betsy when she answered. "How are you this grand morning?"

"It must be just as nice there as it is here in Grand Falls. I am feeling great this morning, thank you very much, Betsy. Would Corporal Tizzard be around?"

"One moment, sir," said Betsy. True to her word, Tizzard was soon on the line.

"Morning, Boss, what's up?" said Tizzard.

"How would you like to stay in Grand Bank?" asked Windflower.

"I would love that," said Tizzard. "But how can that happen?"

"Inspector Quigley is prepared to offer you a six-month assignment as his assistant. You can work out of Grand Bank and go over to Marystown, maybe a day a week. Or work on special projects if they come up," said Windflower.

"Wow," said Tizzard. "That would be great."

"I take it that's a yes," said Windflower.

"Yes, yes, yes!!" said Tizzard. "Thank you, Sarge. That's the best news I've had all week, maybe all year."

"Great. For now, continue what you're doing. When I get back we'll sit down and sort out who does what. Oh, and we've got a new assignee. Rick Smithson is coming in from the west coast. He's a good guy, handy with technology."

"Perfect," said Tizzard. "You are full of good news today."

"This is a good day, Corporal. I plan to enjoy it to the fullest. One more day to clean up stuff around here, and tomorrow night I'll be sleeping in my own bed. Assuming that my uncle hasn't given away my bed to anybody else. How is Uncle Frank by the way? I hear you've been hanging around with him."

"Uncle Frank has been a great help to me," said Tizzard. "I was talking to him one day about a few things that were bothering me. And he's helping me to analyse my dreams. He's a master dream weaver. Did you know that?"

"I did know that, as a matter of fact. So what did you figure out about your dreams?"

"Well, I'm still working on them with Uncle Frank. But I had one where I'm in a fire and can't get out," said Tizzard.

"That's very interesting," said Windflower, not mentioning his own dreams involving Tizzard and the fire. "What did Uncle Frank tell you that meant?"

"He said I was probably playing with fire or danger in some part of my life," said Tizzard. "I'm still thinking about that."

"Maybe you're supposed to slow down when you're driving," said Windflower with a small chuckle.

"I don't think that's what it means," said Tizzard. "Uncle Frank didn't say anything about slowing down. And he's the expert."

"He is indeed," said Windflower, this time with a sigh. "I'll see you tomorrow."

Chapter Sixty-six

Windflower was making a fresh pot of coffee when Lars Lundquist came out of the area where the cells were located.

"Morning," said Lundquist.

"Good morning. How's your head this morning?"

"I'm good," said Lundquist. "I didn't drink too much. I had to come in on relief after midnight. I'm tired, but another cup of java will get me through the morning. Then I'm off for a few days."

"Good for you. I can't remember the last day I had off. I don't think these jobs are built like that. I can't wait to get home and see my woman and my dog."

"I hear she's a great lady and Mayor of Grand Bank," said Lundquist. "How do you make that work?"

"Separation of church and state, at least police and politics. As much as we can, anyway. And it seems to go better the less I have to say."

Lundquist laughed. "I know the feeling. Every time I venture into anything even remotely political, it almost always blows up on me. I'm much better at playing the strong and silent type."

Windflower laughed too. "I'm going over to the industrial park to make sure everything is okay. I was thinking we should probably do a more thorough search at the clubhouse too, maybe tear the place apart and see what turns up. Can you check in again with the judge and confirm we're still good on the warrant?"

"No problem," said Lundquist. "Smithson is out at the park. I'll talk to the judge and round everybody up for early this afternoon to go over to the clubhouse. We'll probably need a posse. Let me know when you're done over at the industrial park."

"Okay. I'm going over now."

Windflower walked to the front and stopped to talk to the receptionist on his way out. "Can you confirm when the Crown Attorney is coming by today? You can call my cell phone when you hear something."

"Yes, sir," said Lynn. "Thanks for being nice to my husband last night. He's a bit shy in these social functions. He said you were a grand man."

"Thank you, Lynn," said Windflower, not really sure what to say in response to that, so he tipped his hat and left for the industrial park.

Smithson and Ezekial were busy loading boxes of stuff from the storage locker into the panel van when Windflower arrived. The drugs were long gone, taken by Pomeroy and his guys to a secure location, and they had left Grand Falls to return to the west coast.

"What are you finding?" asked Windflower.

"We found cases of ammunition, some dynamite and blasting caps, and loot from at least three robberies that the locals were investigating," said Ezekial.

"This box here is all watches, from a smash and grab job at the jewelry store in the mall," said Smithson. "We already took one load back to the shop with computers and other tech stuff that we know is from another break-in."

"Wow. You had a real crime wave going on. You guys will be heroes for finding all this stuff."

"Some people will be pretty happy," said Ezekial. "The stores all have insurance, but we've got a year's worth of petty robberies in here. Corporal Lundquist said we'll have a public viewing of the leftover stuff. Anyone who can prove they own any of it can have it back."

"Then they'll auction the rest off for charity," said Smithson.

"But that'll happen after we get back," said Ezekial. "At least after I go back."

"Yeah, you're coming to Grand Bank," said Windflower to Smithson. "How do you feel about that?"

"I'm looking forward to it," said Smithson. "My great-grand-father was from around the area. He's from Garnish. He was a skipper on one of the fishing schooners. He ended up moving to Boston and my family kind of drifted around after that."

"Garnish is a lovely little town. You'll be coming in time for the annual bakeapple festival."

"That's great," said Smithson. "I love baked apples."

Windflower thought about explaining the difference between bakeapples and baked apples, but realized that he didn't have that kind of time. Nor the words to fully explain what a bakeapple was, or what it tasted like, so he just smiled. "We're going back to the clubhouse later on and we'll need you. Someone will call. Okay?"

"Okay," said both of the RCMP constables.

"Looks like you've got things well under control here," he said as he got back into his cruiser to go to the detachment. His cell phone rang. It was Lynn.

"Paul Fowler will be here in about an hour," said Lynn.

"Thanks. I'm on my way back."

Crown Attorney Paul Fowler was sitting in the command centre talking to Lundquist when he got back.

"Sergeant, good to see you again," said Fowler. "It looks like we've finally got Snow nailed."

"I hope so. From a police perspective I think we've done all we can. Now it's up to the justice side."

"Corporal Lundquist and I have a list of preliminary charges against the others involved in this case ready to go. But I wanted to talk to you about Snow," said Fowler.

"What are the options?" asked Windflower.

Fowler opened a file labeled 'Snow' and scanned his notes. "We've got a great case on the narcotics and controlled substances. In addition to the video we have his name and signature on the rental of the storage locker. It seems dumb that he would leave a trail like that, but it's good for us."

"Maybe he didn't trust anybody else with it. Paranoia is a great motivator."

"Anyway, we'll take it. Now the question is which of the murders do we want to go after him on?" asked the Crown Attorney.

"We have him on tape shooting the Moose," said Windflower. "I'm not sure we can prove his involvement in the rest. The only way might be if Carol Jackson testified to that fact, or if you could get one of his henchmen to roll over."

"The lower guys are not likely going to talk," said Lundquist. "We have little to offer them. They know they'll get looked after if they get sent inside. Truth is, very few of them actually want to go straight."

"Can you talk to your Superintendent in Halifax and see if we can get to Jackson?" asked Fowler.

"No problem. I'll call him right now." Windflower walked out of the room, picked up his phone and dialed Majesky's number, but no answer. He left a message and went back in. "No luck, but I left a message. I'll have to get back to you."

"No worries," said Fowler. "We can charge him with the one murder for now. I'll show the judge the tape at the bail hearing. Snow is not getting out of jail anytime soon."

"I guess we should be thinking about transferring him to a more secure location," said Lundquist. "Maybe you can talk to Majesky about that as well. We can hold him, but you never know what the bikers would do."

"And have done in other areas. They break out their guys all the time in Quebec. I'll check with Majesky about that too."

"Okay, we're good for now," said Fowler. "Thanks for your help, Sergeant."

"Thank you. It's been nice to work with you as well."

Fowler left and Lundquist went to see the judge to get their search warrant updated. He asked Windflower to work with Fitzpatrick to put together everything for their trip back to the clubhouse.

Chapter Sixty-seven

There was a lot to do. Fitzpatrick laid out all the bullet-proof vests and charged up the walkie-talkies. Windflower checked out the Colt and the other rifles and loaded them up. Just in case. They also got out the noise grenade launcher, and found the tear gas canisters. Also, just in case. Fitzpatrick called Smithson and Ezekial to come and join them and by the time they got there, Daniels had come into work as well. They all had their vests on and were ready to go when Lundquist arrived a few minutes later.

"Ready?" asked Windflower.

Lundquist waved a paper in his hands. "We're good to go."

Windflower and Fitzpatrick went together in the lead car, with Lundquist and Daniels following close behind.

Ezekial and Smithson trailed in the white panel van. When they arrived at the laneway that led to the biker's clubhouse, Windflower got them to park the van across the entrance to block it off. And to wind their way through the woods to seal off the back of the clubhouse as well.

Windflower took the Colt and handed Fitzpatrick the launcher,

326 • Mike Martin

getting her to load up a noise grenade. Then he led the four remaining officers up the laneway. When they got near the top, Windflower immediately noticed the door to the clubhouse was open. He motioned to Fitzpatrick to lay down the launcher and to take out her weapon. He cocked his rifle and turned off the safety. He then started moving slowly but deliberately forward.

He whispered into his walkie-talkie, "Movin' in." He got Fitzpatrick and Daniels to flank him on either side and said to Lundquist. "After me."To the others he said, "You follow, right away, as soon as I'm in. But nobody shoots until I call it. Got it?"

All three other officers nodded. Windflower walked right up to the door and yelled "RCMP" as loudly as he could. "Come out now. Hands over your head!" he shouted.

There was a rustle of movement inside the house and then hushed voices. The bikers inside were thinking about their next move. This was always the hardest moment, Windflower thought, because you didn't know how high or how desperate the people inside might be. Anything could happen. Then he heard shouting from the back, which meant that at least some of the bikers were trying the alternative exit.

Windflower could also hear voices yelling at them to "Get down, down on the ground." Then just before the moment of truth, when Windflower would have to lead the RCMP officers in through the open front door to whatever fate lay there, the other bikers starting walking out the front door. They knew the drill and had their hands over their heads and were starting to lie on the ground even as the police officers were yelling at them to do so.

There were three bikers in various states of dress and distress lying on the ground when Ezekial and Smithson came around the corner leading two more handcuffed gang members in front of them.

"Can you take them all in the van?" asked Windflower pointing to the other bikers lying on the ground.

"No problem, Sergeant," said Ezekial.

"Okay. Search them here and get them all cuffed up. Then bring them back and put them all in the drunk tank. One of you stay and keep them company, and the other come back here to help."

Minutes later, the bikers were being loaded into the panel van and were on their way to jail with Ezekial and Smithson. Fitzpatrick had a video camera and was starting to walk through the clubhouse, recording everything before they began the search. For the next couple of hours, the police officers combed through the mess and disarray that the bike gang had created as their special hangout.

Not surprisingly, they found fewer weapons and drugs since their last visit. It was as if the bikers had been expecting a return visit from their friends at the police department. There was a minimal amount of marijuana and a small baggie of what Windflower suspected would turn out to be cocaine. The other officers took the serial numbers off each of the large screen T.V.s that were scattered around the place, in case some of them might be stolen. But there was very little to show for their efforts.

It was a little disappointing, Windflower had to admit to himself. He was ready to pack it in for the day when Fitzpatrick shouted out to him. "Sarge, I think I found something."

"I was walking over this area a few minutes ago and noticed that the rug had a corner pulled up," said the female constable. "Look what's underneath it."

Windflower ran over as she started pulling on a metal ring. It lifted part of the floor up to reveal a secret passageway with steps leading down below the surface. He took out his flashlight and shined it down the hole. "Let's go see what we've got."

Windflower walked carefully down the steps and noticed a string hanging from the ceiling. He pulled on it and the light bulb flicked on. There was shelving along one of the bare earth walls of what seemed to be a dug-out cellar. It kind of reminded him of the root cellars that he'd seen in old farmhouses out west. There was also a row of metal cabinets with combination locks on them.

Lundquist had followed Windflower down the steps and was now squinting to adjust his eyes to the brightness of the light bulb. Windflower pointed to the locks on the cabinets and Lundquist called up for someone to bring the metal cutters from the trunk of his car. While they were waiting, the two men walked towards the shelving on the wall. As they got closer, there was a glint of metal reflecting back towards Windflower's flashlight beam.

Windflower shone his flashlight up and down the shelves and then stared with his mouth wide open. Lundquist came and stood beside him, equally transfixed. On the shelves was the largest number of weapons that they had ever seen outside of an armoury. There were sawed-off shotguns, brand new high-powered assault rifles, at least ten of the same fully automatic MAC 10 machine pistols they found in the original raid, and dozens of other hand-guns of every calibre imaginable. And enough ammunition for these weapons to last a month.

On other shelves were tear gas canisters and some of the same noise grenades that the RCMP officers had put in the back of their car, along with an assorted selection of what were commonly known as street weapons. These included an assortment of knives, brass knuckles, mace and bear spray, thirteen stun guns, two pistol crossbows and a baseball bat that had about ten large nails pro-truding from its end.

"This is amazing," said Lundquist.

"They were certainly capable of creating havoc. It could be to defend themselves. Or maybe they were even getting ready for war."

Daniels came down the steps with the metal cutters. He held them out to Windflower with his mouth also now completely wide open.

Windflower took the shears and snipped the first cabinet open. He shone his flashlight inside to see row upon row of clear plastic bags containing a white powder. He went quickly to the second and cracked the lock. Then the third. Each metal cabinet was full of exactly the same thing. Row upon row of bags of white powder.

The other two officers had followed his actions and were now standing behind him. Windflower couldn't even hear their breathing.

"Okay. Let's seal this place up tight. We'll need the experts for this one." He led his fellow officers back up the steps and motioned to everyone to step outside. "This is now a major crime scene," he started. "Fitzpatrick, I want you to go downstairs and videotape the whole scene. Start a new tape." To Lundquist he said, "Don't move or touch anything until we get some direction. I'm going to talk to Inspector Quigley and see how he wants to handle this."

Chapter Sixty-eight

Windflower walked a little farther away and called Quigley's cell phone.

"Winston, how are you?" asked Quigley.

"We've discovered the biker's arsenal and a large quantity of drugs at the clubhouse," said Windflower.

"I thought you already had their stash," said Quigley.

"I did too. But there are cabinets full of what looks like cocaine in an underground storage area."

"How much is there?" asked Quigley.

"I haven't got a clue. There's kilos. Lots and lots of kilos."

"Holy..." said Quigley.

"And enough guns and ammo to start a war. What should we do?"

"Lock it down tight for now. I'll talk to Majesky and get back to you," said Quigley.

"Okay, I'll wait to hear from you," said Windflower.

Windflower walked back into the clubhouse. "Okay," he said. "Everybody out. Corporal, I want to secure this building and then set up a security perimeter outside the entrance to this laneway. Nobody in or out of this location until we get further orders."

Lundquist nodded and led all the other officers out of the clubhouse. He posted Fitzpatrick at the front and Daniels at the back entrance. He would take the laneway until he could get relieved by Smithson and Ezekial. Windflower took a few moments to go downstairs and take one more look around. It was just as amazing a sight to see now as the first time.

How much money's worth of stuff was in here? He couldn't even get his head around that. How much trouble and chaos could all these drugs and all those weapons cause on the street? It was unimaginable. They hadn't won the war today, but this was a great day for the good guys, thought Windflower. A very great day.

Windflower hung around with Lundquist for a little while, and then headed back to the detachment. If he was going to leave today he had a lot to do, including a lot more of that dreaded paperwork. His one consoling thought was that he had Lynn to help him. Thank goodness for good admin people. The RCMP would be lost without them. He was slowly working his way through some of this with Lynn's patient guidance when his cell phone rang. It was Majesky.

"Good afternoon, Superintendent," said Windflower.

"Congratulations on your discovery," said Majesky. "It sounds like quite a haul. I'm sending down a major crime unit to do the investigation on the clubhouse, and Pomeroy is already on his way back. I phoned Lundquist to let him know."

"That's great," said Windflower.

"There'll be a major media conference on this once we get squared away," said Majesky. "It'll be another great chance for you to get some credit for all the work you've done."

"With all respect, sir, I'd prefer to go back to Grand Bank, if that's okay with you. I've already gotten enough praise for just doing my job. Maybe Corporal Lundquist and his guys could get the profile. They've been on the front line all this time. And they'll have to keep at it for quite a while longer."

"That's very good, Windflower. I like your humility," said Majesky. "I know that I have been a little hard on you through this thing. But I want you to also know that it's because I knew you could do better. And you proved me right."

"Thank you, sir, I appreciate that," said Windflower.

"We're always looking for men like you to move up in the ranks, Sergeant," said the Superintendent.

"I'm quite happy to be where I am. But thank you again."

"You called me earlier about Carol Jackson," said Majesky. "She is an interesting person, to say the least. But I think we're a little closer to the truth because of her. First of all, she's decided to come completely over to our side."

"I thought she was already working for us," said Windflower.

"She was. But she was also working on the side with the Outlaws, and trying to carve off another slice for herself with French," said Majesky.

"The Outlaws. Wasn't that who the first dead guy, Lundrigan, was with?"

"That's likely why he got killed as well," said Majesky. "As we piece things together he and Jackson were trying to take a portion of the trade away from Snow and Bacchus. French is another story altogether. He met Jackson when they were in Northern Ontario and she basically turned him to work for her."

"French brought the Moose in with him and they killed the first pair," said Windflower.

"Correct, at least we think that's what happened. French was ours, but he got off the Force a few years back. Tried some private security stuff and then contacted us about going undercover with the bikers. We knew he was working both sides but he was a private contractor, and he did bring in some small fish for Pomeroy and the drug crew," said Majesky.

"Snow then found out about some or all of this and whacked both the Moose and French?" asked Windflower.

334 • Mike Martin

"Yeah," said the Superintendent. "Although Jackson tells us Snow was particularly freaked about the woman getting shot. She said he still had a thing for her."

"Sounds like Jackson had a pretty good 'in' with Snow," said Windflower.

"That's what she tells us," said Majesky. "So we are going to try her out in court against Snow and Bacchus. In return for immunity from prosecution and a new identity, she will tell everything she knows about the inside workings of that notorious outlaw motorcycle gang."

"Wow. That will be quite a trial."

"Yes, indeed," said Majesky. "But that's also a long time away. In the meantime, I'm sending the chopper back over for Snow. We're going to move him into a more secure location. Can you arrange for that transfer and also let the Crown know that this case is moving up the line? I suspect he won't be disappointed."

"I'll do both of those things. Can I still go back to Grand Bank? I was hoping to leave tomorrow morning."

"Yes, you can," said Majesky. "Lundquist can handle it. He's a good man. I've got a recommendation from your Inspector to make him a Sergeant. What do you think?"

"Absolutely. He's solid."

"Okay, Sergeant," said Majesky. "If you change your mind about moving into management, let me know."

"Thank you again, sir. But I think I'm quite happy where I am right now."

After Majesky hung up, Windflower took a few moments to reflect on what he'd heard and everything that had happened in the last couple of days. A lot of it was foggy and felt almost unreal. What was real, however, was that he felt absolutely sure he was in the right place in his life, and in his career. And he was going home.

He felt a slight touch of sadness when he thought about Carol Jackson, but at this point she was the creator of her own destiny.

That feeling faded when he thought of the quote, 'Oh what a tangled web we weave, When first we practice to deceive'. Not Shakespeare, but not bad. And quite appropriate, considering the circumstances.

He almost bounced back into the room with Lynn and happily completed his required forms. He filled out and signed all of the papers that she presented. The rest of the day was a blur of people and helicopters and phone calls and media. But Windflower didn't just survive, he thrived and smiled throughout everything. A little after 6 p.m. he said goodnight to Lundquist, who was now capably running the command centre, and headed back to the hotel.

Chapter Sixty-nine

Windflower was fully and completely bagged. He knew he was physically tired, but when he stopped or slowed down, he could now feel his emotional weariness as well. He picked up some Chinese take-out on the way back. He also stopped at the front desk to check out and pay his bill, so that he could leave first thing in the morning.

In his room he ate his food without any real relish. Take-out food of any kind was starting to wear on him. He wished he was home and could just open a can of tomato soup. He made a pot of tea after dinner and turned on the T.V., but there was nothing, not even a baseball game on to watch. He picked up his Donna Leon book and that at least gave him the comfort or maybe the distraction he was seeking.

Two hours later he closed the book, completely satisfied. Brunetti had cracked another case and was heading home for dinner with his wife, Paola, and his children. Windflower wished he was too when his cell phone rang.

"Hello, Sheila," he said.

"Winston, are you okay? I saw the news. They're reporting there was a major seizure of drugs and guns out in Grand Falls," said Sheila.

"I'm fine. They're still processing the scene, but it looks like the bikers had enough weapons to fight a small war. Maybe even a big one."

"I'm glad you're coming back. Those are the kind of things that keep me awake at night," said Sheila.

"No need to worry. I'll be back tomorrow. Nothing like this happens in Grand Bank."

"Let's hope so," said Sheila. "We have enough trouble already. Speaking of trouble, is there any news on Carol?"

"In confidence, I can tell you she is safe and likely going to be a star witness for the Crown somewhere down the road. After that, it's unlikely any of us will ever see or hear from her again," said Windflower.

"I guess, given her lifestyle, that's the best that could be expected. I still feel sorry for her though. She'll always be poor little Carol to me," said Sheila.

"I understand," said Windflower.

"So are you in for the night?" asked Sheila.

"I am, but I wish I was there," said Windflower.

"Me too," said Sheila. "See you tomorrow. Call me when you get to Goobies, okay?"

"Goodnight, Sheila," said Windflower.

He turned the T.V. back on and found the Blue Jays game. He lasted until the sixth inning and then started to drift off. He had a short but very hot bath to ease his back and then jumped into bed. He didn't stir until his wake-up call came very early in the morning.

When he pulled back the blinds it was light, but it was also teeming rain. That meant a very short smudge under the over-hang out back and even shorter prayers. Mostly, it was thank you to everything and everybody, but I gotta-get-on-the-road-type prayers.

He grabbed an orange and a muffin and filled his thermos with coffee for the road. Half an hour later he was on the highway. Just after 9 a.m. he stopped at the gas pumps in Goobies. He went inside and got a ready-made breakfast sandwich and more coffee.

He ate his sandwich in his car in the parking lot while the rain beat a steady pattern on the roof of his police cruiser. Then he called Grand Bank. Betsy answered and seemed very happy to hear from him.

"It's good to hear from you, Sergeant. We missed you around here. Corporal Tizzard is very nice, but he's not you, sir."

"Thank you, Betsy. Is he there?" asked Windflower.

"One moment, please," said Betsy.

"Hi Sarge," said Tizzard. "I hear you had some exciting times out in Grand Falls. Can't wait to hear all about it from the hero of the hour."

"We were very fortunate that none of us got hurt. I'll fill you in when I get back. I'm in Goobies now and should be there before lunch. I'll come in for a few hours this afternoon. Then, if you can get by without me, I'd like to take a couple of days off. Maybe even go trout fishing. If the weather improves."

"My dad always said that rainy days were the best for fishing since there'd be no flies for the fish and no competition," said Tizzard. "Yeah, we can get by for a few more days without you. Things are actually pretty quiet around here."

"That's exactly what I wanted to hear," said Windflower as he hung up. He called Sheila and left a message on her cell phone that he was on his way and got back on the highway. He turned off to go down to the Burin Peninsula and put on the classical music station. This morning's concert was a Brahms piano quartet and it was perfect for the rainy day and Windflower's upbeat mood. He made a mental note to see if Herb Stoodley had any Brahms's CDs he could borrow. He was sure he would.

The music and the rain kept him company as he wound his

way south towards Swift Current. The rain also seemed to keep the moose away and Windflower didn't see one all the way along the highway. He passed through Marystown smoothly, despite the morning rush at Tim Hortons, and was safely at the RCMP detachment in Grand Bank just before noon.

He waved at Betsy who was on the phone when he came in, and found Tizzard in the back making some toast and peanut butter for a snack. He took a piece off the Corporal's plate and poured himself a cup of coffee.

"So what's new in Grand Bank, Eddie?" he asked.

"Well, I'm staying in for another few months, maybe longer, which is really good news for me. It also helps me with another decision."

"What's that?" asked Windflower as he munched his toast.

"Me and Carrie," said Tizzard. "We got involved, even though I knew we shouldn't. It was like Uncle Frank said, I was playing with fire. I could have put my career and hers too, at risk."

"So now that's she's there, and you're here, you can deal with that?" asked Windflower.

"Exactly," said Tizzard. "I'm a young soul. That's what Uncle Frank says. In my dream work he said the message was that I have to be careful with my fire, my internal emotional energy, because it might be fragile."

"Fragile?" asked Windflower, a little incredulously. "Where is Uncle Frank anyway?"

"Oh, didn't you know?" asked Tizzard. "He's gone back home. He said he'd leave you a note at your house."

"I thought he was staying for a while, until the wedding," said Windflower.

"Nope," said Tizzard, buttering up another piece of toast. "He had a bit of a falling out with Jarge. Jarge apparently said he wasn't as much fun when he wasn't drinking. Uncle Frank told him that a real friend wouldn't say that. He thought he was plenty fun without the booze. I told him I agreed."

"He's a lot more fun and a lot less trouble without the booze. But it's too bad he's gone. I wanted to talk to him about a few things."

"Was it about dreams?" asked Tizzard. "Because if it was, maybe I could help you out."

"No thanks, Corporal. Did Uncle Frank even suggest you might be driving too fast and should be slowing down? Maybe that was how you were playing with fire?"

"No," said Tizzard, quite seriously. "That didn't come up."

Windflower shook his head at Tizzard and went back out to see Betsy who had the obligatory stack of files for him to consider. He spent a couple of hours going through them and did his absolute best to move his part of the RCMP paperwork mountain along. Shortly after 4 p.m., Sheila called and invited him to dinner. He was very glad to accept.

He drove over to Sheila's about an hour later and was greeted warmly by the main ladies in his life. Sheila gave him a marvellous welcome home hug and Lady wouldn't leave his side. He could smell something absolutely delicious in the kitchen, but couldn't get past the collie to explore the aroma. Instead, he smiled at Sheila, grabbed his raincoat off the hook, and went back outside with Lady.

They walked slowly, but happily, through the many puddles and wandered all over town. On the way back, they came up to the end of Seaview Drive. Windflower almost didn't want to walk up that way, so strong were his memories of the dreams about that place. But when they turned the corner, Windflower got a pleasant surprise. There was a 'Sold' sign on the small front lawn, and scaffolding on the back of the house. The new owners were wasting no time in fixing the broken clapboard and putting in new windows.

Maybe that meant things were being repaired and restored inside him as well, thought Windflower. That was a pleasant thought and if his stomach hadn't started to grumble he might have been content to stand and look at the once nearly destroyed house now being rebuilt in front of him. But Sheila, and that delicious smell from her kitchen, called him back to reality.

He came back in and dried off Lady as best as he could. She finished the job with a vigorous shake that sent a spray everywhere. But nothing could dampen Windflower and Sheila's mood at being reunited.

"It's fish, but it smells like curry too. What is it?"

"Sit down and pour the wine," said Sheila.

Windflower took the bottle of Riesling out of the fridge, got the wine goblets and poured them each a glass. He sat down expectantly at the kitchen table.

"It's Arctic char with a curry sauce," said Sheila. "One of the councillors was up north in Nain and he picked up some char for everybody. This is our share," she said as she laid a thick fish steak on Windflower's plate. She poured an extra ladleful of the curry sauce over the fish and the aroma rose in Windflower's nostrils. He almost felt drunk, it was so spicy and powerful. He took a moment, but only a moment, to savour that experience. Then he took a forkful of the fish.

"Perfect," he said. "This is perfect."

Sheila scooped up a large spoonful of risotto from another pan and added it to his plate along with some steamed broccoli. Then she took a smaller portion for herself and sat to watch Windflower eat. For her, this was pure entertainment. To see how much enjoyment and pleasure her guy, her man, got out of his food, was absolute joy to her.

As usual, there was little commentary from Windflower, other than what sounded like doves cooing, until he had finished his main course, and then his second helping.

"That was great, Sheila, absolutely great. I didn't know you made curry. I haven't had curry since the last time I was over at Doc Sanjay's."

"That's where I got the curry recipe," said Sheila. "Repa was kind enough to give me her family recipe and some of the last of her Bengali curry paste."

"That was the sharp tang I tasted. It burns your mouth a little, but it's so worth it. And the risotto was so smooth and tasty." Windflower went over and gave her a hug and a kiss on the cheek.

"You better be capable of more than that. Although it was pretty nice," said Sheila. "And Moira sent you a little welcome home gift too. It's in the fridge."

Windflower went to the fridge and knew that the small white cardboard box was his surprise. He opened it and looked longingly at a large piece of chocolate peanut butter cheesecake. He almost cried with delight. He offered to share it with Sheila, but she happily, for him, declined. He ate it as slowly as he could, but that wasn't very long. Afterwards, he sighed with satisfaction.

"I am so happy to be home and to be with you," said Windflower as Sheila cleaned the dishes and made them some tea. "'My crown is called content, a crown that seldom kings enjoy'."

"'I believe that the golden age is before us not behind us,'" said Sheila in response.

"You've been practicing," said Windflower.

"I had to do something while you were out gallivanting around the countryside," said Sheila. "Now come upstairs and show me how much you really missed me."

Windflower certainly did not need to be asked twice.

Chapter Seventy

A few months later...

It was Friday morning and Windflower had a jump in his step, and a broad smile for everyone he met in the sleepy little hamlet of Grand Bank. Summer was a distant memory and autumn was starting to bleed into early winter. It wasn't frosty yet, but late October could, and would, bring a range of precipitation. Anything from cold, hard rain to sleet. Even a major dump of the white stuff could happen at any moment. But the coolness in the air did not dampen Windflower's enthusiasm. Tomorrow, he and Sheila Hillier were going to be married.

It had been a long summer for both of them and they were looking forward to getting a break after the wedding. Sheila and Windflower had booked a cabin at Rocky Harbour in Gros Morne National Park. The pair had been there before, and were excited about hiking, and maybe even snow-shoeing on the many trails in the park if there was any snow in that northern part of Newfoundland.

Windflower was almost finished being a witness at the last of a series of trials in Grand Falls. There was one more trial to go, that of the ringleader, Joey Snow, but that would be in Halifax some months, or maybe even a year, down the road. The whole crew in Grand Falls had received acknowledgement from the top brass for their work on this case. Windflower himself received a Commissioner's Commendation for Outstanding Service at a special ceremony in Halifax. He planned to wear his new medallion on his red serge dress uniform for the wedding.

Sheila had a busy fall as well. She had run successfully for re-election as Mayor of Grand Bank and had just finished the planning session with the new Council to set out their goals and objectives for the next four years. That included continuing to preserve as much of the past history and glory as they could, while helping to build a new economy and infrastructure for the future. It was a big job, but Sheila was excited for the challenge these new opportunities presented to her and to the community.

She was coming out of the Mug-Up Café as Windflower was coming in. The pair embraced and had a quick hello before setting off on their daily routines. Last night Sheila had a mini-shower with her lady friends, and Windflower got together with some of his buddies. It was a quiet affair for each of them. A few glasses of wine for Sheila, and some Scotch tasting for Windflower and a few of his close friends at Doc Sanjay's house.

Tonight might be their last night apart for a long time, Windflower thought, as he watched his beautiful lady walk away. He was drinking his coffee and still thinking about Sheila when Eddie Tizzard came into the café.

"Morning, Sarge," said Tizzard. "Are you getting nervous yet?"

"'To fear the worst, oft cures the worst'," said Windflower. When Tizzard looked confused he added, "I'm looking forward to getting married."

Tizzard still looked puzzled, but decided to soldier on anyway. "I saw Uncle Frank at the wharf this morning. He really fits in around here, doesn't he?"

"Frank can fit in anywhere. He has a great personality."

"I met your Auntie Marie yesterday too," said Tizzard. "She's a sweetheart."

"My Auntie is great too. That reminds me. I have to take her over to Marystown. She wants to go to Walmart, of all places."

"The evil empire?" said Tizzard in mock horror, knowing how much Windflower detested the giant retailer, mostly because it often put local shops out of business.

Windflower almost bit, but then he saw the grin spreading across Tizzard's face. "I'll see you later, Eddie."

"Bye, Sarge," said Tizzard. "I think I'll have a little snack before I head back to work."

Windflower went outside to his car and drove to his small house in the centre of town. He picked up his Auntie Marie and soon they were driving along the highway outside of Grand Bank for the forty-minute ride to Marystown. Windflower liked his Auntie a lot. She had been like his mother for many years after his own mother had passed on. She was also part of his touchstone; a connection with his community in Pink Lake, and with his Cree culture and heritage.

He also liked that she was calm and peaceful and quiet. So many things and people in this world were noisy and loud, and more than a little irritating. His Auntie Marie had a solidity to her serenity, and a peace of mind that Windflower craved for himself. The two of them made great travelling companions as they drove in silence almost all of the way to Marystown. Just before they got there, his Auntie sighed. "I am very disappointed, Winston," she said.

"Why is that, Auntie? Did I do something wrong?" asked Windflower.

"Where are all the moose people keep talking about?" asked Auntie Marie. "Frank said the roads were filthy with them. But we haven't seen one yet."

Windflower laughed. "I think the word people use for the moose is 'maggoty'," he said. "Don't worry. If you are around here long enough, I guarantee you will see a moose. Here's your stop," he said, as he pulled into the Walmart parking lot.

"When will you come back and get me?" asked his aunt.

"I'm going to get a coffee at Tim Hortons, and I'll come back in an hour. Would that be okay?"

Auntie Marie nodded her agreement and walked into the store while Windflower drove over to the nearby coffee shop. It was surprisingly quiet, and Windflower spent a pleasant hour drinking his coffee and watching the small world of Marystown pass by. When he drove back to Walmart, his aunt was waiting for him at the entrance.

"Didn't you buy anything?" Windflower, noticing her empty arms.

"I never buy anything at Walmart," said Auntie Marie. "I like to go and look. I can order whatever I need from the co-op store back home."

On the drive back the pair were once again quiet and pensive. That changed just before the first turnoff to Garnish.

"Look, look," Auntie Marie cried.

It was a large female moose standing on the side of the road. As Windflower braked and then slowed, the animal ambled across the highway. When it reached the other side it was swallowed up in the brush.

"Now you've seen your Newfoundland moose," said Windflower.

"Yes, and now I can tell everybody back home," said Auntie Marie. "But they look the same as the ones back in Pink Lake."

Windflower laughed. "Did you expect them to have stripes?"

"No," said Auntie Marie. "But the way people talk about them here, you think they were vicious animals waiting to pounce on unsuspecting cars. They're just like cows."

"I'm sorry we disappointed you, Auntie. But they really are a danger to traffic and people, especially at night. That's why we have this slow-down area," pointing to the 'Reduced Speed' signs. He slowed to meet the new speed limits.

"It's good to slow down anyway," said his Auntie. "That way we can enjoy the beauty Mother Earth has laid before us. We can also see the signs that our allies bring to us."

"Let's stop at the T on the way back. I want to show you one of my favourite places." A few minutes later they were rolling down the rutted laneway that led to the T. He stopped the car and they both got out. The wind was cool but the sun on their faces kept them warm. They each found a nice large rock to sit on, and watched as the ocean rolled up onto the beach.

"This is a powerful place," said Auntie Marie. "Any time that the earth and the water meet in a formation like this means they combine their power. It creates a new source of energy and strength."

"Like synergy. I always feel it here. It is a place I come to think and pray sometimes."

"It is also a good place to interpret dreams," said Auntie Marie. "Because the hand of the earth can reach to the bottom of the ocean, it allows you to see below the surface. You have the gift, you know, Winston."

"What do you mean, Auntie?"

"It's in your family. The ability to interpret dreams, to see below the surface. That's why this place is so appealing to you. It is calling to you from the other side," said Auntie Marie.

When Windflower remained silent, she continued. "Your uncle and I have been speaking about you. We have a gift for you, a wedding gift, if you want to receive it. We want to teach you the language of the dream weavers."

"I would be honoured. Thank you, Auntie."

"Very well, Winston. You will have to come back to Pink Lake for about a week and we will begin the teaching. That will be your gift from Frank and me. I have a nice quilt for Sheila too. And I have a wonderful blanket for the baby," she said with a laugh.

"One step at a time, Auntie. One step at a time," said Windflower. He was laughing as well, as he helped her back into the car. He dropped her back at his house and went back to work.

The rest of the afternoon flew by. He came home a little after 5 and took Lady, for a long walk all over town. When he got back Uncle Frank was sitting in the living room watching T.V. with Auntie Marie.

"How about some fish for supper?" he asked.

"That would be great," said Auntie Marie and his Uncle Frank added, "I'm starved too."

"It won't take me long," said Windflower as he put a package of frozen cod into the microwave to thaw. While he was waiting, he peeled some potatoes and cut up some broccoli. When the microwave beeped he took out the cod and dried it on a paper towel.

Then he rolled it in flour and spiced it up with salt, pepper and a heavy hand of cayenne pepper. He cut up some fat back pork and heated it in an iron skillet to create the perfect medium for the fish. He gently laid the cod into the skillet and let it cook on a medium-high heat for 5 minutes on each side.

Auntie Marie came into the kitchen a little later and set the table. Windflower put potatoes on each plate and poured a little of the pork fat from the frying pan over them. He then placed a portion of the fried codfish on the plates and covered it with the fried pork scraps, called scrunchions. He split the steamed broccoli between the three of them and called his uncle to come and eat.

"This fish is gorgeous," Uncle Frank said, as he forked a portion of the fried cod into his mouth.

"You are a great cook," said Auntie Marie.

"I am glad you came to visit, and that you'll be here for the wedding," said Windflower.

"Are you nervous?" asked Uncle Frank.

"You're the second person who's asked that today. No, what's there to be nervous about? I'm marrying the best woman in Grand Bank."

After dinner Windflower and Auntie Marie cleaned up together while Uncle Frank went to see his friends for a game of cards. Windflower was quite content to sit in the living room and watch television with his aunt. Later on he took Lady for another short walk around the block to do her business. Not long after he said goodnight, and headed off to bed. It had been a long week and he was tired. Within a few minutes of hitting the pillow he was fast and soundly asleep. He didn't stir until he heard the birds in the morning.

When he woke he realized that today was going to be a special day, his wedding day. But first he had an appointment with the second-most important female in his life. He got up quietly and made some coffee. Then he took Lady and her leash and they went out into the early morning.

It was a glorious fall day, sunny but a little cool. Windflower could see Lady's breath in the morning air. She didn't mind and neither did he. The walk would heat them up and the sun was already warming the air around them. They walked all over the Grand Bank from the beach to the wharf. Then they went over to harass the ducks at the brook. It was a grand day to be alive, and both Windflower and Lady seemed to be grateful for the morning and to be together. Lady would not be coming to the wedding. She was staying with Constable Frost at the detachment. But, she was coming on the honeymoon. Windflower had negotiated that with Sheila at the last minute.

When they got back to the house, Windflower got Lady fresh water and re-filled her bowl while he got a cup of coffee and went outside to do his morning routine. First, was a smudge with his special herbs and reindeer moss. He moved the smoke over his head and his heart, and then his body, and finally, his feet. He asked for help and guidance on his journey, especially on this special day. He prayed for a kind heart, and to be filled with love and good intentions.

He prayed for his Auntie Marie and Uncle Frank, prayers of gratitude that they were with him on this day, and for his ancestors who were with him in spirit. He prayed for his friends and his allies, those on two legs and those on four. He thanked them for their help and guidance as well. Finally, he prayed for Sheila, that she continue to be wise and wonderful and that her inner beauty be reflected back to her as she spread her great heart into the world.

When he came back in Auntie Marie was up and already working away at something at the kitchen counter.

"Good morning, Auntie. What are you making?" asked Windflower.

"I am making your breakfast," said Auntie Marie. "It's bannock. We'll have some fruit as well, but bannock is the traditional wedding day food in our community. I had it on my wedding day and so did your mother."

"Thank you, Auntie. Can I help?" asked Windflower.

"Do you have any currants or raisins?" she asked. "Normally we would have it plain, but today is a special day."

Windflower got the raisins and Auntie Marie mixed them into the bowl with the flour, lard, salt and baking powder.

"Too bad, we don't have a fire," she said. "But the stove will have to do." She spread the dough out into a square cake pan. "Why don't you get cleaned up? This will be ready in about twenty minutes."

Windflower had a shower and shaved. When he came back out into the kitchen there was a large bowl of fruit on the table and his aunt was taking the golden brown bannock out of the oven. Uncle Frank had obviously smelled breakfast, and was already sitting at the table, staring at his empty plate.

"Good morning, Uncle. I see you're right on time for breakfast."

"Never miss a meal, that's my strategy," said Uncle Frank.

"That's why all those old fogies are lining up for supper at 4 o'clock. They're afraid they'll die before they eat."

Windflower laughed as Auntie Marie put a large square of the piping hot bannock onto his plate. She did the same for his uncle and took a much smaller portion for herself. Uncle Frank smeared his bannock with butter and started to eat. Auntie Marie admonished him and pointed to the fruit bowl. Reluctantly, he took a small portion of fruit for himself and passed it to Windflower. Windflower scooped out a large helping and laid it aside his buttered bannock.

"Umm," said Windflower as he tasted his first bite of the baked bannock. "This is so good, Auntie."

"Enjoy," said Auntie Marie. "I still wish we had an open fire to cook over. There's something special about eating outside."

"I don't miss the bugs in your face and in your bannock," said Uncle Frank.

"You would get me to pick them out for you," said Auntie Marie. "Like a big baby."

Windflower laughed again at the banter between his relatives. It was all in good fun, and it reminded him again how grateful he was to still have them with him. He smiled at them both as he ate his fruit and bannock. Afterwards, he helped his Auntie Marie clean up, and then he went to get dressed for the wedding.

He took his red serge uniform out of the plastic wrapping from the drycleaners and laid it on the bed. He also organized his post-wedding jacket and dress pants for later and laid them on the other side. That way, he could run in and change quickly after the wedding.

He put on his pants and was doing up his boots when he heard a familiar voice talking to Uncle Frank in the kitchen. Seconds later Ron Quigley poked his head into the bedroom and said, "How's the groom this morning?"

"I'm great, Ron. I'm almost set to go." He pulled on his jacket and got Quigley to put on his service medallion. He grabbed his hat and walked out into the living room.

Auntie Marie came out to give him a big hug, and Uncle Frank shook his hand on the way out. Another RCMP officer was coming to pick up his relatives and bring them to the church for the wedding. His aunt and uncle were going to walk down the aisle with Windflower, to give him away.

Chapter Seventy-one

Windflower and Quigley drove to the RCMP detachment where they were meeting up with the RCMP honour guard. Quigley had arranged for four additional RCMP officers to come over from Marystown. They would be joined by Tizzard, and Windflower's old friend from his Halifax days, Guy Simard, as Windflower's accompaniment to the church.

Tizzard and Simard were finishing off a snack when Windflower came in. Guy Simard came over to give him a hearty handshake, and grabbed him by the shoulder. "Mon gars, this is a great day, a grand day. I'm so happy for you."

"Thank you, Guy. I'm really happy you could make it." Tizzard was quiet for the first time Windflower could remember. He realized that his young friend might be a little emotional too. "You too, Eddie," said Windflower.

Tizzard smiled broadly at his boss's remarks and went to clean everything up. Minutes later, the vanload of Mounties arrived at the office. Quigley went outside to organize them. When Windflower came out they were standing rigidly at attention. Tizzard and Simard joined them, and Quigley and the groom fell in behind. As they were about to start off for the church, Windflower thought he heard music. And it was getting louder.

"Hang on a second," said Tizzard. "They're on their way. I wasn't sure they would make it on time."

All of the Mounties watched as the source of the music became apparent. It was the Salvation Army marching band. Tizzard had made arrangements for them to join in on the way to the church. The band stopped playing and stood in front of the detachment. The Band Major stopped in front of Windflower and saluted. "At your service, Sergeant," he said. Windflower took the salute and nodded to the Major to proceed.

The Major waved his baton in the air as the band broke into music and started marching up the street. Quigley shouted the orders to the RCMP officers to follow, and the procession was underway.

It was only ten minutes to the church but most of the towns-folk of Grand Bank lined the sidewalks or poked their heads out of windows to get a look at this spectacle. The wedding may have been the social and political event of the season, but the band and the dressed-up Mounties marching in formation, was a remarkable sight. Not one to be missed.

When they arrived at the church, the RCMP officers formed up into the honour guard to escort Windflower into the vestibule. They would come out later to do the same when Sheila, the bride, arrived. Windflower nodded his thanks to the RCMP officers, and went inside to wait with Quigley. A few minutes later, Auntie Marie and Uncle Frank arrived.

Together, they took Windflower by the arm and led him down to the front of the church where he and Quigley stood and waited for the arrival of the bride.

She arrived in an antique car, a 1950 baby blue Plymouth Deluxe, driven by Herb Stoodley. He parked the car in front of the church and helped Sheila and Moira Stoodley get out of the vehicle. Then both of the Stoodleys walked with Sheila into the church and towards the altar.

Sheila was a stunning bride, and all heads turned when she came down the aisle. She looked like a goddess to Windflower in her full-length off-white strapless formal gown. She wore her hair up, the way he loved it, in a French twist with a soft sweep of bangs.

She had highlighted her dark brown hair with a russet tint and wore little make-up except for a slight blush that gave her cheeks a healthy glow. Around her neck was a vintage single strand set of pearls that had belonged to her late mother. They were perfect with the set of diamond earrings Windflower had bought for her as a wedding present. They sparkled like her eyes as she drew closer, and finally reached out to hold his hand in front of the Minister.

Windflower didn't recall much of the service. He was mesmerized by Sheila and the moment. He recalled being asked for the ring and froze for an instant, until he realized his best man was trying to hand it to him. He definitely remembered the vows that he and Sheila recited to each other. His was easy, he had practiced it for days before the wedding,

"I, Winston Windflower, offer you my hand in marriage. I will strive to always love and respect you. To be your partner in life and love, and to support you to be the best person that you can be. I will listen to you and hear you in good times and especially when times are not easy. I thank you for your patience with me and for your many acts of kindness. 'Our joining is like a tree to the earth and a cloud to the sky'."

Sheila's was amazing.

"I, Sheila Hillier, promise to always love and respect you. I promise to laugh with you in times of joy and hold you when there is sadness or sorrow. I offer you kindness and compassion, understanding and encouragement. Let us build a life together that is full of love and laughter, a home we can share with others, and a love we can share with the world. I take you gladly and freely as my partner, my lover and my best friend for as long as we both shall live."

Windflower blinked back tears as Sheila looked into his heart and said these words aloud. He couldn't wait to hold her. Luckily, he didn't have to wait long, because the next words from the Minister were, "Ladies and Gentlemen: Let me present the newly married couple. You may show the world how much you love each other," she said to Windflower and Sheila. To the applause of the congregation, they embraced and kissed.

There was one more unforgettable thing at the wedding. After Sheila and Windflower had signed the register and were getting ready to walk back down the aisle, the Minister indicated to them to sit down. She motioned to the congregation to do the same. Windflower and Sheila looked at each other, wondering what would happen next.

Auntie Marie and Uncle Frank rose from their seats and walked to the altar. When they got there, Auntie Marie presented them with two feathers that were tied together. "In our culture this represents your marriage, your new union. May it never be separated," said Auntie Marie.

Then Uncle Frank read a traditional Shoshone Indian love poem:

> 'Fair is the white star of twilight, and the sky clearer
> at the day's end, but she is fairer, and she is dearer
> She, my heart's friend.
> Fair is the white star of twilight, and the moon roving
> to the sky's end; but she is fairer, better worth loving
> She, my heart's friend.'

Windflower and Sheila thanked his relatives for their gifts, and together with Moira Stoodley, the matron of honour, and Ron Quigley, the best man, they all walked slowly down the aisle. All the way, cameras flashed and people smiled but it was much of a blur to Windflower. He was more than relieved the church part was over. Now, they could celebrate.

Outside, Windflower and Sheila were swarmed by well-wishers from the over-flowing church. After about fifteen minutes, Tizzard came up to Windflower and touched his arm. "Whenever you are ready to go, your chariot awaits." He pointed down to the side of the church where a beautiful old wooden carriage with two chestnut brown horses was waiting.

"Where did you get that?" asked Windflower.

"It originally belonged to a doctor who lived here years ago. He brought it over with him from New Brunswick. Paul Herridge from the garage found it and fixed it up. He offers it to people for weddings from time to time. That's Paul with the hat on up front in the carriage." Tizzard waved, and Paul Herridge waved back.

"There is a catch, though," said Tizzard.

"What's that?" asked Windflower.

"Paul wants to drive you all over town to show off his carriage and the famous bride and groom," said Tizzard.

Windflower laughed and shook his head at Tizzard. He smiled at Sheila and took her by the arm. Confetti rained down on them as they walked slowly to the carriage. Paul, the driver, got out and opened the door for them. When the newly-married pair was secure inside, he started to drive off. The streets of Grand Bank were once again lined with well-wishers who cheered their arrival and waved at their departure. It seemed like forever, but it was only about twenty minutes later they arrived at the Lions Club for the reception.

The wedding luncheon was all set to go once the bridal party got there and seated. There was flowing champagne, and after grace by the Minister, the invited guests lined up for the buffet. There were hot eggs and ham, salads of all description, and cold sliced roast beef and turkey, and so many desserts even Eddie Tizzard was overwhelmed. There was also a large white trimmed wedding cake, congratulating Sheila and Windflower on their special day.

After everybody had eaten at least one round, the toasts began. Ron Quigley toasted the bride and groom and made a joke about how he hoped municipal relations would improve after today. Moira and Herb Stoodley stood together to salute Sheila and her new husband. Even Uncle Frank got in on the act with a bit of a bawdy poem that started to butt up against the line of good taste, but thankfully ended shortly just before it got outrageous.

Sheila and Windflower took turns responding to the toasts. They thanked the people in attendance, and the whole community for their support. Sheila acknowledged the presence of Council members and other community leaders. Windflower thanked his friends in the RCMP who were part of his support network, and publicly offered his appreciation to Auntie Marie and Uncle Frank for coming to be with him and Sheila.

After the toasts, there was the cutting of the cake and posing for pictures. Everybody wanted to get their own shot with the mayor and the handsome RCMP officer. Then it was time for the traditional first dance. Even though it was an afternoon affair they had arranged for some music from the club's sound system to lead them. The song Sheila and Windflower had chosen was All of Me by John Legend. Windflower loved the line 'all your perfect imperfections', as a way to express how much he loved Sheila, and more importantly how she put up with him. Sheila liked it too, especially the part about 'you're crazy and I'm out of my mind'. It made her laugh every time she heard it. Including today.

The rest of the afternoon flew by. Windflower and Sheila made the most of their time to connect with their friends and family. Windflower was especially pleased to spend a few minutes with Guy Simard and his wife, and later his good friend Doc Sanjay and his wife, Repa. They made plans for Windflower to come over and play a few games of chess and have some tasty samosas as soon as he got back.

Shortly after 4 p.m., Sheila and Windflower left the party to get changed. Sheila went to the back room where she had left her change of clothes, Windflower went outside to Sheila's car and drove home to change. He picked up Lady from the detachment, and twenty minutes later was back at the hall. They went around the room to say their good-byes and thank you's.

Windflower stopped for an extra minute to say goodbye to his Auntie Marie. He saw Uncle Frank too, but his uncle was busily engaged with his buddies in a corner, so Windflower waved at him along the way.

"You have a wonderful woman," said Auntie Marie.

"I know. I'm a very lucky man."

"Take care of her, and the little one too," said Auntie Marie.

"What do you mean?" asked Windflower. But before he could get an answer, his RCMP friends and a few of the bigger locals had lifted him off the ground and were carrying him outside. Sheila was waiting for him when he got there, and to great cheers they got into Sheila's car and started driving away.

"That was amazing. I love you, Sheila."

"I love you too, Winston. It was a beautiful wedding."

"Now, we can finally get a break," said Windflower.

"I am so looking forward to that," said Sheila. "I feel a bit run down. And I've been sick every morning this week. Can we stop at Tim Hortons in Marystown? I'd like to get a green tea to settle my stomach.

"Sure. Anything for my beautiful wife."

The End

About the Author

Mike Martin was born in Newfoundland on the East Coast of Canada and now lives and works in Ottawa, Ontario. He is a long-time freelance writer and his articles and essays have appeared in newspapers, magazines and online across Canada as well as in the United States and New Zealand. He is the author of *Change the Things You Can: Dealing with Difficult People* and has written a number of short stories that have published in various publications including *Canadian Stories* and *Downhome* magazine. *The Walker on the Cape* was his first full fiction book and the premiere of the Sgt. Windflower Mystery Series. Other books in the series include *The Body on the T, Beneath the Surface* and *A Twist of Fortune. A Long Ways from Home* is the newest book in the series. You can follow the Sgt. Windflower Mysteries on Facebook at https://www.facebook.com/TheWalkerOnTheCapeReviewsAndMore/

Thank you for reading this book and supporting Sgt. Windflower Mysteries. I hope you have enjoyed the story. If you did I hope you will consider doing me a favour by writing a review on Amazon, Chapters/Indigo or Goodreads. The review can be long or short. It can even just be something like "I loved this book and can't wait for the next one." Reviews are how other readers find out about new books. Please help spread the word. Thank you again.

Mike Martin

9 781460 292006